**CROUCHED ON THE FLOOR
OF HER LITTLE GALLERY,
ALL HER PAINTINGS ABOUT HER,
AMARYLLIS WAS WHIRLED BACK
INTO LADYBETH'S WORLD. . . .**

Ladybeth knelt on the bed close to Bay and tightened her arms about his waist, one cheek against his chest. His hands slid up her bare legs, pulling at the bands of her petticoats to whisk them off.

When he lay down beside her, drawing her into his arms, her eyes glowed at him, jewellike. "I shall love you, Bay, and be loyal to you all my life," she vowed.

He shed her of her shift and lifted her, splendidly naked, high in his arms. Huskily he told her, "My darling Ladybeth, one lifetime is not enough for all the love that I have to give you. . . ."

Books by Jacqueline Marten

English Rose
Irish Rose
French Rose
Loving Longest
An Unforgotten Love
Kiss Me, Catriona
Dream Walker

Dream Walker

Jacqueline Marten

SEVERN
SH
HOUSE

This title first published in the U.S.A. 1987 by
Pocket Books, a division of Simon & Schuster, Inc.

This first hardcover edition published in the U.S.A. 1988 by
SEVERN HOUSE PUBLISHERS INC, New York and
published as an original edition in any format in
Great Britain 1988 by SEVERN HOUSE PUBLISHERS LTD of
40–42 William IV Street, London WC2N 4DF.

Copyright © 1987 by Jacqueline Marten

British Library Cataloguing in Publication Data
Marten, Jacqueline
Dream walker.
I. Title
813′.54 [F]
ISBN 0–7278–1700–0

Distributed in the United States of America by
Mercedes Distribution Center, Inc
62 Imlay Street, Brooklyn, NY 11231.

Printed and bound in Great Britain

For
Albert
in Larchmont
(in the sun, in the Sound,
in bed or under the willow)
Ricky, Jonnie, Seth, Ethan
(the house wreckers)
Ruzell (Russ) Browning
(the house preserver)
Junior, Caleb, Holly
(canine house protectors)
and our own particular scouse,
RITA GRANT MILLER

ACKNOWLEDGMENTS

To Anne and Walter Grant of Liverpool; Sylvia Levit of Larchmont, for the artist-on-the-Bowery bits; and to Larry King of Stamford, Conn., who cheerfully (well, maybe not so cheerfully) let me borrow his wife, editor Linda Marrow of Pocket Books, in times of need.

Prologue

A VOICE ON THE VIDEO, HALF ADMONITORY, HALF baby-talk, coaxed, "Try this next exercise as a must for flattening your tummy and taking those naughty inches off your buttocks and thighs. Begin by standing up straight, legs wide apart . . ."

The syrupy accents were wasted on the woman who sat kneeling on her haunches, the upper part of her body in a skin-tight, copper brown Danskin thrust halfway into the fireplace. For the third time she brushed a flaming twist of paper against two stubbornly resisting logs. As the fire threatened her fingertips but not the logs, she let the paper drop, muttering, "Damnation."

Magically, the logs blazed up, hot and roaring.

"Oh, lovely, lovely," she said aloud, yanking the fire screens together. She sat back to toast herself in a state of dreamy contentment until half a minute later the voice on the video, suddenly increasing in volume, broke into her hypnotic trance. "Let's try it one more time."

As she sprang up in a quick, lithe movement, her skimpy nylon overskirt disclosed a stomach that needed no flattening as well as firm thighs and a shapely bottom. Obedient to the exhorting voice, however, she bent. "Right, one, two, three . . . left, one, two, three. Now drop your trunk forward, lower, lower, let your hands touch the floor . . ."

Long, strong fingers slapped the floor, and a fall of brown hair with distinct touches of red, made even more coppery by the firelight, swept back and forth along the carpet, releasing a cloud of dust. The fire gleamed on the fine gold chain hanging down from her neck and struck sparks off the small sapphire set in the middle of its six-pointed star.

"Anyone in good shape should not be winded at all," the video proclaimed self-righteously.

"In a pig's eye," muttered the exerciser breathlessly, falling over onto her back and kicking long, bare legs into the air.

She was unaware of the key turning in the lock until the door opened and slammed shut again. With a start of fright, she turned her head to the man who stood there, staring at her from the open hallway.

Her mouth opened, but no words came out. She struggled upright in a hurry, kneeling on her haunches again and staring back at him disbelievingly.

"C-Cam," she stammered. "Wh-what are you d-doing here?" And at exactly the same moment, he asked her, "Who the devil are you?"

He spoke in the slurred, slightly aggressive voice of the decidedly drunk, which in no way armored her

2

against the knifing pain of his question. She closed her eyes for a moment, shivering uncontrollably, but she could not shut him out. Her trouble was that, from the time she had come to America from England, she had never been able to shut him out. . . .

Height: five feet eleven. Weight: one hundred and seventy-two. No—she blinked a little—come to think of it, he had put on a few pounds. Broad shoulders and a straight back, coal black eyes as easily iced over with anger as alight with laughter. Almost half her life she had waited longingly to see those same eyes resting on her, warm with recognition, hot with passion.

His coal black hair was just now lightly powdered with snow and a single streak of gray; his skin was healthily tanned even in the middle of winter. A rugged face, perhaps even unhandsome, but with an attraction that had nothing to do with hunk appeal and everything to do with bed.

"Rock back and forth on your behind," intoned the voice on the video, and Cam walked over to it with a sailorlike gait—Yes, very definitely he's been drinking, she told herself, as he killed the power.

"I've never known you to get drunk," she said.

"The night is young." He pronounced each word slowly and precisely. "Before it ends, I intend to be a great deal drunker."

"Is—has something gone wrong?"

"My marriage has gone wrong. Or, to put it more correctly, it never did go right. Now it's over. She— thank God—wants out."

I have got him, she rejoiced, as her heart gave another great leap, of exaltation this time. *He is mine now, mine as he was in the beginning.*

She lowered her head quickly for fear that he might

recognize and resent the primitive triumph written on her face.

"Hey, you—you, whoever you are, are you feeling sorry for me?"

She raised her head. "I would never feel sorry for you, Cam. There is nothing to be sorry about."

He peeled off his wet raincoat and tossed it over a Victorian clothes rack in the hallway. His aim was about as steady as his walk, and the coat fell to the floor in a sodden heap. Uncaring, he slouched down in the nearest armchair, stretching out his legs so far that one shoe pinned the net of her skirt.

"You keep calling me Cam," he accused, biting down on his lip and narrowing his eyes. Even drunk he sensed that there was something familiar about her.

"It's your name, isn't it?"

"No one calls me Cam except family or close friends. You're not family or . . . are . . . Have we by any chance ever been close friends?"

"How close—?" She had to stop grinding her teeth to get the rest of the question out—"How close do you mean?"

"Did we ever go to bed together?" he asked her quite crudely.

Even firelight could not conceal the sudden whitening of her face. Her blue green cat eyes glittered up at him. *Oh God, I'll get you for that,* she vowed, even as she answered with a shrug, "Not recently."

Not recently, indeed, she thought, her fury dissolving in sudden wry humor. What would he say if she answered him truly? *It's a century or so ago since we made love.*

He closed his eyes and leaned back against the chair. "I wanna drink," he said, sounding young and pathetic.

4

She was not in the least moved to pity. "I presume that you mean you would like *me* to get you one?"

"Yu-up. If you are interested in saving my life."

"At the moment," she said sweetly, "I really am not, but I suppose I will. Just what exactly are you soused on?"

"Bloody Marys." He opened his mouth and grimaced slightly. "I'd better stick to vodka or I'll be sorry in the morning."

In the kitchen she released a few cubes with a vicious slam of the tray against the sink and jammed the electric opener onto the can of tomato juice as though it were his blasted head getting the guillotine.

Aloud, she said, "You *will* be sorry in the morning, all right, Charles Adam Mailer, only not for the reasons you think."

During the next forty-five minutes they each downed three drinks, but his were all Bloody Marys and hers were plain tomato juice. She was encouraging him to polish off a fourth drink when he fell asleep with the gentle suddenness of a baby, one cheek against the chair back and a half-full glass in his hand.

He looked younger and more vulnerable than the thirty-nine years and four months that she knew him to be. She eased the glass from his grip and set it on a table, steeling herself not to yield to compassion or loving tenderness, especially not to be touched by his little-lost-boy look. In the past fifteen years, where had her own vulnerability gotten her?

"Cam, speak to me." She shook him hard to see if he would waken. "Come on, Cam."

A dulcet snore was his only response, a highly unromantic sound, but one that was somehow endearing. Unable to help herself, she knelt between the sprawled-out legs and leaned her face against his tweedy jacket, tears pouring down her face and dripping through to his shirt.

"Who the devil am I? Oh God, you son of a bitch, why do I have to love you so?" she wept.

He stirred, murmuring something she could not hear, then turned restlessly in the chair. Dislodged from his chest, she sat up straight again, wiping both cheeks with the backs of her hands.

Then she leaned over once again, asking him loudly, "Cam, are you awake?"

He grunted, eyes closed, and one flailing arm landed across her shoulders. She held it there firmly as she eased up out of her crouching position, pulling and heaving to drag him up with her.

When they were both on their feet, with the top half of him bent across her like a wind-tossed tree, she propelled him down the hallway and into the bedroom, panting and pushing all the way. As they performed an awkward two-step through the doorway, she managed with two fingertips to switch on the light.

On arrival at the foot of the queen-sized bed, she gave him one quick shove and then ducked free. He went bouncing backward onto the bed and landed spread-eagled. His eyes opened in quick surprise for about five seconds, then closed again as he settled into a deep, snoring slumber.

Her own eyes gleamed down at him, more catlike than ever, as she knelt beside him on the bed and began unknotting his tie.

"Now it's my turn, Cam," she warned him out loud, and unable to resist, bent over to kiss his unresponsive lips. "You bloody bastard," she added in a loving whisper and then grinned wickedly down at him. "I'll sort you, laddie, just you see if I don't."

Deliberately she tossed his tie on the floor and started tugging at his shoe laces. By the time she had undressed him completely, all his clothes were scattered over the carpet, except for his trousers and blazer, draped artistically across a chaise longue.

She stared down unabashedly at the naked, recumbent body. *Why not?* she demanded fiercely of the fate that had kept them apart. *He's mine. He's been mine since the beginning of time.*

Her hands reached out and started a slow sensuous walk along his face and neck and over his shoulders. Her splayed fingers skimmed through the dark curls of hair on his chest, caressed approvingly the slightly concave belly, but stopped their trembling progress when they arrived at his thighs.

This far and no farther, she thought ruefully.

He was sleeping but not unconscious, his senses aware. Blushing madly, eyes widening as she watched his unknowing arousal, she jerked down the bedspread and bundled him under the blankets and out of her sight.

With her plan for "sorting" him almost fully formed in her mind, she started rummaging in the dresser drawers, starting from top to bottom. Plenty of lingerie but no nightgowns . . . assorted sweaters . . . in the lower drawer a pile of fleecy stoles. Kneeling on the floor, she pawed through the stoles and finally came up with an enormous, loose-knit shawl of many colors, red predominating.

"Hmmm." She pranced over to the mirror and draped it about herself. The copper brown of the Danskin leotard was evident through the wide weave. If there should only be pale skin showing underneath . . . A delicious quiver shot through her. Yes, pale skin would definitely enhance the effect!

In the open doorway, before she turned off the light, she took one last, lingering look at the humped figure under the bedclothes.

"It's a new beginning, Cam," she said softly. "A new beginning for both of us."

While he slept on, she inspected the linen closet and presently returned to the living room with a foam rubber pillow and a child's colorful sleeping bag, which she spread out over the couch.

She squirmed her way out of the leotard and tossed it over the back of the couch. Inching her way down inside the sleeping bag, she wore nothing but her gold chain and star.

For several hours afterward she lay there, watching the smoldering logs and impatiently wooing sleep. The muted firelight danced gently through the strands of her coppery hair, spread in separate tangles over the pillow. It gave a creamy sheen to the pale face with its gleaming green eyes. The logs had crumbled to ashes and the firelight died out completely when the catlike eyes finally closed.

In spite of just four hours' sleep, her mental alarm clock woke her an hour past dawn.

She sat up, instantly alert, and fought free of the sleeping bag, then folded it up and bundled it back into the linen closet. He must never suspect where she had spent the night. It would ruin her entire plan.

She padded back into the bedroom, barefoot and naked and carrying her leotard. She was not the least self-conscious till she caught a glimpse of herself in the dressing table mirror.

Then she stopped and stared, trying to see herself as he soon would. She wore a size 34B bra but was upright enough not to need one. She had been told by several resentful dates who deplored her 'Look! Don't touch' rule that her breasts were commendably shapely. She had a reasonably slim waist, swelling out to a generous length of hips and legs. She was fairly certain about her legs; they had always been admired. She turned, then twisted her head gymnastically to get a good look at her backside. Small . . . firm . . . Not bad, not bad at all, she summed up smugly and gulped deep in her throat at the image turning her mouth dry and her knees weak: Cam's hands slithering down her back and then firmly grasping the muscled tautness of her bottom.

She approached the bed where he lay still quite soundly asleep and slung the Danskin over one bed-post. Hardly daring to breathe, she eased herself down on the bed. Since he didn't move so much as a muscle, with a lot more confidence she slid under the covers and helped herself to one of his two pillows.

"Side by side, Cam," she said contentedly. "You and me, just the way we were meant to be." After a minute of cuddling near to his warmth, she daringly slid one leg closer, bringing them thigh to thigh.

Wake up, Cam, she willed him, *wake up and discover I'm alive.*

He murmured low in his throat and backed up against her, settling spoon-fashion into her curves. She gave a tiny gasp that mingled shock with a guilty pleasure. Her first instinctive movement of withdrawal gave way to instinctive desire as she offered him curve for curve.

Nestling, he slept on while she lay rigid, her knees tucked up in the bend of his, her breasts pressed against his back. Presently she felt a cramp in the arm she was lying on and tried to ease it out from under her, only to discover that she was more or less attached to him by her Star of David. The gold chain had worked its way up her neck and the star was caught in his hair.

"Quite symbolic," she said aloud wryly.

Carefully using her one free hand, she started to pry it loose, only to be struck by a sudden thought. Impulsively she rolled away from him and yanked the chain hard, letting out a small yelp as it broke against her neck.

She moved her pillow an inch or two from him and dropped the broken chain between the two of them. It lay, a little heap of mesh, golden star on top with the small sapphire blinking up at her like a jeweled eye.

"Bring my love to me," she whispered passionately, and turned, cuddling close again, only to find that "her love" had reversed in bed to face her and was leaning on his unsteadily propped elbow, staring, bewildered, across at her.

"Oh, my good God!" he moaned. Then, "Who the—"

She reacted swiftly to cut him off in mid-speech. "Oh Cam, Cam darling, you were wonderful," she trilled, lifting one of his hands and snuggling it against her cheek.

"But you—you—my—my—my—"

"Oh Cam, don't tell me you're tongue-tied now," she reproached him, "not after all those marvelous things you said to me last night."

She sat up, letting the blankets fall below her waist and giving him a widescreen view of everything above. Suppressing a grin at his panicked expression, she leaned forward. "Say them again, Cam," she begged, "especially—"

"Especially?"

"I love that name you kept calling me."

"What name?" he asked baldly. And then, belatedly tactful, "There were so many wonderful names you deserved."

"Oh Cam, you tease, as though you don't know."

Like a contented cat, she rubbed up against his arm, and he accepted this fondling for a minute or two, silently acquiescent. Then suddenly his rock-hard arm snaked around the "reasonably slim waist," and he pulled her to him. Immediately on contact, she discovered that something else was rock hard, too.

"Speaking of teases," he said against her throat, and she fought her rising panic and smiled brilliantly down at him.

On his back, disarmed and unprepared, he couldn't prevent the sudden thrust backward that freed her. In a single adrenalin-inspired bound, she was out of the queen-sized bed and standing at the foot of it, shaking her head in rebuke.

"Now, darling, you know we agreed, no matinees today. I have to concentrate on business."

He swore under his breath, and she chided him as though he were a three-year-old. "Now Cam dear, we've got tomorrow and tomorrow, all the time in the world. Wait for me, love; I'll be back in a jiffy."

She waved her fingers and whirled around, giving him a quick glimpse as she exited of the charming little backside to which he, as she had done earlier, gave his unqualified seal of approval.

Charles Adam Mailer lay back against his pillow and hers, his black eyes blinking bewilderedly up at the ceiling. "Either I am dreaming," he said out loud, "or I have blundered through the Looking Glass with Alice."

After deliberating awhile, *Each alternative is acceptable,* he decided and closed his eyes again. They did not open until she appeared back at his bedside, calling him by name. This time she was balancing a breakfast tray.

"Sit up against both pillows," she ordered practically, and when he dazedly followed orders, she laid the tray against his raised knees.

"Orange juice, eggs scrambled with cream cheese, whole wheat toast, butter, marmalade, coffee . . . I'm sorry, I could only find instant—" She frowned worriedly. "I don't think I've forgotten anything."

"It's a feast." He picked up his fork, adding a meek "Thank you" to her maternal spreading of a flowered cloth napkin across his bare chest. "The eggs are delicious," he mumbled with his mouth full of them. "Thank you again."

"Why, Cam, it's *I* who should be thanking you." Her voice lowered to husky intimacy. "You need something to recruit your strength, my heroic one—after all your exertion last night."

"About last night . . ."

The fork shook in his hand as he stared across at her. She was dressed now in the shawl of many colors and absolutely nothing else. The deliciously insufficient garment was draped around her shoulders and knotted between her breasts. At the sides it came no lower than her thighs; the fringed edges hung just below her knees in front. The open spaces of the loose weave revealed exciting glimpses of key portions of her anatomy.

In his bemusement he deemed this revelation accidental, and he continued to stare while his eggs grew cold.

"Never mind me, darling, get on with your eating," she urged with a happy little laugh. "You've got to stoke the engine if we want a full head of steam."

As he lifted a forkful of egg, she nodded approvingly, then sped out of the room, calling to him over her shoulder, "I'll be back soon."

He was scraping a thick layer of marmalade onto the last bit of toast when she did return, and in his disappointment he popped it into his mouth and down his throat too fast, then started to cough and choke.

All through breakfast his mind's eye had been filled with pictures of the lithe, sensuous figure underneath the many-colored shawl. The pertly jouncing breasts that she had thrust almost in his face . . . the curve of her hip . . . the saucy swing of her backside . . .

It was a terrible disappointment now to see her fully dressed. At least he assumed that she must be fully dressed, or why bother to put on the smoky tweed coat and fur-trimmed leather boots? Also the Icelandic tam pulled at a jaunty angle onto one side of the coppery hair? Unless . . . underneath . . . as with the woolen stole . . .

"I'm all right now," he croaked, and as soon as she stopped smacking his back, he reached out to whip up the skirt of her coat, disclosing a pleated, plaid skirt.

Doubly regretful and still bemused, he tried to lift the tray off his knees and onto the bed, but was prevented by the firm placing of both her hands on his shoulders, followed by a quick, sexless kiss planted in the middle of his forehead.

"Don't bother, darling, you can get up and dispose of it after I've left."

"Where the hell do you think you're going?"

"To work. Where else? Remember . . ." She gave him a gay, cocky smile. "I'm a working girl, not my own boss, like some rich plutocrats who shall be nameless. Don't look so sad, Cam, we'll be together tonight."

She whisked a leather envelope bag from beneath her arm, fumbled inside it, and produced a single key attached to a little white tag. She pressed the key into his numbed hand and folded his fingers around it.

Her smile this time was warm and intimate. "This is my spare. You may as well have it. I have a feeling that from now on, to coin an old cliché, my house is going to be your house."

Her eyes, as she repeated the 'old cliché,' raked him boldly, hinting at remembered pleasure. Then, as though abashed at the stark passion being returned to her in his eyes, her own suddenly fell.

She turned to the mirror, breathing hard, and pretended to be quite absorbed in adjusting the angle of her tam. The red brown hair tumbling from it framed her pale face and high-planed cheeks. . . . Again there had been that flutter of recognition in his eyes . . . gone . . . damn it! gone almost as quickly as it had come.

"Till tonight, Cam," she told him low and tenderly, and swept out of the room.

He shouted, "Wait a minute!" trying to rise up in bed at imminent risk to the tray and its contents.

Either she could not or would not hear him. The slam of the outer door was his only answer.

Savagely he shoved the tray down toward the foot of the bed and pushed back the covers, all the while uttering low-voiced, army-inspired obscenities. In a final stab at relieving frustration, he administered two punishing punches to his pillow. It went skimming along the bed, and he stared down for a moment, then plucked up the broken chain and held it dangling in the air, with the golden star gently swaying to and fro and blue green sparks from the sapphire streaking into the air, sparks that were almost the same color as the cat eyes that had smoldered at him minutes before in the pale, provocative face.

Friend? Lover? Intimate? She acted like all three.

Face and voice . . . they were like something out of his past, out of his dreams. All too familiar . . . and yet . . . and yet . . .

He couldn't put a name to her; he couldn't recall the dream.

Faster and faster he swung the chain, and the sapphire seemed to be staring at him like a third eye . . . those damned all-knowing, somehow daunting, blue green eyes. He had seen them before; he had seen the star before. He was sure of it.

Thank God he had this key. Soon, very soon, he'd see her again, he swore to himself, unfolding his other clenched hand to look at the key with its white identification tag. He was going to ask some questions, and he would damn well get some answers. But first he had to take care of something of the utmost importance.

He examined the tag. It was bare and white . . . no address written down. In a panic, he turned it over. No address there either. Just two words in a fine script hand. *Ladybeth's Apartment.*

"Ladybeth!" He strangled on the name, then repeated it low and hoarsely.

"Good God Almighty!" With a sudden revulsion of feeling, he dropped both chain and key onto the white sheet. A shaft of sunlight slicing through the window formed a halo around the star and stabbed the deep blue sapphire.

As Cam bumped his way to the bathroom, large and naked and with a swelling head that suddenly felt too big for his body, it seemed as though, even through the walls, the eye was staring after him. It was laughing at him, mocking him.

He turned on the bathroom light, and as he thrust his haggard, lightly bearded face close to the mirror of the medicine cabinet, a sudden sharp memory exploded inside his stabbing head.

"Not just Ladybeth," he said to the man in the mirror. "Sweet Jesus! It was Katy. Katy Dingle from London."

He smashed his fist down on the sink, then winced as the sound and motion set up a painful, pounding echo that vibrated all the way down his spine. "Why does she keep doing this to me?" he groaned aloud. "And how in God's name am I going to find her?"

In the same panicked moment that he was splashing cold, reviving water on his face and the back of his neck, in a public telephone booth on the corner of First Avenue and 62nd Street, two blocks from the apartment where they had spent the night together, the green-eyed *provocateur* was talking breathlessly into the phone.

"Hannah. This is Rilla Scott. Is Mrs. Mailer in? No, I'm on the move and I can't call back, and it's terribly important that I speak to her right now. Wake her up, please, there's a dear, you can blame it on me. . . ."

"Maggie? No, don't worry, nothing's wrong; no, I'm fine, honestly. No, no . . . everything at the apartment is fine, too. It's just that I absolutely had to get to you before Cam managed to. Yes, that's right, I did say Cam. Yes, your brother-in-law Charles Adam Mailer. Do you know any other Cam? Look, let's stick to basics; I can't go into all the details at the moment—there isn't time—but any moment he's going to shake the smog out of his brain. And when he finally does get his head together, he is bright enough to make four out of two and two. That means in a very little while from now, he will be burning up the telephone wires between

Manhattan and Larchmont. In fact, I would not be surprised if he were trying to get through to you this very minute and swearing merry hell about getting a busy signal."

"Rilla, what on earth are you talking about?"

"Cam is going to call you soon, Maggie, and ask you who spent last night in your New York apartment. What you have *got* to tell him is that, as far as you know, *nobody* did."

"Nobody. But Rilla—"

"Maggie, I beg you, listen carefully and please remember. You did *not* lend the apartment to anyone last night. Neither—please tell him so—did Ben."

"My husband is out of town on business, some of it your business, I might add."

"He's out of town? That's wonderful!"

"Thanks a heap."

"Sorry, I know it's not wonderful for you, but in this case it will save a lot of lying, and you happen to be much better at that than he is."

"You're really full of compliments this morning. It makes a great start to my day."

"Oh Maggie, you know what I mean. It may all sound crazy, but if you only knew how important this is to me; and hell, what kind of actress would you be if you couldn't put this over with a few little white lies?"

"I will on one condition. A full and complete confession later on today accompanied by a full and complete luncheon at Gino's."

"Deal. What about your diet?"

"For a good confession and a good meal, and in, I hope, a good cause, I will sacrifice my diet."

"Okay. I'll meet you at Gino's at one. And Maggie, one more thing. Cam is not going to be put off easily. When he insists that there *was* someone in the apartment—he'll probably even describe me to see if it rings any bells—you might suddenly have a brainstorm and remember that a week or so ago you lost the key chain with the keys to your apartment, and you forgot to mention it to Ben. Maybe you'd better act sort of alarmed and start talking about changing the lock." She gave a little-girl giggle into the phone. "Two bits he'll try to talk you out of it in the hopes that I may come back there."

"Do I gather that you and Cam spent the night together in my apartment?"

"We did indeed, but not—do clean up your mind, Maggie—not in the way you think." The giggle sounded again, even more infectious than the first one. "As a matter of fact, not even the way that *he* thinks."

"And what do I say when he describes you to a T?"

"You lie again, Maggie dear. Out of your love and friendship for me, and your gratitude for the years I spent with your progeny, you lie like a rug."

"Pull-eeze de-posit thirty-five cents for an-other three min-utes," the operator sing-songed into the middle of Maggie's prolonged snort.

"I don't have ten cents, operator. Gino's at one, Maggie. Don't forget, you don't know anyone who looks remotely like me . . . except . . . oh my God, I've just had a wonderful idea. Operator, don't you dare cut me off. My friend will accept the charges. Maggie, tell her your number."

Maggie recited her number, bells clanged, and the conversation went on.

"Maggie, you might do it this way. First deny knowing anyone who fits the description, then act as though you've suddenly had an inspiration. Don't come up with it yourself . . . sort of make *him* see that you've had an idea so that *he'll* question you. Tell him you seem to remember seeing a young woman answering his description who was at his big gallery exhibition in December."

"But you didn't go to that exhibition. I remember inviting you myself, and you refused very firmly. Even Ben said you acted rather funny about it."

"Of course I did. I couldn't possibly go. He was still feeling married. It wasn't time for Cam and me to meet yet."

"Oh God!" Maggie moaned. "This is no kind of conversation to start the day."

"High tragedy isn't your style, Maggie. I promise I'll explain everything later—well, almost everything," Rilla amended quickly.

There was a slight pause before Maggie inquired politely, "Are you quite finished?"

"I think so."

"You're sure there are no further instructions?"

"For the time being."

"If I were a drinking woman," said Maggie with dignity, "I would have a large stiff brandy. As it is I shall try—*try,* mind you, to return to the sleep from which you so rudely and confusedly snatched me."

"Sweet dreams," said Rilla cheerfully. "I'm on my way to your husband's office myself. I have to see my editor. Oh, Maggie."

"What now?"

"Thank you. Thank you for everything, past, present, and future. Gino's at one."

The gold lettering on the double oak doors read Mailer-Crown Publishing Co. Underneath in smaller letters was a listing of five names headed by Benjamin H. Mailer.

The receptionist displayed two newly bonded front teeth in a wide friendly grin.

"Mr. Mailer is out of town, Ms. Scott."

"I know. I'm here to see Mr. Cowan today."

Eric Cowan came out to reception to usher her into his office himself. Once there, he kissed her lightly on each cheek, said, "I think you'll be pleased with the final effort, Rilla," and handed her a slim book about eight by ten in size.

The cream-colored cover highlighted a plump and huggable koala bear hanging from a eucalyptus tree with two little black-eyed, black-nosed replicas of herself clinging to her shoulders.

With one finger Rilla slowly traced the title, *The Koala Twins,* and then with equal pride of authorship, her own name in print of the same size, Rilla Scott.

"It's lovely," she sighed pleasurably.

"Wait till the promo material comes out. We've got high hopes for this one. I think we could double the sales we had on *The Frog Who Loved a Flounder.*

"*Allevai.*"

"Huh?"

"*Allevai.* That's Yiddish for 'it should only happen,' you poor benighted WASP, you."

He grinned. "You show-off Liverpoolian."

"*Pud*lian. That's Liver*pud*lian. Or, better still, Scouse. Don't they teach you *any*thing out in Des Moines?"

"Sure," he said cheerfully. "How to come to New York and create best sellers for crazy converts. So treat me more respectfully, Ms. Scott, or I'll drop you back into obscurity. How about some coffee?"

"No thanks."

"Lunch?"

"I'm booked."

He shrugged. "For dinner, too, I suppose?"

"Nooo, but my apartment was painted yesterday. I have to spend tonight putting things back in order."

"Tell me something. Is it me—something my best friend won't tell me—or don't you like men? Come on, nourish my male ego, tell me it isn't just that *I* turn you off?"

"It isn't just you, Eric," she told him gently, "it's me. There is . . . Unfortunately, there has only been one man who ever turned me on."

"Did he die?"

"Of course not. He's very much alive and living not so far from here."

"Either that's a lot of bull or your guy isn't doing right by you."

"What do you mean?"

"I may be a hick from the Midwest, kid, but I know a thing or two about women. You've got a tight-lipped look, honey, and a tense, if beautiful, body. You're a stunner on the surface, but there's a lot of stored-up energy in you that isn't going any place useful."

Her smile faded. Tears slid out of her eyes and splashed down onto *The Koala Twins*. "It will be soon," she mumbled.

"Ah, Rilla, I'm sorry. I didn't mean to press the wrong button."

"Don't be sorry. My life is good, and it's soon going to get even better."

"Well, if it doesn't, call on me any time."

"Will do." She held up the book. "May I have this one?"

He said, "Sure," and she gave a brief wave and whisked out of his office, trying to recapture the glow of her mood before she entered it.

The Gordon Gallery was nine blocks north and two

blocks east of Mailer-Crown Publishing. She resisted a cab and trudged there in the cutting cold, huddling down in her coat, grateful for the furry embrace of her boots and wishing they reached all the way to her frozen thighs.

Her wind-whipped cheeks were aglow and her nose an unattractive, frosted red when she thankfully pushed her way through the doors of the gallery.

Mr. Gordon himself came hurrying out to greet her.

"Mrs. Dingle. It must be telepathy. I just this minute got finished telling Zora that she should give you a ring some time today. Late last night we got the last of your client's pictures hung. I wanted your opinion."

"Great minds," she laughed, and followed him to the adjoining room, where three large watercolors dominated the left wall. Pastel shades, but with the strength of more vibrant colors. Oriental in concept. Oriental in style. A waterfall flashing down the side of a mountain. A wonderland of lush flowers, with a small, arched bridge leading from the garden. A forest in the rain, with an ancient farmhouse showing through the trees.

The painter's name on all three, instead of a signature, was in stylized block letters, a single name, AMARYLLIS.

"I don't suppose, Mrs. Dingle," Mr. Gordon said wistfully, "Amaryllis plans to attend the opening tomorrow?"

"Nothing's changed, Mr. Gordon. She still has agoraphobia. There's no way I can get her to leave her house. She hasn't been out of it in five, maybe six years."

"I could visit her at home, maybe?"

"She doesn't like people, Mr. Gordon. Nothing personal, honestly. It's just this fear she has. I'm really sorry, but you always knew the conditions. You want her pictures, you have to deal through me."

"Gladly, gladly, Mrs. Dingle, don't misunderstand, it's always been a pleasure working with you. It's just"—he cast a last, wistful backward glance at the watercolors as he shepherded her away—"I like to meet my artists."

"Perhaps some day," she said firmly and finally.

As they walked around the room, viewing the other paintings, she asked casually, "Can you tell me, Mr. Gordon, have you ever sold any Ladybeths?"

"A Ladybeth? I should be so lucky. They're as rare as hailstones in Tahiti. I saw one auctioned off once at Christie's in London. *The Man in Silver.* Exquisite. Simply exquisite. Coloring. Brush strokes. Composition. Strength with delicacy. It looked as though any moment he would stride out of the canvas to shake hands. Similar, but to my mind superior, to Gainsborough, and pure Constable in her backgrounds." He stopped this impassioned description long enough to clap her on the shoulder with such enthusiasm she staggered. "Don't tell me you have come across a Ladybeth?"

She massaged her shoulder surreptitiously. "Well, I'm not sure, I don't think so, I just heard . . . accidentally . . . possibly . . ."

He clasped both her hands in his.

"If it should happen, give me the first refusal. I promise you, Mrs. Dingle, you do this for me and I'll do right by you as I always have."

"I promise you first refusal," she pledged uncomfortably, wishing she had kept her mouth shut, then couldn't resist asking, *"The Man in Silver,* what was it like?"

"He was sitting at his desk—Hepplewhite, I think—with the chair—a Sheraton—turned around as though he had just moved it back to greet someone who had entered the room . . . someone he liked, judging by his expression. A tall, powerfully built man with thick black brows and keen blue eyes, a prominent nose, not a beak, you understand, but long and straight and strong, more like a Scot's. It dominated the face. He had rings on both hands, which, strangely enough, were a worker's hands, not the hands of an aristocrat. Powdered hair, unparted, and combed back simply in a high wave and clubbed at the back with a ribbon tie."

"Why *The Man in Silver*?"

"He wore a gray suit. Breeches, brocade waistcoat, jacket all a silvery gray with a fall of white lace at his throat and the same lace tumbling down from his sleeves. Handsome devil, not at all a typical English face. A bit of Spaniard as well as Scots, I would say."

For the second time that morning her eyes grew luminous with tears. She blinked them back quickly.

"I'll see you tomorrow night at the preview, Mr. Gordon," she told him, and fled the gallery.

A cab was just dislodging two passengers. She reached it two yards ahead of a man with a briefcase who muttered disagreeably, disregarding her apologetic smile.

"I was ahead of you," she informed his rigid back as she stepped into the cab. "Turtle Bay Apartments, Forty-sixth Street east of Second Avenue," she told the cabbie, and sank back against the seat, suddenly weary and discouraged. Only midmorning, and it felt as though she had been through a very long day.

"Cam, oh Cam," she mourned, unaware that she had spoken his name aloud till the cabdriver asked, "Ya say something, lady?"

"No, no . . . just thinking aloud, I guess."

"Talking to themselves, that's for old people, not a pretty girl like you."

"I'm a lot older than I look."

"Aw c'mon, you don't look more than twenty-five, which means maybe you might be thirty."

She rubbed her temples with the tips of her fingers. "Actually, you're not even warm. Try adding two hundred."

He laughed uneasily. "You're some kidder, lady."

The cab pulled up in front of her apartment house, and she handed some folded bills across to him.

"I'll bet you've never before met anyone over two hundred years old," she said conversationally.

"Nah, nah," he mumbled, doling out change. "Ack-cherly, you're the foist."

"Ack-cherly"—she confounded him by handing over a two-dollar tip—"I'm probably just the foist—first to admit it. There are more of us around than you ever dreamed." She flashed him a dazzling smile.

"Sure, sure, lady, whatever you say," he agreed uneasily as she stepped out of the cab. He started shifting gears before she got the door shut and made a quick getaway. She marched into the lobby unbuttoning her coat.

"Good morning, Miss Scott."

"Morning, Tom." She came up to the uniformed man behind reception. "Is John around? I need to be let into my apartment. I slept at a friend's place last night because the new paint was giving me a headache. I forgot and left my key there."

Tom chuckled. "I never before heard of an artist getting a headache from paint."

She acknowledged this pleasantry with a faint smile, but he continued to chuckle at his own wit as he rang for John, who arrived promptly, passkey in hand, and accompanied her up to the twenty-third floor.

The smell of her newly painted walls assailed her nose and sent little stabs of pain up the back of her neck the moment she entered her apartment. She rushed around flinging windows wide and opening the terrace door. Then she shrugged off her coat, hung it in the hall closet, and walked through the apartment, studying the paint job and trying to recapture the mood of peace and contentment that, even after four years, was always a part of each homecoming.

This was her home, her kingdom, her place of work, her place of rest, the place she had earned, both the tribute to and the award for her own ambition and achievement.

Her studio had once been a greenhouse, and the glass walls and half-glassed ceiling provided her light and space. It was two plush-carpeted steps down to the living room, where friends gathered to talk and eat, or where she sat alone, savoring the quiet, to read or watch television. The kitchen was small but suited her; cooking had never been her favorite occupation. The bathroom was small, too, but the tub, probably installed by a former, more prosperous tenant, was a square slab of marble, ideal for long soaking.

The last stop on the tour was her bedroom, with its raised wooden platform on which lay a king-sized mattress covered by a hand-knit afghan, a gift from her Aunt Bronwyn in England. On that same oversized mattress—which fairly begged for a sleeping partner—night after night, all the years of her life here, she had lain alone . . . just as she had lain alone on all the mattresses in all the apartments for all the years preceding.

She was thirty-three, and except for those few deceptive minutes with Cam this morning, she had lain alone all her life. And, in spite of the bravado of this morning's performance and her phone call to Maggie, who was to say that she might not go on lying alone for the next thirty-three years as well?

She knelt down on the platform suddenly, lowered her head to the bed, and, for the third time in a single day, her eyes were awash with tears. This time she didn't try to stop them. She gave the tears full rein, letting them soak into the afghan as she sobbed out her loneliness and her longing.

The consciousness of his presence was with her minutes before she saw him. Through the long years, knowledge of him had always started with sensation, an awareness that had nothing to do with touch or taste or sight. She could *feel* him there in every throbbing nerve of her body.

She jumped up and whirled around, her glance directed unerringly at the corner where he sat in her old Shaker rocker, smiling gravely, sympathetically, across at her. A man all in silver gray, from his breeches, which tied at the knees, to the fine, fitted waistcoat with its dozen pearl buttons. Even his clubbed hair was powdered a silvery white and tied back with a silver gray ribbon. Lace at his throat, lace at his sleeves. A strong, prominent nose in a devilishly handsome dark face with straight black brows and intense blue eyes, a hard mouth and chin. His hands—surprisingly strong and square and workmanlike—were clasped over one knee, a gold signet ring on one of them, a huge round onyx on the other.

"You!" she said accusingly. "I might have known you would turn up today. I'm only surprised you weren't around this morning."

"I was."

"You—when I was with Cam?"

He nodded calmly, and a vivid blush spread over her cheeks.

"Why didn't you show yourself?" she asked him crossly.

"You seemed to be doing splendidly without me."

Her blush spread upward and downward over her body as she hastily reviewed the morning's proceedings. She blushed more in recollection now than she had when strolling all but nude before Cam.

"Why were you weeping?" the man in silver asked gently.

She gave him a stormy glance. *"You're* supposed to know everything. Why do you have to ask?"

"I'm sorry that you are unhappy, m'dear."

She sank down on the bed, her legs stretched out on the raised platform. "But not sorry enough to help me . . . to free me to find happiness. Crazy, isn't it? I have everything a poor little Scouse could ever dream of. Modest success at not one, but two, careers. A little fame and a very nice start to my fortune. This apartment. Travel. Friends. Altogether an interesting life. And I've never been loved. I can't be loved. There have only been two men in my life—you and Cam. Only two men who ever counted, and a fat lot of good either one of you has ever been to me. Look at me. I'm a virgin, a goddamned virgin at thirty-three because I can't . . . I daren't . . . *You* won't let me live."

"It won't always be this way."

"Oh, for Christ's sake, it's been this way for seventeen—no, damn it, it's been eighteen years. Eighteen bloody years. Do you realize we're talking about more than half my life? How much longer do you think I can wait? How much longer do you expect me to go on like this?"

"Not much longer, little one."

"Oh God, that's what you used to call me. Can't you get it through your head—or your phantom mind—or your psychic senses—or whatever it is that goes on between us—that I'm not a little girl anymore? I haven't been a little girl for a hell of a lot of years. What I am is spelled w-o-m-a-n, meaning big, *big* girl, and I've got a woman's needs and wants."

The stern mouth melted into unexpected tenderness; the intense blue eyes lit up with love and laughter.

"My dear love, I have known you a long, long time. There is nothing you can tell me about your wants and needs that I haven't always known."

"Then hear me, please, help me."

"You have everything the girl from Liverpool once asked for."

"I want to love and be loved."

"You didn't ask for that, Rilla Scott."

"I'm asking now. No, I'm begging." Her voice rose passionately. "That girl from Liverpool didn't know everything. Do you think it's fair to make *me* pay forever just because *she* was young and arrogant and didn't know all there was to know?"

"It's not fair at all, my sweet, and it was never intended to happen. As for that girl from Liverpool, I won't have you speak against her. I agree she was young and arrogant, and sometimes just a bit silly, but I liked her enormously. I still do."

"Truly?"

"Truly."

She jumped up and rushed toward the rocker where he sat so quietly, and he shook his head warningly. She checked her headlong dash.

"Until Cam, there was no one but you. There's still no one like you. You're more real to me than most real

29

men," she whispered huskily, "more man than most I meet."

"That's a rare compliment, Rilla. I wish . . . for one night in all eternity . . . I would like to be a man for you again."

The man in gray started to fade, and she begged him desperately, "Don't go, please, don't go. I'm so lonely without you."

"Not any longer. Good-bye, Rilla. Farewell, my dear."

"Aren't you coming to me anymore?" she cried out in an agony of fear and regret.

"It's either shadow or substance now. You can't have us both. Good-bye. Good-bye till the next time, my own dear love."

Blinded by tears, she started toward him again; and when her eyes cleared, there was only an empty rocking chair, rocking to and fro with no one in it. The man in silver gray was gone, and not only from her presence.

She lay down on the bed and wrapped herself, cocoonlike, in the afghan, feeling empty, abandoned, and afraid, forgetting there was ever a time when he hadn't been her lifeline out of Liverpool. . . .

Chapter 1

I WAS BORN AND SPENT THE FIRST HALF-DOZEN YEARS OF my life in the Dingle, which is a dreary section of Liverpool that stretches for about four miles along the docks. It was a rough section with a rough population, mainly a mix of Catholics and Protestants, who managed to coexist in uneasy amity most of the time; but in my adolescence—in the mid and late sixties—just as they had in bad periods before, they battled each other fiercely both on Orange and on St. Paddy's Day.

The Scotland Road area was even rougher than the Dingle, while Edge Hill was almost tame by comparison. But no matter where you went in working-class Liverpool, you were surrounded by the webs of connected, terraced houses, without so much as a pint-sized garden for miles. Thousands of streets of these houses led off from the main road, breaking down into about ten major arteries, each made up of wall-to-wall neighborhood shops, small, filthy, and permanently crowded.

You had about as much privacy living in a terraced house as in a commune. Street noises drowned out the soap opera lives of your neighbors during the daytime, but the nights—oh God, those nights! Years after I left the Dingle behind me forever, I would awaken in my odd-shaped room in Larchmont, New York (where the loudest nighttime disturbance came from raccoons in the back yard knocking over garbage cans), and I would sweat with nightmare remembrances of how it had been.

At night in a terraced house, your neighbor's life was *your* life. You could hear every sound, imagine every sight to go along with it . . . the creaking of a bed, the slap across a child's face. You could hear every cough, every sneeze, particularly if the man of the house was a docker, a miner, or a factory worker. Asthma was the common enemy of all of them, and the hacking cough from the worker next door could keep you awake for hours.

Most prevalent and most prominent of all the noises was the fighting. Nightly, the men sought forgetfulness of the grimness and grinding poverty of their daily lives inside the local pub. They were off to the local every day after work before they would dream of going home. Often they were getting tanked enough so that they *could* go home.

With a pub on every corner—ask a working-class Englishman for directions, and he'll guide you by the pubs!—it was all too easy. By the time her man came staggering into the house at night (awash with all the pints he had emptied into himself), the overworked, overtired wife had her own bones of contention: the waste of the uneaten food she had prepared for him;

the kids who had misbehaved in his absence; and her anger at the endless stream of money poured down his throat in drink.

Husband and wife would scream at each other in particular and at life in general. They would go on loudly scrapping until they both dropped from exhaustion or, which happened just as often, he decided to silence her with his fists. Then the kids would start squalling, too; and if it got really brutal, which it frequently did, the police would be called to come and haul him away.

It was commonplace during the day to see some poor woman parading through the shops with a black eye or a broken nose as a souvenir of a fight the night before.

Saturday nights were the worst, maybe because Friday was payday. While one group of neighbors was outside boxing each other in the road, others were milling around, shouting obscenities to the contenders, or even making book on the outcome.

Oh God, how terrified I used to be by the fights. I would wake scared and crying and run into my parents' bed, where I would snuggle down against my mother, shaking and sniffling. She would stroke my back and my hair, and my father would say, "Now, don't be taking it seriously, Rilla, my girl; they're just letting off steam. You see if they're not friends again tomorrow."

Somehow, I would be soothed and comforted, as much by his words as by her stroking. It was a marvel to me that Dad was right. The men would half kill each other in the night and be sheepishly friends before the week had ended, sometimes even sitting side by side next day in church as though they had never broken a single Commandment, let alone bones.

In both the Dingle, and especially later when we moved a step up to Cantril Farm (where the houses were separate and each had a Lilliputian garden and, best of all, hedges for privacy), mine was never your average everyday, working-class Liverpool family.

Several things made us different, the first one, I suspect, being birth control. Not that my mother—"me mum," as she was in those days—ever said so. From that day to this she's never even hinted, let alone discussed outright, why in a town where the number of children in a family averaged at least five, and eleven or twelve was nothing out of the way, our family had only two kids, my brother Jim and, three years later, me.

Still, long before I left Liverpool, I was able to put two and two together, remembering those strange little miniature balloons Jim and I used to pinch from under my father's pillow and fill with water to toss at the kids next door.

Much later on I learned that my mother was Rh-negative and had a pelvic build not recommended for bearing children. She fulfilled her religious duty in her own eyes by sending Jim and me to Catholic schools, but in her own quiet way, she was a strong, determined lady, and no church was ever going to tell her how to run her private life.

So there was more of everything for Jim and me, more food, more clothes, and best of all, more loving time and attention from our parents.

I never walked the streets with my stomach grumbling with hunger. My clothes may have been cheap, but I never went to school and had to pretend to smile, as my friends did, when another girl would say maliciously, "Oh, I remember that skirt. Your sister Emily used to wear it."

I never, thank God, slept three or four in a bed meant only for two. Where we lived in the Dingle, Jim and I each had a separate bed of our own; and in the

Cantril Farm house, we had an even more incredible luxury. Never mind that they were closet-sized; we still had a room apiece.

My parents took us for picnics in the woods and sometimes for day outings on the Mersey River. Behind the closed doors of families who bickered constantly and blackened each other's eyes, we were laughed at for this family togetherness.

In the eyes of the Dingle and Cantril Farm—everywhere in insular Liverpool, in fact—my parents were both regarded as "foreigners."

My mother's "foreignness" consisted of being born in Wales of Irish parents, and my father's, though he had been brought up in Southampton, of being a Scot. The speech of both of them was quite distinctively (unforgivably) different, and their English too pure, lacking the harsh Scouse accent.

For many years they were treated as different beings, slightly set apart. This suited them fine. My father was never one of the lads, and my mother was never one of the girls. They had each other, and later on Jim and me.

To create a family unit must have been desperately important to both of them; they had been without one for so long. Both had left home at the same age, fourteen. My mother came away when her own mother died and her father remarried a tough old bird who didn't want any leftovers from the first wife. My father's father died quite young, so as soon as he could, he went to work on the ships to relieve his mother of the care of at least one child out of her nine.

Until he met my mother half his life later, my father was never off the ships for more than a two weeks' leave. Liverpool was where the ships docked, and Liverpool was where my mother finally drifted, after first working in a small hotel in Wales and later on in Cadbury's chocolate factory.

Her only sister, my Aunt Bronwyn, had settled there; but Auntie's husband died of leukemia when he was still a young man, and my mum came to live with her to help out with the three kids.

In Liverpool Mum got herself a job in Vernon's Football Pools; and as luck would have it, Dad came to Vernon's one day on his leave to place a bet. Once he and Mum started keeping company, he never placed another. His philosophy was simple. *If you can't afford to lose, you can't afford to bet.* A man with family responsibilities, he reasoned, could not throw away even a trifling bit of money that his family might need.

This philosophy alone made my father unique, but he had other qualities, my Dad did, to match.

He gave up the ships and worked on the docks after Jim was born, so the family would be together. He worked hard, as dockers must, and every day when he came home from the job, he worked some more. He was an artist at carving in wood, though no one in those days knew it. He constructed almost all the furniture in our home and was merely considered "handy." There was never any money left over, so night after night through the winter months, he would sit in the warm kitchen, he and my mum seeming always to have plenty to say to one another, while he made our toys for Christmas—a fort, a dolls' house, a pram, wooden soldiers.

He was a wonder to all our neighbors, was my Dad. My friends' mothers were perpetually curious about him, as though he came of some strange exotic species.

I can close my eyes and see their eager, somehow greedy faces, remember their avidly questioning me.

Doesn't your Dad ever have a drink then?
Doesn't he ever go inside the pub at all?
Doesn't your mother ever let him?
Do they never fight?
You Dad's real good around the house. Does he help your mother cook and clean?

They would chuckle, these women who often sported black eyes and bruises as tokens of their husbands' love and devotion, half-envious, half-contemptuous that my father was more likely to be weeding in his garden of a summer night than hanging out in the Bow and Arrow; critical that my mother was a tyrant who kept him tied to her apron strings at home. Never mind that *their* men started dying at forty-five and seldom lasted beyond sixty, with the booze and the factory dust and the fabric lime all rotting out their stomachs and their livers and their lungs!

I was seven when my parents decided to make their home on the outskirts of the city, which in those days was considered a pretty adventurous move. Most city-bred people preferred a slum in Liverpool, even the rubble of the war-ravaged Dingle, to the woods and trees and quiet of Cantril Farm.

Auntie Bron stayed on in the old neighborhood, and though I loved my new home, I was always delighted to go back to visit her. During World War II the Germans had used the miles along the dock for target practice, blowing up thousands of houses. As a kid I loved to go to my Aunt's so I could play on the bomb sites and dig for buried treasure. We'd turn up broken cups and plates, shards of exotic glass, buttons, once even a bit of silver.

Hordes of kids roamed around there. They were like wild wolf packs, running through the maze of alleys behind the houses, climbing into yards, pinching the wash off the lines, helping themselves to anything that wasn't nailed down, whether it was wanted or not.

They would sneak in and out of shops, stealing sweets, fruits, or the bread loaf from the shopping bag of some poor old woman who couldn't run fast enough to catch them. They were without pity, without feeling . . . and for a while, I was one of them.

I didn't have the excuse of the tough home life and the lack of love that most of my gang lived with, but to be accepted as part of the street life around me, I had to be one of them.

It's called peer approval now; survival on the streets it was then. There was no room on the streets for love or understanding or compassion. I was almost ashamed that I had these at home. Loyalty to friends was all that counted. To uphold this tradition, fighting became a way of life. Fighting between Catholics and Protestants. Territorial fights—strangers were supposed to stay out of our area. Later, there were the men's and boys' fights over girls, and girls were beaten up for looking at or being with the wrong fellow.

It was like leading a double life: the home life and the street life. I wasn't the only one who existed that way, though most who did had more and better cause. *Their* homes lacked almost everything—money, food, clothing, beds, caring.

The sameness of the home and the ugly street environment was supported by the sameness of the public school system for the poor. God help anyone who showed individual promise or dared to ask questions; damnation and punishment were the rewards doled out to those who bucked the establishment.

Catholic schools in Liverpool, sadly, were the worst. With an undertone of impending religious war always around the corner, our schools were obsessed with prayer, religious fervor, and discipline. The three got all tangled up together in such convoluted confusion it was hard to distinguish one from the other.

We were taught that God was love when it was obvious to even the meanest intelligence that this wasn't true in practice. Layman, nun, or priest, discipline was the obsession of most teachers. We weren't children being educated; we were animals being religiously trounced into awareness of the basics for survival.

My first day in school when a teacher said, "Eyes front," I lowered mine five seconds while I scratched an itch on my right calf. For that I got three smacks on the hand I had scratched with as well as three smacks on the leg that had dared to itch.

After age nine we were graduated to punishment in the grown-up way—taps from a bamboo cane that had been soaked for weeks in a lemonade bottle full of vinegar.

The subtle swift flick of the cane across a quivering palm could inflict a red-hot trail of pain. By age twelve we had learned to show stoic acceptance of six of the best without so much as batting an eyelid. No tears. Tears were an unaffordable luxury, punished by two extra strokes. Animals must not show emotion.

Liverpudlians have a reputation for being hard-faced. God knows, to survive we had to be.

My brother Jim was not only brighter than most, he showed talent in drawing. He had several teachers who took a special interest in him and helped him to prepare for college, which meant higher education after age thirteen.

The student who did well on the eleven-plus and went to college was exposed to a much broader field of study: languages, the sciences, even art and the theatre.

The student who didn't pass the eleven-plus went to a state school, Catholic or Protestant, where what you really did was mark time until age fifteen, which was the day you said good-bye to education.

In effect, this meant that one test alone could determine your whole future. It decided whether there was just the *possibility* that you might rise a little higher in the world, or that you would be forced to spend your whole life in the factories or on the docks. To fail that test meant you could be condemned at age thirteen to the same bleak life as your father and your mother! It was like a foot set on your neck, holding you down and daring you to rise.

Even as a young child, I was troubled by the sweeping cruelty of this system. It was so final. It seemed so unfair.

My father—maybe with some premonition of what was to come—spoke my own secret thoughts aloud. He said often, cleaning it up for my mother's benefit if she was around, that it was horse manure to believe that one examination could be a sure test of anyone's ability to deal with his or her entire life.

He was obviously proud when Jim passed the eleven-plus and went on to college, but he never stopped telling *me* that I could be anything or do anything or make anything of my life that I wanted to. Luckily for me, I had such faith in my Dad as the fount of all wisdom that he got me to believe what I later found out he never really believed himself!

Chapter 2

THE YEARS BETWEEN THIRTEEN AND FIFTEEN WERE tremendously important in shaping my life. I failed the eleven-plus. I got suspended from school. I discovered Boys with a capital B. My skinny stick of a body started blossoming in all directions, and the boys then began discovering me. I found the greatest treasure any Dingle kid had ever uncovered at a bomb site near the docks, and I began the backward journey into my own roots. I nearly died of pneumonia, and the man in silver entered my life.

It would make my story more coherent, I guess, if I began with that day in the Dingle. Me mum—God, how easy it is to slip back! I mean, *my* mom and I were on a visit to my Aunt Bron's. Both the boys were gone from the house, working on the ships, and my Cousin Jeannie had not yet come home from work. Auntie Bron had proudly produced a tin of American coffee

her son Tom had brought home on his last leave. She
and my mum were having a cuppa, and I was restless
and bored, so I took myself off for a walk.

I was scuffling along a whole section that was still left
standing as bare and bombed-out as the day years
before when the Germans blitzed it. The toes of my
shoes scraped the ground. I wasn't really looking for
treasure the way I usually did; I had begun to feel that I
was too old for that kid stuff. All of a sudden I got this
feeling of someone watching me. You know the feeling
I mean . . . there is no one around when you look, but
you feel as though there are eyes boring into the back of
your shoulders.

I turned every which way, but no one was there. Still,
I had that same uneasy feeling. I could hear faint music,
not in the air, but seeming to come from inside my own
head, and there seemed to be one slim shaft of light just
ahead of me . . . you know, like in the theatre, when
the spotlight hits the stage, directed on just one block
of space.

I stayed still, afraid to move, hardly daring to
breathe. I knew, I just knew something tremendous
was going to happen. Whether good or bad I wasn't
sure, and I found myself shaking with the excitement
of it.

I stumbled. How I stumbled I can't figure out to this
day because I was standing stock-still.

I went down on my knees, scraping them against the
rubble, and there in front of me was a large, jagged
fragment of crockery. I picked it up and, hardly knowing what I was doing, began to use it like a scoop,
digging around in the dirt and bits and pieces.

That's how I found my star, so dull and lackluster
then I had no way of knowing right away that it was
pure gold and that the little dull chip in the center was

anything more than a bit of stone. It was the shape that intrigued me. The Star of Bethlehem in our religious books, the gold stars for awards at school—they all looked the same. I had never seen a six-pointed star before.

There was no more music; the shaft of light was gone. There was just me, kneeling in the rubble of the Dingle, but I knew with a passionate certainty, clutching the star in my hand, that this was what I had been meant to find. It was on a chain so rusted and decayed it fell apart in my hands. I let the chain fall away and with the toe of my shoe ground it back into the rubble from which it had come. The chain wasn't important. Only the star.

I don't know why—up to then I had never been much of a keeper of secrets—but I didn't tell Mum or Auntie Bron.

I took the star home with me and that night I tried to clean it up. I soaked it in a glass of soapy water and I rubbed it dry. I went on rubbing it hard with Mum's soft polishing cloth that she used for the silver wedding bowl she had gotten from Cadbury's.

It looked a little better but still not the way I thought my star should look. The next night when Dad got home I waited for him to finish his tea, and then I put the star on the kitchen table in front of him next to his cleaned plate.

"Is there any way to make this shine the way it should, Dad?"

He picked up the star in his own slow, deliberate way.

"Now where would you get a thing like that, our Rilla?"

"I found it in the rubble when I was walking near the docks. I want to make it pretty again."

Mum came to look over his shoulder at the thing lying in his great, horny palm.

A look of gentle sorrow came over her face. "Rilla Cohn used to wear a star like that," she said softly. "A silver one, it was, on a bit of black ribbon around her neck. I never saw her without it."

Rilla Cohn, I knew, was my mother's best friend when she first came to Liverpool. She died of cancer the month before I was born, and Mum still mourned her even after all these years.

Truth to tell, I had a secret grudge against Rilla Cohn. I had been named after her, and her full name was Amaryllis. A sillier one, I used to say, though never in Mum's hearing, I had never heard. Rilla Cohn must have thought so herself because she never used anything but Rilla. Neither did I.

A strange look passed between my mum and dad. His hand suddenly clenched around the star, then just as suddenly released it.

"My mother wore one, too," he said, and smiled a strange distant smile, unlike the usual cheeky grin he was wont to bestow on the peccadilloes of life, mine in particular. "She gave up everything but that when she came away from Cornwall."

The room was full of electricity. Behind their words were strange, hidden meanings I couldn't fathom.

"Why should she have thought of giving it up, Dad?" I asked uneasily. And then, as an afterthought, "I didn't know me grandmother came from Cornwall."

"Aye, she did, and her family before her for several generations, and before that God only knows where they'd fled from to save their skins."

Again I was aware of strange currents in the room . . .

"Why did they have to save their skins?"

"They were Jews," my father said quietly.

My mouth fell open in shock. "Jews!" I squealed. "Me own grandmother was a Jew?"

"Aye."

"And me grandfather. Was he a Jew, too?"

"Not him. He was a Protestant."

"A Protestant!" I sat down at the table, reeling with the horrid shock of it. Protestants were the enemy. No longer ago than last Orange Lodge Day I'd lined up against them in a street fight and come home with a bloody nose and a cut lip, satisfied I'd given as good as I got.

"But you were maybe brought up Catholic?" I queried him hopefully.

My father seemed to have shaken off his somber mood. He looked me over, a distinct twinkle in his blue eyes.

"Now use the brains the good Lord gave you, Rilla, my girl," he admonished me. "With a Jewish mother and a Protestant father, why would I be brought up Catholic?"

"Which were you then? Or are they both alike?"

"No, they're not both alike." My father shook his head meaningfully at my mother. "That's some education the girl is getting, even to have to ask." He turned back to me. "I was brought up Protestant. Why, I don't know, and neither do I care. I don't much believe in any religion, if the truth be known. They're the source of most of the evil in the world: wars, family break-ups, cruelty between people . . ."

"Why did you never tell us?" I wailed.

"Well, girl, think on, you never asked. And have you ever seen me in church except when you and Jim took communion and had confirmation? Haven't I always told you religion's your mother's department?"

45

He gently laid my star on the table and turned up my chin with his hand. "Am I any less your dad than I was yesterday because you've discovered I'm not a Catholic?"

I gave him a rare hug. "You're the best dad ever. I guess I better not fight the Protestants anymore."

He started to chuckle as I turned to my mother to ask, "Your friend Rilla Cohn, she was Jewish, too, then?"

"She was."

I looked at her doubtfully. "Were me granny and granfer on your side both Catholic like you?"

"Irish and Catholic both, and you can't get any more Catholic than that."

I must still have been looking doubtful because she drew herself up straight and proud, all five feet three of her, in a grand dignified way she had, and told me straight out, "I'm as good a Catholic as any, I hope, and I've brought up you and your brother to be the same, but it's my own business who I have for a friend and I wasn't about to let the church choose my husband. I chose for myself"—she looked Dad straight in the eye—"and I've never had a moment's regret over the choosing."

The color flamed up in her cheeks at the way he looked back at her. A year or two later I would have been a bit smarter and maybe had the sense to make myself scarce so they could in all decency go off into the bedroom. As it was, my father made a rare gesture.

"I'll drink to that, Angie, my girl," he said.

He got a bottle out of the cupboard, and my mum produced three of her best glasses, the ones we hardly ever used.

It was brandy he poured into the glasses, just enough in mine to wet the bottom, but even so I sputtered and choked on just the one mouthful. I thought it was nasty stuff.

My father said, as he and my mother drank and continued to give each other that strange soft look, "If you would like me to, Rilla, I'll be taking your Star of David down to the jeweler's near the dock and see if I can get it cleaned up for you."

"Oh, please, yes, you do that for me then, Dad." I stopped to think. "Why do you call it Star of David?"

"Because that's what the six-pointed star is called. It's the symbol of being a Jew."

"Does it make me Jewish if I wear it?"

"You're whatever you want to be," my mother said promptly, then added with typical practicality, "Still, if you're planning to wear it to school, tuck it down under your shirt out of sight and save yourself a bit of trouble."

My father laughed out loud. "Never fear, Rilla. Between your mother and me, we've made you a proper mongrel."

When he brought the star home to me a few days later, I thought it was the most beautiful thing I had ever seen, all shiny and golden, with its dozens of slender, twisted bands interlacing one another and what had seemed a dull, dead stone in the center turning out to be a sparkling, blue green jewel.

"Ooh, Dad, it's gorgeous."

"Mr. Coleman offered you eight pounds for it. Real old it is, he said."

"Eight pounds!" I clutched the star in my hands. Eight pounds was a fortune. When had I ever seen so much money? "You won't make me sell it, will you, Dad?"

"Is it likely I would make you sell what belongs to you?"

"But eight pounds . . . what we couldn't do with eight pounds!"

"There's a roof over our heads, and plenty of good food on the table," he said dryly, his expression making it clear he was not fooled by my show of nobility. "We'll survive as we have all these years without your eight pounds."

I had planned to wear my star to school and, contrary to my mother's advice, to keep it right out in sight, but it wasn't possible. The hook on top was so small that not the narrowest bit of ribbon or piece of string would go through it. So I kept it in my shell box labeled "Souvenir of Blackpool." It sat there on my dresser, and never a day passed that I didn't look at it morning and night.

"Some day when I'm rich and famous," our Jim promised me once in an expansive mood, "I'll buy you a real gold chain to wear it on."

"When I'm rich and famous, I'll buy me own."

"I'm older. I'll be rich and famous first."

"Not bloody likely."

I didn't hear my father come into the kitchen. The first sound and sign of his presence was a light stinging wallop on my behind.

"While you're both waiting to be so rich, try helping your mother get the dinner on the table. And Rilla, watch your language, lass. You know your mother doesn't like to hear you swear."

Chapter 3

P ROMPTLY AFTER I DISCOVERED MY FATHER WASN'T
Catholic, the whole world discovered it, too. I made my
announcement to the twerp of a teacher who taught
religious instruction, thinking in my blissful ignorance
that it might get me excluded from the daily drills of
catechism.

It didn't.

The class got lectured instead, with special emphasis
directed at me, on the evils arriving out of mixed
marriages. The catechism drills became even more
intense, the general opinion being that I needed them
that much more.

Another outcome was a healthy increase in the
length of the weekly visit from dear old Father Mack,
who came by every Friday to pick up our donation for a
new church bell. Only now his visits stretched on and
on, with conversion lightly touched upon. No real

pressure . . . just the merest suggestion that he would be happy to lead Dad to salvation.

It was my mother who finally and firmly and politely told Father Mack to please stay out of the affairs of our household, we were happy as we were.

The next thing that happened to upset the easy ebb and flow of our lives was my failing the eleven-plus.

Only two girls from each school were allowed to pass, and the two from our school that did were only average, whereas I had been first in my class for six years straight, and I knew, I just *knew,* I had done well on the exam.

My father shrugged when I brought the bad news home.

"Annie Casey and Noreen Murray, hmm . . . both their fathers are collectors for the church . . . and our family's not even in good standing in the parish what with the poor old sod of an unbelieving dad you've got yourself."

"You think it's that then, Dad?" I asked him, on fire at the injustice of it.

"Don't you?"

"I've been ahead of both Annie and Noreen all our lives. It seems funny it should change now."

"Not funny, lass, but sad, and the way of the world. But it needn't affect your future. Even if you can't go to college, you can still—"

"Be anything and do anything and make anything of your life you want to," I finished up with him.

"Aren't you the cheeky one!"

Cheeky I was, and something more. From that day on I got harder in my feelings and hard-faced on the surface, too.

I fell from the rank of first in my class to thirty-second out of thirty-three. I had not only lost interest in learning, I had lost heart in the belief that trying would get me anywhere. The system was against me.

Boys suddenly seemed more important than books. All sorts of womanly things were happening to me. My mother explained about them matter-of-factly, though the truth was I had earlier picked up much of the information on the streets.

To show off my figure to best advantage, I flaunted the pitiful beginnings of what I fondly imagined was a burgeoning bosom in sweaters deliberately shrunk one size too small.

The boys started brushing up against me, and sometimes their hands or their arms, even elbows, would "accidentally" touch up against private parts of me.

"Par-dunny-mwa," they would say, straight-faced, but with a gleam of triumph in their eyes.

"Par-dunny-me," I'd answer ever so sweetly as I kicked them in the shins or doubled up my knee if what they had done deserved a real jab.

When I went to the state school, I found a real soulmate, Josie Corbett. Talk about hard-faced, they didn't come any tougher than Josie! She was one year older than I on account of my having started school early since I combined an August birthday with "brightness."

Josie was smart as a whip herself, but she wouldn't bother to study.

"What for?" she asked. "To work in the corset factory?"

She wasn't afraid of anyone, not her drunk of a father, not the biggest bully on the block, not even the meanest teacher in the school. She could take six of the best, laid on cruelly hard, and laugh in the face of the one who was caning her. She would speak her mind in class, no matter what the consequences.

I saw Josie break down only twice; the first time was the day her sister Mary left for America to be a mother's helper. Mary was second oldest and Josie the youngest in a family of seven, but "She's the only one in the whole bloody family I care about," Josie sniffled, swiping her sweater sleeve across her face and under her nose.

Then she said, "Oh, well, it will only be a coupla years. When she puts enough money by she'll send for me, or maybe as soon as I'm old enough she'll line up a job for me in the States. She says she's never coming back."

Josie and I got suspended together by the personal order of the new headmaster, Mr. Creedon, who had gotten his experience in running a school by directing a Boys' Borstal for ten years. A headmaster who went from training delinquent boys to a state school, that was the way of English education in those days.

God, how we all hated Mr. Creedon! If he was alive and in front of me right now, there wouldn't be an ounce of forgiveness for him in my heart. I would still gladly do him whatever bad turn I could.

The first time Mr. Creedon talked to us in Assembly, I knew—we all of us knew—we were in for trouble. He was tall for an Englishman, nearly six feet two, very shinily bald on top but with little tufts of white hair sticking out at the sides and even the back of his round head. He walked ramrod-stiff, with short quick steps; and he talked in short, clipped sentences.

He kept his cane tucked always in his left trouser leg, and he whipped it out suddenly while he was telling us what would be expected of his students.

"I soak my canes for two or three weeks on one side, then reverse and soak them two or three weeks on the other side. It takes about six weeks for a cane to be properly soft and supple." He paused and gave us a seraphic smile, then continued, "There's an art to giving a good caning. It's all in the movement of the wrist."

He demonstrated the proper flick of the wrist for us, cutting the air with a swish and a snap that chilled the blood of more than one of us. "When you crack down straight, you get sound but not substance." Another smile. "No one will ever laugh when they get caned by me," he added softly. "I guarantee it."

In the hushed stillness of the assembly hall his bold gray eyes moved over us row by row; and I don't think it was just my fancy that they lingered a few extra, meaningful seconds on Josie Corbett, sitting next to me.

I shivered in my hard-backed seat; lots of the kids did. Under Mr. Creedon the daily bouts with the cane reached an all-time high. We got punished for coughing too loud, being late for school, not going to church on Sunday, pulling faces in class, talking out of turn. Or there were general sessions when an entire class would get the cane because one person wouldn't own up to an offense and, true to the rule of the streets, no one would tell!

When Mr. Creedon did the public caning—which I think was something he loved to do; his gray eyes glistened with pleasure and little beads of sweat popped out over his forehead even before he began—afterward he made the victim stand before him while he prayed forgiveness for all our sinfulness.

It was probably inevitable that some time in the school year Josie and I would collide in a head-to-head confrontation with Mr. Creedon; I'm only surprised now that it took so long.

We were in class one day, and I had finished my

history assignment early and was staring out the window, daydreaming about the handsome prince on a dashing white stallion who was going to come prancing up the dirty stairs of the school, charge right into the schoolroom, and take me away. I heard some whispering off to the side, but I was too busy with my daydreams to pay attention.

"Josie Corbett! Rilla Scott!" Sister Agatha's high-pitched whine snatched me out of my world of beautiful make-believe. "How many times must I warn you about talking in class? Come to the front of the room."

I got up, shrugging resignedly, pulled down my blouse, and hiked up my skirt. Josie caught my arm, pulling me back, then crossed her own arms belligerently.

"We weren't talking, Sister Agatha, not either of us."

Sister Agatha turned purple and her eyes bugged out. "Three for talking, three for answering back. Come to the front. Fetch the cane."

I was ready to get it over with, but Josie said stubbornly, "I didn't talk, and I'm not going to be caned."

I stood beside her, scared but loyal. Someone in the class giggled nervously and received a gimlet glare from Sister Agatha, who wagged a bony finger at Josie and me as she warned threateningly, "This is your last chance."

She glared at us, and we stared her down.

"Report to Mr. Creedon, the both of you!" she snapped.

"*You* report to Mr. Creedon!" Josie sassed. "I'm going home."

I thought Josie was bonkers, but she was my best pal, so we marched out of that room together, too.

We were dead silent till halfway to our lockers; then we suddenly looked at each other in the hall and started laughing. We laughed till the tears poured down our cheeks and we were doubled over.

The word got around fast. We had no sooner emptied our lockers and pushed through the outside door when Miss Scully, the girls' head teacher, came panting after us. "You girls come back here and leave your school uniforms," she shrilled. "You're a disgrace to St. Jude's. You have no right to wear your uniforms in the street."

Josie turned around and made a rude noise.

"Up your backside with a meat hook. Me mum paid for this uniform and I'm wearing it where I please."

Miss Scully gave a scream at this street vulgarity and, still screaming, ran away. Mr. Creedon promptly sent formal word home to our folks that we were suspended until such time as we were willing to make a public apology and take our punishment—also publicly.

My mum said, "Oh dearie me!" and went off to consult Auntie Bron. My Dad said respectfully, "That's quite a vocabulary your friend Josie has." Then, "Well, Rilla, I'll not force you my girl, but you'll just have to weigh an apology—"

"And the caning," I interrupted.

"An apology and a few licks against a year and a half's education."

"Some education."

"If you learned just one thing in all that time— maybe just one little bit of knowledge that would help you in the outside world, then it could all be worthwhile," he told me quietly. "Think on it, lass. I'll stand by you, no matter what."

If he had ranted and raved like the average working-class father, who just didn't want any bother brought home, why then I might have defied him. But he was so *reas*onable, my dad was, so willing to see both sides.

"All right then, Dad, I'll think on it, but I've got to speak to Josie. I have to stand by her."

Josie came to the house next morning, and my mother made us both fried eggs and potatoes. Josie had to eat hers standing up. Her father had taken his belt to her. She would get the belt every night, he had warned her, until a proper apology was made and Mr. Creedon lifted the suspension.

"We'd best go back today then," I said, butterflies churning in my stomach at the thought of what was in store for us. "No use your taking an extra licking from your dad tonight."

At school, a special assembly was called just for our benefit.

Mr. Creedon made a long preparatory speech. There were some students, he bemoaned piously, who were a disgrace to their school, their religion, even their city. If it was up to him, their contaminating presence would never be permitted back at St. Jude's, but he had to abide by the law of the land, and he could only pray by making the two delinquent girls he was speaking of an example to them all, everyone present would profit by the lesson about to be learned.

He stepped forward to the edge of the platform.

"Rilla Scott! Josie Corbett! Up here on the double!" he boomed.

Josie and I sat paralyzed. It was the only time in my life I had ever seen her scared. One of the teachers hissed at us, not unsympathetically, "Hurry yourselves, girls," and we went forward in a daze and found ourselves up on the platform.

Mr. Creedon made a dramatic gesture of slowly drawing the cane out of his trouser leg. It looked a thicker one than usual. He slashed the air with it a few times, and I tried not to wince at each crack, I didn't want to give him that satisfaction.

It was Josie he hated most, so he took me first to keep her in sick suspense. "Hold out your right hand, Scott." I had hoped to get away with the left. Swish. Swish. He held the cane high in the air and snapped it down viciously, criss-crossing my palm and fingers with flaming welts.

By the time he'd given me six of his very best, my hand was on fire and I was sick and dizzy with the pain. I stood there, gritting my teeth to keep from whimpering, waiting to be dismissed.

Through my misted eyes I could see the curl of his smile.

"Hold out your left hand, Scott."

A concerted gasp went through the auditorium, and then a sighing, excited murmur of sound. Everyone knew the maximum punishment allowed by law was six strokes.

"Silence!" thundered Mr. Creedon.

There was instant, hushed silence.

"Punishment has been given for the first two offenses of talking in class and refusing proper chastisement. However"—the cane cracked in the air like a bullwhip as he flourished it between Josie and me—"there was a third offense. Insubordination." He drew the syllables out slowly. "Not-to-be-tol-erated in-sub-or-din-ation." Then again, "Hold out your hand, Scott."

Who was going to protest that this was an exercise in sadism? That the daughter of a working-class man was being caned beyond the limits set by law? The police? They would've laughed at the notion.

In the breathless, palpitating silence, I bit down on my lip till it bled, willing myself not to give him the satisfaction of hearing me cry out. Rigid, I endured the second set of swift, searing strokes.

It was Josie, to my dismayed astonishment, whom he finally reduced to tears. I wouldn't have believed it. Josie the indomitable, Josie the hard-faced. But then, I excused her to myself even as I watched for the second time in our friendship her face screw up and the tears flow free: she was still stiff and sore from last night's belting; a girl could take just so much.

But it made my already-churning stomach turn over a little bit more to hear his low whispered aside to Josie, "I always knew I would have you blubbering one day, my fine lady."

The assembly ended, and Josie and I were told to report to Miss Scully to be reinstated.

Plans for our return had been very well laid on, indeed.

Nothing in the law stated anything about punishment for a separate offense by a different teacher.

We received six of the best each from Miss Scully, laid on with a slow, grim satisfaction, each blow acting like salt measured out into open burning wounds.

I think we had both figured out by then the full extent of Mr. Creedon's malice and revenge. Neither of us felt any surprise when we got to Sister Agatha's class that she should be waiting for us, cane in hand.

Chapter 4

I DON'T REMEMBER GETTING THROUGH THE REST OF THE day. It's all a vague blur of agony. My whole body seemed nothing but a pair of red-hot hands. I remember someone in the cafeteria giving Josie and me some pills that we gulped down with water. They were supposed to help the pain. They didn't.

Josie and I left school together, our purses strung around our necks and our books in the crook of our arms so nothing made contact with the raw, sensitive flesh of our hands.

The other students made way for us as we went through the hallway; the front doors were pushed open for us. They fell back, whispering and respectful, as we went down the outside steps. Any other time I would have pranced down them like a circus animal, enjoying all the attention, but not this time. The price paid had been too high.

We walked, Josie and I, for about two blocks, neither of us uttering a word. Finally, she spoke first, an unaccustomed quaver in her voice. "I suppose you blame me?"

I looked at her sideways. "Don't be daft."

"It was my fault, I know that," she muttered almost resentfully. "It was me he had it in for."

"That bloody bastard's got it in for everybody who doesn't knuckle in," I said matter-of-factly. "It was only a matter of time for the both of us."

"You didn't expect him to break me. He didn't"—it was a cry of agony for her lost self-respect—"he didn't break you."

"Me dad didn't belt me the way yours did." I tried to offer her a sop of comfort. "At least you won't get the belt tonight."

"Don't be too sure of that," she said starkly. "I'm not. Gawd, Rilla," she burst out suddenly after another minute, "I'm not sure of nothing except that I have to get out of this life any way I can. I can't wait for our Mary to send for me from America. It's too many years."

At the corner where we usually said good-bye, I called out "Ta" breezily, and she returned "Ta" glumly, and we both went our separate ways.

I didn't have to pretend any more after she left. I plodded along feeling sick and full of self-pity and more confused about Josie than I had been willing to let on to her.

I was halfway there before I realized I was headed to Auntie Bron's in the Dingle, not to my own home. Feeling lightheaded and dizzy, I leaned against a parked lorry just as the driver, a feisty-looking little man, came out of the corner pub.

He looked me over carefully. "I'm headed down to the docks. You after a lift, lass?" he asked me with cocky good humor.

I gulped out a grateful "Yes."

"Hop in then," he invited. "You don't think I'm like that fellow Lochinvar, do you, that I'm going to pull you up on my steed?"

I said pretty meekly for me, "I don't think I can open the door," and I turned my bent arms around, easing up my palms so he could see them.

His rough red face went suddenly white, except for a crop of freckles on his nose and forehead that stood out darker than before. "Holy Jumping Jesus!" he breathed through his broken nose.

Then he came around, jerked open the cab door, put his hands on either side of my waist, and lifted me up easily into the lorry.

He slammed the door shut, came around to the other side, and got in beside me.

"Where do you live then, love?" he asked me gently. "I'm taking you home."

"I live at Cantril Farm, but I'm not going there now. I'm going to my Auntie Bron's in the Dingle; it's right along your way."

"I don't mind going out of me way to take you home to your mum, so she can tend you."

"No," I cried out fearfully. "I don't dare let me dad see me."

"You're not saying he'd give you more of the same!" he bristled. "Not when Jack Carden gets through with him, he wouldn't."

"No, you don't understand. Me dad's real slow to anger, but when he gets his dander up, he can be the fierce one. He wouldn't half kill Creedon—that's the headmaster at St. Jude's—for doing this to me. And our Jim's the same way. They'd both be after his blood."

"It's right and proper they should be. I would myself if it were me own daughter this was done to."

"That's just it, Creedon would get back at them. He's a mean one, our headmaster is. Six months ago Tim Donnelly waited after school one day and tried to lay into Creedon for thrashing the youngest Donnelly. Much good it did him. Headmaster did most of the beating up; then he turned around and laid charges of assault against Tim as well. He got him sent up for three years."

I broke down in unexpected weeping. "I don't want me family harmed. Auntie Bron will take care of me. She'll know what to do."

"Okay, love, don't take on, where does your Auntie Bron live? You've got yourself a bloody limousine ride to her door."

I rubbed my wet face and nose against my shoulder and told him Auntie Bron's address.

We drove a little way in silence, then he asked me my name and I told him. Then he wanted to know what had happened, so I told him that, too, making it as short as I could.

He said shrewdly, when my voice trailed off, "This mate of yours, this Josie, you're upset, ain'tcha, that you turned out to be tougher than she?"

"Josie's tough!" I denied indignantly. "Why, Josie's the toughest girl at St. Jude's. She's . . ."

"But you're stronger . . . so what? She's still your mate, ain't she? She's allowed to be human. Maybe if she had *your* mum and dad she wouldn't have broken down neither. Appearances, they can be deceiving.

Looking at me size now, would you think I was a fighter once?"

I grinned feebly. "Yes."

"It's the cheeky one you are, Rilla Scott. Now we're almost there to your auntie's, so do me one more favor. This *Mister* Creedon, your headmaster, what's the bloke look like?"

I described Mr. Creedon from the tufts of hair on the top of his head to the tips of his pants legs with the protruding edge of the cane.

The driver stopped his lorry right in front of Auntie Bron's. I noticed he was writing down the street number. Then he came around and opened the door and lifted me out, careful not to touch my hands.

"Take care of yourself, love." He rubbed his crooked nose. "I have to drive down to London and back . . . arrangements take time . . . Do you suppose that, say Friday night a week, you could make sure your dad and your brother stayed to home, with maybe some family and friends—solid, respectable folk who could swear, if it came to swearing, that they never left the house? That no one connected with you could have been anywhere near Creedon?"

"Couldn't I, though!" I exclaimed, my heart bounding joyfully at what he seemed to imply.

With a wave of his hand, he got back in the lorry, but poked his head out the window as he drove off to shout, "Best of British luck to you from Jack Carden, love."

Auntie Bron took one look at my hands, turned even paler than Jack the driver had, and crossed herself, murmuring, "Merciful Mary." I studied my palms with her and came all over sick; they did rather have the look of unfried steak.

My aunt undressed me and popped me into her own

bed and ran off to the chemist's to get something to use on my hands. It was supposed to be a soothing ointment, but it burned like hell for a bit before it cooled down and she put gauze pads on my hands and bandaged the whole hands, right down to the fingertips.

She knew without my telling her why I had come to her and how needful it was to keep what had happened from Dad and our Jim.

"I'll send a written message by one of the neighbor lads to your mother. We'll tell her I'm off me feed and you're staying the week to look after me. When she comes to visit, she can have the truth. Now drink this, it'll put you to sleep."

I drank and went to sleep and woke up sweating and in a nightmare. I was standing in front of Mr. Creedon and having both hands caned together. This time I wasn't so brave.

Auntie Bron told me later I screamed for real.

I was off my head a lot of the time for a day or two, the pain stabbing me fiercely and the fear almost as bad.

Sometimes when I woke, my mother was there, heavy eyed and tight lipped, but I knew her anger wasn't for me.

"Dad?" I croaked, dry mouthed. "Jim?"

"Don't fret, Rilla. They know nothing. They think you're in school during the day and here taking care of Bronwyn at night so I can be home."

She changed my bandages often. The skin was still tender but healing nicely.

"Mother of God!" she exclaimed once, smearing on the ointment. "If I was sure I could get away with it, I would strangle that man with my own two hands!"

"Angie!" Auntie Bron cried, shocked.

"Don't Angie me, Bronwyn Slater. It's the same as you would do, and well you know it, so don't be starting to toss God's will at me. Religion is all very well and good but where it belongs."

"What day is today, Mum?" I asked her before a quarrel could erupt between them.

"It's Friday."

"He said I should make sure that Dad and our Jim are in the house one week from tonight."

They both stared at me worriedly. They thought my mind was wandering again.

"I'm talking about Jack Carden," I explained. "He's the lorry driver who brought me here. He said we should have witnesses to Dad and Jim being home that night because he might be arranging something for Mr. Creedon."

My mother and my aunt looked at each other, then my mother put the bandage roll away in its box and said briskly, "You'll come to supper then next Friday night, Bronwyn, you and Jeannie and her young man."

"We will that."

"And I'll send a message to Father Mack that I've a fine piece of flounder put by for him, and we'll expect him to stay to tea when he comes by collecting for the church bell. There's nothing he likes better than a bit of flounder, and there's no better witness than a priest of the church."

The next Friday night we had a fine party at our house. Auntie Bron came with Jeannie and her boyfriend Brian. Father Mack was there and the family from next door. Jim had planned to go out with his mates Innis and Sid. Mum and I practically kept him home by force. We wound up having Innis and Sid to dinner, too, and I flirted happily with the both of them.

The police came around asking questions early the next morning. Mr. Creedon had been assaulted and badly beaten up the night before.

"What's it to do with me?" Dad asked him in genuine bewilderment.

"He didn't see faces, but your name was high on his list of suspects. It's natural you—or maybe your son—should hold a grudge after the thrashing he said he gave your daughter."

"It's the first I've heard of any thrashing," Dad said grimly. "Rilla?"

"We was afraid you might get mad and do something daft," I admitted meekly, and held out my hands, healed now, but still pink striped.

"By God, but I would have!" he swore lustily. "The man can thank his lucky stars," he informed the police grimly, "that whoever got to him before I could, left him alive."

A couple of days later a clipping from a Liverpool newspaper came in the mail to Auntie Bron's house. It was all about the headmaster of St. Jude's being brutally assaulted on the streets by a couple of thugs. Scrawled across the headline was a simple greeting. "Best of British luck from J.C."

Creedon was in hospital for nearly two weeks. I passed him in the hall his first day back. I didn't smile or blink an eye. I just looked at him steadily, letting him know full well that *I* knew. I wondered if Jack and his mate had said anything while they did the beating-up.

I never got caned again, and neither did Josie, but she left school just the same not five months later. She was pregnant by Ted Halsey, who was on the ships. Next leave he got, they married and moved into a single room in a boarding house on the Dingle. Ted went back on the ships and Josie went to work in Weatherall's raincoat factory. She had just reached sixteen when the baby was born. She never got to Mary in America.

Chapter 5

I'VE NEVER KIDDED MYSELF THAT I COULDN'T HAVE ended up just like Josie.

I liked the lads, and the lads liked me.

When I lost all heart for learning, I got even more interested in them than before. When I lost Josie, I turned to boys with a vengeance.

Boys had lots of uses so far as I was concerned. Free ciggies, pints of lager or gifts of candy, not to mention being taken to the pictures. To be sure, they expected something in return—not really too much at first. I didn't actually mind their sweaty palms holding onto mine or certain ways they had of touching. In fact, certain ways of touching felt pretty good.

When I didn't like what they did, I wasn't slow to let them know it.

As I got older I noticed that what I objected to was changing. I was beginning to feel some pretty funny wants and needs of my own.

One night when I was fourteen, maybe even closer to fifteen, our Jim was over to Sid's; Mum and Dad had gone to the pictures.

I was watching the telly by myself when Innis stopped by. Innis and I had never dated like, but we had kept a sort of pretend flirtation going on ever since the Friday night supper that was set up to provide us with witnesses.

I brought some cookies in from the kitchen and Innis sat watching the telly with me, and what with one thing and another, pretty soon what was going on between us on the couch got a lot more exciting than what was happening on the twelve-inch screen.

My blouse was unbuttoned in front, and somehow he had managed to unhook my bra at the back. My skirt was up about my knees, and before long I could feel fingers working their way down inside the band of my panties.

I tell you that boy seemed to have as many hands as an octopus, and all of them were very busy about me. The worst of it was my suddenly not minding. Even more, I was beginning to be much too pleased by some of the things he was doing.

I had always been contemptuous of the girls that both sexes labeled "easy." Now I was beginning faintly to see how there was no such thing, just good old Mummy Nature at work, bringing trouble to any one of us.

Halfheartedly, I tried to push Innis away, but he just laughed as though he knew I didn't really mean it. Again and again, his hot mouth returned to mine, devouring me with his kisses. After a while, instead of pushing him away, I felt myself squirming close, wanting even more. More of what?

And then suddenly it all changed. A cold shiver went through me, the kind I had always heard described as "someone walking over my grave." The eerie music I had heard just once before (the day I found my star) began sounding inside my head.

I shoved Innis, but strongly this time, meaning it, so that I succeeded in breaking away from him.

I jumped up from the couch and stood next to it, looking to a dim dark corner of the room which was suddenly all lit up. There wasn't a lamp or bulb anywhere near . . . the radiance seemed to come from nowhere. It was like something tangible, and as I watched, scarcely daring to breathe, a man stepped into the middle of the light.

I think I screamed.

Innis said "What the hell?" coming upright, and I pointed with my trembling finger, quavering, "How did he get here?"

He was like no other man I had ever seen before, at least outside the pages of a book. He was dressed all in a shiny, silvery gray cloth with a kind of pants that were like knickers, only they had bows tied at his knees, and a tight jacket with a fancy undervest done up with pearl buttons. He was tall and strong looking with eyes of a piercing blue, brows that were thick and black, a mouth that was harsh and set. In spite of the lace all about him and the ribbons tying back his powdered hair, he was all man.

He was all man, too, in looking anything but pleased, glaring at me and shaking his head like a stern parent.

I quavered again, "Wh-who are you?"

Innis said again almost plaintively, "What the hell's going on here?"

The answer to my question came, just as the music had, sounding inside my own head.

"What a way to behave! Put your clothes to rights, my girl, and send that creature home."

Quaking with fright, never taking my eyes from the man in silver gray, I said, "Innis, go home."

"Aw, Rilla, what kind of game are you playing?" he cajoled, reaching inside my blouse.

I recoiled, not so much at the contact but at the thought of the strange man's watching it.

"Clear off!" I shouted to Innis. "Go home. Don't ever do that again."

Highly indignant, he slammed out of the house, calling back that it would be a cold day in hell before ever he returned.

"Button up your shirt!" the man in silver ordered me. "Make yourself decent!"

I turned my back, unable to obey in full view of him. Tremblingly I hooked my bra behind me and buttoned up my blouse in front. When I turned back, I was sure he would be gone—this had to be a nightmare—but he was still there, his face still stern and set but his mouth less harsh.

"Now understand me, there's to be no more of this. You're not for the likes of him."

"Wh-who are you?" I asked tremblingly again. "Wh-what are you?"

An indulgent smile played around the corners of his lips, softening his mouth, lighting up his eyes.

"All in good time, my dear," he said ever so gently, and was gone from me as eerily as he had arrived.

The light faded, the music ended. I was alone and more frightened than I had ever been in my whole life. I bolted to my room and dived into my bed fully dressed, trying to hide myself completely—even my head—underneath the covers.

I never breathed a word about the man in silver to anyone. What was there to say that anyone could possibly have believed? Sometimes, thinking it over, I told myself I must have dreamed the whole thing. Yet I knew I hadn't. He had really stood there, admonishing me, talking inside my head.

Something about me was different, not quite like other girls. It was not the first time I had suspected it, but always before I had been smugly pleased that it might be so. I didn't feel pleased anymore, only quietly and coldly terrified.

For weeks, every time the family sat in the parlor I kept eyeing that dark corner of the room, nervously starting at every sound, expecting him to turn up on me any minute.

"For God's sake, sit still, girl!" Dad finally exploded one night. "You're jumpy as a bride on her wedding night."

Mum, though frowning down this description, agreed that I had been unusually fidgety lately.

I made a conscious effort to calm down. Then, since the man in silver didn't reappear, after a while the effort wasn't conscious. He wasn't going to reappear, I comforted myself. Maybe I had just hallucinated him. Hallucinating was a new word I had just come across and promptly taken to my heart; it seemed so to fit my case.

Several months went by. I had a new boyfriend, Marty McHugh. He was a lorry driver and real sophisticated, I thought, a whole six years older than I. I had been partial to lorry drivers ever since Jack Carden.

Even if there hadn't been Jack Carden, Marty was something special, good looking, good natured, well dressed. He took me to my first posh restaurant for tea and to dance places none of the other lads I knew could afford.

Inevitably, I suppose, he took me to the furnished

room he rented, and where, he said, we could have "a bit of a chat" without being interrupted.

We went up the back stairs so as not to disturb his landlady, and a few minutes into the chat, I was sitting on his lap in the room's one big armchair.

He had a way of cupping his big hand around the back of my neck and then sliding it slowly down and around in front, all the way around, with his other hand coming from the other direction to meet it.

I nearly jumped out of his lap in my excitement, but he laughed softly and brought me back, tilting my head back against his shoulder, teasing my lips with little nibbling kisses, not devouring ones the way Innis had.

The first thing I knew we were lying together on the top of his coverlet; but with what was going on between us, I knew it was just a question of time how soon we'd be popping underneath.

I knew it in a hazy back corner of my mind, but still I couldn't do anything about it. I just lay there, madly kissing and being kissed, on fire everywhere his hands touched and probed.

And then . . . and then . . .

I gave a shriek as the music and light and the man in silver appeared all at once.

He was standing at the foot of the bed, looking at me like my Dad used to when I was a kid before he let loose a swipe at my backside.

His blue eyes on me were haughty and disdainful. "I thought I told you," he said coldly, "that the likes of these—these young men you allow to *fondle* your body are not for you."

I asked almost tearfully, "Why are you doing this to me?"

Marty thought I was talking to him and scoffed,

"C'mon, quit yer teasing, you were giving as good as you got."

The man in silver said through clenched teeth, "I will not permit these intimacies you indulge in with any oaf off the streets."

"*You* won't permit. Who the hell are you to permit?" I flung at him.

He crossed his arms and regarded me. "Very well, then, madam. As you please. Let him take you into his bed. Get the business over with."

"Are you crackers?" Marty asked. "What's going on here?"

"Are you crackers?" I demanded of the man in silver. "I c-can't *do* anything with you here . . . watching . . ."

"You can't do anything without me here," Marty pointed out.

"Oh, shut up!" I said to him rudely. "I'm talking to *him.*" I pointed to the man in gray.

Marty looked where I was pointing, quite obviously saw nothing, and shrugged.

"Quit the play-acting. Are you or aren't you?"

I glanced desperately toward the man in silver, and he stared gravely back at me, only not quite so serious as before. I think it was the lurking twinkle in his eye that decided me. For the first time I didn't find him frightening.

"I'm not," I said firmly to Marty.

"Till we meet again," said the man in silver softly. Shivering with a new and different kind of excitement, I watched him fade away.

"Get your shoes on and take yourself home," Marty snarled. "Try me again some time when you're all grown up."

I didn't snarl back because he had some right on his

side. I *had* treated him pretty shabbily. Showing quite unusual meekness for me, I put my shoes back on and went quietly out through his door and down the back stairs.

It was raining hard, and I had counted on Marty to drive me home. Out of vanity I hadn't worn a raincoat —not even a sweater—over my new V-necked jersey dress. The jersey just sopped up the rain, wetting me through and through. The next day I was coughing and sneezing, eyes and nose running. In forty-eight hours my cold had turned into pneumonia.

Chapter 6

THEY TOLD ME AFTERWARD THAT I CAME CLOSE TO
taking a one-way trip straight through St. Peter's pearly
gates. I wasn't unduly bothered since I was sitting up
and eating sausage rolls by the time I was told how
close I had gotten.

Truth to tell I had too much else on my mind.

My family told me that for several days during my
pneumonia I had been out of my head. What they
didn't say—because they didn't know—was that during
those days I had made contact with another world.

I remember lying on my bed in a kind of sodden
stupor, with someone wiping a cool cloth over my face
and forehead. There was the sound of weeping all
about me and then sharp stabs of pain as the music
danced in my brain.

Soft and low as the music sounded, it hurt my head.

"Stop that!" I said feebly, and the cool cloth came

away. My Mum must have thought I was saying it to her.

I tried to close my eyes against the shining light, but it was as though I had no choice. My eyes opened wide, and *he* was there—my man in silver gray.

He sat on the side of the bed as close up to me as he had ever come. He stared down at me with his hard blue eyes and began laying down the law in his usual peremptory fashion, without making any allowance for my illness.

"This nonsense has got to stop. You're not fighting—not even trying. You've been many things not so admirable during your life, but at least never before a quitter."

I tried to sit up and couldn't make it.

Mum, leaning clear through the man, pressed me back down.

"Bollocks!" I said wearily when she had straightened up and he was visible again. "Why don't you just bug off?"

"Your language, like your manners, is execrable," he said severely. "I obviously neglected to school you enough when I had the chance. Since, however, I prefer you bawdily belligerent to wilting like a damned dandelion, this once I will let it pass. Now I *order* you to start resisting this illness and begin getting well!"

"Oh, you order me, do you, your high and mightiness? Well, you can just—"

"Don't say it," he warned.

I swallowed the words; I don't know why, there was no way he could have hurt me. It had become obvious by now we could see and speak to each other's minds but never ever touch.

I asked sullenly, "What's it to you?"

77

His hard face took on a gentleness I had never
dreamed it could show. His eyes were lit with a hundred
flickering little lights I had never seen in a real man's
eyes, only in a film or on the telly.

He spoke in a voice that was soft and low and urgent
and caressed me more tenderly than ever Innis or
Marty's hands had done. "It is close to two hundred
years since I first loved you. I have waited for this next
life overlong. I refuse to allow you to die and make me
wait two hundred more!"

My anger had all melted away. I looked into those
blue blue eyes of love, and my insides turned to mush.
"We loved one another?" I asked him almost shyly.

"By God, but we did. Too much for just once. I—he
is waiting for you again."

A shiver of excitement shot up and down my spinal
cord and then moved slowly frontward.

"I won't die," I promised him solemnly.

"Good, just stick to that."

He sat quietly, and I lay still, and we looked at each
other, both of us happy and peaceful. Presently I
remembered what he had said and stirred myself to ask,
"Two hundred years ago was I like now?"

He chuckled aloud. "No, my little Scouse love"—his
mouth twisted with laughter at some picture he must be
seeing in his mind—"Except for your spirit, you were in
every way different."

"Rilla love, are you awake then?" I heard my
mother's voice ask softly.

The man in gray got up as though to take his leave.

"Don't leave me!" I cried.

"I'm not leaving you, lass. Your mum and me, we're
both here," Dad spoke up gruffly.

Tears squeezed out of my eyes. It was *his* reassurance
I needed.

"I'll always know where to find you," I heard the gray man's voice. "Haven't I been with you and watched over you since the day you found your star? The star will always bring me to you when there is need."

I sobbed, bereft, when he was gone. I wailed, "My star, I want my star." It was the magic talisman that would keep him close.

Voices. Not his.

Her star, the one she found in the rubble on the bomb site.

She keeps it in the shell box on her dresser.

No Father, with all respect, I won't let you be giving her the last rites. Last rites are for the dying. Our Rilla's going to live.

"I promised him not to die," I tried to say loud and clear.

"That's right, our Rilla," my father's voice spoke close to my ear. "Now here's your star in your hand, close your fingers around it, touch it, feel it, it's there the way you wanted."

I clenched my hand about the star, tried to smile, and smiling, fell asleep.

I woke up to the waning sun of the late afternoon. My mother was asleep in a chair by the window. How worn and tired she looked, I thought, moved to love and pity.

I sat up, mouth agape in a huge yawn. I stretched my arms over my head, yawning again, and my mother waked all in a rush and leaped up out of her chair.

I smiled at her, asking, "Is there anything to eat, Mum? I'm hungry."

"Merciful Mother!" she answered, and began to weep.

Then she rushed over to the bed and felt my forehead. She said, "The fever's gone, you're cool as snow," and wept again.

I unclenched the fist lying in my lap to try to give her a comforting pat, and something fell from my hand onto the bed. My star. I looked down at it stupidly, my memory not yet in focus.

I had been sick, I remembered vaguely . . . but what was my star doing clutched in my hand?

I looked down at my palm, and my memory returned all at once. The man in silver, *my* man . . . the star had brought him to me, he said . . . and there was the star right in the palm of my hand, not the solid star of gold but a sketch, deep and red, as though someone had carved on my skin a perfect outline of the six-pointed Star of David.

My mum looked down at my palm, saw what I did, and said again, "Merciful Mother." Then she nodded her head in a strange way, as though she were confirming something to herself.

"I'll put some food together for you from the fridge," she said quietly and left me.

Dad came in from the job not too long afterward, and in minutes he was at my bedside, confirming the good news Mum had already given him.

They both stood over me, talking excitedly. Then Mum said, "Show him your hand, Rilla."

Knowing what she meant, I held out my right hand, palm up. It had faded a little but was still very clear. No one could mistake it for anything but what it was, a Star of David etched into my hand.

"That's the way it was when she came to herself," Mum said quietly, and her eyes met Dad's, and a look of perfect love and understanding seemed to pass between them.

"Life plays strange tricks, Angie," he said, seeming half-glad, half-sorrowful.

"It does that, Wallace," my mother acknowledged.

The next day when my father came home from the docks, he had a present for me, a long gold chain, solid 14 Karat the clasp said, yet slender enough to go through the top hook on my star. For the first time I was able to wear it around my neck.

He fetched a mirror to the bed so I could see it hanging down against my nightgown.

"Coo, it's beautiful, Dad." I hugged him hard. "However did you afford a gold chain, 14 karat like?" I breathed reverently.

He said gruffly, "It costs less than a funeral."

We both gulped a little, thinking of that grim might-have-been. Then I asked, "Can I wear it always, Dad?"

"It's your own choice, lass."

"Even at school?"

"I'll take care of the school, mind. If you want to wear it, you wear it."

So I flaunted my jewel proudly when I was well enough to go back to school, and nobody said anything out-of-the-way. In fact, several of the girls praised the prettiness of the star and admired my fine gold chain. I doubt that they knew what it stood for, and if any of the teachers did, they weren't saying so. My dad had done his work well.

Still, by far the most important thing that happened when I returned to school was that I gave up the boys and took to my books again. My last year there I went from thirty-second in class all the way back up to first.

The beginning of June, with just a few weeks of schooling left to us, a counselor, Mrs. Wilson, came from the education committee to advise us on our futures.

She was a big, blowsy woman with mean little pig eyes, a red nose, and thick, self-satisfied lips. I disliked her on sight.

She stood at the front of the room, and her advice to us all went something like this: "You will soon go to work in the factories and shops hereabouts, and I will do my best to procure jobs for all of you."

She beamed at us, waiting for the gratitude we were no doubt supposed to feel, then concentrated on us one by one.

"What is your name, dear?"

"My name is Sally Miles."

"Stand up and tell us what you would like to do."

"I would like to work in Sayer's, the cake factory."

"Very good, Sally." She made a brief note on the desk pad. "I'm sure you'll like it at Sayer's. I'll do my best to place you there. You next, dearie. What is your name?"

"Joan O'Hare, Mrs. Wilson. Please, I'd like to work at Simington's."

"The corset factory? Yes, indeed, a good choice." The thick lips spread in a smug smile. "I know the foreman well. Keep doing good work, and I'll put in a word for you." She scratched vigorously on the pad. "Next."

"I'm Sheila Dunn," came in a breathless whisper, and then with a kind of desperation, "I want to try to get into Vernon's Pools."

Mrs. Wilson's pen hesitated over the pad. "Vernon's Pools . . . hmm. That's setting your sights a bit high. They take only the best. But I'll see what I can do, Sheila."

"Oh, thank you, Mrs. Wilson."

It went on and on like that, leaving me more than slightly queasy. For the first time in my life I faced the reality of the future. Girl after girl that I'd grown up with reeled off her name and her ambition to work in a green-grocery shop, a cake shop, or a raincoat factory.

And all of them were assured with Mrs. Wilson's thick-lipped smile that they would like it there, she would help them.

It dawned on me frighteningly that I might actually wind up like most of the other women in the neighborhood, five kids, a shopping bag, pushing a baby pram with curlers in my hair, big night out Saturday night. I might get trapped for life in a terraced house in the Dingle and spend my days cleaning the door steps and knockers, going to the shops, gabbing with other women on the corners, fixing my man's tea, waiting hopefully for him to come home from the nearest pub.

I was one of the last to speak because I always sat at the back of the room.

I drew a deep breath when Mrs. Wilson pointed to me but stood up and faced her boldly. "I'm Amaryllis Scott," I said, the first time I had ever openly admitted to the full name.

Her smile was supposed to be encouraging.

"And what would *you* like to do, Amy-rillis?"

"I want to go to America and become famous."

The entire class cracked up, of course. Who can blame any one of them? Where did a lower-class Scouse get the nerve to have any such ambition?

Mrs. Wilson's smile withered. She asked coldly, "How do you propose to get there?"

I thought of my dad with his *You can do anything or be anything you want.* . . . I thought of Mary Corbett in America and Josie a mother at sixteen.

I said clearly and confidently, "I'll work anywhere I can till I'm old enough, then I'll go as a mother's helper."

Mrs. Wilson signaled that my classmates should stop laughing even as she made it plain that she shared in their merriment.

"You will end up like the rest of your friends in a factory and married by the time you're nineteen," she told me with a vicious little flick of her tongue against her lips.

I told Mum and Dad about it at the supper table that night.

"You should have punched her in the nose!" my father said stolidly, cutting into his steak.

"Oh Lord, I hope you don't get married before twenty-five," my mother reinforced him.

Bless them, they were great.

And bless Mrs. Wilson, too, the bloody old cow. Nothing triggered my determination so much as knowing the world was full of people like her trying to keep me down!

Chapter 7

I DID JUST WHAT I HAD TOLD MRS. WILSON I WOULD. I worked anywhere for the next two years waiting till I was old enough to go to America.

My first summer out of school I was a waitress in a resort hotel on the Isle of Man; the next summer I went over the water to Jersey.

In between those two summers I must have been employed in six different sewing factories. My sewing was good, and I didn't mind the work. It was the rules that kept me on the move. I got fired all six times, along with my new best friend Mavis Green, for the sin—shades of Mr. Creedon—of in-sub-or-din-a-tion.

Mavis used to be terrified to go home and tell her parents. Mine just laughed or rolled their eyes at one another. The next day I would go out and find another job.

My highest-paying stint was with Jackson's, the tailor's, where I did piecework, making whole suits, for which I got a big fat weekly seven pounds. My longest-lasting job was Vernon's Football Pools, where I managed not to get myself chucked out for a full four months.When I finally did get fired from Vernon's, it was one month short of my seventeenth birthday.

"Rilla, what's going to become of you?" my mother sighed, not really anxious.

She was her usual cheerful self when I had given her the bad news but burst into tears when I answered her question. It was time, I told her, to shake off the chains of Liverpool. London came next.

I went to Dad on the sly and tried to make him understand. "It's not that I want to leave you and Mum, just that I want to make me own way. And Liverpool—it's not the world. You've traveled lots, Dad. Me, I've never been out of smelling distance of the Mersey."

Dad finally told Mum, "Angie, you know our Rilla. If she's bound and determined to go, then go she will. At least let it be with our blessing, so she doesn't lose touch."

Mum gave her blessing, and before I completed my plans for going to London, I stopped in at an Overseas Domestic Agency and filled out an application that would allow me to be sponsored to the States as a mother's helper. The minimum age was eighteen, I knew, so I had carefully doctored the records I brought with me, pushing my age up by two years.

The agency said that, what with the processing of the papers and getting someone in America to accept me, it might take quite a while.

"That's okay with me," I said cheerfully. "I'm not going any place."

Then I promptly scarpered off to London.

Two days after arrival in the Smoke I had landed a job in a coffee shop in Queens Way, running the cash register. I found myself a two-room flatlet in a once beautiful faded brick Georgian house in Nottinghill Gate. The old lady who owned it had fallen on bad times and converted it top to bottom into flats and furnished rooms.

I had quite a few dates my first six months in London, but they were what you might call short-term relationships. Boys in the Smoke weren't any different from the Liverpool lads. When they took a girl out, they weren't exactly interested in being with a brilliant conversationalist. In fact, it suited them fine if she didn't talk at all. A quick trip to the films and the fish and chips, then a quick hop into bed was what they wanted.

I wasn't about to do any hopping, so most of my dates ended on a sour note. They felt they had been cheated.

I began to feel cheated, too.

The months had slipped by without my even noticing; it had begun to be years.

In all that time I hadn't seen him once, and in all that time, because of him, I had not been able to let myself be kissed or cuddled by any other male creature.

I began to feel quite sorry for myself, and from self-pity, I worked my way up to fury. I was mad at myself for being daft enough to let him run my life, even madder at him for never coming back to me.

Jenny, a young schoolteacher who lived in my building, put the seal on my discontent. She wanted to arrange a blind date for me with her boyfriend's mate. I declined, maybe a bit curtly, but only because it would maybe lead to complications. The mate, I knew from past experience, would probably wind up complaining to his friend about sticking him with a girl who was a dead loss.

"Listen, honey, if there are any two things I regard as someone's private business, it's her religion and her sex life," Jenny told me earnestly, "so don't think I'm prying or casting any stones. It's just that I can't help wondering if you're a Les, and if you are, then I'll stop trying to fix you up. If you're not, though, then I can't understand why you wouldn't take a chance on Doug. He's a good-looking bloke, one of the best, and real generous."

"I'm not a Les, Jenny. It's just that . . . that . . ." I stopped, helpless to say just what it was.

"Then I'd say you have naught to lose," Jenny informed me.

How long was I supposed to stay faithful to a phantom lover who didn't even trouble to stop by for an annual visit?

"Okay then," I agreed recklessly. "I'll do it."

Jenny's description, I discovered, hadn't half done Doug justice. He was more than just a good-looking bloke, he was downright handsome. Tall, dark blond hair, brown eyes, an athlete's body.

I had never known a man with so much money to throw around and quite so willing to throw it. He took me out once, twice, three times. There was no arm wrestling, no dress ripping, just a quick kiss good night, and the kisses as often as not were on my forehead or the tip of my nose.

I began to think I had found my ideal companion until the night of date number four when he took me back to my flat and I invited him in for a cuppa.

I was standing at the table, laying out the cake plates while the tea brewed in the pot, when Doug came up behind me and put his arms around me, running his fingers ever so lightly, ever so gently across my breasts.

I was startled by the violence of my own reaction. Not against him. God, no! After my first startled leap, I reversed into his arms and lifted up my face. I was not just eager for his kisses and the touch of his hands, I was starved for them. I responded with a vengeance as Doug proved himself eager to help the hungry and the needy.

"Jesus!" I heard him murmur against my throat. "Jenny said you were shy-like and only needed bringing out. But this—I have a feeling in my bones this will be a night to remember. You were worth the waiting for, Rilla."

I left the cake to go stale and the tea to grow cold in the pot while I went with him willingly into my little bedroom, where he crushed me down under him on the bed.

The cacophony of music in my mind as he tried to yank up my dress was like a bolt of electricity striking at my head. I was deafened and dazed both at the same time.

I moaned so hard and so loudly that not even Doug could mistake it for passion. He rolled off me and sat up. "Here now," he asked me anxiously. "What's going on?"

I put my hands to the sides of my neck, pressing against the stabbing pain. As it eased a little, I flung up one arm over my face and, with the other, I tried feebly to fend him off. *Him,* not Doug.

A fat lot of good it did me. When I struggled into sitting position, he was still there, standing in his usual cocksure fashion at the foot of the bed, the usual look of insolent disdain on his face, the usual scolding on his lips.

"At it again the minute my back is turned. Will you never learn?"

"The *minute!*" my mind exploded. "Damn you, it's been almost two years. I might as well go into a convent as wait for you. The world's passing me by, but what do you care?"

"Rilla, you look queer-like," I heard Doug saying from far off. "I'll just be going inside and brewing you a cup o' tea."

"Thank you," I said gratefully, glad to see him go. Whether we talked, the man in silver gray and I, with our tongues or with our minds, this was a private quarrel.

"I can't even pass a pleasant evening with a lad because of you," I shouted aloud the moment Doug was gone. "I can't—there's no kissing in my life or—or . . ."

"Yes," he said a bit grimly, "it's the *or* that has me worried."

"Well, why shouldn't I? I'm human, aren't I?"

His eyes took on the steely look I knew so well. "You can do whatever you have a mind to, my girl, but just remember I'll be there watching when you do it. As for the world going by, good God, you've just turned seventeen. Your whole life's ahead of you yet if you'll just be patient."

I looked down into my lap, avoiding his eyes. "I missed you," I told him. "I could . . . I could . . ." I looked up again, biting my lip and blushing madly. I said awkwardly all in a rush, "I could stand being without others if I had—if you—if . . ."

"Good Lord! Tonight was for my benefit?" He studied me ruefully. "You went this far with him only in order to draw me?"

I nodded, unable to speak for the lump in my throat.

"And if I hadn't turned up?" he queried me gently.

"Then it might as well be Doug as any other," I admitted. "Though it's God's truth you're the one I wanted here. It's come to me that I'd rather have your ghost's smile and even your scolding than another man's flesh and blood arms about me."

"Here's your tea, Rilla."

I took the cup and saucer from Doug, smiling at him gratefully. Over his shoulder I smiled a "Ta" to the fading man in gray, and he murmured to me that he would return quite soon.

I can't blame Doug that I never saw him again, not when I heard afterward that the most memorable thing about the night for him was that after I edged him out of my flat he was in such a state, he stopped off for a brief visit of consolation with the prostitute who lived upstairs.

And I can't blame Jenny for her uplifted eyebrows when she saw me the next morning, or that she never tried to get me another date. In her place I would have acted the same.

I didn't blame myself either. It wasn't as though I had a choice.

I got through my work in the Queens Way coffee shop by day, ran up the dresses I sold on the side by night. And I waited. And I waited. Only this time, not for so long as before.

There was a sink in every flat but only one bathroom to a floor. We had to sign up for baths by prearrangement.

I was having a good long soak one Friday evening. I had poured salts that smelled deliciously of violets into the tub, and I was lathering myself all over with my favorite lavender soap when I heard my special music and looked up to see the man in silver seating himself jauntily on the edge of the tub. He crossed his legs and smiled at me, preening a bit.

"See?" he said. "I kept my promise. Here I am."

I gasped, "You're not supposed to be here," and sank deep down into the tub so nothing of me showed below my neck and shoulders.

"My dear girl, the last time I saw you, you reproached me for staying away."

"But not when I'm in me tub."

He studied me with calm interest. "I've seen you before without your clothes."

"You never have!"

"The girl you used to be. It's one and the same."

"Not to me, it isn't."

"Lower-class prudery, my dear."

"You're nothing but an upper-class snob."

"She called me that, too," he said reflectively, seeming to remember it with pleasure.

I flashed at him, "Well, she was right," and that seemed to please him, too.

"The question before the House, my love, is do you or do you not want me to visit?"

"Yes, I do, only not when I'm in me bath," I wailed. "It isn't proper."

He gave me one of his sardonic looks, lips faintly curled and eyebrows soaring up his forehead. "I suggest you keep that in mind, since you're so set on being proper, the next time you are tempted to roll about in a bed with one of your lusty suitors." He got up from the tub and bowed low from the waist. "I shall visit you again, ma'am, when you are not in your bath."

As he disappeared into the fog of the overheated bathroom, I heard the lilt of faintly mocking laughter and then a whisper of sound. "You are a very fetching sight in a state of complete undress, my love. Forgive me for mentioning that just a little extra meat on your frame would not be amiss."

I threw the soap after him, which proved to be a mistake. There was no response at all from him, but *I* slipped on it getting out of the tub.

Chapter 8

Mᴜᴍ ᴘʜᴏɴᴇᴅ ᴍᴇ ᴏɴ ᴀ Wᴇᴅɴᴇsᴅᴀʏ ɴɪɢʜᴛ ᴡʜᴇɴ I had been in London for about five months. A letter had come for me from the Overseas Agency with the offer of a job in America.

I had Jenny call me in sick at the coffee shop, and I flew down to Liverpool on the first morning plane. I went straight from the airport to the Agency.

The prospective employer was a Mrs. Deedham, who lived in a place called Huntington on Long Island, which she said was just a short train ride from New York City.

She had five children, three girls and two boys, but there was other help in the house and I was wanted for just the youngest girl, Dinah, who was five and needed a companion while the others were at school. I was also expected to do some of the light housework, dishes and dusting and such. I would have plenty of time off.

It sounded good to me, and the woman at the agency

said it sounded good to her. Mrs. Deedham had already signed, agreeing to pay my plane fare and sponsor me into the country. Without any hesitation I signed the application agreeing to work for her for a year for the agreed salary, benefits, and bonus. I allowed my signature to be witnessed and the papers notarized.

I spent the day with Mum, stayed to see Dad at tea, and then flew back to London that same night.

Seven weeks later I was on a plane to America, wanting to go, eager to go, but with tears streaming down my face every time I remembered how Mum and Dad had looked when we said good-bye. There were seven of us on the plane being sent by the same agency. One of them, Linda Coyne, I used to know at school when Josie was my best friend. She lived near Auntie Bron in the Dingle and was going to a job in a place called Larchmont, New York.

"It's north of the city, like," she told me, showing me a map she had got hold of. "This Long Island of yours is the other way, I think."

We both pored over the map as our plane zoomed across the ocean, and finally I was able to put my finger on Huntington.

It was a long, tiring trip, and my stomach was churning with excitement and dread by the time we landed at the John F. Kennedy Airport. We girls all stood in a little huddle outside customs, waiting for our prospective employers to find us.

Some of us were identified by pictures that had been sent with our applications. In some cases our names were called out.

I heard a sweet, soft voice say, "Rilla. Are you Rilla Scott?" and I turned with a sigh of relief.

She looked as soft and sweet as her voice, so slim and pretty it was hard to believe she had five kids. Fancy a woman with five children at home looking like that! Smooth young skin, softly curling blond hair, pink cashmere sweater, and a pink and blue skirt of the finest wool.

For once my native Liverpool shrewdness played me false. I had one good night's sleep, thinking I had landed soft, but before twenty-four hours had passed, I knew my mistake.

Behind the soft, sweet manner was a will of iron; the saccharine smile hid a wide streak of meanness. Under the deceptive charm, Mrs. Deedham was as tough a biddy as any I had ever met in Liverpool. About the 'other help' in the house, she fluttered vaguely the next day, "I've just lost her, so you'll have to manage without for a while."

Before long I found out that the just lost help had been gone a few years, and the light housework consisted not just of hard housework but *all* the housework.

My one charge Dinah was multiplied by all her brothers and sisters. I had the full care of all of them.

Either they liked their mother no better than I did and all had emotional problems, or the five of them had weak bladders. They were all bed wetters! Every morning I had five beds to change and five loads of bedding, from the quilted pads to the sheets and blankets, to run through the washer and the dryer. This, in addition to all their clothes.

I was expected to learn to cook for the family, and she was a bit impatient at my slowness in learning to cook American style.

I was expected to iron and vacuum as well, scrub floors, sinks, and toilets, answer the phone, serve at table, and keep her from being bothered by her children.

Thursdays and every other Sunday I was supposed to have off, but the first Thursday came when I'd only been in the house three days. "That's too soon for a day off," she said merrily, though I was already reeling between jet lag, culture shock, and exhaustion. I didn't get the first Sunday either; "every other," it seemed, began with the second Sunday.

The second Thursday I didn't even ask; I just took off right after breakfast. I had debated between going to the branch of the agency office in New York City to tell them I couldn't stick the damn job or to see my friend Linda Coyne in Larchmont. After talking to Linda on the phone, I decided to take the two long train rides to Larchmont instead.

Linda looked all bright and bubbly. There were only two kids in the family she worked for, a girl and a boy. The mother worked in a library, and she had full charge of the house, but no one expected her to kill herself. It was an easy household. She'd had one date already with the gardener's son. She was wildly happy; she just loved America! There was a job with a family called Mailer who lived only two blocks away from her. Their Scots girl had just left on account of getting pregnant and married in that order. Was I interested?

Was I ever!

Linda arranged an interview for me that same afternoon. Mrs. Mailer turned out to be Maggie Mailer, the actress. I had never heard of her in Liverpool because she wasn't in films, but Mrs. Deedham watched her several afternoons on television on what the Americans called a soap program. It was called "Storm Warning," and Maggie played the part of a beautiful, wicked home wrecker called Caroline Marsh.

She looked the part, too, all dark flashing eyes, black hair, and high cheekbones in a Garbo kind of face. She was tall and carried herself like a queen, but underneath, I discovered later, she was all soft and sweet, as Mrs. Deedham pretended to be and wasn't.

When Linda brought me over to the house, Mrs. Mailer was outside playing with a little boy who was maybe between two and three years old. As we came around the corner, she leaned over to a pile of leaves, gathered up a handful, and sprinkled them over him. He laughed out loud and threw as many as he could gather in his hands back at her. His laugh was a sound of pure happiness.

She smiled as we came close to her. Linda did the introducing, and I gave a quick look at the big, round stone house topped by greenish turrets and battlements on each side. It looked like a baby castle.

She saw my glance and laughed deep down in her throat. "Crazy, isn't it?" she said. "But we love it." A single dimple in her left cheek deepened. "Don't worry; you won't have to clean it. Hannah does most of that, and we have a man who comes in twice a week for the heavy work. You'll have to do dishes, dusting, and beds, and be there for the boys when I'm not there. I go to New York about three days a week for my show; you knew about that, didn't you?"

"Yes, Linda told me. It sounds easy enough, ma'am, Mrs. Mailer."

"Don't kid yourself. Easy it's not. I've got four boys. F-o-u-r, four. Do you know what that's like? Perpetual noise. Perpetual action. Perpetual pandemonium. Do you like boys?"

I grinned. "Almost since my cradle."

"You're not frightened by the prospect?"

"I don't frighten easy."

"You look a bit younger than I expected."

"I'm nineteen," I lied valiantly.

"How about dogs? Do you like them, too? We've got two, a big retriever and a small mutt. Also some hamsters, goldfish, and a turtle."

"It sounds cozy."

"Rilla, you seem crazy enough to belong with this family. Do you want the job?"

"I bl—certainly do."

"Do you smoke?"

"Now and then," I lied again.

"Only in your own room, never anywhere else in the house. If you agree to that, then you're hired. When can you start?"

I explained about Mrs. Deedham and my agency contract. She frowned thoughtfully. "It will be best to deal directly with the agency. I'll call and agree to take over your contract." She hesitated a minute. "Are you sure you would have left your job if Linda hadn't—"

I knew what was coming and interrupted hastily, "Mrs. Mailer, I would have scarp—left her, I mean, if I had to knock on every door in Huntington and ask if they could use a scullery maid."

"That's all right then. Let's go in and phone the agency, and you can meet the boys. This one in the stroller, by the way, is Edward, my youngest, but we all call him Chick."

"Hello, Chick," I said.

He laughed his happy little laugh again and flung a handful of leaves at me.

We went into the house and the other three came pelting down the stairs, two of them tossing a baseball back and forth, the third shooting a water pistol.

"Not on the new wallpaper!" their mother shrieked. "Rilla, these are my older fiends. That's Nicky, the oldest, and Jonnie just below him. This one is Jethro."

Nicky and Jonnie were dark haired; Jethro had red

99

blond hair like the baby Chick. They all had large, beautiful blue eyes brimming over with mischief.

We went into the kitchen, and while Hannah, the housekeeper, gave me tea, Mrs. Mailer called the agency. It was reluctantly conceded that she could take over my contract only after I got on the phone and said that nothing would induce me to stay on with Mrs. Deedham. Rather than have me just disappear one fine day, without expenses being reimbursed, which had been known to happen, unhappy agreement was made.

The next week was a nightmare. Mrs. Deedham alternately yelled at me, implored, appealed to my sense of fairness, played on my guilt, and threatened to have me sent to jail or back to England, which she obviously considered comparable.

I stubbornly insisted it was *she* who had broken the terms of the contract. By way of proof I flourished the letter she had sent me about the terms of employment (prudently keeping it on my person afterward), and took my departure the next Saturday after dinner, with a final barrage of insults thrown at me as I walked out the door.

Mr. and Mrs. Mailer were waiting outside in their car for me, discreetly parked a few feet away from the Deedham drive. It was a proper, cream-colored car about half a mile long, this being before the days of gas crisis, not a Caddy but nearly as good to look at.

I breathed a happy sigh as we crossed the grand bridge over the river, leaving Long Island behind. Mr. and Mrs. Mailer chatted easily with me about how it had gone the past week and the arrangements they had made with the agency.

Mr. Mailer was a bit of a surprise to me. I suppose, without really studying on it, I had expected him to be a tall, handsome, glamorous man; instead he was two inches shorter than his wife and stocky, with red blond hair (in the places where it wasn't thinning) like the two younger boys, and the same deep blue eyes as all of them. But so much for good looks; it was obvious she adored him.

When we got to the house, Mrs. Mailer said she had spoken to Linda, who had the next day off, so I should take it, too, to have a bit of a rest and settle in. I could start work early on Monday.

Then she showed me to my room on the second floor, right near to the baby Chick and Jethro but at right angles to what was almost a separate apartment she shared with her husband. Nicky and Jonnie were up on the third floor; Hannah, the housekeeper, had her own little suite adjoining the kitchen.

My room was right under one of the battlements, so it was a funny octagonal shape, small but lovely. There was a shaggy beige carpet on the floor, a solid oak bed and dresser and desk, but what I liked best—through a sliding door, a whole bathroom of my own!

I had one big picture window overlooking the yard, which it was already too dark to see, except for the outline of a giant tree. Mrs. Mailer told me the tree was a weeping willow. I just loved the swish of it, whipping back and forth.

When my new employer left me, I whirled round and round in an ecstasy of happiness. Then I started tearing off my clothes. I wanted to get right into my first very own tub.

I came out of the bathroom nearly an hour later, flushed and rosy and contented as a well-fed cat and wearing nothing on me at all but a towel wrapped turbanlike about my wet hair. There had not been any music to warn me. Or maybe I had been too noisy singing in the bath to hear it.

The man in gray stood at my picture window looking out. He turned to me with one of his rare, heart-stopping smiles.

"Welcome back to America, Ladybeth."

"Ladybeth." I tasted the sound of it. "Was that my name?"

"A slip of the tongue. I meant Amaryllis."

"I don't think you're telling me the truth." As I shook my head, the turban slid off and fell to the floor; a shower of water drops rained over my shoulders, sliding down my back and over my breasts.

I stood before him, naked and not caring. "What was your name?" I asked him.

"It's not important what it was. Soon, very soon, you'll find out what it is. You have come to the right place."

"You mean America?"

"I mean that you've come home, my dear."

"I suppose if you won't explain, you won't, but at least I'm glad that you've come here with me. More glad than you'll ever know."

"Express it, please, by putting on some clothing. It's rather unkind of you to stand there titillating me when I'm physically unable to do anything about it. For a girl who didn't want to be seen in the tub, you seem a mite immodest."

"I'd rather you saw me in me skin than not at all."

"I promise I'll drop in from time to time—either when you need me or sometimes because I need you. Do you like the Mailers?"

"I'm a bit cagey after Mrs. Deedham, but I think so."

"Good . . . because they're very much in your future." He added teasingly, "Ta, my dear," and started to fade.

I said gravely, "Good-bye, my lord," and he returned to me in full form and color, very stern looking, very strange.

"Why did you call me that?"

"I don't know," I answered honestly, puzzled myself. "It just—came to me."

"You may call me Bayard," he informed me with a slight touch of condescension.

"Aye, aye, your lordship," I mocked him.

"Minx!" he retorted, and did his vanishing act.

I let my unpacking go till the morning, snuggled naked between the crisp, fresh-smelling sheets of the bed, and slept a full ten hours.

Chapter 9

I SPENT MOST OF SUNDAY MORNING WITH LINDA WALK-
ing around Larchmont, first promenading in the village
through the streets of closed shops and then down by
the rocks at the shore, watching the sailboats out on the
Sound and the Canadian geese picking their way
through the sand. It took a lot of explaining from
laughing strangers nearby to make me understand how
Long Island Sound got all the way from Huntington up
north to where we were.

That afternoon we went to the city, dirty, grubby,
wonderful, exciting New York. We walked along 42nd
Street, where the prostitutes hustled on the streets and
drugs were sold out in the open. Then we wandered up
to the outskirts of Central Park and took a bus to the
Metropolitan Museum of Art.

I was fascinated by the exhibits and paintings—ever
since we were nippers our Jim and me had loved to
draw—but Linda got bored quickly. I made a mental

note to come back all by myself on one of my days off.

Monday I got up early, put on a plain blouse and skirt, and went straightaway to Chick's room. He was sitting on the floor, playing with his blocks, wearing just one sock and an undershirt, which he had put on backward.

"Let's get you dressed, Chick," I said, pulling out his dresser drawers to see what kind of clothes he had.

I found underpants and corduroys and the mate to his sock and came over to him. "C'mon, Chick," I coaxed him. "I'll help you."

He stared at me, poking out his lower lip. "You tan do it yourself; you're a big boy."

"Huh?"

"The translation," Mrs. Mailer said from the doorway, "is, 'I can do it myself; I'm a big boy.' He says *you* for *I* and pronounces *c* as *t*. You'll catch on soon. Come on Chick-o-lino," she added fondly, "let's get your clothes on before you freeze your tush."

"Tush." I repeated it experimentally. "Is that an American word?"

She choked back laughter. "You might say Jewish-American." She tapped his cute little bottom as she expertly inserted him into the underpants. "It refers to this."

She looked up at me and stared a moment, then an expression of puzzled surprise flitted over her face. "I shouldn't think any girl who wears a Star of David would need an explanation of the word *tush*," she added lightly. There was a slight pause, then she asked me with obvious curiosity, "Rilla, are you Jewish?"

I pokered up, feeling a bit disappointed in her. I had hoped to leave all such nonsense behind me in England.

I answered her a bit stiffly, "I was brought up Catholic, but me father's mother from Cornwall was Jewish, so part of me is Jewish, too. And I've a bit of Protestant in me as well," I mentioned recklessly, giving her the whole bad news, if it was that, at once.

"What an interesting mix for a girl from Liverpool," she marveled. "I suppose"—tugging at Chick's corduroys—"Linda must have told you the Catholic church is just a few blocks away."

"I'm not much on church," I told her straight out, "but I go sometimes to please me mum. Is it the same church you go to, ma'am?"

"I'm afraid I'm not much on church either." She smiled at me. "Unlike you, I'm all Jewish."

I couldn't believe I was hearing straight. "All!"

"Every bit."

"You mean all of you?"

"My husband and me, his parents and mine, our children."

"Gawd!" I breathed. "If that isn't something!"

"Why?"

"I thought Jews would—you know, maybe look different, or act different, or—oh, you know what I mean?"

"No, I don't know. Horns and tails?" she said a bit tartly, and then, at my shocked expression, relented. She pointed out seriously, "You don't look or act different yourself, do you?"

"But I thought it was because I'm only part. I've wanted for years to know how Jews were, how they lived."

"Rilla, we're people, just like any other. Our religious beliefs are different, sometimes not even that, sometimes just our culture."

I swung Chick up in my arms, feeling on top of the

world. "I'd like to learn about your culture then." I wasn't completely sure what it meant, but it sounded a grand word.

That night in my room, as I unhooked the chain around my neck and laid my star on the dresser, I addressed myself to the man who wasn't there. "It must have been *meant,"* I declared to him passionately.

No answer.

"Oh damn, why aren't you here when I need someone to talk to who understands?" I demanded forlornly.

All quiet.

"If you're not more cooperative," I threatened, "I'll just have to find me a fellow around here who is."

He didn't appear, but his voice came loud and clear. *Over my dead body.*

As the extreme silliness of this remark penetrated, he began to chuckle and I began to cry.

"What are you wailing about now?"

"I want you to be real."

"I am . . . you'll find me soon. Be patient, love. Our time is not yet."

Then silence.

No matter how many provocative remarks I uttered, I couldn't tease him into returning or retaliating; and what's more, he stayed away for all of my first half-year in the States. In spite of this defection, never did the autumn and winter months fly by so fast. To use an expression that I heard for the first time in America, I was as happy as a bedbug.

It was an altogether informal and harmonious household and seemed tailor-made for me. Little Chick got to seem like my own kid, and Nicky, Jonnie, and Jethro might have been my little brothers.

I had plenty of friends in the neighborhood, not just

Linda but lots of other girls who had come like me, seemingly from every corner of Britain. Cockneys from London, Scouses from Liverpool, Scots from Glasgow and Edinburgh, Irish from all over, and even a smattering from Wales and the Channel Isles.

Several of us gathered together a couple of nights a week in the houses where we worked, or at local pubs—which the Americans called nightspots or taverns. We shared our days off, walking, shopping, or taking the train to the city.

Chapter 10

THE MAILERS WERE PART OF A LARGE FAMILY, A LARGE and rich family. Aunts and uncles and cousins were always descending on them for meals, holidays, or long week-ends. Mrs. Mailer's two sisters came often with their husbands and children. Mr. Mailer was the oldest of three brothers. The middle brother, Joshua Eric, headed the Mailer Department Stores, with branches in big eastern cities and parts of the Midwest.

My Mr. Mailer, Benjamin H., headed the family publishing business, with offices in New York and San Francisco. I didn't get to meet the youngest brother Charles until the summer. He had gone to Europe on a buying and study trip just about the time that I arrived from England. He was being trained by a much older cousin and would some day run the Mailer art galleries and antique shops.

"This is not a family," Mrs. Mailer used to tease her husband often. "It's a damned corporation."

"At least the work's steady," he would tease back blandly, at which she usually gave a theatrical groan—Caroline Marsh, home wrecker, having been written out of the soap opera, "Storm Warning," via a fiery and fatal car crash.

My first summer in Larchmont was like something out of a book. At high tide the water came nearly to the top of the sea wall in the back yard, and a flight of stone steps as well as an aluminum ramp led down to the water.

The three older boys were half-fish. Even little Chick, with his father beside him, could manage a triumphant dog paddle. My inability to swim produced derisive snorts.

They thought most schools came equipped with Olympic-sized pools and everyone had Long Island Sound behind their houses. I had to explain the hard facts of life about *my* body of water being the Mersey River in Liverpool, where it would have been risking my life from pollution to so much as dip my big toe two inches into it.

The family parties increased in the summer. Everyone came to picnic or barbecue, to boat, and to swim. The three cars—Mr. Mailer's Lincoln, Mrs. Mailer's station wagon, and Hannah's little two-door roadster—in the summer months sat out in the front driveway so that the garage could be converted into what I learned was called a cabana.

A double layer of dark shower curtains were strung up on copper pipes to form a big square dressing room. It contained two wooden chairs, half a dozen unpainted shelves for towels, and a cabinet full of first aid stuff and suntan oil and shampoo.

The entire width of the garage from this dressing-

and-undressing area, which Mrs. Mailer called her house-preserver, was a stall shower rather like a walk-in closet, with tinted plastic board walls so that those showering could not be seen from outside, not even in outline.

"It saves a lot of tracking back and forth in the house in summertime," Mrs. Mailer explained when I was watching in wonder, as the shower was being set up for the summer.

I didn't realize fully what she meant until, starting with the hot weather in June, hordes of visitors descended on us, "like a plague of locusts," my employer said laughingly, not really meaning it. She loved the sun, the water, the summer, and the guests.

So did I. I helped serve the food and drinks. I tossed away the paper plates and carried off the garbage. I tried to keep the kids from getting in everyone's hair. In between I mingled with the guests and took swimming lessons from practically every one of them. I rocked in the hammock and occasionally went out fishing. If anyone had told me I was working on the week-ends, just before I doubled up laughing, I would have stared in disbelief.

In the middle of the first summer, on one of my Sundays off, it was so hot and sticky I canceled my earlier plan to go to New York in favor of a lazy day at home.

I went back to bed and was lulled into sleep again by the hum of the air conditioner. When I finally got up, I put on just shorts and a shirt and went yawning to the kitchen to perch on a high stool, eating cold cereal, sliced bananas, and milk, while I talked to Hannah. Then I got my book and went outside.

There was the usual gaggle of guests, some sunning, some sleeping, some sitting under the willow, helping themselves from the bowls of nuts and popcorn as well as from a huge platter of watermelon slices.

I sat myself on a lounge chair near the sea wall, meaning to read, but Chick came running over to ruin my peace the minute he saw me.

"Tell you a story," he demanded.

"It's my day off from telling stories."

"Please, Rilla." He kicked eagerly at my chair.

I groaned. "Chick, it's your brothers' turn to tell you a story."

"They can't. They went fishing wif Daddy." His lower lip quivered. "They lef' you."

"Why didn't *you* go fishing?"

"You think they're crazy?" asked one of the older cousins, passing by. He put out a hand as he spoke to alleviate the harshness of this remark by tumbling Chick's silky hair on end.

"All right, Chick, I'll tell you a story," I said resignedly, "but only one."

"Only one," he agreed, and climbed onto my lap, where he bounced happily up and down.

"Ugh! What's all over you?"

"You don't know."

"What did you have for breakfast?"

"Pancakes."

"Oh Lord, I should have known. You've got me all-over syrup."

"Some ice c'eam, too," he added scrupulously.

"Ta, Chick, I really needed that."

Another floating relative grinned at both of us in passing, and I delivered a second stern warning. "Now remember, only one. This story," I got going, "is about a fish . . . a really big fish known as a scouse. Now the name of this scouse was . . . er . . . Chickolino, and he . . ."

"Chickolino like you?"

"*Just* like you, and he—Chickolino—was the very last scouse of all the scouses that used to live in the river Mersey. Now one day when Chick—"

". . . olino . . ."

I stood corrected. "One day when Chickolino was feeling very, very lonely . . ."

My story went on for about six or seven minutes, getting more and more creative as I went along. When I was about finished, what with his patting my face and pulling at my shirt and cuddling up against my body, I was about as sticky as he.

"And they lived happily ever after, swimming side by side," I wound up. "Now oops-a-baby, let's go have a shower."

He skipped along with me to the garage dressing room, one syrupy little paw clinging to mine. "We'll have one together," I said, quickly stripping myself of shirt and shorts, bra and panties. "You can keep your trunks on, Chick," I said.

"No," he decided. "You take them off."

I wrapped an oversized towel around me, and we scooted together across the garage and into the stall shower. Before turning on the water, I put my hand outside the door to hook my towel over the handle. Then I lifted Chick high to the spray, while he shrieked with joy and splashed the water. "Wash you, wash Chick," he said.

I reached up to the soap tray and found it empty. "No soap, Chick." I set him down. "How about you just rinse?"

He stuck out his lip at me. "You tan get soap from Hanaha," he said, marching his little bare ass out of the shower. By then I had lived with him long enough to know that this translated into "I can get soap from Hannah."

I sang while I waited for Chick. I don't remember the tune, but the words I made up as I warbled. Something about a boy and a girl from London town, and I sang in my best cockney accent until I heard the opening of the garage door that led to the downstairs area of the house.

"Have you got the soap?"

There was a thumping sound for an answer. Chick, with his hands full of soap, probably couldn't twist the handle of the shower door. I kicked it open for him with one foot.

"Come on in, love," I invited.

No answer. And no entrance.

"Come in here this minute so I can close the door!" I ordered impatiently.

"All right, but just remember, *you* were the one who insisted."

With these words, not my little pint-sized Chick but a full-grown man came into the shower!

Did I hit him over the head or kick him out the door like any sane, sensible girl would have done? No, I just stood there and gaped at him, utterly speechless, completely transfixed.

I don't know *what* it was about him . . . I still don't know . . . I have never known.

He was maybe six or seven or eight years older than I. I couldn't always tell with Americans; they seemed to age so much more slowly. He was tall and had good shoulders, but Marty, the lorry driver who had kicked me out of his apartment and contributed to my pneumonia, had topped him by a few inches, and his shoulders had been even broader.

My shower visitor had a good, healthy-looking kind of face, tanned and strong, but I remembered that Doug, the soccer player in London, had been handsomer.

There was just something about this lad, about his coal black hair and coal black eyes that was . . . oh, I don't know, *compelling*-like. It's the best word I can think of. Altogether, he had a kind of dark, lithesome, long-legged, wonderful Indian look about him.

Like a ninny, like a real nitwit, I just stood there and stared. And you better believe that he was doing some staring of his own. But at least *he* had on a shirt and swimming trunks. He was the epitome of modesty compared to me and my birthday suit of newly suntanned skin.

I didn't know where to put my hands first to cover myself. I spread them over my chest, but he only chuckled. When I immediately lowered them to—well, where they needed to be lowered to—he leaned against his side of the shower and laughed so hard, he wound up crying, too, it seemed, but I couldn't be sure of it with the shower spraying him almost as much as me.

I don't know if our staring contest ended after only one minute or a full ten minutes, that's how dazed I felt. Then it came to me rather slowly that I had the right to order him out.

"G-g-g-get out!" I commanded, holding out my arm and pointing one finger at the door.

Even I couldn't help but realize at once that this had been another of my mistakes. My breasts jiggled up and down as I made this grand gesture, and I didn't need his added hilarity to tell me that he was enjoying every second of it.

In fact, instead of getting out, he just slid his back along the shower wall, down, down, down until he was sitting at my feet.

Sweet Mother in Heaven, he was sitting there and looking *up!* The creature looked as though he had no intention of leaving ever. While still looking at him, I came back to my own senses and reached for the door handle.

"If you are planning to get your towel," he told me cheerfully, "you are out of luck. I removed it. It's in one of the bicycle baskets." Then, as though he had read my mind, "And if you try to streak across the garage after it, you are going to give more than just *me* a grand eyeful."

"Wh-wh-why . . ." I sputtered out, which was as far as I could get with the question, *Why are you doing this to me?* I sank down on my knees, kind of huddled over. It seemed about as modest as I could get.

He appeared to know what the question was I hadn't managed to ask. Reproachfully, he provided me the answer. *"You* invited me. I believe your exact words were 'Come on in, love.' I *did* hesitate at first, if you remember. I'm a modest kind of fellow myself, you understand, properly brought up." His dancing dark eyes dared me to contradict him. "But then you got rather . . . well, I hesitate to call a lady pushy, but if you think back honestly, you may recall that it was *you* who opened the door and all but ordered me to come in."

"If you don't un-invite yourself, I'll scream me head off!"

"No, you won't, me darlin'," he imitated me mockingly. "It would cause too much of a fuss. Lovely hair you have, by the way." He reached for a sopping strand. "And a lovely cockney accent you put on. Are you one of Maggie's actress friends?"

I was so exasperated (under a simmering excitement that I didn't dare think about yet) that I raised both fists to clobber him good and proper. His eyes grew suddenly bigger and darker at the exact moment that I realized what I was doing and what he was seeing.

Instead of getting madder or pretending that I was furious, all at once I began to chuckle. It was as though we had switched places and reversed attitudes. The tide of red, which had ebbed from my face, was sweeping all over his (even the suntan couldn't hide it). I knew the reason immediately as my eyes went down.

"Shall we dance?" I asked, sweetly vengeful, and promptly got my comeuppance. Without any words or warning, he grabbed for me. I was wet and bare and slippery, but that didn't stop him. He got me onto his lap, and there in that closet-sized shower stall, sitting on what was literally the floor of the garage, he gave me my first kiss.

I call it first kiss because any other I had ever been given became nothing . . . was all but forgotten. I had never been kissed completely undressed; so that a kiss wasn't just a merging of two mouths but incorporated all kinds of touch and feel. His bare legs were under my bottom, and presently we moved around and were kneeling together. His hands were on me . . . Oh God, were they ever on me. Here . . . there . . . everywhere.

Under his gentle, loving handling, my muscles became mush, except for my breasts, which were standing out by themselves. Some time or other, he had gotten rid of his shirt, and I was cuddling happily against his hairy, bare chest.

When I saw his hand slip inside the cord of his bathing trunks, I admitted to myself the truth of what was going to happen. Here, on the floor of a garage in America, the mighty Amaryllis Scott, who had prided herself on being stronger, wiser, cagier than other girls in Liverpool, was about to lose her virginity to a stranger. And instead of being doubtful or shrinking or even ashamed, I remember uttering fervent if silent words of thanks to the Lord that the shower water would wash away all the signs.

Probably the Lord objected to being thanked for that particular boon. Perhaps He, or maybe someone else, had other plans for me.

Just as my stranger loosed the cord of his trunks and was about to pull them off, there were footsteps in the garage, and then Mrs. Mailer's voice, "Rilla, is that you?"

"Y-y-yes," I quavered, while he, without needing me to tell him, hunkered down on the shower floor and flattened himself like a snake.

"Have you seen Chick?"

"In the house," I gulped.

"Thank you."

Her footsteps faded away, and I looked down at him. His bathing trunks were securely around his waist again when he got up, and he was retying the cord. We exchanged glances of equal desperation and regret, knowing, both of us, that the magic moment had passed. The moment of hot impulse and the peak of passion were over for now.

He quietly turned the handle of the shower door, whispering, "I'll bring back your towel."

As I nodded, he took a quick look at me, a rueful good-bye sort of look, then another quick peek outside.

I guess the garage was clear because in a second he was gone and the door closed. Then, in another couple of seconds, I heard a fumbling at the door and figured that he was hooking my towel over the handle.

I didn't hear the sound of bare feet, but I sensed he was out of sight, out of hearing.

I leaned against the shower door. I wasn't sad, I was exalted. The spark that had been ignited between us was no puny, flickering flame.

Soon I would step outside and meet him. We would both smile in secret knowledge of each other, perhaps even while we were going through some form of introduction.

Regrets were foolish—and futile.

What was to have been . . . would ultimately be!

Chapter 11

I WAS SICK WITH DISAPPOINTMENT WHEN I WENT OUT-side, walked all around the back yard, down the ramp to inspect the swimmers, and then to the lawn in front.

He was nowhere around.

I chided myself for being such a fool. He was probably in the house, maybe using the bathroom. I strolled aimlessly into the steamy kitchen, where Hannah stood basting chicken parts. Chick, still unself-consciously bare, was seated at the table, all sticky again, devouring a bagel from which peanut butter oozed.

"Thanks for the soap, Chick."

"You forgetted," he told me, unconcerned.

I realized what a wonderful twist of fate it was that he had "forgetted" and bent to kiss his silky blond hair. "Tomorrow," I promised recklessly, "we'll go to the dime store and you shall choose a present."

I heard footsteps and stood there, shaking with

happiness. I didn't even have to turn around. I knew. I just *knew*.

"Top of the morning, Hannah," said the warm, vibrant voice that thrilled me through and through, and I turned around slowly, almost shyly. I think my whole heart must have been in the happy little smile barely trembling on the corners of my lips. And if I was any judge, that was a lovely secret smile in his challenging eyes.

"It's afternoon, in case you didn't notice, sleeping the day away like you do," Hannah said with high good humor. I could tell there was fondness behind the brisk words.

"You met Rilla Scott yet?" she asked him. "She's our new mother's helper from England. Rilla, this is Mr. Mailer's younger brother, just recently back from England hisself."

"Pleased to meetcher," I said, more for Hannah's benefit, and looked up at him from under my lashes.

"How do you do?" he said ever so politely, and a silence fell between us. Not that I didn't want to talk to him, just as he must have wanted to talk to me, but there was Hannah, and Chick—and we had gotten so fast and so far from the beginnings of acquaintance in that garage shower I felt more awkward about trying any of the kind of small talk you go in for when you first meet someone than I would have if he had suddenly taken my hand or kissed my lips again.

Chick had finished his bagel. It gave me an excuse to get away. "Let's get you into some pants, boyo," I said, swinging him up in my arms.

As I bore him off, I swiveled my neck around quickly, just a passing glance to see if he was looking after me. He was—but not in any way I could figure out. There was a really odd expression on his face.

I took Chick up to his room, cleaned him up while he howled protestingly about my thoroughness, then tugged a fresh pair of swim trunks over his little tush. Together we went outside again.

He was standing at the outside trestle table with Mrs. Mailer, dipping crackers in a cheese dip.

"Hi, Rilla. Have you met my brother-in-law? He's just recently come from England, too. Cam, this is my mother's helper from—"

"London, yes, we've met," said the younger Mr. Mailer coolly, looking not so much at me as at the horizon beyond me.

"I'm not from the Smoke," I corrected him blithely. "Sure, I lived there a whiles, but Liverpool is me proper home."

"I beg your pardon."

"No need to," I answered him cheekily. "Americans always think English accents are all the same."

"Not precisely," he said dryly.

For some reason the way he said it frightened me. For the first time in the last happy half-hour, it dawned on me that perhaps what had happened in the shower might not be a beginning, but an end.

In England, I knew, there would have been an impossible gulf between an employer's worker and his brother. Except, a small, insidious voice whispered inside me, for a quick tumble in the hay.

But this was America, I argued with myself, land of the free, where you were not supposed to be divided into classes. Would Mr. Mailer mind if we . . . if we . . . Or *Mrs.* Mailer? Or, how about the person most concerned, young Mr. Mailer, known to his family as Cam?

Just as I was about to speak, he turned carelessly

122

away from me and spoke to his sister-in-law. "Here comes Ben in the boat."

They moved away together toward the ramp, leaving me feeling like a fly speck on a window: small, and not of much account . . .

Part of me didn't want to do it. Part of me could no more keep from following after them than I could have kept from leaving for America.

The boys jumped out of the boat onto the dock, and Nicky tied it to the boat hook. Jonnie and Jethro swung full pails under my nose. "Look, look, we've got more than a dozen."

"I got the biggest one of all," Jonnie boasted.

"*I* got the biggest one on my hook," Jethro told me mournfully, "but it swallowed my bait and then it wriggled free."

"*Almost* doesn't count," Nicky told him patronizingly.

"If it was on the hook, it does. Isn't that right, Uncle Cam? Doesn't *almost* count?"

"I'm afraid not," his uncle answered a bit strangely. I looked up at him from under my lashes while pretending to study the pails of fish.

In that single instant, the family resemblance would have been obvious to anyone; but what made me catch my breath sharply was the almost identical expression of intense regret that made Jethro, wailing over his lost fish, and Cam, maybe inwardly wailing over a lost opportunity in the shower, seem an older and younger version of each other.

I was as certain in that moment as I had ever been certain of anything in my life that, without even having had me, Cam Mailer had let me go.

Apparently, there were some rules in America, too, about that sort of thing.

Well, too bad, America, I vowed, with the same determination that used to make my parents groan and my brother Jim call me a stubborn sausage. I was not about to give him up for a silly scruple!

I ran up the ramp and rescued my book from the lounge chair, where I had left it earlier, unread. It was a suspense story that Mrs. Mailer had recommended. I still wanted to read it, but it could wait. I replaced it on the bottom row of shelves in the living room bookcase and looked through the history books to see if I could find something about this American Revolution of theirs that they seemed to set such store by.

In England it had never rated more than a paragraph in most of our history books, sometimes only a single line. *By a peace treaty signed in Paris in 1783, Britain relinquished her colonies in North America.*

I wanted to read up on this revolution. Maybe it would give me a clue to what went on inside their heads.

I skimmed through the shelves of history. There were a number that seemed to be all about the revolution, but when I flicked through the pages, they looked dry as dust and too many of the words were strange to me. I would have to start with something easier. At the very end of the shelf, I was sure I had found what I wanted.

There were two little volumes side by side, one bound in crumbling leather that was called *Heros and Heroines of the American Revolution*. The other was called *Loyalist Exiles In London*. I was about to pass it by when I noticed, on the first page, a description that went: *Being the story of those faithful few, Loyal to their King and Crown, who went to England during the Civil War between Britain and her North-American Colonies.*

I would try that one, too, I decided. As long as I was

learning about their fight, I might as well hear both sides of the story.

Much to my surprise, the heros and heroines book made fascinating reading. It was almost eighty years old, that book, and the language was formal and quaint, but I kind of got the hang of it pretty soon. I even got so interested that after a while I almost forgot to look around to see what Cam was doing . . . sometimes I forgot for as much as ten minutes.

During one of those forgetful interludes, I looked up as a shadow fell across my page. It was *him!* He had come to *me!*

"May I?" Even as he asked the question, he was bending to take the book out of my hands.

He read out the title and his eyebrows scaled his forehead in a funny way; first one went up and then the other, instead of both at once.

"Self-improvement," he murmured. "How laudable."

I didn't altogether understand the meaning, but there was no mistaking the tone. He was making a May-game of me, and so far as I was concerned, taking *that* never came with any salary.

"I read thrillers, too, and magazines. Does that make you easier in your mind?"

A dull red crept into his face. "I beg your pardon, Miss Scott. I—"

"Just Rilla will do. I'm the hired help here, remember?"

"You have made your point." As he returned the book, one of his hands suddenly covered mine all too briefly. "I sincerely beg your pardon, little one," he said softly, then walked away.

My heart sank. It had been a sincere apology, but there had been such finality in the way he said it that I had to believe it was his way of saying, Good-bye, best of British luck to you, but never the twain shall meet!

I returned resolutely to my book. There was a passage in it that provided my second shock of the day.

Patience Wright, the wax sculptor, practiced both her art and her patriotism in London. Her efforts on behalf of her countrymen are perhaps better known than those of the painter Ladybeth, who it is believed—though proof has never been presented—acted as a spy in London during the Revolution. She is presumed to have reported directly to Benjamin Franklin, who was then posted to Paris.

Ladybeth! The name that my man in silver had called me the day I arrived at the Mailers'. God! Where was he now when I needed him? There were so many questions to ask . . . so many answers I was waiting for!

Chapter 12

T HERE WAS JUST ONE MORE CONFRONTATION BETWEEN Charles Adam Mailer and me that afternoon.

I was swimming around the dock with the three older boys, wearing my bulky, orange life vest, as I usually did. Presently my employer joined us, watching me critically.

"You know, Rilla," Mr. Mailer said after a while, "I think you could safely get rid of that contraption now."

"Honest?" I gasped. "You're certain-sure I wouldn't be over me head in water?"

"I'm pretty sure, but I'll stay close—just in case."

I untied the series of bows holding it on me, while treading water and swallowing some as well. Much to my joy, when I was out of it, I could paddle my hands and feet and stay up just the way I wanted to.

"Wait till I write home I can really swim!" I gasped, seizing hold of the "contraption" to keep it from floating away. With a backhand sweep of my hand, I sent it flying over the sea wall. Halfway there, it sort of boomeranged and landed on the dock. To be precise, before falling onto the dock it first landed hard against the back of a male guest.

The guest turned around as I came swimming up to sputter my apologies. I might have known it would be Cam. "Ever so sorry, sir," I said stiffly. "I meant it to go the other way. My aim was a bit off."

"Tom Seaver you ain't," he agreed with perfect good humor, in the clear, vibrant voice already as familiar as though I had been hearing it all my life.

I shook the damp strands of hair back from my face, blinked my eyes clear of saltwater, and propped my arms on the dock the better to look up at him.

One look, and I lost my grip on the dock's edge, dropped down into the water, and came up choking and gasping. A hand tangled in my hair and another in the front straps of my swim suit, getting a generous handful of breast in the process. I was pulled painfully up, with an extra boost from his knee beneath my bottom as soon as that portion of me was available. It was—in spite of all the familiarity—an entirely impersonal touch. Believe me, I already knew the difference.

I slumped over on the dock where he'd dumped me like so much baggage, leaned over to upchuck back into the Sound from which it had come about two quarts of saltwater, looked up at Cam again, and suddenly understood.

The stranger in the shower, the remote brother-in-law, the casual uncle, the regretful fisherman who had to let me get away, and finally this last minute's rescuer . . .

They were all one and the same person, and I had fallen in love with him. Devastatingly in love.

I never fell out again!

Don't ask me why love hit me the way it did. I could no more tell you that than why whales beach themselves or guppies eat their young. Sure, I wanted to be held in his arms again, remembering how it had been, knowing that he wanted me, too, *feeling* that he wanted me.

But, ah, hell! It was more than just a thing of the body. So much more. I heard him speak. Even though it was totally impersonal, I had felt that bond between us when he hauled me up. When the simple fact of it was clear to me, I just looked at him mistily, knowing that whatever *was* was meant. The world—*my* world—became well lost for love.

Having politely seen to my well-being, he dived off the dock and went swimming away. I knew he was making a point again, but I had already decided in my mind what the solution was to be.

If, in America, there wasn't any more likelihood of a happy ending between a mother's helper and the boss's kid brother than there might have been in England, so be it.

In the dizzying space of ten minutes I went from noble relinquishment of what had never been mine to a shattering compromise of what had never been asked for. Okay then, I told myself stoutly, no one but the two of us need ever know. I would be his mistress. Some way or another—soon, if not today—I would find a way to tell him.

Feeling almost noble in this resolve, I went up to my bedroom, combed out my hair, changed into a short white cotton skirt with a print of pink and blue umbrellas, a hot pink knit blouse with a round neck that dipped low enough to show a touch of cleavage, and my white cross-strap clogs.

They were all new, bought at a summer sale in the

same store where I had gotten my little white enamel earrings in the shape of butterflies. The perfume I had brought with me from England.

Feeling utterly pleased with myself and my grand appearance, I went back downstairs and outside. Many of the guests had left with the tide; only the close family had stayed on for a barbecue dinner.

Mr. Mailer and Cam did the cooking, but I helped Mrs. Mailer serve. Cam and I ate last, and I flushed with pleasure when he filled a paper plate for me before serving himself. Just like in the films!

He sat beside me on the grass, talking easily about life in England, where he seemed to spend a lot of time, comparing it with life in America. How did I like it here, he inquired politely.

"Oh, ever so!" I said fervently. "I'll never go back!"

His eyebrows lifted in that satanic, one-sided way. "Never?"

"Oh, to visit, of course. To see me Mum and Dad and our Jim. I miss them something fierce. But never again to live. This is the life for me."

I was babbling. I knew I was babbling, but I couldn't help it. I was drowning in those searching black eyes of his. I didn't see why it couldn't be more simple. Why couldn't I just tell him, *I'm yours, Cam. Any way you want me, I'm yours forever.*

When we had finished our outdoor meal and the mosquitoes began to feed on us, everyone decided to go indoors. Chick was tired and getting a bit cranky, so I hefted him up in my arms and told Mrs. Mailer I would put him to bed.

He practically fell asleep in the bath, and I held him cuddled against me while I dried his soft round body, slipped on his pajamas, and tucked him up.

I had a date to go dancing, with Toby (the lad hired to fix the Mailer roof) but he wasn't coming for me till nine. I was drawn irresistibly downstairs to the voices and the laughter in the living room. I pretended to myself I was just going to pop down to ask Mrs. Mailer if there was anything else I could do for her. Even as my mind wrestled with this proposal, I knew I was being a prize hypocrite. To be helpful just then was the last of my intentions.

The second floor, like the first, was thickly carpeted, so I made no sound as I approached the head of the stairs. Just below me I heard Mrs. Mailer's low-pitched, actress's voice and then the resonant masculine one that set my pulses fluttering.

I paused to listen. I didn't really mean to eavesdrop. I just wanted a moment's joy in listening, undetected, to the sound of his voice.

Talk about eavesdroppers hearing poorly of themselves!

Not immediately, though. At first all I heard was Mrs. Mailer regretting that he must leave so early and joking that she supposed a family party with all four of her sons was enough to drive any bachelor into a speedy retreat to the city.

He joked back that he was advancing into the city, not retreating.

"I should have known," said Mrs. Mailer with mock resignation. "Who is she?"

"A new one. I don't think you know her. Miriam Forsythe."

"Beautiful, I suppose?"

"Ravishing."

My insides knotted up with a strange new discomfort, a combination of dull nausea and stabbing pain. It took me a moment to identify the feeling for what it was, something I had never before experienced, the acute agony of jealousy.

"You've only been home from Europe for two weeks; that's fast work."

"The Mailers are all fast workers, as you should know. What was it—a full ten days before Ben proposed?"

There was the smacking sound of a non-lover's kiss, and then Mrs. Mailer's voice again, purring with self-satisfaction and good-humored affection.

"Oh, go along to your heavy date. You're every bit as bad as Ben. I'm going up to tuck Chick in."

"Speaking of your offspring," he said casually, "aren't you afraid they'll pick up that horrible Cockney accent from the cute new nanny creature you've gotten them?"

My hand tightened on the banister. Somehow, the way he had described me reduced me to nothingness.

"She's not Cockney. Cockney is London; she's a Scouse."

"What the hell is a Scouse?"

"Not what, *who*. It's apparently anyone who comes from Liverpool. There was a fish called scouse that, in prepollution days, was very plentiful in their River Mersey and formed the chief staple of a Liverpudlian's daily diet."

"Well, whatever, her accent is almost as atrocious as her clothes. And that hair!"

"Her hair is beautiful!"

"In color, yes, or wet hanging down her back, but not the way she arranges it, or should I say, doesn't arrange it, straggling all over her face, like one of the witches from *Macbeth*. Even covering her eyes—her one feature, by the way, that should never be covered.

Now *they* have a witching kind of appeal. Can't you give her a few gentle hints about grooming?"

"She's a very bright girl. Given time, she'll learn all she has to."

"How about the boys while she's in the process of learning?"

"The boys," Mrs. Mailer defended me, "aren't going to be corrupted by either Rilla's accent *or* her clothes. She's warm and loving and romps around with them as though they were her little brothers. You know what wild Indians those four are, much too wearing to be left alone with Hannah. When I'm working, I feel better knowing Rilla is here with them, too."

For a few seconds, I heard nothing, and then Mrs. Mailer spoke again, adding with a touch of impatience, "Goodness, Charlie, I didn't dream you were such a snob. In fact, if you must know"—her voice seemed to change subtly—"once or twice this afternoon I had the impression you were rather attracted to her."

"Of course, I'm attracted to her," he answered coolly. "I'm attracted to any girl with a gorgeous figure. She has got that, Maggie dear, in case you haven't noticed. But as for the entire package, complete with cheap perfume and stale cigarette aroma, to say nothing of the Cockney accent—"

"Scouse!"

"Scoose—Scouse. Whatever. Don't worry about your little exile, Maggie. She doesn't even tempt me to exercise *droit du seigneur.*"

I canceled my date with Toby that night. When he came to the kitchen door, I really must have looked awful, because it didn't take any effort to convince him I was too sick to go out.

Like a sick animal, seeking only loneliness in which to lick its wounds, I stayed in my room with the door locked. I felt too empty even to cry, but after a while I turned on the overhead light, then the big lamp near my bed and the smaller study lamp on my desk.

With the room shiningly bright, I approached the floor-length mirror on the inside of my closet door.

It showed me up mercilessly, and I wondered why I hadn't noticed before that the skirt with the pink and blue umbrellas had neither cut nor style. Like the hot pink shirt, it was both cheap and garish. How obvious now that the clumping clogs were in poor taste.

Even the butterfly earrings of which I had been so proud! I ripped them ruthlessly off my ears, bringing tears of pain to my eyes. I lifted up a window screen and tossed them into the night. I stripped down to my underwear, and even that seemed suddenly offensive, the color too pink, the lace edging too phony.

I bundled up everything and stared at my naked reflection in the mirror. Naked and not talking—that's when he had been attracted.

I got into the tub and I scrubbed and I scrubbed myself, but I could still smell the perfume.

"I hate you, Cam Mailer!" I sobbed, knowing all the while that what I really hated was the picture of myself he had made me see all too clearly. What I sorrowed for was the fantasy of future happiness he had stolen from me.

I went to the library next day and I asked about *droit du seigneur,* which I said I had come across in a history book. By a miracle, I remembered the pronunciation enough for recognition. When I copied it down, as it was shown to me in the dictionary, then I really started to hate Cam, too.

The only trouble was that, even as I hated him, I went right on loving him.

Chapter 13

I WAITED A FULL MONTH BEFORE I SPOKE TO MRS. Mailer, wanting to be sure that she would make no connection between her conversation with her brother-in-law and this present one with me.

"You mean some kind of *charm* school, Rilla?" she asked me doubtfully. "Those things are mostly cons. What you need"—her forehead wrinkled in concentration; then she suddenly brightened. "Connie Lackland!" she came up with triumphantly. "She's the one for you. She's an ex-actress, ex-model, ex–costume designer turned make-up artist. In her own way, she's something of a genius."

"Does she run a school?" I asked, doubtful in return.

"No, she doesn't need to, but she takes an occasional apprentice. She enjoys a challenge. I'll bet I can get her to take you on."

"Would she be very expensive?" I asked, determined to pay whatever it was.

"I doubt it." Her tone was brisk, dismissing such unimportant matters as expense. "I'll call her and let you know."

Mrs. Lackland was out of town. It was three weeks before I was able to get an appointment with her. She lived in the city in an apartment in the west fifties near Carnegie Hall with a doorman who had unnerved me completely by his assumption that I belonged at the tradesman's entrance. Shades of the English class system!

"I'm here to see Mrs. Lackland at her express invitation," I sauced him smartly, "so you be announcing my name then, bucko, which happens to be Miss Rilla Scott, and none of your lip neither, if you please. You're working class same as me."

Mrs. Lackland turned out to be a tall, almost gaunt woman with great, gray eyes, chopped-off white hair, and a deep, throaty voice. I rather wondered at first how she could ever have been a model till I noticed the fine bones of her face, her delicately porcelain skin, and the long, slender, well-shaped hands.

I found out later that she had mostly been in detergent commercials for her hands and soap commercials for her skin.

I stumbled over her doorstep and held out my hand, staring at it sort of stupidly and making a gauche effort to get it out of the way when she made no move to shake it. She brought me into her living room.

"Well, well, well." She walked all around me several times. "Maggie was right. You are a challenge. Sit down." She pointed to a chair.

I sat, paralyzed, on the edge of it.

"Say something," she ordered.

"P-pleased ter meetcha," I stammered.

She shuddered. "Good God. Forget it. Say as little as possible."

I stood up, what Dad called my mongrel temper flaring. "Happen I'm not a guest here seeing as how I've come to pay for your services," I told her tersely, "but even in the Dingle—which is no fancy place like this, mind—when a bloke, even maybe one you don't like, walks into your house, you still offer him a pint then, you don't start insulting him."

She laughed heartily and clapped her hands. "Sit down, Rilla. Maggie said you have spunk. I'm glad to see she was right. I didn't mean to insult you. I was just trying to shake you up a bit. We're not going to get anywhere if you're scared of me."

"Scared of you!" I scoffed, still smarting. "There're lasses I know of in Liverpool who could eat two of the like o' you for breakfast."

She said softly, "Not of me personally, but of what I represent."

"Ba—" I bit the word back, remembering just in time where I was and what I had come for.

"Exactly," she agreed pleasantly. "We can stay here trying to score points off one another or we can try to accomplish what it is you came for. How about talking it over in the kitchen while I fix us a sandwich?"

"I wouldn't mind," I admitted. "I'm feeling kinda peckish. I was that excited about coming here, I skipped over me lunch."

"I presume the translation of that extraordinary speech is that you are hungry, meaning, in need of sustenance. From now on, say so. You are *hungry*. And it's not *me* but *my* lunch, *my* chair, *my* house, *my* nasty manner. *Me* is the personal pronoun, *my* is the possessive form. I'm sure the Mailers have a good dictionary. Look through it. Follow *me!*"

137

In the kitchen she opened her refrigerator and contemplated its sparse contents. "Would you like a bologna sandwich?" she asked apologetically. "There doesn't seem to be much else."

I shouldered her aside and poked into half a dozen little containers of leftovers.

"Sure there is," I said. "I'll fix us a nice mixed salad. You put the kettle on for tea."

"The kettle on for tea," she repeated delightedly. "How very English sounding."

"Why shouldn't it?" I asked, searching for the salad dressing. "England is me—*my* country."

"You're a fast learner, Rilla Scott," Mrs. Lackland said approvingly.

I was! I was indeed.

There is nothing that makes for fast learning quite so much as being what is now called highly motivated. The way I thought of it then was that I nourished a burning desire to make Charles Adam Mailer choke on his own damned patronizing words. Someday he'd be begging for his damned *droit du seigneur*.

I went to see Connie Lackland every Thursday that she was available for the next three months. She taught me to dress from the skin out, constantly preaching the virtues of quality over quantity, suitability to the individual over current fashions and fads.

I learned from her that soap and water were pearls beyond price, and cheap perfume was dross; that a bargain wasn't a bargain if it didn't do anything for me; that daily brushing was the greatest gift you could give your hair; that a good diet did more for your skin than all the make-up in the world. A monthly date with a masseuse—more often, if it could be afforded—was more of a pick-me-up than a new dress. Half an hour of exercise and ten minutes of meditation every morning did more for body and soul than a church sermon.

Connie corrected assiduously what she called my "quaint misuse of the Queen's English," but she couldn't seem to do anything about my accent. For that she finally sent me to a speech teacher, who took me for half price as a special favor to her.

Even at half price he dug a big hole out of my salary, in spite of the expanded wage that was agreed on for my second year with the Mailers.

Shortly after I was nineteen—the Mailers still believed I was twenty-one—I went home to Liverpool for a month's visit. All the family met me at the airport, Mum and Dad, our Jim—now working as a carpenter—Auntie Bron, my cousin Jeannie, big with child, and her husband Brian holding their oldest Timmy by the hand.

There were hugs and kisses and tears and exclamations all around.

"Our Rilla! I can't believe it!" Jeannie cried. "You talk American."

It made the hard, weary lessons and the endless practice and the money spent all seem worthwhile.

In all those years I hardly caught a glimpse of Cam, or maybe it would be more accurate to say he hardly ever caught a glimpse of me. It wasn't hard in winter because when he came to formal family dinners, Hannah served. If I was around, I stuck to the kitchen or stayed upstairs.

The second summer he was on a business trip through Europe, and I timed my visit home for early autumn just as he got back.

During the following winter Mrs. Mailer was very busy as part-time hostess on a morning talk show.

That's when she and Mr. Mailer decided to rent an apartment in New York, since three mornings a week she had to be at the studio by six o'clock.

She had a long talk with me before they rented the apartment. She wanted to make sure she could count on my sticking around for the next year. "I'll be away a lot, and they'll need you more than ever," she admitted frankly.

When I agreed to stay—little could she know the reason why nothing would have dragged me away—a handsome raise in pay was offered to me, and a bonus with it.

"I want you to take some secretarial courses at night and on your day off, too, if you can. I'll pay all the costs," Mrs. Mailer offered firmly.

"Why ever for?"

"Rilla, you can't be a mother's helper all the rest of your life. God knows I'd be glad to have you stay with us till the boys are all through college," she said honestly, "but you've got too much on the ball for this to be your life forever."

"I'm content," I maintained stubbornly.

"For the past two years . . . maybe the next two . . . but the rest of your life? Is this what you came from Liverpool for? You told me once you wanted to break out of the class system. You're not going to do it in my kitchen or taking care of my kids. Don't you want to make something of yourself?" she asked. "Isn't that why you came to this country?"

Don't you want to make something of yourself?

That last was a shrewd thrust. It cut deeper into my soul than she ever dreamed.

She was right, of course. Cam would surely not be seeking me out in her kitchen. Her kitchen was where I had been hiding myself away so he could not so much as see me. I had been trying all this while to make something of myself so that one day I could look into his eyes as an equal, spit in his eye for the things he had once said of me.

Connie had done her best for me; my speech therapy was finished. It was time to move on to the next lessons.

I went up to the high school to register for a typing course three nights a week. The typing course was already filled up.

"Is there any other course that's open?" I asked, thinking perhaps I could begin with shorthand and try again for typing in the next term.

The registrar looked down at her list. After a long while she came up with, "We've got an opening in Yoga I, Monday and Thursday nights at seven."

Connie always said, "What's good for the body is food for the mind."

"I'll take it," I said. "Is there anything else on the same nights?"

She studied her list again. "Beginners' Art?" she suggested dubiously. "Mondays and Thursdays at eight."

Beginners' Art . . . Our Jim was the one considered good at art, though I had always enjoyed drawing little sketches myself. God, the caning I'd gotten in the fourth grade for making a big drawing on the blackboard of the teacher's face attached to the body of a donkey. He'd caught me at it as I made the final flourish in chalk.

Beginners' Art . . .

"Put me down for that, too," I told the registrar.

By just such flimsy threads are sewn the most important fabric of a life!

Chapter 14

Nicky, Jonnie, Jethro, and Chick thought I was the world's greatest bedtime story teller. I seldom got away at night with fewer than three.

After I started my art course, I amused myself and them by sketching little illustrations and funny drawings to go with the stories. The drawing, which they watched with fascinated, childlike absorption, helped give my throat a rest, too.

By the time I was taking my Art III course, and Beginners' Typing had finally replaced Yoga, the boys had quite a thick portfolio full of my drawings.

I came home from New York one Sunday, after an afternoon symphony concert and tea with Connie Lackland. Despite the difference in our ages we had remained friends when the crash course was over, and at every opportunity she continued to cram me full of culture.

There was a light on in the living room, and Mrs. Mailer came out to the hallway as I turned the key in the lock.

"Rilla, would you come into the den, please. My husband wants to see you."

I hung up my coat and scarf and followed her into the den. Mr. Mailer sat there at his office-sized desk rummaging through the portfolio of my drawings.

"Rilla, did you do all of these?"

"Yes, Mr. Mailer."

"Without any help?"

"With no help at all!" I stated quickly, my pride stung.

He grinned. "You sound touchy enough to be an artist," he told me, and then more seriously, "Do you realize, Rilla, you have talent enough to be one, too?"

I stared at him. My art teacher, Mr. Gresham, praised my work, but he had never gone so far as *that!*

"You knew, didn't you, that I publish children's books as well as my other lines?"

I nodded.

"I have illustrators for those books. Half of them"— he thumped the portfolio with his fist by way of emphasis—"do work that can't compare with yours."

I looked at him with eyes of shining delight.

"The stories . . . the little bits of them that I got from the boys," he went on, "they sound professional, too. Do you think you could write them down? Let's say one to start with; I'd like to see how it would read. I could assign you a good editor after you got finished, but I would want it to have your own particular flavor."

"Mr. Mailer, are you saying you might be willing to publish a story of mine . . . a story that I wrote and did the drawings for?"

"I can't make you any promises, Rilla. I would have to see how it turned out, but it's something I'd like to try."

He flipped open the cover of the portfolio and pointed to the first gay-colored illustration of what appeared to be a plump talking fish. "Chick said this was supposed to be the last cow in Mercy. I think he must have that wrong."

I broke out in a fit of giggles. "He means 'last scouse in the River Mersey.' It's the very special fish from which we Liverpool Scouses take our name. I made up a story about what happened when there seemed to be only one left in all of Liverpool."

"Will it be hard for you to write the story part?"

I shook my head vigorously. "I don't think so. I'll just write it down the way I tell it to the kids. Oh, Mr. Mailer, do you really mean—"

"Rilla, you'd better understand one thing. Even if we both get a good book out of this, you won't be rich overnight or even over the years. A mother's helper, I'm sorry to say, often makes more than a hard-working writer. Juveniles—children's books—isn't a tremendously well-paying field. A few exceptions, of course, for a few exceptional best sellers, but—"

"I don't care about the money, but to see my name in print . . . on a real book . . . with my real drawings. To be able to send it home to my family."

Within a year I was able to do exactly that—send half a dozen copies of *The Last Scouse in Liverpool* home to my family. The extra copies after Mum's and Dad's and Auntie Bron's were for our Jim, who promised me he would deliver one personally to Mr. Creedon, headmaster at St. Jude's, and another to Mrs. Wilson of the Educational Committee, if she was still around. I autographed the inside cover of her copy *"From Rilla*

Scott, who didn't wind up in a factory or married at nineteen."

The Last Scouse in Liverpool got good reviews in the papers and enjoyed a mild success, but it couldn't support me the way being a live-in mother's helper did. The same was true of the next one, *A Monkey in Buckingham Palace.*

Just the same, it was extra money, most of it to put away in a special nest egg and the rest to finance my art studies. I went to art classes in New York every Thursday, and I took private evening lessons with an artist in New Rochelle that Mr. Mailer had found for me.

In the cellar playroom, where the children had their ping-pong table, a little corner near the window had been sectioned off as a kind of art studio for me. I set up my easel there, with an old kitchen table for my papers and brushes, turps and paints.

Toward the end of my fifth year in the States, I had my first exhibit. Seven of my paintings were shown, and three of them were sold straightaway.

Mr. and Mrs. Mailer took me out to dinner that night to celebrate—and to tell me it was time for me to move on.

In my heart I knew what they were telling me to do was right. I had buried the secret awareness of it deep down for a long time because, after all these years, I was frightened at the very thought of leaving the safe, snug haven of their home to brave the dangerous world outside on my own.

"I love it with you in Larchmont," I told them defensively. "I do my books, and I paint, too."

"Rilla, if I were thinking of myself, I'd try to keep you with me by hook or by crook," Mrs. Mailer told me fondly. "The boys will be devastated, and I'll miss you terribly myself. But you don't belong here anymore. You should be working full time at your career, both careers, not sandwiching your work in between taking Chick to ice-skate or helping Jethro with his homework, drying dishes for Hannah, and carrying down the wash."

"The sale of these pictures should set you up for a while, together with what else you've put by," Mr. Mailer calculated for me. "You've another book coming out next year that will at least keep you in eating money. The way I figure it, even if nothing else came in, you could manage in a modest apartment for at least two years. If it doesn't work"—he reached across the table to pat my trembling hand—"you can always come back to us, but I feel quite sure you won't have to."

They continued to plot my life's course quite cheerfully, but a scant six weeks later, confronted with the reality of my "modest" apartment down on the Bowery, Mrs. Mailer wrung her hands and lamented as loudly as though she were the traditional, overprotective Jewish mother.

A taxicab disgorged her at the building, which had once been a factory, between Grand and Hester Streets, just as I came strolling along from the small market in Little Italy two blocks away.

She offered to take one of my two big bundles of groceries, but I wouldn't allow it.

"You'll need your breath," I advised kindly.

Inside, she looked around at my tremendous loft, with its two fireplaces (one of which worked), fifteen-foot-high ceilings, and gray painted deck floor. A succession of lights hung from the pipes the whole length of the ceiling. I pulled the strings to light three of them and started putting the perishables into the brand new refrigerator I had bought along with a slightly used gas stove. There hadn't been any kitchen when I moved in, just fittings for installation.

When I finished unloading my groceries, I pulled a hassock (formerly hers, too) over near Mrs. Mailer and invited her to put up her feet.

"There's an artist in the place next door. He's going to build me kitchen cabinets for just a little over the price of the materials. And a closet, too, down at the other end." I waved vaguely in that direction.

She peered down toward "the other end" about a quarter of a mile away.

"You can't live here," she informed me flatly and burst into tears. "Your mother would k-kill me."

I applied myself to soothing her troubled conscience.

"It's so ugly," she moaned.

"It's so cheap," I reminded her. "Where else would I get all this light and space and privacy for $275 a month? And it isn't really ugly. When I get it fixed up with wall hangings and scatter rugs and lots of plants, you'll be surprised how lovely it will look. There are lots of artists and writers in this house and the ones on either side of me. You should see how attractively they fix up their places."

"But the Bowery." She shuddered. "It's not safe."

"Safe as Larchmont," I assured her. "Safer. My grocer in Little Italy told me I don't have to worry. They take care of their own here; women are protected."

She dabbed at her eyes. "What's that supposed to mean?"

"Well, I asked Steve—you know, the guy who's going to build my cabinets—he says all these blocks around Little Italy are Mafia-protected."

"Maf—oh, my good God!"

"Would you like some tea or something? I made a tuna fish salad."

"No, I'd rather take you out to lunch as soon as I get my strength back. Is there any place decent nearby?"

"Oh, lots of wonderful Italian restaurants. They're so reasonable, I eat my main meal out every day."

She applied herself to her make-up. "You can stand the weight, I can't."

"Oh, I divide between Italian food and Chinese. Chinatown is just a few blocks' walk from here, too. There's this one little place we all go to for lunch, where for a buck fifty you can get a bowl of won-ton soup so hefty it's like a full meal."

She put her make-up kit back into her purse. "Tell me, Rilla, is there anything going on between you and this Steve?"

I grinned. "Sure. A covered walkway that leads from his building to mine, so in bad weather he can get here without going outside."

"You know what I mean."

"Yes, I know, sorry for teasing, and no, there isn't, so you needn't worry."

"I worry because there isn't, not because there might be," she told me tartly. "Your lack of interest in the male sex isn't natural."

If she only knew!

"Tell me, Rilla," she pursued. "How old are you now? Twenty-four, isn't it?"

"Twenty-two and a half," I admitted for the first time, looking her straight in the eye. "I lied about my age to get to America. I wasn't even eighteen when I first came to you."

"My God!" She struck her head theatrically. "You

were a baby. I never would have hired you if I had known."

"I figured." I grinned at her. "That's why I lied."

She pulled herself together. "Well, twenty-four, twenty-two, it makes no difference. Any girl in her twenties should be interested in men."

"I like men," I told her. "If you want the truth, I like one man in particular, only he doesn't like me. While I'm waiting for him to see the light, I concentrate on my work. Don't worry about me, Mrs. Mailer, please don't. I expect to have it all one day."

She stood up and cast one last disparaging look around at my new setting all full of what was mostly her own discarded furniture. "You're not my employee anymore; we're just friends now. I suggest you call me Maggie. Let's go to Chinatown."

"All right, Maggie," I said shyly, "but in honor of friendship the lunch—it will be cheap, I promise you—is on me."

She gave me a rueful, maternal smile and the same kind of pat on the cheek followed by a slightly harder pat on the bottom that she might have bestowed on Chick. "In honor of friendship," she agreed.

Chapter 15

I LIVED IN MY BOWERY LOFT FOR A BIT OVER THREE years, and despite Maggie's grim foreboding, they were reasonably happy and good years.

I produced a half dozen books, which sold well if not fabulously and kept me afloat. I painted fifty or so pictures—mostly wishy-washy landscapes—a small percentage of which I sold, enough to keep me in art supplies.

The surroundings may have been ugly and dirty, but there was beauty there, too. We were a community of young artists and writers struggling to achieve a foothold in the world of art and books, too poor most of us to afford Soho, some of us barely able to hang on to our Bowery flats.

I was one of the luckier ones, I suppose. I had modest success, a little backlog in the bank, and always cash enough on hand to afford the cafés of Little Italy and our favorite spots in Chinatown. I could always afford a bottle of wine or some sandwich meat to contribute to the parties held almost nightly. Relationships were casual and easy, someone to talk to or a shoulder to cry on always at hand. The only things in meager supply were food and money.

Two things happened in my third year on the Bowery. I had my first best-selling juvenile, *The Frog Who Loved a Flounder,* and Maggie's brother-in-law Charles Adam Mailer came home from a long stay in England to take over the family antique shops and art galleries and to announce his engagement to shipping heiress Irene Courtland.

I hadn't seen Cam, except at a distance, in more than five years. The one time we accidentally came to Larchmont the same night for dinner I managed to acquire a splitting headache and go to sleep in my old room upstairs until he and his date had left.

It was crazy that the prospect of his marriage should make a difference to me. He was no more lost to me than he had ever been. Except in wishful dreams, he had never been mine at all.

Whether it made sense or not, I cried agonizingly and alone the night I heard the news, and when Steve came over the catwalk and down the fire escape on his almost nightly visit, I invited him first into the apartment and, minutes later, into my bed.

For three years he had been making halfhearted attempts, in between his other commitments, to make love to me, never after the first month much daunted by my persistent refusal.

This time we reversed roles. *I* tried to make love to *him.*

I was twenty-five, going on twenty-six, a reluctant

virgin living in a world where bed-hopping was as casual as breaking bread. Yet I wasn't even sure how to go about it.

I tried, though, God, how I tried, and Steve appeared satisfied with my eager kisses and attempts to rip off both my clothes and his.

It wasn't him or me but the man in silver gray who came between us. He had been as much out of my life these past busy years as Cam, but then I had never done anything in all that time to draw him to me. Evidently he could take in his stride the good-night kiss after a date or the roving hands at a party. Obviously, my rolling about on a bed half-naked, with a nearly undressed male, still came in a different category.

There we were, and there he was, standing over us, haughty, disapproving, and disdainful—blast his soul!

"Damn you to hell!" I cried out in rage and frustration, and Steve sat up and moved away from me.

"What did I do?" he asked, half-indignant, half-concerned.

Nothing that I hadn't wanted him to . . . but how explain it?

"Do you believe in ghosts?" I asked him.

"I can't say as I do."

"Well, neither do I, but just the same there's one here with us now."

"Where?" He gave a nervous jump away, more away from me than the supposed ghost.

"Two feet to the left of you."

"What's he doing?" He asked it in a whisper, leaning toward me, as though maybe that would make us both invisible and hard to hear.

"He's glaring at us."

"Why?"

"He doesn't want you to make love to me."

He forgot to whisper. "What's he got against me?" he asked indignantly.

"Nothing. Nothing that he doesn't have against any man of my choosing. There's supposed to be some super special one from the past I'm being saved for. I expect," I added bitterly, "he'll come along by the time I'm eighty."

Steve was getting back into his clothes with unflattering speed.

"Jeez, Rilla, all you had to do was say no. I'm used to it, you've been saying it for two-three years now. You didn't have to go in for this weird put-on."

I pulled the blankets up to my chin, and the man in silver nodded his approval at this display of modesty. When Steve disappeared through the window onto the fire escape, I turned to vent my frustration and my temper on him only to find him gone.

"You bastard!" I shouted into the empty silence, but no answer came.

I lay where I was and, with the lights still on, fell into a troubled sleep. Dreams came and went, flashing through my brain, like the scenes in a film. The man in silver gray was there, though his clothes were different . . . he seemed to be wearing a uniform . . . there was another man dressed in clothes of the same period, but older, kinder looking. He held out his arms to me, and I ran into them, laughing and happy. There was a woman with enormous gray eyes and one thick braid of rich chestnut hair hanging down her back. She held out her arms—to him? to me?—her face was all soft with love. There was a chain around her neck, and when she leaned forward, I could see what hung at the end of the chain. A star. *My* star.

I woke up hungry, thirsty, tired. The sun was high and the lights were still on. My electric clock read 8:11.

Twelve hours since Steve had left and I had fallen asleep, and I felt tense, tired, muscle-bound, as though I hadn't had so much as an hour's rest.

I got up and padded wearily to the bathroom. I brushed my teeth, and it wasn't till I went to take off the underclothes I had slept in that I noticed they were paint-spattered. I pulled them off, threw them in the hamper, and got under the shower, frowning. There had been no paint on me when I began to strip for Steve.

This was getting damned ridiculous. I skipped out of the shower, wrapped a towel around me, tucking it firmly under one arm, and went to the middle section of my loft, the part set up as a studio, with the big floor-to-ceiling windows left uncurtained.

I was in the middle of a painting of Umbrella Point in Larchmont, this one from the angle of the Sound. I had painted it a dozen times before, from the front, from the back, from the sides.

The painting of Umbrella Point no longer occupied my easel. It lay carefully on my large wooden work table, and staring at me from the easel was the face, done in oils, of the gray-eyed woman who had haunted me in the night. Her face was at least twenty years younger than it had been in my dreams, and against the velvety bare skin exposed by the low-cut bodice of her dress gleamed the blue green sapphire in the middle of the sparkling gold Star of David. It was a rough, almost crude drawing, in the style of an American primitive, but it showed the girl vibrantly alive.

I stood before it shaking with the terror of the unknown, my hands pressed against my lips, holding back a scream. The towel slid slowly to the floor, and I knelt naked and trembling, while a voice out of nowhere, *his* voice, the man in gray's, seemed to be telling me lovingly, tenderly, *Do not be afraid, Ladybeth.*

I looked all about me, but he wasn't there. I looked back at the painting and read the small, sprawled signature in the corner. *Ladybeth.*

I whispered the name aloud. *Ladybeth,* I cried it out to the nameless ghost that haunted me. Ladybeth, who might or might not have been a spy.

I said her name a third time, bending slowly to pick up my towel, and as I did, a great weight seemed to be pressing down on me. I was lying on the towel, curled up like a baby in its mother's womb. There was a humming in my ears and a buzzing inside my head, as though hundreds of flying creatures were beating their wings all about me.

The pressure inside my head increased. I breathed in deeply and felt myself falling . . . tumbling . . . drawn helplessly into the vortex. I was swirling downward into a huge conelike tunnel, at whose narrowing end was a brilliant, burning light. I stopped struggling. I stopped whirling. I stepped forward into the light.

She was waiting there for me, the woman with the great gray eyes and the braided rope of chestnut hair. She held out her hands to me, and I walked toward her, no longer afraid . . .

Chapter 16

T HE SHOP FRONT ON THE OUTER FRINGES OF 'CHANGE
Alley bore a simple inscription in the window, Eleazar
Ben David, Jeweler and Merchant Banker.

Two gentlemen paused before the shop a moment.
The older of the two used the window as a mirror to
straighten his powdered wig and smooth out a wrinkle
on the sleeve of his satin jacket.

"Merchant banker," he sneered. "'Pon rep, these
Hebrews give themselves airs. The fellow's naught but
a common money lender like all his race."

"If you seek his favor, Sir George," the younger man
suggested mildly, "your belligerence may be mis-
placed."

"Upon my word, Edmund"—his friend pushed
through the door, raising his voice over the sound of a
jangling bell—"since when does an English gentleman
kowtow to a demned clothes peddler?"

The sun was in their eyes, so that at first there appeared to be no one in the shop.

As their eyes grew used to the dimness, they detected a movement behind the counter. Then a dark figure stepped forth before them, and they beheld a vision in lush green velvet: a slender girl of marvelous shapeliness and a porcelain-fair face that boasted as creamily soft an English skin as ever they had seen. Her hair was unfashionably braided into one thick plait, sun gold as any Saxon's. It curled around her shoulder and fell against one swelling breast.

She was warmth and light and loveliness. Only her large, gray eyes, studying them as she might a mouse in her pantry, contained an icy hardness. Even as the younger man Edmund drew in his breath at such beauty, she addressed them in a voice to match the cold of her eyes.

"If you seek an old clothes man, *gentlemen*"—she stressed the courtesy title with gentle irony—"you are come to the wrong part of town. Have you tried Monmouth Street?"

"'Pon rep, girl," Sir George asked her indignantly, "what use, think you, would I have for an old clothes man?"

"I'm sure I do not know, sir." The eyes were suddenly limpid, her expression blankly innocent. "What use *would* you have?"

He snapped his fingers impatiently, unaware that he was being made a mock of. "I seek this . . . this merchant banker, as he calls himself, the Hebrew who owns this shop."

"Ah, you seek Mr. Ben David!" she said in the tone of one suddenly enlightened. "If only I had known sooner. Mr. Ben David left here but five minutes gone by."

"Run after him then, girl. Perhaps it's not too late for you to fetch him back for me."

"If it's a jewel you wish to buy for your fine lady, I can summon Jacob from the back to give you every assistance."

"I don't wish a jewel, by Heaven. I wish a loan from the demned usurer, demn it." His cheeks puffed out, getting redder and redder as he choked on this admission. He seemed on the verge of an apoplexy.

She studied these physical manifestations, seemingly grave but with the glitter of amusement now warming up her eyes. "Oh sir, how sorry I am. But Mr. Ben David *never* consults with gentlemen about a loan except by appointment in his own house in Aldgate. This shop is where he conducts his sales of silver and gold, though never in person. He has an able staff at his command to serve you. If you care to leave your card and call again, you will be informed if— that is, *when* Mr. Ben David may be willing to receive you."

Sir George seemed to hesitate on the verge of an ugly retort, then pulled out his card case, tossed a card onto the counter, and went striding out with one curt question over his shoulder. "Are you coming, Edmund?"

"Not just yet."

"Are you a member of Mr. Ben David's staff, ma'am?" Edmund asked, when the slam of the door announced the departure of his friend.

She bowed her head slightly. "I am a member of his family, sir."

"I must apologize for my friend."

"There is no need, sir. I have met English *gentle*men before."

"The need is mine."

"One is responsible only for one's own actions," she stated slowly. *"You* have paid me no hurt or insult."

"I have my thoughts of the past to atone for."

"I, then, too, sir. In the past, I have thought no better of your people than you may have thought of mine."

There was a long pause before she hinted gently, "Give you good day, sir."

He shook off his abstraction. "No, if you please, would you help me? I would like to pick out a fine ornament for—for a lady."

She straightened proudly. "I will summon Jacob."

"No, please." He put out a hand to detain her as she would have turned away. "I would like your aid in choosing."

"I do not deal with the buying and selling, sir. I come here but once a week to deal with the books and accounts."

"You—a woman—do the books?"

She smiled faintly. "Mr. Ben David does not believe ability is a male prerogative."

"A most unusual man."

"My father *is* a most unusual man."

"Ah, I thought so. The way you bear yourself . . . the way you speak . . ."

"I am Deborah Ben David." She curtsied deeply. "I would not expect an Englishman to understand that, though we came from Portugal to your country more than a century ago, our own House goes back a thousand years or more."

"Since my family came to England from Normandy with the Conqueror," he said, bowing even lower than she, "I do understand, Miss Ben David. I am Edmund Henry Crozier, third son to the fifth earl of Shirley."

Gray eyes locked with brown, and the gray fell first, even as she said firmly, "Our meeting has been pleasant, sir, just as our farewell would be timely."

"After you help me pick a jewel for—my lady."

She said colorlessly, moving toward a case of ornaments, "Have you any preference, sir? A bracelet? A brooch? Perhaps an ornament for her hair?"

"Her hair shines golder than the sun; it needs no ornament. I think, perhaps, a chain for her neck with a pendant hanging from it."

"There is this diamond sunburst."

"Beyond my purse, I fear."

"These lockets, then?"

"They are nothing out of the common, and *she* is special."

"Would a cross of gold please her?"

"I fear not." His brown eyes locked with hers once more. "The lady I have given my heart to is of your faith. Would not such a one desire the star of the Israelites?"

Her cheeks had gone white, but her eyes never wavered from his.

"'Tis called the Star of David," she corrected quietly.

"May I see your selection of stars?"

She called out the name "Jacob" and then a few words in a language strange to him. In a minute or two a young bearded man came from the back of the shop carrying a long, velvet-covered tray.

He inclined his head respectfully to both of them and placed the tray on the counter. Edmund came closer to survey its contents. His choice was almost immediate.

"This one," he said, and held up a star that seemed made of woven threads of gold intricately braided together. A small, blue green sapphire sparkled in the center.

"A fine choice," approved Jacob. Then delicately, "As to price . . ."

Deborah Ben David walked away from them into the back room, trying to still her pounding heart. When she returned Jacob was stringing the star on a fine linked chain and Edmund Crozier was returning his purse to his pocket.

"I think you said your father's house is in Aldgate?" he asked Deborah softly.

"He will receive you there by appointment on business, but not— You must understand," she explained in a swift undertone. "He is a proud Sephardic and does not wish to mingle with your people any more than yours do with mine."

He smiled at her with a good deal of understanding. "I understand that he is much like my own father," he conceded. "I shall not let either of them stand in my way." He studied her gravely. "Will you, Deborah Ben David?"

She gripped the countertop with the fingertips of both hands. "You know not what you ask of me!" she cried out in such anguish that Jacob, who did not hear her words but only the tone of them, looked at her curiously.

Edmund walked over to the door after Jacob left them. The bell jangled once more as he opened it. He turned for a last look.

"I will!" she cried impulsively. "I mean, I will not."

"Ah, my little love." He laughed aloud exultantly.

"But come not to my house." The words tumbled out in her hurry. "I will be here in the shop this day a week at the same time."

His eyes pledged all that his heart would have said. "We shall meet again."

Chapter 17

Every week it was the same. Jacob greeted him courteously in front of the shop and spoke the exact words, his voice a little lower in the presence of customers.

"Good day, sir. If you will be pleased to go into the office, Miss Ben David is expecting you."

He would walk in back of the counter, proceed past the storage room through a short, dark corridor till he reached the larger of the two offices.

It was a small room dominated by a large desk heaped with ledgers. At a smaller wooden worktable, books and papers had been pushed aside to make room for the ornate Queen Anne silver tea service.

They would sit sedately opposite one another on the straight-backed office chairs, so close their knees all but touched, each holding a small plate of cakes.

They drank their tea and ate the cakes, they talked

and they were silent; their lips dealt with one language and their tense bodies spoke another.

From time to time his eyes rested possessively on her, proudly on the only ornament she wore, a golden star with a blue green sapphire. She had accepted it on his second visit, leaning forward in her chair, face hidden, while he fastened it about her neck, his fingers trembling when they touched her skin.

On his third visit he brought a little miniature he had painted from memory. It showed her sitting very upright in her chair, the star gleaming against the green velvet of her dress. He had captured the creamy texture of her skin, the fine bones and sculptured features, the grace and elegance of her form.

"Edmund, can this be your work?" she cried out in delight.

"Your surprise is hardly flattering," he teased her laughingly. "My art master used to say if I had not the misfortune to be born a gentleman, I could make my living with my paints. I am quite willing," he added meaningly, "to cease being a gentleman and take up the brush—any time I have a motive."

He saw by the shaking hand pressed up against her breast and the quick alarm in her eyes that he had gone too fast for her.

"'Twas meant as a small gift for you, Miss Ben David," he said, pressing the miniature into her fingers, "but I find myself strangely reluctant to part with one Deborah if I cannot have the other."

"Then keep it by you," she urged, returning the small portrait to him, "until—"

"Until?" he prompted, heedless of her confusion.

There was a spirit about her that could not be intimidated long. "Until you no longer need it," she told him tartly.

"When I have the original?" he suggested.

"When you have the original," she agreed, her eyes responding boldly to the challenge in his.

On his sixth visit, into one of the exquisite understanding silences they had both come to treasure, she spoke sudden troubled words.

"Jacob is distressed."

"Jacob?"

"In his mind."

"I am sorry, but—"

She put her plate and teacup onto the table. "He doesn't wish to betray me," she said, leaning toward him, "but in aiding us, he feels that he betrays my father, who has been good to him. For him it is a moral dilemma."

He rid himself of his own cup and plate to lovingly still the hands she was kneading in her lap.

"There is no dilemma except yours, my love," he told her. "It is in your power to put an end to both Jacob's distress and my own." He paid no heed to the gulping intake of her breath. "I have known what it was I wanted of you from the first day we met. Can you say the same?"

She answered almost pleadingly, "It is not that I do not want . . . You must know that I *do* have a feeling for you, only—only—"

"For me there are no onlies. I love you. I want you to be my wife."

"Impossible!" Lawrence Crozier, fifth earl of Shirley, roared, purple faced. "Are you a Bedlamite? You dare expect me to approve your allying the noble blood of our forbears with the get of a Jew merchant's breeding."

"I should like to remind you, sir," Edmund said in a

calm, reasoning voice that roused his sire's rage to an even higher pitch, "that our Crozier forbears seem to have sprouted from the seed of one Henri De Croix, a ne'er-do-well younger son who was outfitted with horse and weapons by his loving Norman family when he came with William the Conqueror to England. It is a matter of family record that he received enough stolen lands here to fulfill their fondest hopes by never returning to Normandy to harass them further."

"I have only this to say: if you marry this wench, then you cease to be my son."

"You would abandon your people and your faith for one of these Englishmen who spit upon us!" thundered Eleazar Ben David over Deborah's bowed head. "When your ancestors were kings in Israel, the English were walking about these isles as barbarians painting themselves blue."

"My people are my people. My faith is my faith. I would not abandon either to wed with Edmund."

"The day you wed Edmund Crozier, I will rend my garments and cry my sorrow aloud to the God of our fathers that I mourn the death of my daughter."

Lady Elizabeth Crozier had a soft spot in her heart for her third son. True, she had never seen much of him since there were nurses, governesses, tutors, and schools standing between the normal intimacy of mother and son.

But she loved him enough to shed bitter tears when it was certain that he would leave England. She was wise enough to keep her tongue from the Israelite girl and caring enough to empty her jewel case of all but family heirlooms to make up for the inheritance he would never now get from his father. Since Lady Elizabeth was still lovely enough to attract generous lovers, it was a not-inconsiderable fortune Edmund Crozier took with him to America.

Deborah fared nearly as well. Esther Ben David was unable to understand her daughter's passion, but she loved her with no need to understand.

All her own life had been bounded by the tight, secure walls of home, first her father's, then her husband's. Although she had been born in England and never known want, she had been reared in the tradition of having always something laid by if the knock came in the night that spelled danger and exodus. The stocking that she gave to Deborah was packed with silver and gold pieces hoarded all her life long.

On the day they set sail for America Edmund Henry Crozier and Deborah Ben David were joined in marriage by the ship's captain, with no member of their families present, no friends, only strangers and sailors watching curiously.

Their first child was conceived during the stormy, eight-week passage. She was born one week short of eight months after they landed in New York Harbor.

They named her Elizabeth Esther after both their mothers and the two great queens of their peoples. It was too large a name for such a slip of a girl and was soon shortened to Beth by everyone except her father. To him she was always "my little Lady Beth," which somehow became Ladybeth alone.

Chapter 18

EDMUND CROZIER WOULD HAVE BEEN THE FIRST TO admit that the prosperity and well-being of his little family rested squarely on his Deborah's small strong shoulders.

Together they found the house on Bowling Green that was to be their permanent home. Then Deborah took over.

In the front room, where the charming bow window permitted an attractive display of wares, she had placed a series of raised boxes and draped them with a rich ruby velvet cloth.

On these small steps were set a series of framed miniatures that Edmund had painted on the ship: two of herself, one each of the ship's captain and a common seaman, a half dozen of the other passengers, including several children. Mounted in elaborate oval frames, the miniatures made an impressive display.

Passersby, stopping to study them, could not miss the

two handsome cards mounted on child-sized, hand-carved easels. "Edmund Crozier, Portrait Painting in the English Style" read one in flowing calligraphy. "Private lessons by appointment" read the other.

Edmund had argued against advertising his work as in the English style. It smacked, he asserted roundly, of snobbery.

"Precisely," Deborah retorted smugly. "What do you think that someone who can put down two guineas for a miniature, three for a half portrait, and five for a full portrait wants if not a bit of snobbery? From what I can see, art in these colonies is quite primitive and undeveloped. The colonials—or at least their wives—regard any goods or services that are English as the best."

"My cynical little Solomon. Sometimes your wisdom frightens me," he told her, half in awe, half in consternation.

"Recollect, Edmund dear," she reminded him, eyes sparkling, voice teasing, "that the gentleman was left behind in London. However genteel the occupation, the fact remains you are now in trade. A man is in trade to make his bread the best he can. I am enough a merchant's daughter to know *that.*"

He swept her into his arms.

"My devil's advocate and heavenly angel all in one, have it your own way then, and we shall see."

So the cards remained as they were, and Deborah proved to be correct in her calculations.

The merchants and shipowners of New York, accustomed to the harsher, more primitive techniques of American artists, were enraptured by the finer artistry and greater elegance of Edmund's work.

They did not care or even observe that his creative powers were limited, that he repeated his compositions and lacked the ability to organize the light and space properly in his landscape backgrounds.

What pleased his subjects was his ability not only to catch a likeness but to improve it. Whatever they were in real life, when framed on a wall, they wanted their women to appear lovely standing beneath a tree, their men handsome and virile with ships' masts rising behind them, their children plump and appealing as they tumbled about in a garden.

Edmund Crozier gave them not works of art but the romanticized portraits they felt proud to hang on their walls, and they paid handsomely for the privilege.

They paid well, too, to send their daughters to him to learn this newest ladylike accomplishment, occasionally even their sons.

The women bought from Deborah, too, for, without ever setting up shop, the front room always contained several tables of appealing wares, at first the original stock she had brought from England, wisely investing some of her mother's gold and silver coins. Fine trinkets for ladies such as lockets, jeweled combs, brooches and bracelets, men's watch fobs and stick-pins, fine bolts of satin and lace, velvets and ribbons.

In later years, when from time to time her stock was replenished, she advertised in the Gazette the latest arrival by ship from England of the finest and newest in English goods.

Each business fed on the other. Those who came to buy from Deborah often wound up commissioning portraits from Edmund. Those who came to be painted often wound up buying from Deborah.

They were prosperous as well as happy. Ladybeth grew up in the studio and the shop, loving nothing so much as the smell of her father's paints.

She was five when her brother was born and letters

went out to England apprising two families of the existence of Lawrence Ben David Crozier, named after his two grandfathers.

No letters from the fathers came in reply, but Lady Elizabeth sent a heavy gold signet ring with a large onyx stone that the tiny recipient in the cradle would not be able to wear until full manhood. From Esther Ben David came a tear-blotched missive, evidently written in fear of her own daring. It protested her love and devotion and proclaimed her husband's unwavering determination to disavow his daughter. She enclosed a bank draft.

With a smile and a sigh and not a few tears, Deborah Crozier locked both ring and letter away. Then with practical common sense, she converted the bank draft to hard cash to be used for the purchase of a wagon and horses.

In buying a wagon she had two objects in mind: the first, to get away from the putrid, unhealthful air of New York when summer came; the second, to expand her husband's business, not quite as thriving as in earlier years. Competitors had not only begun to advertise their work as executed in the manner and technique taught in the London school of art, but work was always slow in the summer when the wealthier families fled the diseases of the city for their summer homes on Long Island and in West Chester. The buying of Deborah's wares suffered equally.

She had read of the itinerant painters who traveled throughout the countryside, seeking business wherever it might be, at country homes, wayside inns, farm houses . . .

"We need not aspire to the prices you charge in New York," she urged Edmund eagerly. "Indeed, if we could only meet our expenses . . . and get the children away from the malodorous air of summer. It would be so healthful . . ."

Her voice wavered; her eyes filled up as she glanced down at the child in her arms. The baby Lawrence Ben David, unlike his more sturdy sister, was frail, prone to every passing ailment, a constant source of anxiety.

The notion of traveling about appealed to Edmund's eager appetite for new sights and sensations. The notion was irresistible when it could be combined with pleasing Deborah and protecting his children.

When summer came, the wagon was carefully chosen, one set up to travel, sleep, and eat in, as well as store provisions and Edmund's art supplies. Two hardy work horses gave him greater ease and speed in travel than most journeymen painters boasted.

He never gave any thought to the irony of holding the reins behind such a pair, he who had once been mounted on the finest horseflesh in England.

He never gave any thought to England at all.

His life was America, and during the next nine years they saw vastly more of it than most colonials ever did.

Eight months of the year they resided and worked at their home on Bowling Green. From the time that Ladybeth was six and the child Lawrence just under one year, starting off in late May, staying away till mid-September or sometimes Indian summer, they journeyed about the country, stopping in whatever place took their fancy or wherever work was to be had.

They traveled through upstate New York, all about Connecticut and Massachusetts. Over the years they covered most of the New England colonies, Rhode Island, Vermont, the Hampshires, one month on Nantucket Island.

They went south through the Jerseys and Pennsylvania, reaching as far away as Virginia.

They ate in farmers' fields and in inn kitchens, in tents at country fairs, sitting on logs in lonely wooded areas, on rocks at oceanside and along sandy beaches.

Edmund learned to set up his easel in a farmer's parlor or the common room of an inn, in a country garden or a sewing room.

Deborah, after the first year, carried a little trunk of assorted clothing: silks and satins and London breeches. The poorest farmer's wife did not want to be painted in her work clothes or even her Sunday dress if there was better to be had. She wanted to be portrayed as a lady; she wished her husband to be painted "looking like a gentleman."

Deborah could not help laughing often at the absurdity, woman after woman in the same neighborhood painted in perhaps the selfsame dress, with just a change of lace collar or muslin fichu to make a difference.

After a while it began to seem that even the faces in the portraits were alike, too, one farmer much resembling another, the wives differing only as to slimness or to fat.

She buried this disloyal thought as quickly as it came to her. Edmund Crozier was not a great painter. She was too clear-headed in spite of her overwhelming love for him not to recognize this truth. The best work he had ever performed was the first miniature of herself, in which love more than talent appeared to be his inspiration.

It was unimportant. Edmund's work took care of them all. It made him happy. It gave pleasure to those he painted, none more so than the country people they encountered on their journeys, where often they were paid, not with money, which such people lacked, but in barter. Fresh-baked loaves, produce from the garden, a chicken with its neck yet to be wrung, hay for the horses, food and lodging overnight as a change from their outdoor campfires and wagon cots.

As she grew older, Elizabeth Esther Crozier became increasingly aware that their life in New York, though not a season of penance, could in no way compare to the freedom and joy of their life on the road.

By the time she was nine she was drawing along with her father and helping him to mix his paints. She knew that indigo combined with white made a blue sky in his backgrounds; the same colors with pink added could be used for grass. For the deepest black she learned to take the whitest ivory and burn it, so that the ashes produced the desired shade.

She was taught by the farmers' wives to make dyes from herbs, and from an ancient Indian who dwelled unaccountably alone on a lake in Connecticut, she learned to mix colored earths with the gum of trees as binder to get wondrously different paints.

She painted her first pictures with her fingers and fashioned figures out of clay or even flour dough. As soon as he realized her talent, her father began supplying her with paper and brushes. Then she started painting in earnest, beginning with crude, innocent studies of farm creatures in a style that was totally American, totally her own.

"It has nothing of me in it," Edmund confided to Deborah when Ladybeth was twelve. "I may have been her teacher and her mentor, but she is her own painter just as she has always been her own woman. She derives nothing from my technique, and before she is adult, she will surpass me. When I am dead and forgotten, *her* work may well live on."

Deborah made a small sound of protest, and he smiled and shook his head. "Come, love, let us be honest. We have both long recognized that my talent is no great thing. I am reconciled. What I do suffices me so long as it suffices you."

His trailing voice made it a question, not a statement, and her glowing eyes and warm embrace were answer enough.

"When she is older, we must try to send her to England to study," Edmund said. "Nay, love," as Deborah pushed away from him, panic in her eyes, "not for many years yet. But you would not for love of her, would you, deny her any opportunity or advantage that belongs to such gifts as God has bestowed upon her?"

"Not that, but—"

"The set of sketches she did on Farmer Ludwell and his wife," he swept on, unaware in his enthusiasm that he had interrupted her. "Did you note the clean, sharp lines of her drawing, the almost masculine quality of robustness? It was positively Hogarthian in its satire." He added dreamily, "I hope we are so fortunate as to be alive to hear her fame trumpeted. I would not mind being pointed out as the father of the great American painter Ladybeth."

Chapter 19

THEY WERE NOT DESTINED TO BE THAT FORTUNATE.

By one of fate's strange ironies, it was the very way of life that had been intended to preserve their health and lives that placed them all in jeopardy.

The summer before Ladybeth reached fourteen, they were journeying through Pennsylvania. At a country inn outside Philadelphia, Edmund was commissioned to repaint a handsome sign for the tavern.

Pleased with the result, the innkeeper asked for portraits of his two sons, the younger just a toddler, the older a handsome boy of eight or nine, the same age as Lawrence. They had played together while the sign was being painted.

They were difficult subjects, the younger child fretful and the older one complaining endlessly of pain in his back and head from sitting. Edmund finally sent them away with their mother, saying he would try again the next morning. He busied himself until evening filling in a landscape background.

They shared supper in the kitchen that night with the innkeeper's family. The next day the two boys could not sit for their portraits. They were both down with a fever.

The Croziers continued on their travels, promising to stop by again if they came the same way on the return journey.

Lawrence sickened first, complaining of pains in the head and the back, then came the fever, the same as the innkeeper's sons.

Deborah nursed him in the wagon, insisting that Ladybeth make her bed beside a campfire off the road, while Edmund unhitched the better of their two horses to ride into Philadelphia in search of a doctor.

When he returned the next day, haggard and exhausted but with a doctor riding alongside him, his son was already dead, and his wife lay in the wagon, tossing in delirium, with Ladybeth placing cloths cooled in the brook onto her red-hot head. The doctor, after a brief examination, shook his head sadly, knowing her past all help. She died within four hours.

With her father slumped on the seat beside her, half-dead with fatigue, shock, and grief, Ladybeth—too numbed to feel—drove the wagon with its grievous burden. The doctor rode into Philadelphia ahead of the sorrowful little procession.

Edmund roused himself when they reached Philadelphia, stopped along a busy street, and stepped down from the wagon to make some inquiries. When he returned to the wagon, he took the reins from Ladybeth.

Deborah Crozier of the house of Ben David and her

son Lawrence, descended from the earls of Shirley, were buried side by side in the old Jewish cemetery, acknowledged in death as they had not been in life.

Walking through the graveyard after the simple service, Edmund Crozier unclenched his right fist, showing Ladybeth the Star of David with its blue green sapphire, her mother's most precious jewel.

"By rights this should be yours now," he said huskily, "but I cannot bear to see it about any neck but hers." Slow tears trickled down his face and further clogged his voice. "And neither can I bear to part with it."

He reached up, his movements like a tired old man's, to fasten the chain around his own neck and tuck the star away beneath his shirt. He was to wear it that way for all the rest of his life.

They slept in lodgings that night and left in the gray dawn, stopping only to eat and sleep until they reached the house on Bowling Green.

When Ladybeth suggested tentatively that he make some work stops along the way, Edmund just shook his head.

"Let us go back to New York. I yearn to be home."

They arrived in mid-August, one month ahead of their usual time, Ladybeth as eager to arrive now as Edmund so that the father she loved and revered would be returned to her.

He never was.

Without Deborah, the house on Bowling Green was no longer home to Edmund. It was a house and nothing more. A house full of empty spaces and empty dreams.

He missed his small son achingly, agonizingly, but the loss of his wife destroyed the meaning of his whole life. Ambition faded, purpose died.

Sometimes he heard his dear-loved daughter coaxing

him back to life, but the effort was too much, he always slipped back into indolence again. He dressed sloppily, carelessly, he who had always appeared in public, even to paint, as a son of the earl of Shirley should. He remained unshaven for days, changed his linen less often than had been his wont, and the number of empty wine bottles brought down from his bedroom grew and grew.

After some months, murmuring about a new commission, he went out one night. Several hours later when he returned, Ladybeth started up hopefully. One look at his pale face and tormented eyes, and she asked no questions.

Later that night she heard him weeping aloud in his bedroom. "Deborah, forgive me, it would never have happened if you had not left me. God forgive me, I cannot forgive myself."

Several weeks afterward the same thing happened, only this time when she went up to his room to bring him a cup of hot tea and put an end to his self-torment, she noticed that he reeked of an over-sweet perfume.

Then she understood.

She had spent summer days at too many farms not to know the needs and behavior of all male creatures. Her mother had been the first to see the sketches she had drawn, depicting the attempts of Farmer Hatfield in Rhode Island to have his indifferent cow Betsy serviced by his neighbor's prize bull Rufus.

Deborah had thoughtfully viewed the three sketches, which showed the doubtful beginnings of the bovine romance through to its ultimate triumphant conclusion. They were done in the robust manner her husband called Hogarthian. Calmly she suggested to the youthful artist that the nature of the subject, perhaps, made it unwise that her signature be affixed to the sketches.

To an indignant Ladybeth, who knew an artist *always* signed a painting, she explained the nature of society's viewpoint. Then, acquainted only too well with her daughter's insatiable hunger to know and explore, she went on to explain the nature of man.

Ladybeth listened carefully.

"You mean men behave like the animals?" she inquired with interest when her mother was done.

"The physical act may seem the same, but the love that a man and woman feel for each other makes a vast difference."

Ladybeth cocked her head, considering. "You mean—" she paused delicately—"you and Papa—"

Deborah's color rose, but her great, gray eyes met her daughter's candid gaze unflinchingly. "Yes," she said, "and of such acts of love, children are sometimes born."

"I'm glad I was born of love, Mama," Ladybeth told her with a bright smile, "and though I think it's silly that people don't understand nature"—she shrugged cheerfully—"I'll take off my name if you think it's best." As she spoke she was erasing her signature by scribbling it in as part of the background.

Ladybeth never forgot. In the happy old days her father was wont to tease that she never, worse luck, forgot anything.

The memory of it enabled her now to hand her father his cup of tea, to look at his haggard, ravaged face, try to conceal her distaste of the sickly sweet perfume smell, and say to him, "Papa, you mustn't blame yourself."

"Wh-what do you m-mean?" Edmund Crozier stammered out.

"Mama would have understood," Ladybeth told him

firmly. "She told me more than once that a man must have the—the comfort of a woman."

Edmund had drunk too much wine.

"A cheap woman who s-sells her favors for a few shillings to t-take p-place of your m-mother," he hiccuped.

"No one does that," stated Ladybeth calmly. "Your shillings bought you a little ease of mind and body. Mama would have understood," she repeated.

Edmund swayed a bit on his feet, and she rescued the cup and saucer and placed them on the table near his bed. In some fogged recess of his mind, he was aware that this sturdy little daughter, with her new dignity and understanding and her mother's lovely, clear-sighted gray eyes, had far outdistanced him in age, just as she had done in talent.

Chapter 20

O<small>N</small> L<small>ADYBETH'S</small> <small>FIFTEENTH</small> <small>BIRTHDAY,</small> <small>WHICH</small> <small>HER</small>
father forgot, she determined that their roles must be
reversed.

His commissions were falling off to nothing. More
money was going out than was coming in. Their capital
was being eaten into. She was enough her mother's
daughter to know this state of affairs must be stopped.
Someone had to take charge, and clearly it would not
be Edmund.

The first step she took was to dismiss their two
servants and hire one strong maid-of-all-work in their
place. Next, she advertised in the Gazette the sale at
great bargains of all her mother's wares. She knew that
she was not good at trade, and it would be best to end
this aspect of their business life, accumulating as much
hard cash in the process as was possible.

For a full week a steady stream of shoppers, drawn
first by the advertisement and then by word-of-mouth

from the early customers, streamed in and out of the house. When the last one left and she pulled her mother's business card out of the Bow Window, there was not one thing left to sell in the house and the cash box was pleasantly heavy.

An apathetic Edmund, playing at painting in the back room, appeared not to notice. Ladybeth hid the cash box with a small supply of coins and paper monies in her bedroom; the rest went to the bank.

Next she advertised herself as a teacher of drawing who would give private instruction in the home to "Very young girls and boys with an aptitude for the arts." Repeating this advertisement weekly for one month, she procured herself five pupils.

She refurbished the front room as Edmund's studio, so that those who stopped by the Bow Window could see his easel set up and sometimes the artist himself engaged on a portrait, his jacket pressed, his cravat neatly tied—his daughter having bullied him into work.

As a result of these efforts, Edmund received enough commissions to pay their house expenses. Ladybeth's pupils paid for their servant and little extras. Their capital remained intact.

Most of her life Elizabeth Crozier had dwelled within the narrow world of her family and her painting. Alone so much now, she subscribed to Mr. Noel's lending library and discovered the wonderful world of books.

She embraced reading with the same wholehearted-ness with which she approached most things in life. Not only books contented her. Magazines, newspapers, broadsides—anything that was printed, she read.

She had always known that both her parents were English-born, and she and her brother Lawrence were English, but colonials. Through reading, she discov-ered new pride in being American, anger at the British who from five thousand miles away trampled on American rights.

New York had more than its share of Tories and an outstandingly large number of the British military. In the midst of them all, fiercely individual as always, Elizabeth Esther Crozier read herself into a state of rampant patriotism.

It inspired her into sketching the series of political satires that brought renewed business and fame to Edmund Crozier. A large new pen and ink sketch appeared each week in the Bow Window, signed simply E. Crozier and naturally assumed by everyone to be the work of the portrait painter.

When Ladybeth saw how people crowded about the window each Monday to view the new display, she whisked the portrait miniatures off to the side and featured the political cartoons.

King George, standing on a map of Britain, with one long leg stretched out across the ocean to reach his New World colonies, where a working man in a tricorn hat, stooping to pick up a piece of firewood, presented his bare behind labeled *American* to receive a royal kick. . . . A caricature of Lord North, crouched behind a group of obvious Americans, busily picking their pockets. . . . An obese gentleman, decked in the robes of the House of Lords and waving a flag marked Parliament, held prisoner beneath his arm a small boy whose sailor hat bore the label *American colonies*. The gentleman was belaboring the child with a large wooden paddle, an expression of glee on his face. The caption beneath the cartoon read, "This hurts me more than it does you."

Her political cartoons—bawdy, obvious, and robust —were an overnight sensation. Edmund demurred at accepting credit for her work, but Ladybeth held firm.

Copies of the cartoons, she pointed out, not only brought in welcome income, but even better, fresh commissions for portraits by Edmund Crozier, suddenly the most talked-of painter in New York.

"They will accept political commentary from *you*," she said with a flash of her mother's wise cynicism. "From *me*, a sixteen-year-old girl, they would consider it impertinent."

Reluctantly Edmund agreed, but by way of amends to her, he started painting with renewed vigor. Ladybeth acquired three more pupils and continued to draw a new cartoon each week. They were happier than at any time since her brother and mother had died.

About once a month in the evening, Edmund made a discreet disappearance. Ladybeth never questioned him, he never explained, but he no longer came home from such expeditions, wild-eyed, imploring his Deborah's forgiveness.

On one such night, it had grown quite late, and he did not come home till long after his usual time. It was past midnight before the anxiously waiting Ladybeth heard sounds outside the front door. She sped through the kitchen, where she had been sitting with a book beside a dying fire, to fling open the door.

Her father stumbled across the threshold on the arm of a painted woman. Ladybeth seized his other slack arm, and they helped him to a chair.

"Is he sick or drunk?" she asked the woman sharply.

"A little of both, I think," came the woman's reply. She looked at Ladybeth belligerently, defying her to lay any blame.

"It was kind of you to see him home," the girl said quietly. "Would you help me get him upstairs? I think he would be better off in his bed."

"I suppose so," came the grudging answer, but she

proved efficient, possibly experienced, in getting an inert man up a steep flight of steps and into his bed, then stripping him of his clothes.

"Do you think I should send for a doctor?" Ladybeth whispered when they had him under the covers.

A head was shaken in reply. "I think not. He's already coughed up everything inside him. Let him sleep it off. He hasn't any fever."

Ladybeth snuffed the candle, and they left the room together and went downstairs.

"I'm much obliged to you, Miss—Mrs.—Ma'am," she stumbled awkwardly.

"I'm Ruthanna Cummins, *Miss* Ruthanna Cummins, and I'm a friend of your father's. I've been a good friend of his this whole past year," she announced with studied insolence.

"I know." Ladybeth smiled faintly. "I recognized your perfume. I'm very grateful to you."

"Huh!" gulped Ruthanna Cummins, considerably taken back. Gratitude was hardly the emotion she expected to arouse in a customer's womenfolk. She tossed her head of obviously dyed yellow hair. "I better be getting on my way."

"It's too late. You can't go walking the streets alone at this hour of night." Ladybeth realized, even as she spoke, that her turn of phrase had been unfortunate. She blushed vividly at Ruthanna's blunt return.

"It's part of my business to walk the streets late at night."

"Why do you try to make yourself out so much worse than you are?" Ladybeth protested.

"I'm a whore, honey. Dressing it up in pretty language ain't going to make it any different. Being your father's whore don't make it any better."

"It's late and it's cold, and I insist you stay the night.

There's a little chamber off the kitchen where you'll be warmer than in any of the upstairs rooms. They haven't had fires lit in them for quite a while. There's hot water in the kettle on the stove and tea in the pantry. You'll find matches and candles on the sink. Thank you again for bringing my father home."

"Well, if you don't beat all!"

But Ladybeth had already whisked herself back upstairs.

Chapter 21

EDMUND RECOVERED FROM HIS ILLNESS IN JUST A FEW days, but a malignant fate was not yet done with him.

Early in December Ladybeth sat in the kitchen rocker, swathed in shawls, quietly reading. She could never sleep, knowing her father was abroad, but as soon as she heard a key turn in the lock announcing that he was safe home—to save him embarrassment—she ran upstairs. By the time he made a stumbling progress to his bedroom, she would be closed in her own.

Outside the house the sound of several pairs of boots, loud and clumping, halted her in her tracks the moment she got up from the rocker. Her father was obviously not alone. Perhaps Ruthanna Cummins had brought him home again, in which case she would be needed. Discretion be damned!

She flung open the kitchen door and cried out in anguish. Her father stood there, supported on either side by a husky, hatless sailor, one tow-haired, one redheaded. Actually, each man had an arm about Edmund and was carrying so much dead weight, since his head lolled about on his neck and he was only half-conscious. This semi-stupor was just as well for him, as blood streamed from his nose, his torn lower lip, and one of his swollen eyes.

"Bring him in!" Ladybeth called out, and when they did so, "Oh, God! What happened?" she asked them.

"Best get him into bed, Missy. Doctor's fast on our heels. Our mate went to fetch him."

"Oh, yes, of course. Can you manage him up these stairs?"

"Naught to it, ma'am." One of the sailors took on the full weight of Edmund, hoisting him easily over his shoulder and mounting the steep staircase, as agile as though he were climbing up a mast.

Once they had him on the bed, Ladybeth (because they seemed to expect it) turned her back modestly while they stripped Edmund to his smalls. His best blue breeches were handed to her along with his coat and bloodied shirt.

"I'm afraid they're past saving, Miss," the redheaded sailor said apologetically. "We came to help him a mite too late."

Ladybeth laid aside the ruined clothes and asked in a shaking voice, "Can you tell me what happened, please?"

"We was all in a tavern," said the tow-haired sailor.

"Perfectly respectable place," volunteered the redhead.

"Everyone there, your pa included, just having a harmless bit of fun."

"Then up comes this big chap—towered over your

father, he did—and he starts talking to him kinda wild, but it being a bit noisy and all, no one pays much attention."

"Then the two of them got to squaring up to one another, and first thing you know, the big one, he's a-knocking your pa about something fierce, and all the time accusing him of setting fires."

"Setting fires!" cried Ladybeth. *"My* father! That's ridiculous."

"Well, at first no one thinks to interfere in a private quarrel, but then it didn't seem fair, this other chap being so much younger and bigger than your pa, so Eddy and Nolan and me come over, and we was mighty glad we did because it seems—"

"—because it seems," broke in his friend, "that it was a political argument, and the big chap"—he spat expertly into the fireplace four feet away—"he was a thrice-damned Tory and it was some 'insensiary cartons' he was talking about, not setting fires."

"Oh, dear Lord!" whispered Ladybeth, pale as death. "Incendiary cartoons!"

"That's it, miss. That's it exactly," said the sailor, pleased to find her so quick of understanding. "All the good Whigs there, they later on said as how your father he draws these cartons that really jabs the stinking British bastards just where they need jabbing, and I beg your pardon for speaking so free in front of a real lady."

"That's all right," said Ladybeth on a low sobbing breath. "I can't think of any more accurate description than stinking British bastards!"

The sailors grinned appreciatively just as a loud knocking sounded from below.

"That must be the doctor," Ladybeth said, and

walked swiftly out of Edmund's room and down the stairs, both sailors following in her wake.

She admitted the doctor and turned to reward the sailors, but both backed away from her offered coin, the towhead saying apologetically, "We're only sorry we didn't get to him ahead of the bashing."

"It was our pleasure to help a real patriot like your pa," declared the redhead.

The doctor and Ladybeth together washed Edmund's poor battered face before soothing salves were applied to it and to other parts of his body as well.

Promising to return the following morning, the doctor then dosed him with laudanum and left. Ladybeth set up a cot in her father's room, so that while she tended him she could get what sleep she might. Even as she tossed and turned and fretted, knowing she must husband her strength to nurse her father, the pangs of remorse and the canker of self-loathing kept her awake for many more hours than she slept.

She was to blame that her father lay there, semiconscious, wounded, and in pain. She was the cause of his having been abused and beaten.

Her dear, happily carefree father—as he had been while Deborah lived—and the gentle, loving, helpless man he had become ever since she died, was as English now as the day that he was born. *She,* Ladybeth, was the American patriot. *She,* Ladybeth, was the American zealot!

She had drawn the cartoons, glad not only of the money, but gleeful at the chance to twist the British lion's tail! And because of her impudence, her imprudence, her father had paid a fearful price.

How often had he not said that Ladybeth's own signature should appear on her cartoons? And how firmly, always, she had declined, never considering what such a decision might cost *him*. Why, oh why, had she given no thought to how *she* would feel to have *her* name attached to work that was none of hers? Every instinct rebelled against it. Perhaps Edmund's own brand of patriotism as well as his pride had been violently repulsed by such double deception.

When Edmund slipped from his unconscious state into pneumonia, Ladybeth, aided by the doctor, waged a ceaseless, vigilant fight to keep him alive. He was all the family she had, and she loved him dearly. She could not bear the thought of life without him; but she was too honest not to acknowledge to herself that, if he died, she would be unable to bear the burden of her own guilt and remorse.

Torn with anxiety, as well as with fear and regret, Ladybeth shared the nursing of him with their servant Elsie and reluctantly sent messages canceling lessons. She managed to finish all the portraits Edmund had begun, carefully imitating his romantically stereotyped style, but she abandoned the cartoons completely.

If ever she were to return to drawing them, she vowed more than once in the cold December nights as she watched over Edmund's sickbed, it would be under her own name, flying her own flag. In the words of the two kindhearted sailors, she would be doing it to jab the stinking British bastards exactly where they needed jabbing!

On Christmas night Ruthanna Cummins knocked at the kitchen door. She entered the house with nervous haste in answer to Ladybeth's eager invitation.

"I haven't seen your father in quite a while," she began awkwardly, "not since that night I brought him home. I suppose I shouldn't have come like this, but I

heard how he had been set on to, and I wondered was
he still hurting."

"It was kind of you to come to inquire," said
Ladybeth gratefully. "He has been very ill with pneumonia. The doctor tells me," she insisted as much to
herself as to Ruthanna, "that he is getting better. Only
he seems so weak."

"You look like death yourself, honey."

"I'm a bit tired from not enough sleep and the
nursing and the painting and . . . you know . . ."

"Listen, if you don't like the idea, just throw me out,
but if it don't bother you, I'll sit up with him tonight. I
was"—she colored up a bit under Ladybeth's steady
gaze—"taking the night off anyways. I could sit up with
him and you could go to bed. You don't have to worry.
I'm a good nurse, I am. Back at the farm I used to nurse
all my sisters and brothers."

"Farm?"

"Hard to believe, huh, but that's where I grew up. A
farm in Jersey. I was the oldest in a family of ten. I got
so tired of cows and chickens and pigs and kids, when
the farmer next door proposed to me—a nice steady
man, good-looking, too—it was enough to make me
run screaming. I didn't want that kind of life. Just at the
right time, or maybe it was the wrong one, this horse
trader came along. Lord, what a smooth one he was.
He could talk the britches off a preacher, smile, and
rob him at the same time. He brought me to the big city
and dumped me inside of two weeks. I was too proud to
go home. I didn't have the money to go even without
the pride. So." She shrugged philosophically. "Here I
am, and for God's sakes"—her voice changed—"here
you are, dropping on your feet with exhaustion. Go to
bed, missie, I swear I'll take good care of your pa."

Ruthanna stayed the night and never went back, except to pack up her things and bring them to the house on Bowling Green.

When Ladybeth woke rested and refreshed for the first time in six weeks and a knock on her door announced the arrival of a succulent-smelling breakfast tray, she decided that Ruthanna was heaven-sent.

"Did you learn to cook like this back on the farm?"

"Sure did, though I haven't had too much practice these last years. Cooking," she said wistfully, "was one of the things I used to like to do."

Ladybeth said slowly, "Not me, and I do most of it. We have Elsie for the heavy work, but she's not too good a nurse. I have to get back to my pupils soon or I'll lose them all. It's been worrying me because we need the money. I have to go on with the painting, too; I don't want business to fall away. Maybe you're not even interested . . . I couldn't pay you much over room and board." She colored up. "You probably earn a lot more."

Ruthanna laughed in genuine amusement. "You don't know British soldiers if you think *that!* Who do you think comes to the likes of me, *officers?* Not bloody likely. Now look. Give it to me straight. Do you mean," she asked incredulously, "that I could *stay* here, *live* here?"

"Yes, of course, it wouldn't be any help if you didn't."

"Your pa would skin me alive."

"No, he wouldn't. Not when he understood what a help it would be to us both and what a burden it took off me. Of course, you'd have to give up painting your face, *and* the perfume, maybe even wear a cap on your head to look older and more like a housekeeper, if you were willing."

"Honey, I'm willing."

So Ruthanna moved into the little room off the kitchen, and by the time he had fully recovered, Edmund was reconciled to the fairly bizarre situation. He could not help noticing that the meals were vastly improved and that his daughter had recovered her usual vigor and good spirits.

Ladybeth herself never questioned the relationship between her father and the new housekeeper. If there were occasional visits between the small downstairs chamber and the master's bedroom, they were discreetly arranged so that she never knew.

Deborah, she told herself, would have understood.

The arrangement continued happily until the middle of 1774 when Ladybeth was seventeen and Edmund Crozier suffered a sudden heart seizure while he was painting a portrait of Jacob Ver Loop, who lived in one of the grander houses on the Bowling Green.

Ladybeth came home from giving a lesson to find the Dutch merchant standing in the front room with the brandy bottle trying to pour a drink into the weeping Ruthanna.

"Miss Crozier," he said in heavily accented English, "I fear we haf bad news for you."

"Ruthanna?" Ladybeth implored her.

"He's gone," Ruthanna whispered back.

"Gone." She repeated the word stupidly, refusing to acknowledge its true meaning. "Gone where?"

Ruthanna rocked back and forth. "Oh Ladybeth, he's dead, your father's dead."

"No!" said Ladybeth. "No!" And she sat down in a chair, looking so white and shaken that Mr. Ver Loop abandoned Ruthanna to rush the brandy to her. But even as Ladybeth kept repeating, "No!" denying aloud what she did not want to hear, she knew in her heart it was so.

Ever since his beating-up by the Tory who objected to his American-biased cartoons, ever since his pneumonia, Edmund had been living on borrowed time. His death might be the greatest grief of her life, but it was not truly unexpected.

So Ladybeth drank her father's brandy, went alone to say good-bye to him, and then fell to making plans. Although she would have given all she possessed to have him lie beside Deborah and his son, for all practical purposes, Philadelphia was as far away as England.

Edmund Crozier, third son of the earl of Shirley, was laid to rest in the cemetery of New York's Trinity Church. The funeral service was short and simple, but Ladybeth could never afterward recall a single line of it. She was too busy with her own vengeful thoughts.

It wasn't just the pneumonia and your weakened heart, Papa. It was my cartoons that killed you. My cartoons and the beating-up from a damned British-loving Tory. I'll even the score, Papa. Somehow, some way, if it's the last thing I do in my life, I'll even the score!

When she and Ruthanna came back from Trinity Churchyard, Ladybeth unclenched her right hand as they came into the house together. She had slipped the chain from around her father's neck before they closed the coffin and clutched it so tightly throughout the service that the pointed star had slightly cut her palm.

The star was more than the symbol of a faith to her. It was the living symbol of the love that had been between Deborah and Edmund, of the life they had all shared. She remembered Edmund's words in the ancient cemetery in Philadelphia. *I cannot bear to see it about any neck but hers . . . and neither can I bear to part with it.*

She knew that she could not bear to part with it either. She would wear it all her life long and perhaps hand it down to *her* daughter, she decided, as she slipped the chain around her neck, fastened it, and settled the star against the lace of her collar.

While Ruthanna set a light supper on the table, Ladybeth sat in the kitchen rocker, brooding.

"I suppose," she heard Ruthanna say dully after a while, "you won't be needing me anymore?"

Ladybeth's mournful rocking became a bit brisker.

"If I go back to my own cooking," she said, "I'm likely to starve to death."

The silver tableware slipped from Ruthanna's shaking hands.

"You mean you want me to stay on?"

"You surely don't think I want to live here alone with only Elsie coming in by the day? Ruthanna, I need you as much as you need me."

"Sit you down," said Ruthanna abruptly. "Supper's on."

But when Ladybeth slipped into her usual seat, tears were streaking down the cheeks of both.

They picked at their food in silence for a while till Ladybeth looked up, wiped her eyes with a linen napkin, and asked curiously, "What would you have done if you had had to leave?"

"With the references you would give me! Why, I'd get the best housekeeping job in New York," Ruthanna said swaggeringly. Then she shrugged and grimaced. "Who'm I joshing? We both know how long I'd likely last with any other family. It would be back to the old life for me . . . there's always lonesome soldiers needing a bit of home comfort."

"My God!" Ladybeth flung down her fork. "That's it. Ruthanna, you're a genius."

"What do you mean?" Ruthanna cried out in alarm. "Not you, Ladybeth, I'd never allow it."

"Ruthanna! For heaven's sake!" Ladybeth couldn't help but laugh. "I wasn't proposing to—to—well, I wasn't proposing *that*. I want to paint. It's all I've ever wanted to do. But if we're going to be able to stay on in this house, I have to earn some money, and no one wants to give commissions to a female, let alone a girl as young as I. Except maybe—you gave me the idea—lonely soldiers with not enough money for a high-priced painter."

She rushed from the table and sped out of the room, returning in minutes with pen, paper, and an inkwell.

She scribbled busily on the paper for several minutes, crossing out, scratching in.

"There!" She read it over once to herself and then aloud. " 'E. Crozier respectfully informs the military that miniature paintings of all ranks will be executed at most reasonable prices. These small sizes are suitable for shipping home, and their striking likeness to the subjects will gladden the hearts of your loved ones. Also half and full lengths.' "

"It sounds well," Ruthanna admitted cautiously, "but what makes you think the soldiers, too, will not object to being painted by a girl?"

"Because you, dear Ruthanna, will see them before I do, and having reduced them to tears by the prospect of the joy that will be sustained on receiving such miniatures by their sweethearts, wives, and mothers, you will complete the business transaction."

Laughing at Ruthanna's dumbfounded expression, she planned on. "I'll make up half a dozen or so samples of varying backgrounds and prices for them to choose from. *You* will take the order, collect the money in advance, and hand out a receipt previously signed by E. Crozier before they ever see who E. Crozier is. By the time you show them into the back room, where my easel will be set up, they will have no choice but to accept being painted by me. That or lose their money. Besides"—she laughed exultantly—"did you not say the soldiers here are lonesome? I will be *so* sympathetic to them, *so* understanding of their problems."

"That could cause trouble, too."

"Not," said Ladybeth sweetly, "with you as my chaperone, gliding in and out of the room often enough to ensure no liberties are taken."

Ruthanna weighed further objections. "Have you ever considered," she asked, "that some of your customers may turn out to have been *my* customers, which could cause trouble for both of us?"

Ladybeth paused a moment to consider, then maintained stoutly, "Nonsense, no one would recognize you now. You've put on weight, and you have good natural color on your face instead of all that white paint plastered over it. Your hair's gone back to its natural brown—that yellow dye gave you a very different appearance. With your cap and your new gowns, there isn't one chance in hundreds anyone but me would know you from before. You're a respectable housekeeper, a—a—you know, I think you should be a widow woman. There's something so respectable-sounding about a widow. Why don't you change your name?"

Ruthanna gave that suggestion a moment's thought, rubbing her forehead. "The farmer who wanted to give me his name fifteen years ago was called Fielding, Sam

Fielding," she mentioned humorously. "Mayhap I will accept from Samuel now what I was foolish enough to refuse then. Mrs. Fielding. It sounds well, I think."

"It sounds very well," agreed Ladybeth. "I will start my sample sketches tomorrow, and as soon as I have a sufficiency for display, I will take this advertisement to all the newspapers."

"I'm sure I don't know what your father would have said," Ruthanna lamented. "I wish I could feel sure you were doing the right thing."

"He would have said, 'When my little Ladybeth gets the bit between her teeth, there's no use trying to stop her.'" She twirled the paper with her advertisement around in the air. "What's more, he would have been right. Stop borrowing trouble, my dear Mrs. Fielding," she wound up buoyantly. "I tell you a wonderful new life is beginning for both of us."

Chapter 22

WITH THREE HUNDRED PEOPLE SCHEDULED TO AT-
tend the Mailer-Cortland wedding, it wasn't surprising
that my name had somehow slipped onto the invitation
list. I must have been among Maggie's fifty most-
wanted friends. Cam's intended, the Mailer grapevine
informed me, was being very gracious to Maggie.

"Even a shipping heiress is impressed by a TV-star
sister-in-law," Nicky said with youthful cynicism one
day.

I didn't bother to reprimand him, nannylike, which
I'd never gotten out of the habit of doing. Nor, I
couldn't help noticing, did Maggie. Neither of our
hearts was in it.

I sent a polite note of thanks and refusal, stating that
it just happened I would be out of town on the joyful
day. I not only intended to be out of town; I intended to
be out of the country. The day the invitation came, I

had bought a plane ticket for Liverpool, and I planned a month's visit home. The only way I could figure to get through the wedding day without falling apart was to put an ocean between Cam and me.

Two weeks before I left for England Maggie and I had a farewell lunch at the Russian Tea Room. Then we walked east to Mailer Publishing.

Ben bestowed a hearty smack on his wife's lips, a fatherly buss on my cheek, and burst out jubilantly, "Maggie, I've just got word from Boston. McNeal turned up that painting at the agreed price. It will get here before the wedding."

"How wonderful!" Maggie enthused in her deep, throbbing actress's voice. "Cam will be so pleased. But I wonder"—she raised her penciled brows in speculation—"somehow I don't quite see Irene's taste running to American primitives."

"Screw Irene!" said Ben succinctly. "I'm buying a wedding gift for my brother."

"Well, Irene *is* part of the wedding package," said Maggie mildly, "and there happens to be a young lady present."

"I'm sure Rilla has heard the word before in her Bowery retreat," Ben mentioned dryly. "As for Irene, even if she doesn't like the artwork of a Ladybeth, she'll appreciate the dollar value. In fact, I think— Rilla, for God's sake, Rilla, what's wrong?"

I was in a chair. Maggie was unbuttoning my collar, and Ben was fanning me so vigorously with a folded newspaper my hair was in my eyes and in my mouth. In the almost forgotten words of my childhood, I had come all over queer.

"Sorry," I choked, picking strands of hair off my tongue. "I'm all right now. It must have been the heat."

They both stared at me. The temperature outside stood at a bare thirty above. Then they glanced at one another in the unspoken communication of good marriage.

"No, dear," she said, "she's too young for that."

They suddenly seemed to be struck by another terrible thought about something I *wasn't* too young for, and they gave me simultaneous stares of panic.

"I'm *not* pregnant," I denied indignantly. "It was probably the—the fish at lunch. I thought it tasted funny," I said with a reckless sacrifice of truth. "I feel fine now."

I got up and went striding about the room to show them just how fine I felt, picking up ornaments, shuffling through magazines.

"Tell me about this Ladybeth, Ben," I said casually. "I—I've never seen one. Actually, I don't know much about her."

"She's one of our earliest folk-art painters and has not been that well known till fairly recently. Her more prominent works are signed Ladybeth, but it's now accepted that she painted under other identities as well."

"Cam—I mean, your brother likes her work?"

"He more than likes it. Sometimes I think he's obsessed with it." He tapped a pencil thoughtfully against his desk. "It began with two little miniatures he found in a flea market sale in some small New England state he was just passing through. One was of a British redcoat in the 1700s, one of a colonial girl. Frankly, they never seemed very outstanding to me. Interesting period pieces, of course, but no great art. But Cam went wild over them."

My throat was constricted, and my chest, too. I felt as though I couldn't breathe.

If I had ever needed anything to prove that space and time and distance didn't matter—single, engaged, or married—that there was something between Cam and me that nothing and no one could get in the way of, this was it. Whether he recognized it yet or not, we were tied together with invisible bonds that could not be cut or broken.

Moments like these were the ones I needed every now and then, both for love's sweet sake and for sanity's sake. I had to be reminded that I wouldn't spend my entire life as a lady-in-waiting. One day, I would unsuspectingly turn a corner and find fulfillment waiting for me.

Maggie had been subjecting me to the kind of scrutiny she gave one of the boys when she knew he had been up to something forbidden. Prudence dictated I keep my mouth shut, but I could no more have kept from asking than an astronaut could turn down a shot at a moon walk.

"Wh-what is this Ladybeth you bought for him? You talked as though it might be something special."

"It is. At least Cam will think so. I haven't even seen it. I'm no art expert. I have to accept an expert's advice. It's supposed to be a portrait of her father."

"Her f-father," I faltered.

"So McNeal says."

"Is it—is it—I mean, how do they know?"

"The name was written on the back. E. Crozier. That's considered to be—For Christ's sake, Maggie, get hold of her, she's going to faint."

"No, I'm not," I said, just before I did.

I woke up to a coffee mug with brandy in it being held to my lips, and my legs up and stretched out on the couch. I took a few seconds to get my bearings, accepted a few sips of brandy, managed a weak grin, and muttered, "Just like in a novel, only it's the hero who supplies the brandy."

"Then I," said Maggie somewhat tartly, "should be the one drinking it."

I held up the coffee mug. "Have some. It doesn't really go well with spoiled fish."

"Rilla," said Maggie dangerously, "if you say one more lying word about that fish, I will personally clobber you with the brandy bottle. Now get up; we're going to go downstairs and find a cab so I can take you home."

"I can take myself home."

"Over my dead body—until we do some talking."

As she dragged me out of the room, nothing on this earth could have stopped me from turning to ask Mr. Mailer over my shoulder, "Ben, when the painting comes, b-before you give it to C—your brother, could I see it?"

"I'll give you a ring."

There was a thick silence in the cab while our daredevil driver, a moonlighting actor, battled the traffic of the fifties and forties. Once we got below 34th Street, Maggie stopped bracing herself for a collision, ended her discussion of the theatre with our actor-driver, and uttered one ominous word. "Well?"

"Maggie, I—I can't tell you—not now. The truth is, there isn't anything to tell unless you want to hear my dreams, which I think I'd be better off telling to a psychiatrist. If it ever begins to make sense to anyone, especially me, you know you're the one I would turn to."

She put her hand over mine, lying on the seat, and squeezed it hard.

"I hate Irene's guts," she said quite clearly, "and I think she's all wrong for Cam, but *he* doesn't, *he's* marrying her. I know it's none of my damn business and Ben would be horrified at me for interfering, but you are very dear to us and we want to see you happy. I just can't," she burst out defensively, "stand by and see you waste your life over a schoolgirl crush."

I smiled at her with amused admiration and affection. "You never did miss a trick, Maggie. I won't waste my life," I promised.

"There are other good men out there."

"I hope I find one."

"You have to *look* if you want to find."

"I *look* all the time, Maggie. I just can't hop into bed with them, and that always seems to be the bottom line to furthering acquaintance."

"Well, not that I'm advocating promiscuity, but it happens not to be the most terrible thing in the world at your age to lose your virginity. I mean, virginity just for virginity's sake . . . Yours is, I believe, still intact?"

We stopped for a traffic light, and the taxi driver turned for a long stare, first at her and then at me. Maggie has a particularly penetrating voice, so I wasn't surprised that his interest appeared to be concentrated on me now a trifle more than it was on her. After that question, who could blame him?

I felt as though I owed them both an answer. "Yes, I *am* a virgin!" I stated loudly. "Come to think of it, why shouldn't the whole damn city be let in on this exciting little bit of gossip?" I rolled down the cab window. "Hey, New York," I shouted, "forgive me, but I'm a virgin!"

Chapter 23

THE PAINTING OF E. CROZIER BY LADYBETH, PRE-
sumed to be her father, did not arrive in New York
before I left for Liverpool. I flew to England, not
knowing if it was a portrait of the Edmund in my
dream.

I kept myself almost frantically busy with Mum and
Dad, so proud of their daughter Rilla, who, as the
neighbors put it, "had gone to the States and made a
success of herself."

I attended a wedding of our own, Jim's to his
childhood sweetheart Heather. Church ceremony and
lunch for twenty afterward.

While Jim and Heather traveled to Brighton, and
Cam and his Irene were honeymooning in the Caribbe-
an, Mum, Dad, and I went on a bus trip to the
Cotswolds.

I needed something to make me forget about that

man of mine, who just couldn't get it through his head that he belonged to *me*. If only he knew that he didn't need a Caribbean island or an heiress. With *me*, even in my loft on the Bowery, it would have been the kind of honeymoon that the poets write about!

We came back to Liverpool to find the copy of a wireless from Mr. Mailer collecting dust under the door. It was three days old and announced jubilantly that *The Frog Who Loved a Flounder* had been bought for an animated television special, to be aired the following Thanksgiving. He had negotiated the contract himself; come home quickly and sign the papers.

I flew out the next day.

The special was shown, with plenty of previous fanfare and promotion, on the first Thanksgiving after contract-signing, also the one after that and the one after that. Whenever it was shown, Ben explained to me in the beginning, I would get royalties or residuals or whatever. I didn't know the terms so well in those days, just that it meant more lovely lucre.

Ben was anxious for me to come up with something else while *The Frog* was still a hot property and my name was before the public, so my painting moved to the background, and I concentrated on juveniles—story and illustration by Rilla Scott.

Boat in the Barnyard was the first, I think. Then came *Josie of the Dingle*. The one I enjoyed most didn't ever get printed—*Birthday Party for a Beatle*.

"Sorry," Ben told me, "the lawyers say we could be sued."

"But it really happened, Ben," I protested. "I was there. It was Paul McCartney's eighteenth birthday at Hambleton Hall in Huyton, and he was wearing that old blue jumper of his he was so crazy about. All the things I wrote about really happened. The fight and—"

"I can't argue with the legal department, and I don't want to be put out of business." He grinned comfortably across at me. "Try something else, hon."

So I tried *The Twin Bulls.*

It was an enormous success and the start of my twin animal series. I bestowed twinship on pigs, kangaroos, buffalo, and even members of the marine kingdom and insect world. The porpoise and the crickets were my favorites.

During the next several years I built up a portfolio to ensure my future and had more money pass through my hands and over to accountants, the IRS, and my business manager than I had ever seen in my life. I was by no means rich, but I could safely be called comfortable.

"My husband would kill me for this," Maggie told me one day over our monthly lunch in Little Italy— mostly we met uptown—"because I might kill the goose laying some of his golden eggs, but you're definitely in a rut."

"Don't be ridiculous!" I said it all the more hotly for knowing she was right.

"Ridiculous?" she repeated, all actress, her face registering pain, shock, and disdain. She managed to trill out that single word with the dramatic impact of King Lear's denunciation of his daughters.

Into the moment of silence that followed she dropped a ruthless challenge.

"When did you last paint a picture? Not an illustration for one of your cutesy stories but a painting of your own that gave you satisfaction?"

I couldn't remember, but I had my revenge for the question.

When I gave up the loft, leaving Maggie's stuff and the Salvation Army pieces for the next grateful tenant, my own precious furniture journeyed up to Larchmont by truck to be stored in Maggie's attic.

I went home to England, first to Liverpool for a few weeks' visit, then to London to live for the next few years.

I rented a two-room flat, unfurnished, with eating space in the kitchen. Besides a small round table and two chairs for the kitchen, my furniture consisted of an easel and an armchair and a big worktable in one room, a bed, a bookcase, and a dresser in the other. Several big floor lamps were scattered throughout.

The bookcase was empty the day it got moved in. At the end of four months it was full. I bought another. Bigger. By the end of the year I had three bookcases. By the end of two years, I had five.

The first time I added to my collection, I figuratively thumbed my nose at Cam, remembering his mocking voice on a summer's day in Larchmont: *Self-improvement. How laudable.*

And then, as though it were yesterday, all the other memories came flooding back, *I sincerely beg your pardon, little one* . . . the water from the shower dripping down on the two of us, entwined in our lusty embrace . . . Cam and I kissing . . . Cam and I touching . . . Cam and I . . .

It was all completely real to me until the salesman's voice finally penetrated my glorious trance. It's a wonder I didn't wind up in a kneeling position on the shop floor, as he asked for perhaps the third time, "Do you want the oak or the walnut veneer, madam?"

So I spent the greater part of those two years just reading, at first for Cam and later for myself. I read classics, contemporary, and trash. I read English, American, French, and Russian writers.

Lots of what I read was literature; quite a lot was

junk. I took courses at London University, mostly so I would get an education about whom to read and what to read.

By the second year I didn't need anyone to tell me what was good or bad. I decided for myself. And I acquired the education that had passed me by after I failed the eleven-plus.

In my spare time I painted—not the kind of work I had done before, pastel paintings of Umbrella Point and sailboats on the Sound.

I was working on a series of the Bowery . . . then and now . . .

The idea had come to me suddenly, thinking of something Maggie once said as we strolled down Hester Street on our way to Chinatown.

"I don't know why I'm such a snob about this place. My grandparents lived right here, who knows, maybe on this very spot. When they first came over from Poland, my grandfather had a little street stand where he sold pots and pans and kitchen oddments. He was the most beautiful, dignified-looking old man, short, pointed white beard and deep-sunken blue eyes. Away from the stand, you'd have taken him for a successful businessman."

Funny how the words had stayed in my mind, shaking around there till they made an impact on my brain. I kept thinking of all the ethnic groups who came before and after, inhabiting Hester Street, the Bowery, Little Italy, Chinatown. . . .

I began my American ethnic series while I was still in London. The Bowery bum who sat on my doorstep every day and stood up to bow and open the outside door and sometimes helped me carry my bags of groceries upstairs . . . Steve in his paint-spattered jeans climbing down the fire escape . . . the frequent religious festivals of Little Italy, with every kind of food being sold and eaten on the streets . . . Hester Street of old, its peddlers, one of them a dignified old man with a short, pointed beard and deep-sunken blue eyes who sold pots and pans . . .

I painted mostly in oils, using stronger, bolder colors, and I no longer signed my paintings Rilla Scott. I wanted this new work to stand apart from what I had done before. I signed myself Amaryllis.

I didn't try to sell my work, I just let the paintings pile up till I got back to America.

The last few months of my second year I thought often of going back to the States, but it was so much easier to drift. There always seemed to be one more book I wanted to read, one more painting I had to work on, one more university course to attend. Mum was so much happier having me an hour's plane ride away. Jim and Heather had a little boy named Gregory, my godson. I simply had to fly down to see our Greg every month or so.

Over in the States Cam and his Irene had become parents of a little girl. I didn't want to see or know about her. Even just knowing her name gave me a fearful pang. Bethany. No need for me to ask who had picked *that* name. It was crazy how everything, like his having a daughter by a woman who wasn't me, should only bind him more closely to my heart instead of creating greater distance.

It was paradise of a sort I was living in, a calm, lifeless, soulless paradise perhaps, but there was something to be said, I kept telling myself, for peace and escape and ease of spirit.

None of these can ever be permanent. No matter how far or fast you run away, the world eventually intrudes.

The particular intrusion in mine came in the shape of an auction catalogue from Christie's. I flicked through it casually, carelessly, then my fingers froze in the middle of a page. "Group of miniatures by E. Crozier, considered to be the American folk artist Ladybeth. British soldier, two colonials."

I couldn't read that night, I couldn't paint. I called a friend I knew from London University, and we managed to get ballet tickets, which turned out to be wasted effort and money. My mind blocked out the music, my eyes blotted out the dancers . . .

All I could see was a British redcoat. Later that night I fell asleep to troubled thoughts of the miniatures on auction, and in my sleep I dreamed I saw the soldier's face.

Young, good looking, but with no strength of character, smooth cheeks, liquid brown eyes like a puppy's, a chest puffed out with pride in his new uniform.

"I just ordered it from Hercules Mulligan, about the best tailor you have in New York."

I woke up tense, tired, irritable. What made me think I had heard those words? Who the devil was Hercules Mulligan?

I pushed back the covers and saw that the hands I had just raised to rub my eyes were paint stained. I looked down in panic. There were paint stains on my pajamas.

Barefooted, I ran to my easel.

I had been working on a scene in Chinatown the last time I used it. The Chinatown scene was gone, replaced by the portrait of a young man in red uniform. A British soldier of the 1700s. Young, handsome, a bit weak looking. Brown eyes. Smooth cheeks.

The portrait was signed E. Crozier. The E. Crozier was scribbled in the same sprawled script as in that other picture, carefully crated and stored at Mailer Publishing: Ladybeth's painting of the gray-eyed girl with my star.

"Oh God!" I whispered aloud. "Oh God, I'm almost twenty-eight. How long before I know what this is all about?"

I closed my eyes and was swaying slightly when the sound came, that sound once heard that could never be forgotten. Hundreds of wings were beating all around me. Before, behind, and above, in great waves of sound, they engulfed me. I tried to open my eyes and found the lids shut tight. I tried to run, but there were hands on my shoulders, gentle hands but strong ones, pressing me down. I went onto my knees, bent over. The hands stroked soothingly along my back, and the superstitious dread melted away, replaced by the most marvelous sense of peace.

I was curled up in a little ball, and the man in silver gray was there. "Wake up," he told me lovingly. "Open your eyes. This is what you wanted to know."

Chapter 24

PORTRAITS OF SOLDIERS BY E. CROZIER SET RUTH-anna's qualms to rest and proved more successful than the young artist's most roseate predictions.

Ladybeth herself freely acknowledged that part of their good luck could be attributed to the new Mrs. Fielding, who conducted the business side of each transaction with a stately majesty that impressed even the British military.

The soldiery, Ladybeth decided after the first month, were no different from the farmers' wives in New England and Pennsylvania way. They wanted to improve on both nature and fact when they were painted. Stripes as well as decorations were sometimes added before a sitting began. Uniforms were brushed, and ranks were upgraded.

She decided to invest in a small stock of uniforms, certain that discreet word would get around for those who wanted their families at home in New England, other middle colonies, and the South to see them as something more than they were.

She walked uptown late one spring afternoon to the shop of the popular Irish tailor, Hercules Mulligan, spoke to his head clerk, and waited a quarter-hour while he finished measuring a British officer for a new uniform.

"Sure, it's sorry I am to have kept you waiting so long, ma'am."

Ladybeth turned quickly on the high stool. He had a bright round face, a merry smile, and shrewd watchful eyes.

"I recognize the name E. Crozier from the political cartoons. Is it any connection you have with him?" he asked directly.

"M-m-my father," Ladybeth stammered, stricken by the same pangs of guilt and remorse that always affected her when she remembered the cartoons and how they had ultimately, if indirectly, led to her father's death.

"A sad loss both to you, m'dear, and the country. His cartoons did us much good."

"Is that really true?" Ladybeth couldn't help asking eagerly, and then at the remembrance of how much harm they had already done, her face became shuttered and expressionless.

It was left to Mr. Mulligan to pursue the subject, which he did at once. "Very much good. I only wish there had been more of them. Did he, perhaps, leave any unpublished ones before he died?"

"A few," Ladybeth said reluctantly, recalling all she had burned or bundled away out of sight in her blanket chest.

She could have cried aloud with vexation at her own

stupidity when he immediately said, "I should like to see them published, too."

"Mr. Mulligan," she told him, changing the subject firmly and without finesse. "I am here because I wondered if you have any military uniforms for sale, worn but in good condition."

He rubbed his knuckles along his chin. "I just might have some old ones," he mentioned cautiously, "but the military doesn't take too kindly to the handing out of their uniforms for no reason."

"Oh. Oh, I never thought of that. It's just that . . . Look." She unfolded a newspaper and showed him a copy of her advertisement. "See, I'm a painter, too, like my father. I've discovered the soldiers like to put on better uniforms—you know, improve the way they look—"

"Upgrade their rank?" he suggested, grinning.

"That, too, I suppose. It's none of my business. It doesn't hurt anyone. They just want the miniatures they send home to—to add to their consequence."

He said abruptly, "I am expecting an important customer for a fitting soon. If you will leave the advertisement with me, I will visit you, perhaps tomorrow, with whatever I have."

"I don't want to put you to so much trouble."

"No trouble at all."

"I cannot afford to pay very much."

"I am sure we can reach an agreeable price."

She smiled, vaguely troubled by such an excess of good will. He came up close to her as she prepared to leave the shop. "Miss Crozier, ma'am, your father made it clear with his cartoons where his sympathies lay in our struggles with Britain. Are you of like mind?"

"I am American-born, American-bred!" she retorted. "My father and I were of one mind."

All the way home Ladybeth wondered why her fervor seemed to please him. That night after supper, she finished work started long ago on a cartoon divided into scenes showing George III and Lord North dining together. The main dish ceremoniously served on a huge platter by a servant was a scroll labeled *Magna Carta for Americans*. The King and his minister were carving up the Magna Carta, chewing the pieces, and spitting them out.

The cartoon, carefully dried overnight, was in the Bow Window when Hercules Mulligan arrived at the house on Bowling Green the next morning. It bore the name E. Crozier, but it was Ladybeth's scrolled signature, not her father's.

Ruthanna, in her role of Mrs. Fielding, received him graciously and served him a glass of cider while Ladybeth finished with her first sitting.

As he passed into the studio, he heard the soldier's eager words of thanks for his miniature.

"If you'll just be seated while I mix a little white and vermilion," Ladybeth said, hearing footsteps. Then she turned her head. "Oh, Mr. Mulligan, how—how nice of you to visit so soon."

"I brought you two uniforms, hats, and some insignia. I left them with Mrs. Fielding."

"I thank you, sir. Did you receive your monies from her?"

He ignored the question of price. "I enjoyed the new cartoon in the window."

"Thank you."

She knew she should let it rest at that, but there was something compelling about those watchful eyes of his. They seemed always to induce her to say too much.

"It's not so new. I mean, the sketch was done before he died. I just—"

"You just, I suspect, sketched it yourself."

She stared at him, in relief at the end of deception, even as she asked with genuine curiosity, "How did you know?"

"Your father was not well before he died, not for some time," he told her softly. "We believe he was not in condition to—shall we say, execute much of the work attributed to him. You and Mrs. Fielding, as you both prefer to call her, did your best for him."

Ladybeth's eyes flashed an angry challenge. "Why should you know so much about us? Or even care?" she demanded. "What are we to you? Who are you?"

He answered lightly, "Let us say, a patriot, like yourself. You did name yourself a patriot, did you not?"

"Yes," said Ladybeth belligerently, "but—"

"I brought you your uniforms. You could bring me something of far more value. Information."

"Information?"

"Speak more softly, my dear. Yes, information. You deal every day in the most innocent way with our soldiers and with citizens we suspect to be British sympathizers. Some day soon you may be dealing directly with the British military. You would be in a unique position to speak to them of homes and families; in their loneliness, they might share much more with you. Assignments. Barracks gossip. General orders. All the bits and scraps that, put together, make for a bit of wheat amongst the chaff."

"My God! You want me to *spy* for you?"

"Not just for me, Miss Crozier. For your country," he said cheerfully. "I happen to be one small link in a chain of agents being gathered to channel information directly to General Washington."

Ladybeth clasped her hands to stop their shaking.

"Most people don't talk politics while I paint them," she whispered.

"They need not. Their politics are of no interest to us. 'Tis their daily activities, as I told you, barracks gossip and tea-party gossip which will tell us the most. Don't fret about the value of what you hear, just remember and be able to repeat as much as possible."

"You have a glib tongue, Mr. Mulligan, but you go too fast for me. I have yet to give my consent to this wild plan of yours."

"You will," he told her softly. "You've a feeling for our cause, I can tell that by your cartoons. You're a lass of strength and spirit, though you try to hide it behind that artist's sack. You will help us," he repeated confidently. "Will you not, Miss Crozier?"

"Yes, Mr. Mulligan," she answered slowly. Then she smiled the warm reckless smile of a much younger Ladybeth, embarking on a piece of mischief. Deborah and Edmund had known it all too well. It was a smile of happier days that Ruthanna had never seen.

She was about to twist the tail of the British lion most cruelly. She was about to fulfill the vow made the day Edmund died to jab the stinking British bastards just where they needed jabbing!

"I will help you, sir," she said again, gladly, more confidently this time. "Pray tell me how."

He saluted her laughingly, but with respect, one soldier to another. "Just as I indicated, ma'am, by lending any persons who come to your shop a sympathetic ear. Do so, and believe me, they will pour information into it, much of it useless but here and there something of value. Listen and remember all. We will determine the worth."

"Must I bring the information to your shop?"

He shook his head. "After today, there should be no direct contact between us. Your code name is Pepper. A fish peddler will come to your door tomorrow and bring you a supply of stain."

"Stain?"

"'Tis an ink that becomes invisible in the writing but on reading can be made to reappear. You can conceal it among your paints. This will protect you should you ever have to put anything in writing. Do so only in emergency. I prefer that you deliver your information by mouth to—let us say a peddler of fresh vegetables who will come to your door twice weekly. He will identify himself as Culper III."

Ladybeth was no longer smiling but rather pale and serious. "What if I have something important to tell you and the peddler does not come?"

He nodded approvingly. "I think it's a fine head you have for this business, my lass. A good point. Signal us if that happens . . . say, by three white handkerchiefs hung up on your clothesline, with a petticoat on either side of them."

He interrupted as she seemed about to speak. "Never fear. Your signal will be seen and contact made."

They stared at one another, his eyes bright, hers a bit shadowed.

"Never fret, my lass," he comforted her. "It will come to seem as nothing. Now you had better start your painting."

"Painting?"

"Of me. I've been here overlong; it's as well to have a good reason. Haven't you noticed I've me Sunday best on to be painted by E. Crozier?"

She stepped over to her easel. "A miniature?"

"Nay. Something a bit bigger, I think, to hang up in my shop and impress the lobsterbacks when they arrive."

In her portraits of the soldiers, Ladybeth tried to stifle her own bold style and emphasize her father's romanticism. She knew it was what her subjects preferred.

For Hercules Mulligan, she gave free rein to her own artistic impulse, showing the round merry face with its full mouth and reckless pirate's eyes, portraying him for the daring, adventurous soul he was.

He looked long and hard at the finished portrait. "For sure," he told her in awed admiration, "my tongue is not so glib as your paint brush, me dear girl. It's the wicked witch you are to look clear through to a man's soul like this."

He departed, painting in hand, with one last admonition. "Take the cartoon out of your window now, Miss Crozier. It has served its purpose. As far as New York is concerned, the cartoonist E. Crozier is dead and decently interred. For our purposes, we prefer gradually to establish you as leaning toward the British side. So draw no more cartoons, not even for your private pleasure. It would be better—certainly safer—in fact, if you toss all you may have about the house into your kitchen fire."

Exhausted, not so much by painting as emotion, Ladybeth was ready to call a halt to the day's work, but an eager soldier—just made sergeant—Ruthanna announced, had been awaiting her for about an hour. More than just money was at stake now.

Ladybeth squared her shoulders. "Please send him in, Mrs. Fielding," she said out loud.

She smiled dazzlingly at the soldier who followed quickly on the heels of this invitation. "My felicitations,

Sergeant, on your promotion," she murmured. "Has it been a long time coming?"

"Too bloody long by half, begging yer pardon, ma'am. But you know how it is in the army."

"Actually," confided Ladybeth in the friendliest manner, "I know little about the army. You can educate me about it while I work. It will make the time pass for both of us. Turn this way . . . hold your head so . . . a little more to the left. That's fine, Sergeant. Just right. Are you expecting to stay long in our city? No, what a pity! Where do you go next?"

Thus started a second career for Ladybeth that, in the beginning, appeared more mundane than adventurous. Later, as the political climate heated up somewhat, so did the atmosphere of New York; and she began to feel that she really served her country.

She waited with particular eagerness one day for her regular "peddler" and breathed a sigh of relief as he came up the winding path to the kitchen door.

"They're good fresh vegetables, ma'am," he assured her a few minutes later, "just brought over from Long Island. Look at these fine tomatoes."

"Beautiful. I want a full dozen, as well as all those greens. Mr. Ver Loop is coming to sup with us tonight. He's very partial to stewed tomatoes."

"Yes, ma'am, Miss Crozier, I know. I sell to his housekeeper regular. Allow me—I'll choose the best for you."

He picked the tomatoes, testing each one, inspecting and discarding several as not without blemish. While he took his tedious time, Ladybeth whispered, "Thank God you saw my signal. There is a plot afoot to kidnap General Washington."

"That's common knowledge here in New York."

"They intend to take him from his New York headquarters together with his own guard. Two of the general's personal bodyguard—I know not which ones —are involved. The agents for the plan are housed at Corbie's Tavern, near his headquarters, and at the Sergeant's Arms."

The last tomato changed baskets, money changed hands. The peddler tipped his hat respectfully. "Thank you kindly, ma'am."

Ladybeth walked briskly into the kitchen with her basketful of vegetables.

"*More* tomatoes!" said Ruthanna. "I've preserved enough to see us through the next two winters."

Ladybeth flushed slightly. "You know how much Mr. Ver Loop likes fresh stewed tomatoes."

"If he supped with us every night instead of his once a week, he could still never eat his way through your supply. Ladybeth, haven't you done enough already? It has been nigh on two years."

Ladybeth turned from storing the tomatoes to stare at Ruthanna. "You have known all this time?"

"Of course."

"And kept your own counsel. What control and fortitude. *You* should be in the business." Ladybeth smiled lovingly at her friend. "No, I cannot stop. Not especially now when our own army may soon leave and the British army—with so much more information to give—march in. I am needed, useful. And I love it. It gives a spark to life."

"Excitement and danger. I knew it," Ruthanna groaned. "That's why I never troubled to say anything. I didn't delude myself you would pay me the least heed."

"Dear Ruthanna." Ladybeth rubbed her cheek against the housekeeper's in a rare show of affection. "I would heed your wishes about most things, on my honor, I would, but I cannot do so about this. It's true that I enjoy the challenge; but it is equally true that I am of service to the American cause. Nor do I ever forget"—both her face and her voice hardened—"just *how* and *why* my father died. I'll never let *them* forget either. Any harm I can do them, any rub I can throw their way, I promised over Papa's grave that I would pay back the British." Even now, remembering, her hands became tight fists. "This isn't just a patriot's dream with me, Ruthanna!" she cried out. "It's my own private, personal war. I promised Papa."

"Your Papa would want you to be happy," said Ruthanna in a subdued way, impressed in spite of herself by Ladybeth's passionate conviction. But a moment later she was off on another tack. "When the stupid men with their stupid fights are finished, what's to become of *you*, I should like to know. Nineteen, going on twenty and not a beau in sight. It's a husband should be on your mind, not a general."

"It seems to me the pot is labeling the kettle," Ladybeth retorted. "Did *you* want a husband at my age?"

"So where did it bring me to?"

"Housekeeper to a painter-spy. But not for long, I think." Ladybeth smiled slyly. "Not if Mr. Ver Loop has his way."

"I'm sure I don't know what you mean."

Ladybeth looked at Ruthanna's reddened face and became convulsed with laughter.

"I take it back. You would make a terrible spy with a giveaway face like yours. And what a hypocrite you are, too, Ruthanna. Or are you going to pretend that Mr. Ver Loop's Sunday visits and Saturday night suppers these two years since Papa died are for the sake of *my* charms? Why don't you put the poor man out of

225

his misery and answer the question before he comes around to asking it?"

"You think I would desert you after all you have done for me?"

"Ruthanna, never say that. Don't you dare to refuse him because of me. A husband and a home of your own. A fine man. A fine home. And the children, too. Those girls of his need mothering more than I do."

"You come first," Ruthanna persisted doggedly.

"I will close up shop and leave you if you think to make a sacrifice of yourself on my account," Ladybeth warned her. "This is everything you ever wanted, everything I want for you. I'm earning good money now; I could hire a housekeeper in your place. It's not as though we would be parted either. The Ver Loop home is just down the road. We would be living close by one another."

"We will discuss it another time," Ruthanna said, at her most decided; and Ladybeth shrugged, aware that this usually meant, *We will not discuss it again.*

Chapter 25

THE WARNING JANGLE OF THE BELL THAT ANNOUNCED the entrance of a client into the front room sent Ladybeth scurrying into the studio, while Ruthanna, smoothing out her apron and straightening her cap, made her sedate way to the parlor.

They were much more formal since the Americans had left and the British occupied New York. In the stately, measured manner that was now the so-called Mrs. Fielding's, she walked toward the cloaked officer.

"May I be of assistance, sir?" she inquired.

He turned from studying the full-length wall portrait, which depicted a swarthy, thick-browed man in dark breeches and heavy dark jacket, a wool cap set at a rakish angle across his forehead, a single lock of black hair curling out from under it. The brightest splashes of color in the painting came from the red lips and the white teeth in the broad slash of his smile.

The soldier turned smilingly to indicate the portrait. "He looks a proper rascal."

"He's a moon-curser, sir."

"Moon-curser?"

"Smuggler, you would say."

"Moon-curser. I see." He laughed pleasantly. "An apt phrase. I must remember it when I go home. In Sussex, where I was born, 'tis an active trade." He inspected the portrait for another few seconds. "E. Crozier. I like his strong, bold style."

"Were you wishful to be painted yourself, sir?" Ruthanna asked softly.

It was not her job to explain the sex of the artist. Ladybeth handled that with ease and competence.

"I would be grateful for an interview with Mr. Edmund Crozier."

"Mr. Edmund Crozier," she repeated faintly, turning rather pale.

"Yes," he said again, somewhat surprised at the effect of such a simple request. "Mr. Edmund Crozier. He lives here, does he not? And this"—he indicated the painting—"is his work?"

"If you will follow me, sir."

She stepped aside when they reached the studio where Ladybeth stood at her easel, her back to them.

"Miss Crozier, this soldier"—she corrected herself with a glance at his officer's insignia—"this gentleman . . ."

"Captain De Croix," he supplied helpfully.

"Captain De Croix requested an interview with your father, ma'am."

Ladybeth turned swiftly as Ruthanna withdrew, and they stared at one another in mutual astonishment.

He had been prepared to greet a man of middle years rather than an amazingly young woman. She was tall, slender, and well formed, and what must be a great quantity of chestnut hair was twisted into a thick knot atop her head. The forehead and nose and chin were all familiar. He had seen them before in portraits of the Croziers hanging on the walls of the earl of Shirley's ancestral manor house. The great, sparkling gray eyes were part of her own individual beauty.

A homegrown belle in the wilds of America, he marveled to himself. As amusement glistened in the watchful gray eyes opposite, he had the strange, uncomfortable feeling that she had guessed his thoughts.

Ladybeth inspected Capt. De Croix with the candid, critical look of a painter. Good bone structure, face and body. An outdoor man. Strong shoulders, capable hands. Broad forehead. Chiseled, Roman nose. Decisive tilt to the chin. Keen intelligence in the deep blue eyes.

"What is your business with my father?" she asked abruptly.

"When he presents himself," he snubbed her gently but firmly, "I will be most happy to explain my business to *him*."

"I would be more happy than you can imagine," Ladybeth retorted pertly, but with a flash of anger, "if the possibility of my father's presenting himself existed. Unfortunately, Captain, he has—he is dead."

"Dead!"

"Yes, Captain, dead for these two years." She added forthrightly, "You are a stranger to me, sir, and I had thought I knew all of my father's acquaintance. Why should it be a matter of such moment to you?"

"I—not precisely to *me*, Miss Crozier, although I offer you my sincere condolences; but this news will be a great grief to some of his family at home. When it was made known there that my regiment was coming to

America, I was requested most urgently by his mother and the family attorneys to locate him. My business then is with your brother. I believe his name is Lawrence—er—Ben David?"

"Lawrence Ben David was his name."

He was quick to comprehend, unexpectedly compassionate. "I am very sorry, ma'am. Your brother, too?"

"Some time before my father."

"And your mother?"

"At the same time, of the same fever as Lawrence," she answered softly.

"I am most deeply distressed for you, Miss Crozier." Indeed, she thought, surprised, he really did look distressed. "If his surviving family in England had been informed of these tragedies, I assure you that long before this they would have sent for you."

Her eyes narrowed in displeasure. "I saw no need to inform the Croziers in England of something that was none of their concern," she told him haughtily.

"The death of a son and a grandson!"

"Good God!" she exploded. "For more than twenty years the relationship existed in name only. I could not conceive of informing them, and I would have considered it a presumption for them to send for me!"

"A presumption! Miss Crozier, you sound both emotional and ridiculously prideful. It is the duty of the earl to see to the well-being of *all* of his dependents."

"Then you have proven my own case," she announced blithely, in a sudden, swift change of mood. "You see, sir, *I* am not a dependent, not of the earl nor of anyone else. I earn a comfortable competence by my painting, more than enough"—her bright smile mocked him—"to satisfy the simple needs of my household. I am not without skill, believe me, Captain. Did I not hear you just a few moments since admiring my bold, strong style?"

He subjected her to an even closer inspection than on their introduction, his astonishment more marked than before.

"*You,* not your father, are the E. Crozier who painted *The Moon-Curser?*"

"My name, both my names, begin with an E, too. Elizabeth Esther." She curtseyed in the parody of a grand lady. "If you can spare a guinea, kind sir, I will paint you a portrait that will delight the hearts of your family at home. And you may even show it to the earl of Shirley and my family to prove they need not feel troubled in their hearts for me. That is, if they have any hearts, which I have long doubted."

"I am sure that when you return to England, the Earl of Shirley will be deeply interested in that opinion."

"Perhaps he would, perhaps he would not be. How sad that we shall never know. You see, Captain"—she curtseyed laughingly again—"I have no intention of visiting him in England."

"I fear that he will insist."

Her gray eyes glinted in anger; the smile died away on her lips. "The earl of Shirley may insist till the oceans run dry. I would see him in hell before I obliged him in that or any other way."

"You do not understand," he said, after half a minute in which he waged a silent battle for control of his temper. "*You* are the daughter of the sixth Earl of Shirley."

"I am—*what?*"

"Your grandfather, the fifth Earl, is dead, too. Edmund, your father, inherited the earldom."

"Impossible. He had two older brothers."

"The oldest son Lawrence succumbed to a wasting sickness, leaving three daughters, no heirs. The second son George had entered the diplomatic service. He was on a mission to South America when his father died. No effort was made to notify Edmund here in the colonies, everyone having assumed that George would inherit. Efforts to contact him were all unavailing. Only recently was the final proof received that he had been killed some time before in an accident on a scientific expedition along the mouth of the Amazon River."

He looked at her, frowning slightly. "You say your father died two years ago—what month?"

"October 9, 1774."

"George Crozier died some time in August, your grandfather, the fifth Earl, in September. Your father was, therefore, for some three to four weeks, the sixth Earl."

"Who has the earldom now?"

He said, frowning, "There are several cousins, distant connections. I will have to notify the attorneys at once and send legal affidavits regarding your father and your brother. *Your* status, I assure you, remains unchanged by all of this, Lady Elizabeth. As the daughter of the sixth Earl, you will have a portion equal to that given to Lawrence Crozier's daughters. The seventh Earl will undoubtedly welcome you home."

"Either your hearing is deficient," responded Ladybeth coolly, "or you choose willfully to misunderstand me. Here, where I am now, *is* my home, not England, never England. The seventh earl has no voice in my affairs. If I am legally entitled to any monies, I will accept them gladly. As for the title . . . am I truly my lady?"

His lips had tightened at her deliberate rudeness, but he said, "Yes, Lady Elizabeth, you are."

"Then that is the happiest news of all."

"So overjoyed about a title?" he asked ironically. "It does not suit your professions of democratic independency, my lady."

She laughed aloud exultantly. "We seem doomed to misunderstand one another, sir. If I can use my title to increase my business, yes, I am overjoyed. When I advertise now, I do so as E. Crozier, who paints simple portraits of the military. Truth to tell," she confided with a genuinely warm smile, "most of my clients arrive here thinking—as I intend them to—that I am a man. All that subterfuge may be finished with now. My new identity will appeal to the ultimate snobbery in most people. Have you any idea of the commissions I will be able to obtain when I advertise that the Lady Beth—I prefer it to Elizabeth—daughter of the sixth Earl of Shirley, will accept commissions for full-length portraits at—oh, perhaps as much as twenty guineas the portrait?" Her laughter pealed out again, full and joyous. "Of course, by appointment only. So, *you*, sir, are the very last gentleman I shall paint without prearrangement. Pray take off your cloak, sir, so I may determine what pose suits you best. I must do full justice to your uniform. Have you just lately come from England, sir? Does your wife . . . or sweetheart . . . prefer your right or your left profile, do you know?"

He could not help but smile, though other, more powerful emotions already burned in his breast. "No wife, and no sweetheart either, ma'am."

"Oh, Captain, you would not try to fool an innocent little colonial miss, now would you? Especially one who is all at once a ladyship?" She shook her head in reproach. "Impossible that you should be without one or the other."

She had been readying her paints and her brushes as

she spoke. Now her eyes narrowed. "A pity," she said, "that the uniform is so commonplace. I could fancy you myself, when you are not being so very properly English, as a pirate with a sash around your waist and a knife between your teeth. But I shall—sit down, please, no, there, facing east." Not satisfied, she came and turned his shoulders and then his chin to suit her. "As I was saying," she continued, "I shall do my humble best. No, don't pucker up your lips. Stay quiet and . . ."

"You direct *me* to stay quiet. Good God, Lady Elizabeth!" he exclaimed, the laughter in his eyes giving the lie to his pretense of dismay. "Do you *never* give your tongue a rest? You have hardly stopped speaking since I entered this room. Even when you ask questions, you give me little opportunity to answer. Are all painters so verbose?"

"I cannot speak for others, sir, only for myself. Alas, it is true," she admitted mournfully, "that my tongue seldom stops wagging. 'Tis part of my stock in trade, you see. I am not only expected to paint my subjects; military gentlemen seem to require that I amuse them as well."

He started to speak and was again interrupted. "I assure you, I feel the injustice of the arrangement as much as you do. After all, I do not get paid extra for all the conversation"—she gave him a languishing glance —"that I delight them with. But you have given me fresh heart, Captain. It occurs to me that *now* I may forevermore be elegantly silent whilst I work. Lady Beth, unlike poor, unaristocratic Miss Crozier, will not have to provide conversation with her expensive, *very* expensive paintings."

"It is my own impression that Lady Beth can—"

"Please don't move about so," she interrupted with a frowning look at her last brush strokes.

"Lady Beth cannot be still ever!" he continued firmly. "In token of which, I am prepared to wager double the usual price of a portrait that she cannot remain silent a full ten minutes by that handsome piece." He pointed to the tall, baroque Philadelphia case clock.

As though by a secret agreement, the clock struck as he finished speaking. "In substance," he repeated, "my wager is that Lady Elizabeth Crozier is completely unable to keep her tongue between her teeth for a full ten minutes."

Ladybeth bowed her head in silent, sparkling acceptance of the bet, made a deliberate business of seeming to pin her lips together, and went on with her painting.

While she worked, she had a habit of cocking her head to one side as she glanced at him every so often in a way that seemed to indicate she was rather looking *through* him. Except by a schoolmaster, ferreting out some act of omission or commission, he could never in his life remember being subjected to such a searching scrutiny. And at the same time, it was an exceedingly indifferent and impersonal, strangely daunting inspection.

He experienced a sensation of pique that a simple colonial miss—for, after all, her title, to her own knowledge, had existed a scant half-hour—should be so . . . so . . . When he discovered that the word that leaped into his mind was "unimpressed," he became irritated more at himself than at her.

"Coxcomb," he muttered under his breath, compounding his exasperation when he realized by the lift of her eyebrows that she had heard him.

Luckily, Ladybeth glanced from him to the clock and observed that eleven minutes had passed since their wager was placed, adding, "My trick, sir, I believe."

A moment later, just as he was congratulating himself that she had overlooked his slip, she added innocently, "Coxcomb? I am sorry you think so, sir. How have I displeased you?"

"I was not referring to you," he answered with as much dignity as he could muster.

"Thank the Lord!" She placed her hand dramatically against her palpitating bodice. "How relieved I am!"

"You, my new-made lady, are a minx."

She looked so entirely delighted by this accusation that he could not help but join in her infectious laughter. After a minute or two of hilarity, she hushed him again.

"I am sorry, Captain De Croix, but you *must* be serious or I cannot complete today's painting. Alas, I have portrayed you as the extremely proper English gentleman that I thought you to be when first you entered the room and spoke to me. I fear such a model of decorum as I have before me could never be quite so merry and unbending."

Some time later she laid down her brush. "I await your opinion, sir."

He came forward to inspect his likeness; and in the short, awful silence before he turned to her, Ladybeth found herself experiencing (most unusually) a great deal of shame as well as some regret.

"As you say, Lady Elizabeth, a very model of decorum," he agreed finally. "Not to say exceedingly starched-up and stuffy." With great deliberation, he took a small leather purse from inside his coat. "Pray what is your price, my lady? I think you mentioned a guinea; and since you have won our wager as well, then I must, of course, double it."

"You owe me nothing, Captain," Ladybeth told him, flushed and repentant. "I did this portrait just for the—the sport of it," she finished lamely. "Well, you *were* acting stuffy in the beginning," she defended herself clumsily, "so I thought . . . I thought . . . Besides, some people don't even know when they—"

Realizing in time that she was about to make a somewhat infelicitous explanation, she broke off uneasily.

"I collect you mean to say," he told her calmly, "that some stuffy Englishmen are also too stupid to recognize that they are being ridiculed? That was the point you were about to make, was it not?"

"Well, as a matter of truth, ye-es, but truly . . ." She looked up at him and finished ingenuously, "I was liking you a great deal before I was halfway done, but I didn't wish to abandon the project. After all, *stuffiness* might well be one of your many facets, just like the pirate look. You haven't forgotten that earlier I saw you as a bold adventurer, have you?" she asked in the coaxing voice of a child begging for a treat.

"No." He could not help but grin. "I have not forgotten *that,* Lady Elizabeth, and you should be grateful for it. I promise you, it is the only reason you have not been visited by the just retribution you deserve, my dear, for a portrait that I consider not only denigrating but defaming. Nevertheless, I insist on paying you, both for this libelous portrait as well as for our wager."

When he would have forced two gold coins on her, she put her hands behind her back and shook her head. "The portrait is a gift, yours to take away or tear apart.

It is my farewell, sir, to being simply E. Crozier, an unsung painter. As for the wager, twice nothing remains nothing, so let us cry quits, Captain. If you come again by appointment, I shall charge you an enormous sum, I assure you. More, I believe, than a captain in his Majesty's army can afford."

"Ah, but this is *one* Captain in his Majesty's army who would find no price too great to pay for such a privilege, Lady Elizabeth."

He was the one mocking now, or perhaps just teasing a little. She looked at him somewhat uncertainly. Did he by any chance mean to be taken seriously?

She looked at him, doubtful, uneasy, and encountered such a warm, glowing look as to send her three steps backward.

"Good day, Lady Elizabeth."

She put out her hand unthinkingly as he came toward her. She was surprised to find his own hand so cool and his lips so warm when he took her half-extended hand and kissed it.

Chapter 26

RUTHANNA WALKED INTO THE STUDIO SOME TIME later to find Ladybeth standing still in the middle of the room, with her right hand supported by the palm of her left. She was staring at it with the oddest expression on her face.

"Heavens!" Ruthanna's starched petticoat swished under her skirt and apron as she hurried to Ladybeth's side. "Have you hurt your hand?"

"Oh, n-no, it's nothing," Ladybeth stammered weakly, adding for the other's benefit, "I—I thought I saw a—a mole forming."

Ruthanna went about the room, straightening a cushion here, an object out of place there. "Captain De Croix seems a very pleasant gentleman," she mentioned casually.

"Captain De Croix?" repeated Ladybeth at her most vague, as though she had never before heard of that particular British officer. "Oh, yes, very pleasant.

He—he arrived from England recently, but he did not so much come here to be painted as to make contact with my father's family."

"How strange."

"Strange, indeed!" repeated Ladybeth somewhat bitterly. "More than twenty years of silence and all at once they are all agog in England to have us come, as *they* call it, 'home.' "

"Fancy that," marveled Ruthanna, who needed to fancy no such thing. When she was not in the room chaperoning Edmund's beloved daughter from any impudence or impropriety, she was always within hearing so she could, if needed, come at once to the studio. And finally, she was always nearby to ensure that, if any person stepped into the shop while Ladybeth was getting or giving information, the newcomer would be unable to hear anything suspicious. A short series of bell rings became their signal.

Since there was almost nothing Ruthanna did not know of what went on in the house, just now she chose to pretend ignorance.

"Fancy it, indeed!" said Ladybeth, striding about the room. "Just like that. The brothers between my father and *his* father have died, and there is a dearth of sons, so all at once they are eager to let bygones be bygones. They want us back in England."

"Well, it's the way of it in those great families," Ruthanna told her in what Ladybeth considered an annoyingly complacent manner.

"You don't understand!" the younger woman flung at the older. "My father became an earl before he died!"

"An earl!" Ruthanna seemed suitably awed. "Do you mean we would have had to call him Lord Edmund?"

Ladybeth allowed her attention to be diverted. "Not you or me," she grinned, "but all the rest of the world."

"Then maybe it's just as well I didn't know," said Ruthanna philosophically. "I might not have felt the same . . . being with an earl."

Ladybeth's grin became a laugh. "Oh, I don't know . . ." She pretended to ponder. "It might have its moments."

"You're about to be vulgar," said Ruthanna with dignity, "and I shan't stay to listen."

"Just look then." Ladybeth stood up very straight, with her stomach pushed out to simulate a great belly, her cheeks quite puffy and full as she strutted up and down.

"Good evening, my lord. What can I do for you, my lord? Oh, my lord, I cannot believe . . . Oh, my lord, you make me blush. I should, my lord? I must, my lord? Oh! Oh! Oh, my lord!"

"Oh, my Lord, indeed!" said a voice behind her that never in a hundred years could she have mistaken for Ruthanna's. *"You* make *me* blush, Lady Elizabeth! I had heard that American girls were different . . . perhaps a little more free and open than our own, but this—*this* passes all belief!"

Ladybeth whirled about, her face scarlet with confusion, to encounter the laughing, mocking, deep blue eyes of Captain De Croix.

"H-how did you g-get in?" she asked stumblingly. "I did not h-hear the bell."

"I am afraid I left the door ajar as I left." His offhand apology and his dancing eyes both proclaimed full knowledge that he had gotten the upper hand of her. "I forgot to take my painting," he explained.

"I—I had thought you wanted it destroyed."

"No, indeed. I shall use it to look at myself instead of in a mirror any time I think I stand in need of humbling."

"It is—the paint is not dry. If you could—if it would not be too much trouble . . . another day, perhaps. Ruth—Mrs. Fielding can tell you wh-when."

He bowed as courteously and soberly as though her last few minutes of bawdy indiscretion had never been. Still redfaced, Ladybeth plumped herself down on an upholstered chair, only to see his neck and head poke through from the entranceway a moment later. "Now I understand," Capt. De Croix said virtuously, "why you chose to portray me as stuffy and starched-up. I shall endeavor in the future to be much more . . . shall we say, much more American in my actions and speech?"

He disappeared again from sight, laughing quite audibly.

"Damnation!" said Ladybeth with feeling as she fanned herself vigorously with a folded copy of yesterday's Gazette.

Several minutes later, concerned with more than her momentary embarrassment, she was back in the front parlor.

"Ruthanna," she said abruptly, "I have been careless. It was of no moment this time, but it might have been. From now on, either one or the other of us must see our visitors off the premises and make certain they are gone and that, when need be, the door is locked."

Ruthanna nodded her understanding, and they both checked the door together, then Ladybeth trailed her friend into the kitchen.

"Do you realize," she asked chattily, perching on an edge of the kitchen table while Ruthanna poured out fresh water to wash the vegetables for their supper,

242

"that from now on I will be called Lady Elizabeth or Lady Beth or my lady?"

"I realize it," Ruthanna answered placidly. "Am I required to do it, too, my lady?"

"Only if you want to be out of a position!" Ladybeth told her emphatically. "But there's no denying it will be good for business."

"No, there's no denying *that.*"

During another short silence, Ruthanna cut up the vegetables and Ladybeth fidgeted with her apron strings. Then her new ladyship said offhandedly, "Captain De Croix will return another day for his painting."

"Yes, I know."

"Oh?"

"He said so when he made the appointment for his next sitting."

"He wants another miniature?"

"No, he mentioned a half-portrait."

"Oh, then—"

"Yes, Ladybeth?"

"Nothing, I just—When is he to come?"

"Friday morning, I believe. He said the mornings are best for him because his duties are lighter then."

"Oh, very light, indeed!" She was once again on fire with the zeal of Ladybeth, the patriot. "That's when his respected general has nothing better to do than to take to the streets with his entourage, riding recklessly as lunatics, all of them, scattering children and livestock and any passersby, in their eagerness to get to the billiards table or to any other sport they fancy that day."

Ruthanna looked at her keenly. "He's a British officer, Ladybeth," she pointed out. "He does his duty as he sees it, as you do yours."

"I suppose so," said Ladybeth softly, then sighed a little.

She looked up to encounter an encouraging and slightly enigmatic smile from Ruthanna. "Friday will come sooner than you think," said the housekeeper.

Unfortunately, it proved untrue. The three days till Friday dragged out long and tediously, and by the time they were over, Ladybeth was as greatly enraged at herself as at Capt. De Croix that this should be so.

She decided to behave very differently at their next meeting, not unnaturally cold or aloof, or in any way that would indicate lingering resentment or embarrassment. There was nothing to be resentful or embarrassed about, after all. She would merely maintain a proper dignity and distance and set the tone for . . . for . . .

Lying awake at night, she realized that what she meant to set the tone for had become a bit confused in her own mind.

Friday, as most Fridays do, eventually arrived.

"Good morning, Lady Elizabeth."

"I prefer Lady Beth."

"Good morning, Lady Beth."

"Good morning, Captain De Croix."

Without being requested to, he removed his helmet and put it on a table. "How do you intend to paint me this morning, ma'am?"

"Have you seen the new schedule of my fees in the Gazette?" she asked, very much the shopkeeper.

"I saw it, Lady Beth," he assured her solemnly, "and I sold out some of my investments so that I need not go into debt with you. Mrs. Fielding has already accepted my payment for a portrait. Would you like," he asked solicitously, "to see the receipt she signed?"

His dancing blue eyes contradicted his affected, drawling British manner of speech. Her own eyes sparkled with the pleasure of their continuing duel of words.

"I will accept your word as a gentleman of honor that you have made payment," she said gravely. "Now how"—she fastened a fresh sheet to her easel and began mixing paints briskly—"do you see yourself today?"

"I thought"—this time his eyes were boldly challenging—"that it was more a question of how *you* saw *me*."

"You are willing," she asked demurely, "after your last . . . er . . . experience to trust my judgment?"

"I will accept your decision as a lady of honor."

They exchanged laughing glances. In hers there was something more than just lightheartedness. In his there was something that, just for an instant of mixed pleasure and panic, made the breath catch in her throat.

The session lasted more than two hours, during which he stood with extraordinary patience, one leg bent high, his foot on a wooden chair, and his head thrown back. It had taken some time before she was satisfied with both the pose and the smile that she demanded.

"May I see?" asked Capt. De Croix when she finally put down the brush and indicated that he should rest.

"I would rather you did not until it is finished. I need another session . . . if you don't m-mind?"

"I have never minded anything less, Lady Beth." Not just the voice but his very words caressed her.

Frightened, Ladybeth withdrew a little in spirit. "You may fix the time with Mrs. Fielding," she said colorlessly.

"I shall look forward to it, Lady Elizabeth." Once more he came forward and took her hand. Once more he kissed it. Once more she studied her own hand after he had gone, wondering how such a quick, such a fleeting touch could linger on and on as though she had been branded.

They had two sessions more before the half-portrait was finished and Capt. De Croix was finally allowed to see it. When he came around, by invitation, to face her easel, Ladybeth studied his face as carefully as he was studying his likeness.

She breathed a sigh of relief when he turned to her at last, remarking, "I confess that I greatly prefer this interpretation to your last one."

She had used the pose but not the uniform, instead painting him as the pirate of her earlier impression, with a devil-may-care air, a reckless smile on his face, a sword in one hand, a knife in the other, and gold rings in one of his ears.

Capt. De Croix was intent on the painting again. "It's witchery, ma'am, the way you can look inside a man. Do you truly," he inquired with genuine curiosity, "see this as one of my facets?"

"Occasionally . . . in flashes. If you don't like it," she told him boldly, "I shall return your money and exhibit this one on my wall as a sample of my work to show to prospective customers."

"I will not take back my money, and I will not give up my claim to this portrait. It shall never adorn any wall but my own. My grandchildren will be told that it is their venerable sire, Bay, the pirate, in the occupation of his spirited youth."

"Bay?"

"You are Beth for Elizabeth; I am Bay for my middle name, Bayard."

"I like it, I think. Not Bayard—that's for the first portrait—but Bay. It suits you."

"Thank you," he said a bit gravely. "What a pity I am not a lord."

She looked at him a bit doubtfully. "Why so, sir?"

"Because then our names would sound so well in combination," he answered promptly. "Lady Beth and Lord Bay. Don't you think yourself, ma'am," he asked her very innocently, "that they go well together?"

To say no invited a teasing argument that she was all at once not in the mood for. To say yes might cause him to assume . . . Prudently, Ladybeth forbore to answer, only to be accused after a few minutes of silence, "Coward!"

"I am—" began Ladybeth, and then broke off.

She had been about to declare indignantly, *I am not!* But *he* knew and *she* knew it was not the truth.

She had become hideously afraid of her own feelings and aware, too, that he understood what they were only in part.

It was not the ocean between their countries that bothered her so tremendously. It was the wide and threatening gap between their beliefs. He was an English officer and she an American spy.

As a British soldier, he should be regarded solely as the enemy to whose downfall she had dedicated every breath in her body, every ounce of her energies.

She had come to believe that to do so, just as she had sworn she would over her father's grave, was as much a sacred duty as a fierce, flaming desire!

In none of her calculations, however, had she allowed for this very human complication: the coming of Capt. Henry Bayard De Croix to America.

Now she wondered a little hysterically if it was the duty of an intelligence agent to inform her immediate superior . . . in this case, it might be Hercules Mulligan, tailor, or perhaps even the unknown peddler. They might even need to consult the commander-in-chief of all the army to the effect that Ladybeth Crozier, their previously trusted ally, was in the process of losing her heart to an enemy officer!

Chapter 27

LADYBETH HELD OUT HER BASKET TO BE FILLED WITH potatoes.

"The secret Tory uprising that's planned," she whispered, shaking her head over a potato to indicate that it was spoiled, "is intended to extend north along the Hudson and over to Long Island, not just here in the city. Kings Bridge will be cut off so that our forces cannot escape into West Chester."

"That confirms Culper Senior's report," he whispered back, then much louder, "Do you have any special orders for next week, ma'am?"

"More potatoes, of course. I hope you are able to procure some of better grade than these." She pitched her voice high. "Really, one expects Long Island potatoes to be of better quality. Apples, too. I would greatly enjoy some York apples. I keep a full bowl of them in my studio. During the rests my subjects find them quite refreshing."

"Why, Captain De Croix." She pretended to notice his approach for the first time. "I hardly expected to see you back so soon. What a large and loving family you must have to need so many portraits to send home to England. That makes . . . let me see, three miniatures, one quarter-length, two half-lengths . . ."

She turned a moment to dole out some change to the peddler, and as he tipped his cap and went down the steps, she called after him, "As soon as the pumpkins come in, Mrs. Fielding wants a half-dozen for pies and preserves."

She turned back smilingly to the man who had occupied so much of her working time during the last few months as well as so many of her thoughts.

"What can I do for you today, Captain?"

"Firstly, stop calling me Captain. My name, as you know, is Bay, and I would greatly like to hear the sound of it in your lovely American voice."

"I leap to oblige you in your slightest wish, Bay*ard*," she said dutifully, and he groaned as he took the basket from out of her hands and followed her into the house.

"Good afternoon, Mrs. Fielding." He handed over the basket.

"Thank you, Captain. But I think," she explained apologetically, to both of them, consulting her book, "that there has been some error. I did not schedule a sitting for you today. Mrs. Wertenbacker is due in a quarter of an hour."

"I want only a few minutes of Lady Elizabeth's time," Capt. De Croix said easily. "Put me down for a sitting whenever you wish, Mrs. Fielding. I will make myself available."

As he followed Ladybeth into her studio, there was something about him, an air of suppressed excitement, not altogether pleasant . . . his eyes were so serious. Ladybeth found her heart beating fast, much too fast for present comfort. She tried to hide herself behind the easel she was getting ready for Mrs. Wertenbacker so that Bay would neither see nor suspect her inner turmoil.

"I would like you to paint a full-length portrait this next time," he said unexpectedly, and Ladybeth came out of hiding, enormously relieved and determined to make him pay for her last few minutes of suffering.

"Certainly," she said, facing him challengingly. "That will require several long sittings, though I may be able to use some of my previous sketches. My fee will be twenty-five guineas."

"I thought you charged but twenty."

"Formerly, that was true, but I have so many commissions now—all fashionable New York is eager to boast of being painted by the Lady Beth Crozier—that I am in the happy position of being able to ask for and receive higher fees. I am sorry," she added in a voice that proclaimed her not the least bit regretful, "if my price is beyond your purse."

"It is high," he agreed, "but somehow, I shall contrive. Would you prefer to be paid beforehand?"

"Mrs. Fielding," Ladybeth called out loudly, "at our next sitting, I will commence a full-length for Captain De Croix. Will you be so kind as to make out a receipt for half the fee of twenty-five guineas and accept his money as he leaves?"

"Twenty-*five!*" They could both plainly hear the startled surprise in Ruthanna's voice. Capt. De Croix smothered his grin and Ladybeth her scowl.

"Yes," she said even more loudly, "the *new* fee of twenty-five guineas."

"You have painted me in my uniform, with helmet, hatless, cloaked, and as a pirate. This last one will be the first time as an ordinary English gentleman."

"Oh?"

"Yes, I have sold out," he said abruptly. "This is my last week with the army, and I will shortly return to England."

Ladybeth felt as though every drop of blood in her body had all at once descended to her feet. He was going away—and that sudden, hurtful knowledge brought her closer to an understanding of her own feelings than she had come in a score of sleepless nights.

"I am sure your family will be happy," she said numbly, hardly knowing what words she spoke, only determined he should never guess her pain. "How soon will you leave?"

"Within weeks, I believe, unless . . ."

When he seemed not to intend to finish, "Unless?" she finally asked, dry-mouthed.

"Unless, Ladybeth"—it was his first time of making a single word of it instead of according her the shortened title—"unless you give me the hope that by staying on a little longer, I may hope to take you back with me."

"Take me back?" she parroted.

"As my wife."

"I—I—I could not possibly go to England, Cap—Bay," she stuttered, hardly knowing what she said, "I—I'm an American." She was shocked as much by the prospect of his leaving as by this offhand proposal.

"It's a fairly old and common custom for Englishmen to marry Americans," he pointed out mildly.

For one wonderful moment, an entire sixty seconds of forgetfulness, Ladybeth's traitor heart told her,

Why, so it is, and then, even more perfidiously, *Why can't I?*

The next moment it all came back to her, who and what she was, and even more painful, the remembrance of what *he* was.

She was back in time, standing beside Edmund Crozier's bedside, Edmund, who was of Henry Bayard De Croix's own blood. Before her mind flashed the picture of her father's face, bloody and battered and bruised.

In another fleeting mind picture, she was standing in Trinity cemetery, where Edmund's gravestone, like so many others behind the blackened ruins of the church, had been pulled over and laid flat for a paving stone. On pleasant afternoons, while their military band played lively concerts, British soldiers and their ladies—for all she knew Bay might have been one of them—danced on the grave sites of New York's beloved dead.

Remembering such things made it easier for her to deny her own heart.

"Not when their countries are at war!" she flung at Bay. "Not when the American is me!"

"I take it then that you will not have me?"

"Not *will* not." She made no effort to conceal her tears. "I—I cannot."

"And you do not encourage me to stay on in hopes of a change in your heart or mind?"

"How can I, in all fairness, encourage you to do any such thing?" Ladybeth asked in a low, shaken voice. "It would be wrong of me to ask you to wait around for what might be an indefinite period. I am sure you yourself would be unwilling."

"I admit," he said with a slight grin, "that I don't

have the patience of Job. Even for *you,* Ladybeth, I doubt I am capable of serving seven years. I was thinking of something more like seven months, and even that seemed an eternity. So my answer is to be no?"

"I am sorry, Captain."

"Not Captain again, please. I like to hear you call me Bay. If you won't have me in marriage"—his voice had become lightly mocking—"at least I will have *that* memory to take home, along, of course, with my many paintings."

Ruthanna marched into the studio as soon as the captain departed. "You refused him!" she said. "Ladybeth Crozier, you *are* a fool!"

"Not such a fool as all that!" Ladybeth said, with something of a quiver in her voice. "Did you ever see a man make so fast a recovery from what was presumably a great disappointment? Did you—in your overhearing —catch any word of love? Was there any real warmth in the way he asked me?"

"It was strange, I admit," Ruthanna said reluctantly, "but he *does* love you. Any want-wit can tell *that,*" she went on belligerently. "You could at least have taken time to consider, not just give him his marching orders out of your life."

"He has not gone out of my life yet," Ladybeth reminded her wearily. "He is coming back to sit for a full-length portrait."

The bell in the front room jangled. "Perhaps the captain has returned," Ruthanna said hopefully, rushing out of the studio. But their caller proved to be Mrs. Wertenbacker; and Ladybeth pinned on a professional smile as she welcomed her new subject.

Nearly a week later, Ladybeth came back from a morning walk to the silversmith's, where she had gone in search of a trinket for Ruthanna's birthday. The housekeeper met her at the door, all bright and smiling.

"Captain—*Mr.* De Croix is waiting for you in the studio," she whispered happily, and Ladybeth's still-traitor heart leaped high in her breast.

She had always marveled at how much regimentals did to improve the looks of so many men, making the most mundane fellow appear handsome. She had not believed till this moment that the opposite might be true, too—that ordinary clothes could so become a man!

He was sitting at her father's scarred old desk, dressed in a suit of silvery gray. Breeches, waistcoat, and coat, they were all of the same color, with a fall of white lace at his throat and the same lace falling from his sleeves. He turned in his chair smilingly when she came into the studio, his face warm and welcoming.

Ladybeth studied him with a painter's eye as well as a lover's, no longer able to deny even to herself that, willing or not, this man had her heart. She noted his new wig of powdered hair, combed high, unparted, and simply tied at the back. The keen blue eyes, the black brows, the strong Scots nose dominating his face, and the contrast of the strangely workmanlike hands, on one of his fingers a heavy gold signet ring. He was a handsome devil, and she loved him. It was her misfortune that, gray suited and magnificent, he was still the enemy.

But enemy or not, oh what a subject for a portrait!

"I want to paint you just as you are now!" she burst out without a word of greeting. "Wait for me; I will return soon."

True to her word, in less than ten minutes she was back, her walking gown changed to the muslin dress and long apron she used for work.

"I want you to wear this on your other hand for the sitting, Bay."

He looked at the onyx ring held out in her palm, first one eyebrow and then the other raised in question.

"My grandmother sent it for my brother when he was born," she explained. "Poor little Lawrence. He never even lived to grow into it. I have no idea if it was bought new or a family heirloom; but it will suit you, I think, and add a nice touch to the portrait. "Ah yes," she said, as he slipped it easily onto his left hand. "Just so. Now hold your hand here . . . and that one there . . . and if you could, recapture the expression that was on your face when I came in."

"I will if I can recall it," he said agreeably. "Can you perhaps describe it?"

"You looked"—she hesitated—"rather glad."

"As glad as a man, perhaps, seeing someone he cared for come into view?"

Ladybeth bit her lip. "Something like that."

"I will do my best," he said unsmilingly, then suddenly looked at her, his face all aglow. He may never have spoken his love, thought Ladybeth numbly, but it looked out at her now from his eyes, from his face. It was in the very air about them.

"Stay as you are," she whispered. "Stay just that way. Do not, I beg you, move."

And that was the last time she spoke for several hours. There were no false starts, no hesitation, none of the usual bad moments during work. It seemed to her at times, as sitting followed sitting all through the week, that other hands than her own wielded the paint brushes, that in every stroke of her work she was being guided by a power she could not begin to comprehend, only that it lifted her to heights she had believed impossible.

When she made the last brush stroke and painted the little scrolled "Ladybeth" in the corner, she stood there, exhausted, wrung out, and supremely happy.

If I never painted again, she thought, it would not matter. If I had never painted anything before this one, it would still be my . . . Dear God, am I just imagining that this is a masterpiece?

"I am finished," she said to Bay in a strange husky little voice, and he came at once, standing almost shoulder to shoulder with her.

For a long moment he stood and looked at it, while she waited with her hands clasped together tensely and a rapid pulse beating like a bird's in her throat.

"By God!" he said. "It is . . ." Words seemed to fail him. "Girl," he asked her incredulously, "do you know how good it is? How good *you* are?"

She nodded, happy tears standing in her eyes. "Yes," she sniffled happily. "Yes, to both questions."

He examined the painting again. "I see that, like a good fairy godmother, you have made the desk Hepplewhite and the chair Sheraton."

"I had to do justice to the gentleman in silvery gray," she said lightly.

"Yes, indeed, the gentleman in silvery gray. Your portrait makes him very much impressed with himself. You have made him look no end of a dashing fellow. No, come to think of it, not merely dashing." He cocked his left eyebrow. "Handsome?"

Ladybeth nodded.

He cocked the right brow. "The devil of a man with the ladies?"

Ladybeth nodded again.

"All," he said ruefully, "except *you?*"

She colored deeply. "That isn't fair."

"One isn't supposed to be fair in love, remember?

Nor in—I am afraid I must bring up a subject you never have liked."

"What is it?" asked Ladybeth, both angry and defensive that he could skip so readily from love to a subject she disliked.

"It has been more than three months since I wrote to England about the changed status of the earldom. I expect any day to have a reply from the attorneys and from your grandmother, too, regarding your own circumstances."

"So?"

"Would you be willing to go to England only for a visit? Just to see your grandmother," he added persuasively. "I would promise not to harass you with my attentions. She is very old, you know."

"No, I do not know. I know nothing about her," she said, "except that she has managed without me for all of *my* life and may therefore continue to do so for the rest of her own."

Something in his expression prompted her to add defensively, "The last occasion on which we heard from her was my brother's birth, when she did not trouble to write but sent him the ring with the onyx that you are wearing now."

Reminded, he returned it to her, and she slipped it on her own hand, then shrugged in disdain. "I have no false sentiment regarding blood. Ruthanna—Mrs. Fielding, my housekeeper—has shown me more loving-kindness than I have ever received from my kin in England."

"I agree with Capt. De Croix," Ruthanna's voice proclaimed suddenly from behind them. "If the earl wants you to visit England, then I think you should go. A ladyship should mingle with her own kind, not go on like this, painting soldiers and merchants and silly ladies of fashion. Not only that"—she nodded sagely, handing a receipt to the captain and bobbing her head in thanks for the monies he counted out—"you should try to marry among them, too. There's no one here for you, growing up as you did, no matter the title you have now."

"Mrs. Fielding, you are a woman of rare good sense," Bay told her heartily.

Ladybeth untied her apron and flung it down. "Ruthanna, you traitor!" she cried, dismayed. "You *want* me to leave you?"

"I want what's best for you," the other returned stolidly.

"I suppose it would make it easier for you to wed Mr. Ver Loop if I were to leave? Oh, Ruthanna"—she ran after her to fling both arms around her—"I'm sorry," she said contritely. "That was spiteful of me. I didn't mean it. I just can't see myself living in England. I hate them there for what they did to my parents."

"You didn't want the posset I brewed when you had that terrible cough last winter. But it healed you all the same."

"Our countries are at war."

"Forget the war for a while. You should meet your family before you throw them off."

Ladybeth walked about the room in an agony of indecision. Across her head, her suitor's eyes and Mrs. Fielding's exchanged a look that blended complicity with complete understanding.

Chapter 28

A CARPENTER ARRIVED AT THE HOUSE ON BOWLING Green a few days later to wrap the full-length portrait of Bay in protective layers of straw and then crate it for shipment over the seas.

"You'll never tell me a young lady like yourself made a picture the like of this!" he exclaimed admiringly.

"Oh, but I did," said Ladybeth lightly, then ran out of her studio and into the kitchen. "You supervise him, please, Ruthanna," she mumbled.

The truth was, she could not bear to stay and see the portrait be packed away. It would be almost like saying a final good-bye to Bay. The pain she felt now, she knew, was a grim foretaste of the pain she would feel a hundredfold in the future. The light would go out of her world when he was no longer in America.

Half of her—the eager, loving, adventurous half—wanted to accept the only other alternative for this heartsickness and go to England with him. The half of her that was patriotic and prudent insisted she would forever lose her self-respect if she trotted off to the enemy country in search of magic and moonbeams. In time, her saner self might turn her love for Bay into hate. To say nothing of Bay himself. Englishmen might, as he had pointed out, often wed Americans, but not—at least, not knowingly—American agents. If she married him without owning up to her activities as a spy and he later found out, then it might well curdle his love into distrust and dislike that she had used him.

She stayed in her room till she heard the noise of movement downstairs and a glance from her window showed the carpenter gently setting the crate into the back of his cart.

The same glance showed Bay coming up the walk, dressed in sober mulberry and a plain cravat, his tricorn under his arm.

Ladybeth closed her eyes briefly. This might be his farewell visit. She thought of slipping into her new silk gown and brushing out her hair, then frowned in the mirror at her own ridiculous vanity. If this was good-bye, then let it be his good-bye to what she was, Lady Beth Crozier, portrait painter, in her working muslin and apron, with smears of green and vermilion on her fingers and her knot of chestnut hair slightly askew.

Ruthanna came to the foot of the stairs to call up to her just as she was coming down.

"The captain—I mean, Mr. De Croix is waiting for you."

"I know," said Ladybeth sedately, though her palms were sweating and her heart beating uncomfortably fast. "I hardly expected to see you today, Bay," she told him in the studio a moment later. "When Mr.

Tobias came to crate and take away the portrait, I thought you might be busy with your packing. Is the date of your journey set?"

"Not yet, but it soon will be. Since I am leaving my army gear behind and only buying what I need for the ship, my luggage"—he smiled engagingly, inviting her to respond in kind—"consists mainly of crates in several varying sizes that contain all my portraits."

Ladybeth forced an answering smile.

"I hope that your family will be pleased with them, particularly your grandchildren with Bay, the Pirate."

"May we sit down?"

"Oh, of course. Forgive me."

She took the desk chair that she had "turned" to Sheraton in his portrait and waved him to the only upholstered chair in the room.

"Would you like some refreshment, Bay? A beverage, or an apple from the bowl?"

He waved away both offers impatiently, saying curtly, "This is not—though I am always eager to see you—a social call. The fast packet came from England today with the letters I had been expecting."

"Oh?"

"There will be ten thousand pounds settled on you."

"Good heavens!"

"The seventh Earl has been named, and he guarantees the payment, as do the attorneys for the estate. I have legal documents to that effect to give to you. You may wish to show them to your own attorney."

"It passes belief, something wonderful for me out of Merrie Old England," said Ladybeth, trying to appear flippant and succeeding only in sounding rather uncivil.

"Your grandmother is longing to see you."

"A pity."

"And," he wound up softly, "the Earl of Shirley has ordered you home."

She almost strangled on her own breath. "The earl has *ordered* me to do what?"

Softly and steadily, he elaborated, "On the first available ship and under my escort."

She strove to keep her voice calm. "How obliging of the earl and how fortunate the army relieved you just in time for such trivial duty . . . or is it that an earl commanded?"

"It so happens that I had already resigned my commission, effective this next month. The earl, knowing this, was most happy to take advantage of the circumstance that freed me for this—this obligation."

Her eyes flashed at the calculated insult of this word, but before she could properly blast him, as he knew she was preparing to do, he stood up, crossed the room, and seized both her wrists, crossing them one over the other, holding her fast.

"Stay your tongue and listen for once, Lady Beth, listen well, please, I do not intend to repeat myself. No temper tantrums, my little American savage, just a word of advice. *You have no choice!* You are under age, ma'am, and the earl, as the head of the Crozier family, has had himself appointed your guardian. There is still English rule in these colonies, and willing or not, you will obey it."

He watched her, not without sympathy, as she dazedly rubbed her wrists together, staring down in bemusement at the bruise marks from his fingers.

As he bent his head, she suddenly felt a light kiss against each reddened wrist.

"Forgive me," he said huskily. "I did not mean to hurt you. I only meant to make you listen and understand what you must do."

She went to the window and stood looking out, unwilling to let him see her tears.

"I know what I must do," said Ladybeth not much above a whisper.

She had known exactly what that was almost immediately after the instant of shocking gladness when he had said, *You have no choice!* She had wanted to have no alternatives. She had been fiercely, primitively glad that it was in his power to force her to throw off every shackle that bound her to her present life . . . and follow her heart to England.

The revulsion of having allowed herself, even for such a little while, to be so weak, so craven, so forgetful of her greater obligation, hardened her heart and stiffened her determination even more than before, if such a thing were possible.

As soon as Bay took leave of her, in the deluded notion that she would cave in to the forces of law and reason and command, she carried a basket of laundry out to the clothesline to hang three handkerchiefs, with a petticoat on either side of them, to signal to her unseen courier, URGENT!

Several evenings later at the theatre, Ruthanna stayed in her box seat during intermission while Ladybeth braved the crowds in search of refreshment.

"Allow me, madam."

Hercules Mulligan, strolling through the antechamber, bent to pick up the concert program she had just dropped. "Culper Jr. told me your plan, and we considered it carefully, but it will not do. As E. Crozier, you might have followed in the wake of the British army, painting soldiers. The Lady Beth Crozier is far too prominent a person to do that. In respect to your going to another colony, the arm of the law could still reach you, particularly if an English earl were shaking the arm. If nothing worse, you would be too conspicuous, which no agent can afford to be."

Ladybeth stood in silence. She knew that she had been useful to them. How could they relinquish her services so easily?

"Nay then, cheer up, my lass; we have gotten as much good out of your painting as we can here, but over in England . . . 'tis another story. The time may be coming when you can serve us even better."

"In England!" she said, shocked.

"Hush. Yes, in England. Think, Lady Beth, you would be the cousin of an earl, not mingling with the common soldiers anymore, but with all manner of grand folks, lords and ladies and the like. English politicians."

He paused impressively to allow his meaning to sink in.

"You mean—"

"I mean, my lady, you would be supping with them and dancing with them as well as painting their pretty English faces. Very few Americans would have your own unique position as a close relation of the Earl of Shirley. You might be of far more use to us there than here in America."

"But how—"

"Your reports could go direct to old Ben Franklin in Paris and from him on to us. There is plenty of time to determine the ways and the means. Well, lass, what do you say? Will you serve us still?"

A pair of determined, deep blue eyes flashed before her face. Unconsciously, she rubbed her wrists.

"If there are five handkerchiefs in a row on my laundry line tomorrow," she said in a low, choked voice, "you will know that I agree to go."

Long after Ruthanna was in bed that night, Ladybeth wandered restlessly about the house, clad only in her flannel nightdress and slippers. She laughed, she cried, she talked aloud. One moment she was twisting her hands together, and the next pounding a fist against her palm.

Now she truly had no choice. It was no longer a case of the earl commanding and Bay carrying out his instructions. Her own country, too, asked, demanded really, that she go to England.

Everyone, it seemed—those who loved her and those who did not, those who knew her and those she had never met—each and every one of them wanted her to be in England. And none of them, it also seemed, cared a farthing about her own wishes in the matter. All of them, it appeared to Ladybeth, had something of their own to gain.

Bay wanted her there as his wife and the earl to fulfill his family obligations. Her grandmother wanted her belatedly to ease her own conscience. Her country wanted her services as a spy; Ruthanna wanted both of them to have husbands.

In the end, it was all quite simple. Edmund and Deborah and Lawrence were dead, and Ruthanna would have a new family of her own. There was nothing now for her in America, and Bay, whom she wanted, was going to England. Even if she could consign her country's needs to perdition, the truth of it was that she loved Bay with all her heart and wanted him as well with all of her being.

So to England she would go!

There were five handkerchiefs in a row on her laundry line in the morning, and Henry Bayard De Croix—sent for by urgent message—regarded Lady Beth Crozier in stunned astonishment.

"You will go with me on the first Snow Mercury packet?"

"I still don't want to go," lied Ladybeth, "and the earl will rue the day he tried to force me, but it is the only way Ruthanna will consent to wed Mr. Ver Loop. The first banns have been read, and the marriage will take place in a fortnight. I insist on staying for the wedding. Any time after that, I am agreeable to going with you. Pray, sir, why do you look so perturbed?" She smiled saucily up at him. "Are you not getting what you wanted?"

"That is what perturbs me," he told her grimly. "I got it much too easily. No battle, hardly even a struggle. Why the sudden change of heart, my Lady Beth? I do not flatter myself that it was either my strength or my logic that convinced you."

"Ruthanna convinced me. She said it was what my parents would have wanted me to do," she told him in a sad, pitiful way. And without her"—she looked over at him with large, sorrowful eyes and sighed deeply— "now that she is marrying Mr. Ver Loop, home doesn't seem so much like home anymore."

Even as his eyebrows snapped together suspiciously, her voice hardened. "Understand one other thing, Bay De Croix. This house on Bowling Green remains my home. I shall have the Ver Loops put it up for rental while I am in England. Remember, I am only going for a visit. When I am twenty-one, if I wish to return to America, then I shall. Not you, not any earl in the world will keep me from here if that is my desire."

"A bargain." He held out his hand, and a bit reluctantly, she put hers into it to receive his warm, hard clasp. "When you are one-and-twenty, you may choose for yourself where you will live."

Chapter 29

I PUSHED THROUGH THE BABBLING THRONG AT THE
entrance to Christie's, catalogue in hand. By the size of
the crowd, anyone might have thought that the paintings and objets d'art were being given away instead of
sold at vastly inflated prices.

A deep, carrying voice, an *American* voice somewhere to the left of me, was inquiring, "Can you direct
me to the set of miniatures by E. Crozier?"

"Certainly, sir, it's just down this—"

I missed the directions, all my thoughts and feelings
concentrated on the owner of the voice.

Cam, I thought dizzily. *Oh Cam, I can't believe that
it's really you.*

Believable or not, when I whirled around, I found
that my foolish remembering heart had not misled me.
It was Cam, all right, looking not that much different
from the day nearly ten years before when I had

decided that my world would be well lost for love of him.

Oh, he was a bit heavier than the young man who had cradled my bare body in his arms on a garage floor and later heaved me up out of Long Island Sound, but not really ten years' worth. There were lines on his face that hadn't been there then, but that was to be expected of a man approaching his mid-thirties.

On rubbery legs I weaved in and out, following him down a corridor. Running around a corner to catch up, I barreled straight on into him. He had stopped to look at a mural.

"Steady there." His hands were on me, keeping me upright. I could feel them through the heavy gabardine of my raincoat right through to my shoulder bones, and I shuddered with exquisite delight at their light touch.

"Dear God, dear God!" I whispered to myself. How could someone I hardly knew anymore and hadn't seen in years do this to me?

"Do you know if the Ladybeths are down this way?" I asked, trying to sound casual.

"Yes, I'm looking for them myself," he answered, his eyes narrowing.

In one quick, comprehensive glance, he took in my rubber boots, eight-year-old London Fog raincoat, and the silk scarf tied around my hair and hanging down my back like a golden banner. With that one look I felt him decide I would be no competition in the auction bidding.

Even as I marveled that I should know so well the way his mind worked, I was resenting that quick, dismissing summation of my physical assets. At the same time something in me was crying out in rage and grief that he had not a single remembrance of the wild-haired girl with the atrocious accent and clothes.

Unreasonable? Of course it was. Had I not spent a good many years working to wipe out that very girl? But love is not always reasonable or wise.

"I was told the E. Croziers—they have not been authenticated as Ladybeths—are at the end of this wall." His smile was impersonal. "Come with me."

We stood side by side looking at the three miniatures. He studied each one carefully while my eyes flew along the row.

A young British redcoat. Next, a round, merry face with the smile of a born adventurer and the daredevil eyes to match it. Lastly, a finely dressed Dutch merchant in an old-fashioned white wig, with three sausage curls on either side of his plump square-jawed face.

"They're Ladybeths," I said in a croaking voice that seemed to be coming from someone else.

"How do you know?"

I looked at him helplessly. What could I say? *I saw her paint them in my dream.*

"I've studied her work" was all I could come up with.

"Many people have studied her work without being able to identify it at a single glance." He smiled as he said it, an indulgent, patronizing smile that made me itch to slap him.

I said rapidly, "The soldier is Sergeant William Morrison of the Welsh Fusileers. The man in the middle is Hercules Mulligan, who happened to be New York's most popular tailor. Originally recommended by Alexander Hamilton, he was one of Washington's trusted secret agents during the Revolution. Ladybeth painted several bigger portraits of him. The respectable-looking gentleman is Jacob Ver Loop, merchant and ship owner and widower. It was painted the year before his second marriage to Mrs. Ruthanna Fielding."

He had stared at me all during this speech with his mouth agape, but the moment I finished my rapid-fire delivery, he whipped a small notebook out of a side pocket and requested, "Would you mind repeating that, please?"

Obligingly, I said it all again and watched him scribble notes.

"Now would you mind telling me how you can be so positive about your information? Some of the experts don't seem to know it."

"Yes," I said contrarily. "I would mind." I gave him a dazzling smile and walked away.

I saw him again at the auction. We were sitting on opposite sides of the room, three rows apart.

I was conscious of his twisting around in his seat quite often to look at me. Baffled looks, and something else . . . as though he were trying to trace a resemblance to someone, something. Or, I asked myself, was that just a wishful dream of my own?

Whatever the reason, whyever the look, each one was balm to my soul.

I looked straight ahead, pretending not to notice his fixed stares. I found myself wondering idly why Irene wasn't with him. Was she home with their daughter, or had there been just a hint in one of Maggie's recent letters of trouble in what had never, even at the beginning, been paradise?

The miniatures came up for sale midway through the auction. They were put up in one lot, and the bidding finally narrowed down to Cam and one other tall, cadaverous man who looked as though he would not live long enough to enjoy them.

Once, just for a second, Cam seemed undecided about increasing his bid. He was half-turned in his chair; our eyes met and locked. I felt the leap of every pulse in my body and gave a short, sharp nod. His fingers went up in what proved to be the final bid. The miniatures were his.

I stayed till the end of the sale. Then I stood, feeling his eyes on me still. I moved along my row of chairs and through the crowded aisles.

One block from the gallery I heard brisk footsteps and had no doubt who was behind me. I kept up my own quick pace till his hand landed on my shoulder. Then I stopped and turned my head, pretending surprise.

"Will you go to dinner with me?" Cam asked.

"Why?"

"Why?" he echoed, a bit disconcerted.

"Yes, why," I repeated belligerently. "Because you're bowled over by my looks? You're not. Because you have no friends in London? I doubt it. Because you're on the lookout for a woman? You're married. Because you want to pump me about Ladybeth? I have nothing to say."

"Try these on for size. I'm hungry, and I hate to eat alone. You're an attractive, if slightly pugnacious young lady. You're here with me now; my other friends are not. If you don't want to talk about Ladybeth, we won't. No, I'm not on the lookout for a woman, though aren't you a bit naïve to think being married would prevent me if I were?"

His eyes were alight with laughter; his smile was half-tender, half-mocking. It made my insides dissolve.

"Well," said Cam, "have you made up your mind?"

"Yes," I answered abruptly.

"Yes, you've made up your mind, or yes, you'll go to dinner?"

"Yes, I'll go to dinner." And without thinking, "Stop laughing at me, Charley."

Knowing he actively disliked that version of his name, in a teasing mood Maggie used to call Cam Charley when she wanted to annoy him.

He stared at me, a slight frown between his eyes, the way he had in Christie's when I spouted off the bits of information about the Ladybeth miniatures.

"How did you know my name?" he asked quietly.

"I didn't," I bluffed. "Is your name really Charley?"

"Charles. My family and close friends call me Cam, a combination of my initials."

"In England," I lied easily, "we use Charley instead of fellow, you know, the way you Americans call everyone Joe." I changed the subject abruptly. "I've just discovered I'm hungry, too. Where are we going?"

He named several places, all of which I vetoed firmly. I steered him instead in the direction of one of my favorite pubs, where, at a slight sacrifice in ambience, the food would be twice the quality and half the price. Frankly, I preferred the pub atmosphere.

Cam seemed to prefer it, too. He looked at me approvingly across the scarred oak table of our private booth.

"I see you don't pick your restaurants for their PR value."

"Not when I want to eat," I said, letting my raincoat slide back from my shoulders and wishing I were wearing something more exotic than a dark knit jersey shirt.

While Cam ordered two beers from the waitress, I pulled the yellow scarf from my head and knotted it around my neck, sailor-style, to add a touch of color.

At my recommendation, we made it a double order of rare roast beef, fried potatoes, and Yorkshire pudding, with two more beers.

When the waitress was gone, Cam looked me square

in the eyes. "Why were you sure I was married?" he wanted to know.

"All the good men are," I said airily.

"That doesn't answer the question."

"You just have a married look to me," I said, smiling sweetly, to which he responded with a short, blunt, "Bullshit!"

I tried to look affronted and didn't succeed.

"You're a liar," Cam told me matter-of-factly. "A lovely one, but still a liar. I lived in England several years myself. It's not a British habit to call all men Charley. Maybe I do—God help me!—have a married-man look, but that still is not how you happened to know I was one. The E. Croziers may be genuine Ladybeths, but you didn't find it out by studying her history. So let's get down to basics: First, who are you? Second, your accent's not completely English. Where are you from and what are you doing here? Why—"

"Here in this pub?" I interrupted pertly.

"No, here in London. There at the auction."

"Looking at the paintings. Sorry to disappoint you, but I'm an art student. I attend London University. I lived in the States for a number of years—as an exchange student—which slightly diluted my accent."

"And your name is?"

I had given myself time to think of one on the extremely slight chance that Rilla Scott might ring a bell for him. "My name is Catherine Dingle," I told him, suppressing a giggle at the pained expression my last name produced. "Otherwise known as Katy." I held out my hand. "Hi, Charley."

He grasped my hand. "I prefer Charles, Catherine."

"I prefer Katy, Charles."

We were still holding each other's hands when the huge platters of roast beef, not so rare, were held over our heads. We severed our hand-hold reluctantly to give the waitress room to set the plates on the table. Our eye-lock remained unbroken for several seconds more, then Cam lit into his food with relish while I just played with mine.

"Hey," he said, halfway through, "I thought you were hungry."

I couldn't exactly explain that, all for the love of him, my stomach was somewhere up in my chest, leaving no space at all for food. It was obvious he didn't suffer from the same ailment.

"I'm not as hungry as I thought," I managed to utter from between stiff lips.

"Too bad," the insensitive brute sympathized with his mouth full. "You were right. It's a fabulous cut of meat." He plied his knife and swallowed some beer with the gusto of Henry VIII.

"Would you like mine, too?" I gritted out when his platter was clean.

"If you're sure you're not going to eat any more. It seems a shame to waste it."

I felt like sticking my knife and fork into him, but I passed my plate over instead, and he helped himself to the generous portion of beef still remaining on it.

He gave a deep sigh when he was done, the sigh of a contented man. "That was a feast for the gods. Who says the English don't understand good food."

"Only overfed, overweight, over-here Americans."

"Touché." He grinned good-naturedly.

The waitress presented our bill, and he asked me as he counted out bills, "Are you a good walker?"

"The best."

"Having Americanishly overeaten"—he bent toward me in the burlesque of a bow—"I would like to walk it off."

275

It was misty outside the pub, with the kind of damp and chill that cuts through to the bones. I buttoned up the collar of my coat, then reached inside it to pull up my scarf and fasten it around my head.

"Here. Let me." He pushed aside my clumsy, gloved fingers and tied the scarf, kerchief-style, with a strong knot below my chin.

His hands were quick and deft. One of them cupped my chin when he was through, tilting my face up for his inspection. The rain fell lightly onto both of us. It trickled down his cheeks like tears.

God knows what he saw or thought he saw in my face, but I heard him suck in his breath and I shut my eyes tightly, afraid of revealing more. It seemed the most natural thing to happen when he drew me into the closed shelter of his arms. Had I not waited ten years to be there where I belonged? Had I not waited all that time to feel his mouth take mine?

His kiss was light, my response was not. His kiss may have been uncaring, the kiss of any man to a pretty, compliant girl. Standing there on the street, with occasional people passing by, I kissed him back with passion undisguised. I didn't care what he thought or what the watching world might say. All the yearning of my hungry heart was in the pressure of my lips.

"Good God!" he said, when I finally let him go.

"Shall we walk now?" I asked collectedly, and set off before he could answer.

We walked for about twenty blocks without a word, but with one of my hands in its wool mitten wrapped round by his hand in its fur-lined leather glove.

Through the layers of wool and fur and leather, I could feel the strength and warmth which our hands gave to one another. It was as though our blood flowed together in a single stream.

Just that joining of our hands made us one. Oh, why, *why* couldn't he have recognized years ago, as I did, our inescapable belonging?

"This is my hotel."

Those were the first words he had spoken since our kiss.

I blinked, came out of my dream, and focused my eyes. "Yes, I know," I said groggily. "You always favor the Dorchester, don't you?"

"Yes," he said evenly. "For quick trips over, I do. How did you know?"

"Instinct, Charley. The way I knew you would prefer the pub."

He didn't accept that. I knew I would be challenged later, but for the present he let it pass.

"Are you coming up with me?" he asked directly.

In anyone else I would have been either amused or offended by the lack of finesse, but with him I wasn't. Behind the abrupt approach, I sensed a sudden, still desperation. He was terrified that my answer would be no.

"Yes," I said. "I'm coming up."

Chapter 30

HE GOT HIS KEY FROM THE DESK WHILE I WAITED AT the elevator. In the elevator we stood at the back, tugged off our gloves, and our hands reached out again and clasped and clung.

I followed him into the luxury suite. He went around switching on lamps and then hung up both our coats.

"Would you like a drink?"

"Vodka and tonic, please." Then, remembering what lay ahead, "Maybe two," I gulped.

He smiled at me a bit quizzically and went to the phone. I put my hands to my burning cheeks while he spoke to room service, wondering in panic how I was going to explain to him that the eager passion I had shown came from love, not from experience.

I was almost sick with the longing to go to bed with him, but I felt ridiculously embarrassed at having first to inform him that I was, lamentably, a virgin.

"I have something to say to you . . ."

"There's something I have to tell you . . ."

Absurdly, we both spoke together, and then still more absurdly, went through an Alphonse-Gaston routine, with each of us trying to get the other to speak first.

I won.

He stood a few feet away from me and said his piece quickly, looking down at his feet. "I couldn't say this outside the hotel or before we came up in the elevator. It would have sounded like a pitch, a phony line. But now that you're here, I very much want you to know I don't make a practice of this."

"Of what?" I whispered, dry-mouthed.

"A practice of picking up girls in galleries and wining and dining them in pubs. In fact, it's the first time. I've been married for two years, which haven't exactly been the high point of my life, but I have a baby daughter I dearly love, and I more or less believe that if you're going to stay married, you should act married."

"I haven't asked you for any promises, Cam."

"I know that. I—it's just that I want you to know. I asked you because you're *you.* I didn't want a girl, any girl. I wanted—I want *you.*"

"I know that, too, Cam." I moved toward him with my hands out. "I want you, too," I told him breathlessly, "and I wouldn't have come to just anyone's hotel room. It could only have been with you."

He swooped down on me, kissing me at such length and with such strength I wound up leaning against him, shaken and dizzy and needing his body for support.

It pleased me greatly to discover that *his* fingers were shaking as they wound the scarf from about my throat. It wouldn't be fair to have the breathless trembling excitement of my feeling for him all one-sided.

He tossed the scarf onto a chair and brought me up

279

against him with my hands pulled behind me in one of
his. His free hand he used to track through my hair and
down my back, releasing unutterably delightful sensations to whatever bare skin it managed to touch. Then
he proceeded to kiss me again with such passionate
thoroughness, from head to toe, I was one big, quivering dish of jelly.

Moments later I heard his muffled laughter. "Katy
darling, do you have an open pin somewhere on you?
I'm being stabbed in the chest."

We broke apart and discovered that our energetic
movements had twisted up the chain around my neck,
causing my Star of David, instead of lying flat against
my shirt, to stick straight out. One of the pointed edges
of the star had done the stabbing.

Cam unraveled my chain and patted the star down
between my breasts, his fingers lingering not so much
on the star as on what surrounded it.

"Your star is unusual," he told me, not really thinking of my jewelry.

"It's very old," I said, swaying to his rotating hands.

"I can see that," he murmured. "So you're Jewish,"
he sighed, working my shirt out of my skirt band.

"Almost."

The hands paused momentarily, and I had to still my
impulse to cry out, "Don't stop, please don't stop."

"How does one get to be *almost* Jewish?" he asked
me humorously.

"Lots of ways, including choice."

"And you have chosen?"

"Almost."

"My little mystery woman." He laughed softly. "You
have a great deal of explaining to do. About a number
of things. Only not right now. Not tonight."

His hands reached up under my shirt again, unhooking my bra. Then they traveled round in front, trying to free my breasts. I felt one of my bra straps break and began giggling like a teen-ager on her first date.

"Sorry," he apologized, breathing hard.

"Break the other one," I whispered, and after one dazed, astonished look at me, he ripped at it, breathing even harder.

My bra, with its two torn straps, joined my yellow silk scarf on the chair.

When he took me into his arms again, I wanted to sink right down on that sponge-soft carpeting and take him with me. What stopped me was not common sense or even shame but a light knock on the door.

I broke away from Cam guiltily.

"It's only room service," he soothed me, striding to the door.

I flushed up and averted my eyes, and seeing this, he suggested kindly, "Perhaps you'd like to freshen up" and pointed a little to his right.

"Thanks." I fled the room gratefully before he admitted the waiter.

There was a small lamp lit in the huge bedroom. It showed me the way to the bathroom. I fumbled around for a light switch, and as soon as I found it, I closed the door and leaned against it, breathing as though I had just come back from a five-mile jog.

I should have felt wildly happy. Was I not about to have one of my heart's long-cherished desires?

But it had come on me so fast and so suddenly I was unprepared, bewildered.

I would be fine, I avowed to myself, as soon as I was back in Cam's arms, as soon as I stopped thinking of practical details, like remembering that he was married.

It's not something easily forgotten, a little unpleasant reminding voice inside me kept whispering.

I opened my purse and took out my comb and make-up kit. As I approached the mirror of the medicine cabinet, I resolutely determined not to listen to the voice.

I might have succeeded if I had not heard the words out loud.

A wife is not so easily forgotten.

Even as I gave a panicked cry, a misty face and body swirled up behind me in the mirror. My man in silver gray.

I forgot my doubts and fears. I remembered only that *he* was the spoiler in my life.

"Oh, no! Oh, no!" I wept and whirled about to confront him. "Not this time. Not with Cam. Oh, please. I love him so, and I've waited for so long."

"You have waited overlong," he admitted. "But surely not for this? One or two nights in his hotel room, three or four if you are more fortunate. Can this be what you have waited for all these years? A few tumbles with a man who, no matter how you please him, will eventually return to his family?"

I leaned against the sink. "He's not happy with her." Even in my own ears, my voice sounded more weak than defiant.

"He is not yet ready to be happy with you, my dear girl. When the day comes that he is, then I promise I will not make a third in your love scenes."

"My love scenes with Cam, you mean?" I asked wonderingly.

He nodded gravely.

"Then it *is* Cam I was meant to be with? I mean, he *is* the one you made me wait for?"

Again that same grave nod.

"You know something?" I came upright in a burst of energy. "I feel good about knowing that I haven't been crazy all these years. I damn well wish you wouldn't interfere in my life, but I'm glad to know there is a reason for what's been going on. Not just with you but in my mind."

Suddenly I sagged back against the sink, tears filling up my eyes and splashing down my face.

"How can I leave him now?" I sobbed. "There's no way I can possibly explain it."

His smile was half-teasing, half-tender. "Your tongue has never failed you before now, Amaryllis, or your ingenious mind."

For the first time in our long acquaintance, he made me a courtly little bow. Then he was gone, leaving me alone and bereft.

A chill of loneliness and longing swept over me as I bent toward the mirror, applying fresh make-up to cover the tear stains and bring color to my cheeks.

It was no sooner done than I destroyed it with a fresh bout of tears. I had to blow my nose resolutely in some tissues and start all over again. It took quite a long time.

There was a tap on the door.

"Katy. You okay?"

"I'm fine," I sang out. "I'll be right with you." Even as I managed to infuse some warmth and gaiety into my voice, I was marveling at my own acting ability. "Keep my drink cold."

I joined him in another two minutes, immediately reaching for a drink. He held it out to me but made me come close before he would let go of the glass. He looked doubtfully at the repair job to my face.

"Have you been crying?"

"Crying?" I hedged. "How silly. Why would I have been crying?"

"I don't know. I asked you."

He gave me the glass, and I hid my face behind it, taking a sip now and then, rubbing my lips against the frosted surface of the glass with slow, sensual unawareness till Cam said huskily, "Will you put down that damn drink." He seized it, putting it down himself.

Then he seized *me* and showed me a far better use for my lips than they had ever been put to. "What the hell?" I thought in desperation, and gave myself up to those all-too-short, rapturous moments, knowing they would not soon come again. Knowing, even if he did not, that his kisses were for good-bye.

I might have gotten carried away completely and forgotten what it was I had to do, but the man in gray must have sensed danger. Coming up for oxygen between kisses, I felt his presence once again.

"I'd like to finish my drink, Charles," I said, and it must have been the sudden primness in my voice following fast on the heels of all the passion that made him sound so joyously teasing when he answered.

"If you really want it, Katy."

"Yes, please, I do."

To prove it, I gulped down my vodka and tonic like lemonade and asked for another. After the second quick drink, it wasn't so much play-acting when I got up and stammered, "If you'll ex-excuse m-me, I n-need— Excuse me—"

Cam's eyes and smile both mocked my excess of gentility.

"Take your time," he said. "I'll straighten up here."

He added as I stumbled on my way, and there was a wealth of meaning in his voice, "Then I'll wait for you in the bedroom."

I tried to smile at him, but how do you smile good-bye at someone you love and want and only *hope* ever to see again?

Chapter 31

I CLOSED THE CONNECTING DOOR BETWEEN THE LIVING-room and bedroom. Then I made straight for the outside door that I had noted on my previous trip. I opened it carefully, quietly, then closed it behind me in the same manner as I stepped out into the broad corridor.

I had my purse with me, but, of course, my raincoat was left hanging in the closet. There had been no logical reason for taking it with me, as Cam supposed, to the bathroom or later to bed. My scarf and torn bra remained behind me, too.

I didn't know how much time I had or whether he would come after me, but there was no way I could take the chance.

I sped down the hallway to the nearest stairway exit and bolted down three flights, then emerged to take the elevator. When I got to the lobby floor, I took a quick look about, then dashed straight past reception and out through the front doors.

A cab was just discharging a man in a tux and a woman in evening gown. I squeezed past them, cutting off a whiskered gentleman who had a prior claim.

"Victoria Station. Quickly, please," I told the driver, huddling down in the seat out of sight.

Then, as he swung away from the curb and picked up speed, I couldn't resist kneeling and peering out the misted back window for one last look. There was no sight of Cam. I bent my head over against my knees and cried and cried.

After a while the driver asked uneasily, "Anything I can do for you, miss?"

"No, thank you," I sobbed. "I'll be all right."

"You get a good night's sleep, love," he offered. "Amazing how much better things can seem in the daylight."

"Yes, I know," I said dully, not believing it for a moment.

After I paid him off at Victoria, I went into the station by way of one entrance and exited immediately at another. Maybe it was silly of me to believe Cam would try to trace me, but in case he did . . .

I caught another cab and felt safe this time in giving the address of my flat. I sat bra-less, coatless, and shivering all the way home, making plans for my future.

Mrs. Catherine Dingle, who was an art agent—not Cam's Katy Dingle—was born in that London taxi. *She* made the plans for selling paintings by Amaryllis. Rilla Scott's writing and illustrations would go on as they had before.

I made one last trip home to Liverpool to see Mum and Dad, Jim and Heather, and my little nephew. Then back to the States for a few weeks in Larchmont until I found my Turtle Bay apartment and launched my new lives and careers.

All during the weeks and months that the new-made Mrs. Dingle devoted energy, effort, and vigor to turning years of work by Amaryllis into an overnight success, the same old me—Rilla Scott—went around with a leaden weight that was about the size of the Hope diamond lodged somewhere between stomach and chest.

I couldn't get over the sickness of loving Cam. I couldn't stop missing the belonging we had never known. I was terrified that the opportunity would never come again.

The man in silver gray saved my sanity. He came to me one night when I was alone in my half-furnished apartment, too unhappy to paint, too tired to read, too indifferent to call a friend, too queasy to eat.

I sat. That was all I did most evenings after a day of frenzied activity. I just sat. And brooded. Or cried. Mostly both.

I was curled up on the couch. He chose the big armchair opposite.

I stared at him distantly. "Welcome through the Looking Glass," I invited disagreeably.

"The Looking Glass?"

I shrugged. "Never mind. It's past your time. You're eighteenth century, aren't you?" I asked him, past the point of caring.

"I was the last time round."

I sat up a little, interested in spite of myself. It was the most revealing thing he had ever said.

"I don't understand," I told him slowly.

"Of course you understand," he contradicted in a brisk, no-nonsense manner. "You merely don't choose to at the moment. You are too occupied these days in feeling sorry for yourself."

He carefully adjusted the ruffles at his sleeves and brushed away a tiny spot of lint on his brocade waistcoat. "If you want to weep your life away," he continued offhandedly, "it is, of course, your own affair. It makes me sadly disappointed in you, I must admit. In the past you showed more courage."

"Ten years of courage seems to be about my limit," I returned sullenly.

"*Ten* years!" He looked me over, all amazed, then surprisingly his laughter sputtered out. "My dear girl. It has been more than two hundred."

This time I sat all the way upright. "What are you talking about, more than two hundred?" I demanded.

"You have accepted my presence since you were a young girl," he explained gently. "Did it never occur to you to ask yourself, 'Why me?'"

"Not at first, but sometimes, when I got a bit older."

"And what did you answer?"

"I never did!" I retorted. "And you would not! So what choice did I have except to go on wondering."

"I shall try to answer now, Rilla."

"Okay then, why me, for God's sake? Who are you, and why me?"

"Who *I* am is for the future . . . 'why you' has to do with our past." He smiled at her very lovingly. "We shared a common past, you know. People who love and live again frequently do."

"Oh, my God!"

"I missed you the last time round," he said softly. "I was not about to let another century pass by."

"I don't believe this."

"You mean," he corrected, "you are fearful to believe this." He stood up. For a moment he stood over me, closer than he had ever been before. "You were beloved as few women are beloved. It will all be yours again if you have the courage to wait."

He held out his hands, almost as in a benediction. Love and warmth seemed to come from him in great waves. They flooded my body; they flooded my being. As he faded into nothingness, the leaden weight inside me dissolved, too.

I felt not the aching tiredness of before but a wonderful welcome sleepiness. As I lay back on the couch, eyes pressed closed, I was engulfed by the familiar, no longer frightening vibration of the beating wings. The ripples became a swelling roar, breaking over and around me till both my head and my body were caught up in the dizzying whirlpool of sound and motion.

When I awoke, it was daylight, and I knew at once I had dreamwalked again. I looked down at the proof of my paint-stained hands and my paint-spattered corduroy slacks almost with joy.

Then on stumbling feet I made for the studio.

Dream-walked. Dream-painted.

There had been a large blank canvas on my easel all set up for my next working session. It was blank no longer. The neat array of jars and cans on my worktable had been disarranged. My brushes, stiff with paint, not neatly cleaned in turps, lay carelessly nearby.

None of it seemed important. Only the painting.

Slowly I approached the easel.

The girl who smiled back at me from the canvas might have been alive, so vivid was her portrait, so vibrant did she seem. For someone so tall and slim, she had surprisingly voluptuous breasts. They seemed ready to burst the confining bodice of her rather simple green gown. There was humor and more than a hint of sensuality in her smiling mouth; strength, not to say stubbornness, in the firm, straight lines of her nose and chin and her high broad forehead. Her great, gray sparkling eyes were full of laughter and wisdom. She was exactly like the girl in all my dreams. Even the green gown with the light-flowered stomacher was one she had worn.

I choked out just one word, "Ladybeth."

Then a wave of nausea passed over me, and I kicked at a hassock with one foot to bring it close so I could slump down on it, eyes closed, till the nausea passed.

When I looked up again, she was still there, smiling at me all-knowingly from her portrait. Ladybeth by Ladybeth.

I jumped up and ran to the canvas to confirm the little sprawled signature in the corner. Yes, Ladybeth. The best damn portrait I had ever painted, and no one could ever see it but me. No one could ever know. Mine may have been the hand, but hers was the guiding spirit.

"Come back!" I cried passionately aloud to the man in gray. "I need to know more."

I waited, but when did he ever come to my command?

I waited, and the wings beat round me again, so loud and so fiercely this time that I huddled on the hassock with my arms over my head, rocking back and forth . . . back and forth . . . back and forth . . .

Chapter 32

THE NIGHT BEFORE THE WEDDING, THE RESPECTABLE
Mrs. Fielding and Lady Beth Crozier sat down alone to
supper in the kitchen. For each of them an old life was
ending and a new one beginning, a prospect which kept
the two unwontedly silent.

Chicken with dumplings was a favorite dish of both,
but neither had much appetite when their plates were
set before them.

"Ruthanna"—Ladybeth came out of a deep reverie
—"I've arranged that the rental money for the house
shall come to you so long as I am in England."

"You didn't have to do anything so foolish." Mrs.
Fielding's ladylike voice trembled and broke. "You've
given me enough—all my clothes and linens and the
extra house furnishings, and two hundred pounds besides, so I wouldn't have to—to go to him empty-
handed."

"Ruthanna," asked Ladybeth softly, "what's troubling you?"

"We've been together a long time now."

"I know," said the younger woman, reaching across to take one of the older one's roughened hands. "And I shall miss you dreadfully. But it's something more, isn't it?"

"It don't seem right," Ruthanna half-moaned. "Mr. Ver Loop thinks he's getting a worthy widow woman, but—"

"Well, so he is," Ladybeth interrupted sharply. "There's no reason this side of heaven for him to find out any different."

Ruthanna covered her face with her hands. "He would never be a-marrying me if he knew the truth."

"Ruthanna." Ladybeth smacked her own hand down on the table. "He is *not* going to find out."

"It's wrong to cheat such a good man. I feel like I ought to do right and tell him."

"You'll do no such thing!" Ladybeth shouted. "After tonight it will never again be mentioned anywhere outside this room."

Ruthanna wiped her eyes with the edge of her muslin apron. "I'll have it on my conscience all my life."

"Good. On your conscience is where it belongs. Let it stay there." When a prolonged sniff was all she got by way of answer, she added persuasively, "Ruthanna, tell me, would you call Mr. Ver Loop a man of—er—strong passions?"

Ruthanna said with dignity, "Mr. Ver Loop has always been a perfect gentleman to me."

Ladybeth laughed out loud. "That's not what I asked, and you know it." She grinned impudently. "Are you looking forward to your wedding night, Ruthanna?"

Somber brown eyes stared starkly into sparkling gray.

"Like I'd never known a man before. Would to God I never had!"

Ladybeth leaned back in her chair and said reflectively, "Mr. Ver Loop's been a widow man, how long now? Two years? Three? Four? Do you think he's been celibate all that time?"

Ruthanna drew herself ramrod straight, her mouth primmed up. "It's not for me to know."

"Do you care?"

"What's past is past and has naught to do with me."

"Then you don't expect any confessions from him or apologies for the past?"

"Certainly not. He's a good man, I'll take him as he is."

Ladybeth jumped up and ran to kiss Ruthanna's cheek. "See?" she cried jubilantly. "You've answered all your own doubts. Just take it in reverse. It's not for him to know what's in your past. It has naught to do with him. There's no need for apologies or confessions. You're a good woman, and he must take you as you are."

The reflection of the candles shone in Ruthanna's happy eyes.

"You have your father's knack of making difficult things seem simple. Thank you, Ladybeth. I will remember."

"See that you do. I'll be miserable over there in England if you're not happy here on Bowling Green."

Ruthanna said wisely, giving Ladybeth a great hug. "Miserable? You? Not likely. One way or another, you'll find your happiness. But just take care, Ladybeth, over there in London among strangers . . . don't put yourself in danger."

"As though I would," Ladybeth protested, and then, catching Ruthanna's skeptically lifted eyebrows, smiled a rueful acknowledgment. "Very well then. I will take care. How did you know?"

"That you would not stop working for the American cause? Credit me with having my wits about me," Ruthanna scoffed. "And Mr. De Croix, poor man, does he really believe he and I talked some sense into you?"

Three weeks later, aboard the packet *Nancy,* a fortnight into a stormy New York–to–London crossing, Bay De Croix answered the same question.

They were walking about the deck together in one of the rare lulls between storms. Her arm was firmly tucked in his to anchor her down, and the wind whipped bright color into her cheeks, while occasional gusts sent her skirts flying almost to her knees.

"Will you ever tell me the truth about what magic Mrs. Fielding used to induce you to come home to England with me without my having to invoke the law?"

"Why, Bay." She opened her eyes wide at him, even as she remembered, *You have no choice, madam . . .* and wrists held firm. *Well, lass, will you serve us still?* and five white handkerchiefs dancing on a laundry line. "'Twas your own persuasive arts induced me, with a threat or two thrown in, if you recall."

"I wish I could flatter myself you were that much in awe of me. I cannot. You were as greatly intimidated by my threats as Captain Dillon by those six-foot waves of yesterday's storm."

She laughed deep in her throat. "It is my observation," she said provocatively, "that Captain Dillon enjoys a good storm. He seems to regard each one we encounter as a personal challenge."

"Exactly," he murmured, and once again her laughter was carried away on the wind.

He tightened his grip on her arm as the gusts got wilder and the deck heaved under their feet. "We had best go down to the cabin."

"I think so," she gasped, the wind at their backs sending them scurrying.

In the parlor cabin, he hung her cloak over a chairback and warmed her chilled hands between his so naturally she felt no embarrassment at all. It had become a habit of his after their daily walks.

She sighed deeply, looking at the sparse bookshelves. "I wish my library was not packed away in the hold," she said wistfully. "With so few books, if the weather continues like this, the next month or so is likely to be boring."

He bowed. "Thank you for that charming testimonial, Lady Beth."

"Oh, do not be provoking. You know what I mean. One cannot talk *all* day, and I am not accustomed to being idle. If only I could paint. How I would love to do studies of the sailors."

"Captain Dillon tells me it does not always storm this time of year. Perhaps there may be calm enough later on for you to essay some painting."

"I hope so." She sat, chin in hand, reflecting. "Tell me about my grandmother."

"I met her once when I was a child and again just before I came to America. I remembered her as beautiful and smelling of violets. Her scent is the same, and she can still claim traces of beauty."

"Do I resemble her at all?"

"You take more after your grandfather's family. I

noted the first time I saw you a number of features from the Crozier side: the forehead and nose and"—he smiled slightly—"the stubborn chin."

The "stubborn chin" jerked up as he continued. "Your eyes you must get from your mother. I have never seen their like in any Shirley portrait."

"They are my mother's eyes," she acknowledged quietly. "I am much more my mother's daughter than I appear."

"I think that you are perhaps uniquely yourself, Ladybeth."

She bowed her head ever so slightly in more of a gracious, queenly quality than she was aware.

When she raised her head, she became conscious of his steady, intent gaze, of a little light flickering in his pupils that set her pulses fluttering erratically.

She half-turned away from him. "Tell me about the earl," she said in a dry, husky voice hardly recognizable as her own.

"The old earl, your grandfather? I hardly knew him. You must remember, Ladybeth, that I was such a remote connection, there was very little intercourse between our branches of the family. I come from Sussex, and my family was seldom bid to Shirley Manor, the earl's main seat. When I left Eton to enter the army, on my way to join my regiment I was invited to spend two nights in London at Shirley House."

"Did you meet the present earl?"

"I am afraid he was not invited any more often than I."

"A most warm and hospitable family. Will my welcome, think you, be equally generous?"

"You must leave your prejudices behind you." It was kindly said but an unmistakable rebuke. "The warmth of your welcome is not in any doubt. The earl need not have sent for you unless he truly wished you to come. He was assured that you were not in want."

"I thank him for nothing!" she flashed.

"He was a child when the family estrangement occurred," he told her, suddenly irritable. "You are unreasonable."

She answered with six words she had learned just the day before from a sailor on the lower deck who had dropped a wooden bucket on his foot.

Bay De Croix stood stock-still, his eyes incredulous, his nostrils flaring. "What did you say?"

She started to repeat the words, saw the expression on his face, and with belated prudence retreated two steps back from him.

He followed after her and seized her by both arms. "Do you have any idea at all what you just said?"

"None at all." She smiled sunnily. "But it sounded so powerful, I just could not resist."

"I can't resist *this,*" he said with perfect good humor, and gave her a couple of healthy shakes. "Never say that again," he admonished as he let her go. "It's more powerful than you imagine."

She swept him a deep curtsey. "I shall endeavor to be a perfect English lady, Bay," she answered blithely from her half-kneeling position.

He went to lift her up. "I think," he said ruefully, "I prefer my little American portrait painter. English ladies seem all to be poured out of the same mold. It is hard sometimes to tell one from the other."

"Little American savage you called me once, I believe."

"Even so."

"You deplored my temper tantrums."

"I still do."

"You think the earl will be able to control me."

"I fancy he will. He is said to have the family chin."

The "family chin" jerked up again. "Would you care to make a wager about that?" she asked in a voice of silk.

"No," he said. "No wagers. I have not the guineas to lose. Right now my only wager would be that, at twenty-five guineas a full-length portrait, so far as hard cash goes, you are at this precise moment the wealthier of the two of us aboard this ship."

He continued to stare at her, at first pensive and then brooding.

"What are you thinking of, Bay?" she asked him softly.

"That there is something else I do not intend to resist."

With the words, she was once again taken by her shoulders, but this time he scooped her a few inches off the creaking floor only to yank her into a hard embrace. One arm banded her shoulders, the other her waist, and his mouth took firm possession of her lips.

Presently he lifted his head. "You have never been kissed?"

"Not like this."

He laughed softly. "Well, my little one. Allow me to teach you how."

"Put me down then."

The instant he did, her arms went around his neck. As she pressed hard against his chest, she smiled up into darkening eyes. "Teach again," she invited once again, raising her lips to his.

Chapter 33

BAY GRINNED LAZILY AND RATHER POSSESSIVELY across at her, as they sat on the upper deck together, enjoying a rare hour of cloudless, breezy weather, with now and then a moment of sunshine.

"I never had occasion to study the mating habits of the Americans," he said almost idly, "but in England it is still the custom to approach the head of the family about marrying, and it is legally necessary to ask a guardian for his ward's hand. Luckily, since the earl occupies both positions, I need make only one appeal."

"Are you proposing marriage again, Bay?"

"It surely cannot come as a surprise to you, little one."

"Well—"

Her voice was dubious. He stood up and over her. "Did you think it was my custom to teach all lovely young ladies how to kiss?"

"I'm the only *young* and *lovely* lady on board," she pointed out.

He crossed his arms and looked at her in some amusement. "Have you such little faith in your charms," he asked, "as to believe it is your exclusive availability on shipboard that prompts my attentions?"

"Having only so recently joined the British aristocracy," she replied sweetly, "I would express it a bit differently."

"To wit?"

"There's an old saying we have at home, 'A potato in the cooking pot is better than a pig in the marketplace.'"

"That"—he eyed her coldly—"is an extremely vulgar remark."

"And I"—she returned his frosty glance indifferently —"am just a vulgar American girl. I suppose," she added thoughtfully, "I should be grateful that you have stooped so low as to overlook my origins. Or is it that in England the name Lady Elizabeth Crozier carries social standing? To say nothing of my dowry?"

He unfolded his long length from the wooden seat to pull her up out of her identical chair, compelling her to meet his angry eyes. "You forget I am a member of the family, too, so my social standing compares to the Lady Elizabeth's. I may belong to the poorer branch, ma'am, but not so poor I need your damned ten thousand pounds."

She said demurely, not the least dismayed by his temper, "Then why, sir, do you wish to marry me?"

"Hellcat!" He snatched her to him and flattened her lips with his kiss. Lifting his head, he smiled with satisfaction at the limpness of her body in his arms and the dreamy, slumbrous sexiness of her expression. "I love you," he muttered against her throat. "God help me, witch-woman, I love you."

"Now that," she said, sweetly reasonable once she recovered her breath, "is a reason that appeals to me. It's a pity that I had to drag the admission out of you."

"Was *that* what all the provocation was about?"

"Aye, aye, sir."

"I had not thought you so dull-witted, my lady. My love for you was obvious from the first day we met. Even the first minutes. Certainly Mrs. Fielding . . . Mrs. Ver Loop, I should say, perceived it."

"How lovely," she sighed, her upturned mouth inviting repetition.

He pushed her back from him.

"No," he said decidedly. "No more rewards for you until *I* have mine."

"I thought you had already had it."

"Not quite. I asked you a question, and I made you a declaration. I haven't yet received one in return."

"I love you . . . I think," she said almost in a whisper, looking out to sea rather than at him, ashamed of the spoken half-truth that made her declaration a half-lie.

She was aware, if he was not, that she loved him with a passion fierce enough to consume them both, but she was not free to make either him or herself that happy. She had given her word to Mulligan, who had pledged to convey it to Gen. Washington, that she would serve the interests of her country in England in whatever way she could and at whatever cost!

"You only think?" His hand gentled her hair and the back of her neck. His smile broadened as he felt her tremble.

"You see"—She turned her head and managed to make her tone sound apologetic—"I have never before loved anyone except for my family, my c-country, and Ruthanna." She added quite smilingly, "Oh yes, and once, for three whole days a farmer's son in the Hampshire Grants. It is a bit difficult for me, this business of giving one's heart away."

He frowned a little, continuing to stroke her hair gently. "Most of the time, you are so sturdily independent," he said, "I forget about your inexperience." The frown lightened. "Especially in view of your somewhat passionate nature."

She jumped a little at what seemed almost a reading of her mind. "Am I truly passionate?" she asked with pretended naïveté, and he gave a great shout of laughter.

"Very naturally and unashamedly so, thank God. Tell me about the farmer's son in the whatever-grants."

"Hampshire." She laughed happily, too, gladly done with being serious. "He gave me all the best apples from his father's orchard. I ate six and suffered terrible stomach pains. I did a pen and ink sketch of the prize hog he was raising. It nearly broke my heart when we had to move on to Massachusetts."

"And you have never forgotten him?"

"How could I—when he was my only love?" She added dreamily, seeing the slight rigidity of his expression, "He was fourteen, and I was all of eleven."

He gave another shout of laughter and caught her to him. "Your only love?" he demanded.

"Till you," she whispered, surrendering herself recklessly to his arms to receive her just reward.

Some time later when the winds once again drove them down to the parlor cabin, he asked as he chafed her chilled hands, "You will marry me, won't you, Ladybeth, as soon as possible after we come to England?"

He said it in a casual, proprietary way that proved to be her undoing. It brought home to her as nothing had done before why she was there on the packet *Nancy,* the ostensible reason that she was bound for England. God forgive her, she had gotten so wrapped up in her love as to almost forget her mission!

"Ladybeth!" His tone sharpened. He seemed to sense her qualms and doubts, though not her motive. Dear God, she reminded herself, he must never know that. He might no longer be an officer in his Majesty's service, but still he was an Englishman, with all the casual certainty and arrogance of the breed.

Their hearts might not be at war, but their countries were. Her own unswerving vow of allegiance had been given to Hercules Mulligan in the name of the thirteen new states. His was just as certainly devoted to the imperious little island across the seas from America.

Seeing his intent and once more frowning gaze as she pushed away from him, she said hurriedly, trying to buy some time to marshal her thoughts, "I am not yet one-and-twenty. Did you not say the earl must give his consent?"

"Lack of consent did not stop your parents." His hands slid along her arms and then with exquisitely pleasurable insolence over the fullness of her breasts and slowly downward till they gripped her waist. "It would not stop me."

After a moment of silence, he addressed her bowed head. "Would it stop you, my love?"

It was agony to draw away from the seeking hands.

"Not if—" Under his unnerving gaze, she bit her lips and began again. "If I were sure . . ."

"What are you unsure of?" His face became a mask, his voice turned cold.

Impulsively her fingers touched his sleeve.

"Not of you, my love, but . . ."

After another short, unhappy silence, she spoke up calmly, quietly, and with renewed courage.

"I cannot commit myself to England, sight unseen. As a nation, it is the enemy of my people. For a lifetime, I do not know if I may be at home there. As to family, it holds only two for me, and both of them threw off my parents and sentenced them to exile."

He drew her into his arms again, dealing judiciously with each of her objections. "As to the war between our countries, it has nothing to do with us. You will be amazed, my dearest, to discover how many Englishmen, high-born and low, are sympathetic to the American cause. On the personal side, my darling, I had thought that you were rather committing yourself to *me* than to England. I had hoped that where I would settle could be home for you. Our families will be one now; cannot the past be forgiven?"

"Could you give up *your* roots, *your* past so easily? Let us suppose that I said, 'Bay De Croix, will you leave England for America? For love of me, will you give up your home, your country, your customs, and take mine instead?' *Would* you, *could* you then settle across the broad ocean without a backward thought or look?"

He felt his way with caution. "Such sacrifice is customary," he began, only to be interrupted.

"Customary?" she asked, no longer needing to pretend to doubts. "Customary?" she repeated, genuinely aflame at such commonplace masculine logic, the injustice of the sacrifice he thought it only natural to demand of her. "If you expect *me* always to do what is customary," she said disdainfully, "then, indeed, Bay, you have chosen to love the wrong woman, and I"—she turned away abruptly to look out to sea—"and I to love the wrong man."

More heartened by her last giveaway words than by anything that had gone before, he asked her quietly, "What are you saying, Ladybeth?"

His question once again reminded her of her role, which too often, she told herself, she forgot. Aboard ship, as well as in England, she must make her precarious way along the tightrope that seemed to be extended between her love for Bay and her obligation to serve America.

She looked up at him from under her lashes, a flirtatious, un-Ladybeth look. "I did come with you, Bay," she said saucily. "I came in dutiful obedience because the earl, my guardian, ordered me to."

As his own brows lifted, first one and then the other, to tell her how skeptically he regarded this last bit of piety, she allowed herself to become serious again, to explain carefully, "I do not adhere to the notion that if sacrifice is to be made, the woman must make it all, and that the man must inevitably have his way. Are not my sentiments and emotions as much involved as your own? Are they not to be accorded equal concern?"

"Would you separate from me forever for the principle of showing that a woman's rights are no less than a man's?"

"Would *you* to show the reverse?" she countered swiftly.

"My real competition is, after all, your country," he said more truly than he knew. "So we reach an impasse." His tone was light, but the laughter had gone from his eyes.

"Not really," she relented, feeling herself already tottering on the edge of the rope. "Bay, dear Bay, all I ask of you is time. Let me accustom myself both to England and my new position. Let me make the acquaintance of my family and enter into your society so that I may see if it is possible for me to tolerate either or both."

As his face lightened, so did hers.

"Who knows?" she went on airily. "I may enjoy England so much I will never wish to return to the primitive society I have known."

Then she pressed close against him, allowing him to see her wistful eyes and drooping mouth. "I love you, Bay, and I would not wish to be unreasonable, but neither do I believe I am asking too much."

"I love you, too, my Ladybeth, and I don't wish to wait for you. If the choice were left to me, I would call the commander down from his quarterdeck to marry us this minute; but no, my love, though it goes sadly against my inclination to admit it, your request is not unreasonable."

Chapter 34

It was impossible to go on holding a grudge against that fading beauty, her grandmother, the Lady Elizabeth Crozier.

From the moment that she cried "My beloved Edmund's daughter and my own dear namesake," dabbing with a lace handkerchief at the tears raining prettily down her cheeks, Ladybeth accepted her for what she was—shallow, empty-headed, lovable, charming.

They spent two weeks in London replenishing Ladybeth's wardrobe, Lady Elizabeth having consigned her trunks to the attic with the comment that they contained not one garment fit for her granddaughter to wear in public.

She was peculiarly unconscious of the possibility of inflicting any hurt with this frank comment. Like a child, she said whatever came into her head, without regard to its effect on her listeners.

Ladybeth accepted the wardrobe that had been decreed by both Lady Elizabeth and the new earl, knowing if she were to be of any use in gathering information among the aristocracy, then she must by all means be suitably gowned.

Nevertheless, she was overjoyed to have the two weeks of incessant shopping and wearying fittings finally finished with and to be on her way to Shirley Manor to meet the earl.

As the well-sprung, comfortable carriage took the road out of London, she settled herself against the cushions with a wriggle of delight, asking her grandmother not for the first time, "Is it certain Bay will be there on our arrival?"

"Oh, I am sure . . . or very soon . . . he did say he would . . . I'm sure we can count on him," fluttered Lady Elizabeth.

Ladybeth sighed and stared out through the window, hoping these vague twitterings meant yes.

She missed Bay. She had missed him unbearably from the moment that he left her. The day after their arrival in England he had gone into Sussex to visit his own family and to allow her time alone to make her grandmother's acquaintance.

It had been time and enough. Her grandmother was a dear, but there was just so much conversation that could be devoted to gowns, shoe-roses, and reticules.

She had hoped to learn about her father as a boy, but questions about Edmund more often than not produced the smiling answer, "Nurse would have remembered, but she's been dead, poor thing, these eight years and more."

Comments about their life in America elicited a deep sigh and a "Dear Edmund, how handsome he was, how obliging, he could turn such a pretty compliment. I missed him so when he left us to go to those horrid colonies."

Her grandmother's conversation, she decided reluctantly, when it turned from salacious gossip, had about as much interest as the rattle of the chaise wheels.

Certainly it contained nothing worthy of being written to Benjamin Franklin in Paris.

"Bay, my beloved Bay," she mouthed silently, pressing her lips against the cold window of the carriage, "please be there, waiting."

As her grandmother chattered on of balls and beaux and frocks and flowers, Ladybeth wrestled silently in her mind with another problem.

If indeed Bay was at the manor waiting for her, how was she going to be able to steel herself to resist his pleas for a speedy marriage? Or, indeed, must she do so?

The small, easily silenced voice of her conscience said it would be a shameful thing to marry a man and work behind his back against his country. The much louder voice of desire kept tempting her with memories of his strong hands and kisses, and afterward the wicked light in his eyes when he looked at her with the full knowledge of how his touch had roused her.

Remembering, she shivered and sighed, and her grandmother, in complete misunderstanding, patted her hand and comforted her. "I know, dearest Beth. I find traveling vastly wearying, too, but 'tis just a few more miles, and Shirley has excellent chimneys. There will be a blazing fire in your chamber and no smoke either. And perhaps we can have old William send you up a glass of brandy—just for medicinal purposes."

"Who is old William?" Ladybeth asked idly, smiling a bit to contemplate her grandmother's horror if she should say that her blood and body were almost too hot right now rather than cold.

"The butler, dear, of course. He was here at Shirley when I came as a bride."

"Then he'll remember my father?" said Ladybeth with quickened interest.

"Of course, Beth. Everyone at Shirley remembers Edmund. The old retainers, that is, like Mrs. Nesbit, our housekeeper, and Harley and . . . let me see, yes, James. Bakersfield in the stables . . . he taught him to ride. Mrs. Nesbit's granddaughter Lucy is going to be your maid."

"My maid! Do I need a special maid in a house so full of servants?"

Lady Elizabeth stared at her in horrified amazement. "You did not have a lady's maid of your own in America?"

"But grandmother"—she could not keep back the laughter bubbling up inside her—"in America, till just toward the end, I was not a lady. I was a painter. I earned my living, as my father did, painting portraits and murals."

Her grandmother pressed one hand against her heart and with the other employed a confection of ivory and lace to fan herself most vigorously. "Never tell me you had no servants!" she implored.

Ladybeth thought amusedly it was the tone someone might have used to cry out against the commission of a dread crime.

"We always had someone to do the rough work," she admitted, "and then with Ruthanna as house-keeper . . ."

"Thank God!" Lady Elizabeth interrupted, sniffing at her vinaigrette.

In view of this pious pronouncement and the attitude it conveyed, Ladybeth decided against enlarging on Ruthanna's special status as her chosen friend and her father's former mistress.

She wondered idly what her grandmother would have said about Ruthanna's special relationship with Lady Elizabeth's "beloved Edmund." One thing her two weeks in London had taught her was that Lady Elizabeth had not always been so straight-laced.

"None so straight-laced as a reformed rake," her father used to say. She wondered if he had known the truth about his own mother and decided rather sadly that he had.

"We are on Shirley land now," her grandmother's voice interrupted her wandering thoughts. She looked up eagerly and shook off her melancholy. After another moment, Lady Elizabeth told her, "The house is just over the rise."

Ladybeth looked eagerly out the carriage window and in a few moments beheld an imposing and handsome stone building, half-covered in ivy and standing on an eminence all surrounded by trees and woods.

In the distant fields several horsemen had put their mounts to a gallop. One of them seemed to wheel about at the sound of the carriage, pull up his horse, and head back the way he had come.

Was it just her foolish, lovesick fancy that the form of the turnabout rider seemed to be Bay's? She must not be so ridiculous, Ladybeth scolded herself, and as punishment leaned back so she could no longer see the horseman.

All was bustle and confusion when the carriage arrived in the driveway of the house. The coachman pulled down the steps, and old William himself hurried out to lend her grandmother escort while Mrs. Nesbit led Ladybeth into the house, shedding copious tears.

"I can't believe it after all these years," she sobbed enjoyably. "Mr. Edmund's own daughter come back to us."

Though feeling not the least bit tired or incapacitated but eager to be shown over the house, introduced to the earl, and—yes, most of all, damn his eyes!—discover if Bay was yet on the premises, Ladybeth allowed herself to be led tenderly upstairs to rest and recruit her strength.

Lucy, her lady's maid, was there, equally eager to unpack her wardrobe or divest her of her clothes and bathe her in the big tub of hot water being prepared by two shyly smiling maids.

Ladybeth recoiled from the notion of being undressed and bathed like an infant. "You may unpack for me a little later," she said firmly. "I will bathe and dress myself."

They all looked scandalized but had no choice except to obey when she firmly shooed them out of her room.

Ladybeth looked around in wonder at a chamber which would have housed a regiment, and then at the bed, with its hangings and coverlet of blue silk, which could have slept a large family.

She ran to the huge, floor-length windows and looked out. More woods and between two rows of trees, a swelling stream meandering down a rocky incline, conveying the impression of a succession of small waterfalls.

It's beautiful! she thought, and wondered with a pang if it had been hard for her father to leave all this behind.

Had he not done for Deborah what Bay wanted her

to do for him? But then, she reminded herself, my mother sacrificed home and family, too.

She undressed and soaked till the water in the tub began to cool. Just as she was wrapping herself in a huge towel, Lucy returned and at once began rubbing her briskly.

Then she led Ladybeth to the dressing table, where she sat her down and proceeded to arrange her hair.

After a bit of a struggle, Ladybeth was permitted to put on her own stockings and undergarments. Lucy helped her into her petticoats and buttoned up one of the new gowns, a green silk with flowers brocaded in velvet.

Her grandmother had bestowed a number of pretty ornaments on her, including a fine string of pearls and several gold pendants and diamond earrings. But when Lucy's hands hovered over her jewel case, Ladybeth shook her head.

"I will wear only this," she said decidedly, and took Deborah's star from her dressing table and, with her own hands, fastened it around her neck.

She descended the staircase and looked about the great hall helplessly, uncertain which way to go.

"My Lady Beth." William came toward her with slow stateliness. "Tea is being served in the small drawing room. The earl asks that you join him there."

"Thank you, William."

She followed behind him meekly till a door was flung open.

"My lord," William quavered, "the Lady Beth is here."

For a moment as she stepped forward the bright rays of the descending sun, streaking into the room from four long windows, obscured her vision. She could see at the far corner of the room the table all set for tea.

The man standing up to greet her was garbed in silver gray silk breeches and a matching coat with pearl buttons that fit close to his fine figure. His brocade waistcoat was handsomely embroidered, and his cravat was edged in the finest lace, as were the ruffles of his shirt sleeves. His powdered wig was combed back simply and tied in a queue.

"My lord," Ladybeth acknowledged him and dipped in a modest curtsey. As she rose up, blinking her eyes against the sun's rays to make out his features, he came forward into the shadows of the room.

"My very dear Lady Beth," he murmured in the same moment that she saw his face and everything became quite clear to her.

Henry Bayard De Croix, seventh Earl of Shirley, smiled across at her with great and loving tenderness while the Lady Beth Crozier delivered her own message of devotion.

"You scheming British bastard!" she flung at him furiously.

Chapter 35

Two CUPS OF TEA, FIVE SMALL CREAM CAKES, AND half an hour of sound kissing had somewhat calmed Ladybeth.

"You must see," the earl pointed out, "that I had no choice."

"I don't see it at all," she replied untruthfully.

"Then you don't understand that the whole situation was as much a shock to me as it was to you. I had no idea that I had inherited till our first meeting when you told me both your father and brother were dead. Mine was a very distant branch of the family, still bearing the original name De Croix rather than the anglicized Crozier. There had always been so many sons in direct line of descent, with the possibility of grandsons, I had never dreamed that Shirley and the earldom would come to me."

"But why did you not tell me then?"

"With you so antagonistic? Impossible. I sent word back to England about the changed status of the two of us, but I had no intention of telling you. I was too fearful if you discovered *I* were the earl, there would be no way—law or no law—that I could drag you back to England with me." He smiled possessively. "And I had already determined that if I were to be the earl, then you must be my lady."

She helped herself to another cake, while her mind raced furiously with teeming thoughts of the possible changes this might make in her mission. She was infuriated to find that uppermost in her thoughts was the question she asked with studied nonchalance. "Did you really fall in love with me at that first meeting?"

"I really did," he said, smiling into her eyes, then added blandly, "I can't imagine why. For a more fiery, hostile hoyden I had never before encountered."

As she choked on her sixth cake, she heard a soft query. "Would you be so kind as to tell me when your own affections were first engaged? You gave me so little hope before we sailed."

She looked down at her clasped hands. "To a woman it would have been obvious."

He reached out and plucked her up out of her seat, right across the tea table, and onto his lap.

"But since I am not a woman, and you—thank God!—*are*, then I insist that you tell me." He shook her slightly for added emphasis.

"Very well then, my lord." She flung her arms about him. "If you must know, I realized you had my heart when you agreed to give me twenty-five guineas for a full-length portrait." She pretended to scowl. "If I had known you were the earl, I swear I would have charged you fifty."

"My love," he reminded her, "I am prepared to give you much more than fifty. You know it is my heart's desire to endow you with *all* my worldly goods."

She answered by turning in his arms, squirming deeper into his lap, and offering him her eager mouth. They were still rapturously entwined when Lady Elizabeth entered the room.

"Good God!" she cried, fanning herself. "Upon my word. Very pretty behavior, I must say."

Ladybeth slid off Bay's lap and onto the floor and faced her grandmother, unabashed.

"These free and easy American ways will not do!" she was told severely.

Lady Elizabeth confronted the earl. "Bay, as her guardian, you should know this is no way to behave. You had better marry the girl."

"I intend to, ma'am."

Lady Elizabeth clapped her hands together like a schoolgirl. "Oh, excellent. It is what I have wanted to contrive ever since she came to me."

"It took no contrivance of yours, Lady Elizabeth," he told her good-humoredly. "It is what I have wanted to contrive myself since the first time I saw her."

Lady Elizabeth could barely wait for the finish of this speech to issue all her plans. "We can announce your betrothal at her come-out ball in Shirley House . . . and the wedding can be at St. George's in . . . let us say, three months' time. I will need at least that long to arrange her trousseau. As for the honeymoon—"

"No, no, please, I beg you, ma'am," he interrupted laughingly. "At least allow me the privilege of arranging my own honeymoon."

"And me my own wedding," Ladybeth added, much alarmed by the speed with which things were getting out of hand. "I am sorry, Grandmother, but there will be no betrothal"—she cast a quick sideways look at the earl and amended—"no *formal* betrothal, that is, for the present. I am—I am—we are not planning to be wed just yet."

"Indeed!" Lady Elizabeth said icily. "What are you waiting for?"

Ladybeth cast another rather desperate look at the earl, who gave her no help at all but stood, head bent, with abstracted air, contemplating his jeweled snuff box.

"W-we w-would like to b-be better ac-quainted," she stammered out.

"Indeed!" said Lady Elizabeth again, her voice, if possible, even frostier. "By what I saw when I entered the room, you already appear to be very well acquainted. Almost too well, I would say."

"That is my affair, ma'am."

What else she might have answered remained unsaid. The earl spoke her name just once, checking whatever other impetuous words were on her tongue.

Then he smiled his own particular winning smile at Lady Elizabeth. "She has been raised in America, ma'am. Her ways are not our ways. It would be unreasonable of us to expect otherwise. I think we must give her the time she needs. Be easy, my lady. The marriage will take place."

"Just so that it takes place in time, Shirley," Lady Elizabeth returned snappishly. "I want no counting on fingers when your heir is born."

Before Ladybeth could open her mouth, the earl said coldly to her grandmother, "Your comment was unnecessary, ma'am, as well as crude. The honor of the Crozier name," he continued smoothly, "is as safe in our hands as ever it was in yours."

To Ladybeth's surprise, dull red color crept into Lady

Elizabeth's painted cheeks, making the rouge stand out like patches. Instantly Ladybeth was contrite.

"I'm sorry, grandmother," she cried, taking the older woman's hand. "I'm afraid I have a very quick temper. If it pleases you," she promised mischievously, "I will agree not to kiss Bay any more."

"But it would not please Bay," the earl announced firmly, "so kindly don't be so generous with your promises."

Solicitously, he showed Lady Elizabeth to a chair. "Would you prefer tea, ma'am, or a glass of wine?"

Lady Elizabeth accepted a glass of wine, and while he went to pour it, Ladybeth studied him thoughtfully. Lady Elizabeth's strictures had produced in her undutiful granddaughter exactly the opposite effect of the one she desired.

Bay wanted her kisses . . . he wanted *her!* This, perhaps, was one way in which she need not cheat him. She must think on it, she decided, even as they discussed plans for the future.

It was the earl's decision that they enjoy a quiet week at Shirley Manor before returning to London to deal with the attorneys for the name change and the transfer of the estate.

"Why must you change your name?" puzzled Ladybeth.

"Whenever a De Croix inherits—it has happened twice before in the last several hundred years—he takes the English version of the name, thus making it easier for you, my love."

"I don't understand how it affects me."

"You were born a Crozier," he explained gently, "so when you wed me, you will not have to change your name. Only *I* am obliged to do so. I would think, knowing your dear, devious mind, that this should please you greatly."

This only-too-accurate description left Ladybeth momentarily tongue-tied. If he only knew . . . if he should ever learn just how dear and devious her mind not only *was* but *must* be.

How was she ever going to learn to live with this constant internal warfare between love and inclination on one side and hate and another kind of inclination on the other?

She was not just walking the tightrope, Bay kept constantly shaking it. Oh God, if they could only, the two of them together, take hands and say *A plague on both our countries!* and then search out an island somewhere whose people had never even heard of England or America.

But the world was not an island, it kept intruding. She could no more be indifferent to what happened at home than Bay could be to the fate of England.

Casting about for a new topic of conversation, she asked quickly, "What shall we do in London?"

"I, for one, shall enter the Lords."

Think, Lady Beth, you would be the cousin of an earl, not mingling with the common soldiers anymore but with all manner of grand folks, lords and ladies and the like. English politicians . . .

"I should love to attend a meeting of the House of Lords," she enthused. "The Commons, too. And meet some of your great men." She raised limpidly innocent eyes to his, half-ashamed, half-amazed at her own skillful duplicity. "Will that be possible, do you think?"

"I daresay it can be arranged."

"Your Edmund Burke and Charles Fox are greatly admired in America."

His mouth quirked. "We appreciate their worth even over here, if we are not always in agreement with their sentiments."

"All sensible persons must recognize the truth of what they say," she told him hotly.

"Please." Lady Elizabeth held up her hands. "No more of politics. Such a boring subject."

"Whatever you wish, ma'am," Ladybeth agreed quietly, reflecting that perhaps it were better so. To talk overmuch of politics with Bay might not be expedient.

She opened her mouth to admire the beauty of the wood paneling over the fireplace as her grandmother suddenly demanded, "Is that the Hebrew star you wear?"

"The proper name is Star of David," answered Ladybeth quietly. "This one"—she held it up for Lady Elizabeth's inspection—"belonged to my mother."

Lady Elizabeth made a little moue of distaste. "It is to be hoped," she said piously, "you do not follow her faith."

Ladybeth's ironical glance included them both.

"I do not see why any such thing is to be hoped," she said. "There is, after all, as much Ben David blood in me as Crozier." She waited for further comment, but none was forthcoming. Her grandmother stirred restlessly while the earl treated her to a cold, hard stare that dared her to judge him.

She continued a shade less belligerently, "No, I do not follow my mother's faith, nor my father's either. In the name of religion, both families disowned their children for loving. God may be in His Heaven, but I do not look for Him in church or synagogue."

She was suddenly overwhelmed by the desire to return as speedily as possible to London. Her work and her duty lay there. Here in this beautiful manor, with these alien people—however beloved one of them—it would be all too easy to forget her primary obligation.

Chapter 36

A MESSAGE FROM THE STABLES ANNOUNCED THAT THE new mare on which she would be taught had been sent home from Tattersall's. Ladybeth immediately donned her smartly cut green habit, fresh from the dressmaker's, and walked around to the stables.

A groom brought out the mare for her inspection, supplied her with two lumps of sugar and some low-voiced instructions. After a time Ladybeth asked impatiently, "Cannot I mount her now?"

"I am sorry, Lady Beth, but the master gave strict orders that only he was to teach you."

In a much lower voice he added, "If you have any orders of your own, Lady Beth, I am your man."

She stared up at him, astonished, alarmed, and he whispered still more compellingly, "I know that you are to write direct to Franklin in Paris, but if ever there is need for more urgent communication, I will undertake to deliver your messages, written or verbal."

"I have been a month in England and done nothing at all," she whispered back forlornly. "With the exception of the earl, the men I have met thus far are foppish fools with no information to give me."

He smiled encouragingly. "Patience is the name of our game, ma'am. You must not be—" His voice changed, grew coarser and louder. "You will not find a better-tempered mare in any stable in England, my lady, take Tom Binkley's word for it."

"Thank you, Tom." She smiled graciously at the other groom who had come near to them. "I shall ride daily once the earl has taught me."

Under cover of accepting the coin she gave him, he winked at her. "Thankee ma'am, thankee very kindly. If I might just mention it, to call me Binkley would be more English."

"Thank you, Binkley."

The earl rode with her most days after that, but when he could not, Tom Binkley took his place.

"I feel utterly worthless," she confessed to him one morning as their horses moved sedately through the park. "I have attended balls and routs and teas and parties till I am sick to death of them, made calls, I vow, to every silly society woman in London. They hardly know a war is going on," she wound up bitterly. "What is of life and death importance to us is of no consequence at all to them."

"I think perhaps you are taking the wrong tack, Lady Beth."

"If you have any advice for me, I will be pleased to hear it. I grow desperate."

"You must not," he warned. "In desperation lies danger. No, it is my notion that you are mingling with the wrong people. You used your portraiture at home as a means to an end. Do it again. If it won't bring you

325

the generals and the politicians, it may still bring you their wives, almost as good a source. Mingle with writers and artists. They would be more profitable than society fops."

"Good God, but you're right!" she cried, unthinkingly tightening her hands on the rein. Tom Binkley reached out to protect her as her mare took a quick, nervous plunge.

"No, no, thank you, I have her under control, Binkley. Let us go home. I wish to see the earl."

"Bay," she announced to him at luncheon, grateful that her grandmother did not join them, "I am bored to tears. I cannot endure any more of this social routine."

He grinned across at her and helped himself to a lamb cutlet.

"I am surprised that you have endured it for so long."

"Oh, you beast!" she declared indignantly. "If you knew, why did you not say something and end my misery?"

"I thought it prudent to await your own decision." His eyes twinkled engagingly. "I knew full well you would not remain miserable for long. I was content to leave up to you what you wished to do and when you wished to do it. Has boredom by any chance moved you in the direction of marriage?"

She looked across at him, and even as she tried, she could not hide the love written plainly on her face.

"I cannot wed you out of boredom, beloved," she said clearly. It was an acceptable reason, if not the true one. "I wish to paint again. Painting has occupied the greater part of my life. I feel lost and useless without it."

As she said the words, she realized with something of

a shock that she was not engaged in her usual play-acting. What she had said was true. The hungry yearning to feel a paint brush in her hands and the joy of seeing pictures come to life on her canvas amounted almost to physical pain.

"What would you like to do?"

"I would like to rent a studio—out of the interest of my own money—and advertise, just as I did in New York, for those who would like their portraits painted by the Lady Beth Crozier."

"I am very much in favor of your painting. I would prefer that you did not advertise. Nay"—as she seemed about to object—"listen to me, my love. By word of mouth we can let it be known just as speedily as in any news sheet that your services as a portraitist are available. They will flock to you, believe me. As for your studio, there is no need to hire one outside. The old stables in the mews back of the house shall be converted to your use. I will call in an architect this very day to set the project in motion."

"Oh, Bay!" She cried out his name in love and longing, despising herself, as she always did at the times when his goodness and understanding overwhelmed her most with guilt and remorse.

"Why on earth are you crying?"

"Because you are so good to me," she said, meaning it with all her heart.

"It seems a peculiar reason, but then I have noticed that women incline to be somewhat peculiar."

"Not nearly so much as men," stated Ladybeth, wiping her eyes.

"A very quick recovery from your gratitude," he commented wryly. "Perhaps I should bid Mr. West not come to dinner with us after all."

"Mr. West?"

"Mr. Benjamin West, the American artist who has resided so long in London. He is unusually generous, I have been informed, in promoting the careers of promising young artists."

"I have been told so, too," said Ladybeth breathlessly. She forbore from mentioning that Mr. West's other claim to fame was his ability to keep the favor of the king despite his pronounced American sympathies.

"When is he to dine with us?" she asked.

"On Wednesday next, if it so pleases you."

"It pleases me greatly, my lord," she answered demurely.

Extract from letter originally written by Agent Lady Beth Crozier in England to Benjamin Franklin in Paris:

1776

I assure you, sir, that despite his long Years in London, Mr. West remains a steadfast Friend to America. He has procured me Introductions to notable People I might otherwise have had Difficulty in meeting, among them Mrs. Catherine Macaulay, whose Theme in her many-volumed History of England is that royal Rulers such as the present King have corrupted traditional British Liberties both here and in English Colonies. She does our cause infinite Good. I have obeyed Instructions given to me to make Friends among the Refugees here in London from America. There has not been as great an Influx of these Exiles into England as there was last Year (no doubt because of the British military Successes at Home) but they are enough in Numbers to be worth pursuing. I have found it expedient, in establishing Friendships among them, to maintain the Pose of being loyal to the British Side. My cousin's Rank makes this Position plausible. They speak most freely, and indeed show an Eagerness to cultivate me that cannot be wondered at in view of their own precarious Position. They are beset by financial Worries and much disappointed of the warm Welcome they expected to find here from the Ministry.

As soon as her maid was gone, Ladybeth ran to lock the door and bring her bedstand candle to her writing desk. Then she wrapped herself in a shawl and sat down to write.

Her fingers were stiff with cold, since her fire had been let die out, and she would not summon a footman with more logs. When Lucy had been sent away, she was already sliding down into a properly warmed bed, wearing one of the flannel nightdresses brought from America for shipboard.

Having finished her letter and sealed it, Ladybeth locked it away in the handsome jewel case, a gift from her grandmother, along with the Crozier pearls and several fine brooches and rings. She would slip it to Binkley when her horse was brought around for her morning ride with the earl, which had become an established habit.

With a sigh of relief, candlestick in hand, Ladybeth walked back toward her bed. Passing the largest of the three mirrors hanging in her room, she could not help laughing softly at the sight of herself. How Bay would laugh if he could see the fashionably dressed Lady Beth Crozier at this instant, in the unfashionable, unflattering drab gray flannel gown.

Instead of getting into her bed, Ladybeth perched on

top of it, tucking her chilled feet under the generous folds of flannel.

Bay! If only Bay could see her now . . . be with her now . . . alone as they had so often been in the studio in New York or on the *Nancy,* crossing the Atlantic. It wouldn't matter what she wore . . . or if . . . She drew in her breath and then suddenly expelled it on a great sigh, acknowledging honestly at last what was in her mind.

It would not matter greatly if she wore nothing at all. In truth, to wear nothing at all was her preferred choice. She wanted to be with Bay; she wanted to give him her love and receive his! She yearned as much as he did for more than public encounters and chaste kisses. She desired him as much as he desired her.

She wanted desperately (she, who while he was otherwise engaged, went through his desk papers and his private portfolio) to make amends to him in this one way at least for all the other ways in which she cheated him.

Although he had so innocently and so truly designated as "devious" the mind, which was dedicated to the service of America, her body at least was hers to use as she chose, to give, if she wished, to Bay.

She unlocked her door and set it slightly ajar while she brushed out her chestnut hair until it crackled and gleamed in the candlelight.

When she heard the sounds she had been awaiting, she walked catlike to the slightly open door and peeped out to confirm that Bay's batman Wilkerson, who was now his valet, was closing the door of the earl's apartment and walking down the long hallway, a coat over one arm and a pair of boots in his hand.

When Wilkerson disappeared up the stairs, Ladybeth

made her move, carefully closing the door of her own room behind her and running barefoot to the earl's, which she opened without knocking.

She had thought to find him in bed, but he was standing before his fire, looking a bit pensive. He was bare-chested and bootless but still wearing his breeches.

As he turned sharply, eyeing her in growing astonishment, Ladybeth closed the door.

"I—I came here," she began breathlessly, only to stop, uncertain how to proceed.

"You came here," the earl encouraged her obligingly, though the corners of his mouth quivered with the effort to keep from laughing. "Yes, I can see that, my lady," he told her solemnly. "You came here, perhaps, for a reason?"

Ladybeth glared at him in frustration. Since all his best efforts had failed, it was obvious that he was highly amused, which was not, she felt, providing the proper atmosphere for a romantic encounter.

"Really, Bay, it's not like you to be obtuse," she said to him crossly. "It must be obvious to anyone of the meanest intelligence that I came here to seduce you."

The earl's jaw dropped; he stared at her blankly for a few seconds. Then his shoulders shook; he bent over from the waist and started laughing so hard and so loudly that the panicked Ladybeth could only say, "Oh, hush! Someone is liable to be listening. Think of the fuss if I am found here!"

"No one will find you," said Bay, as he wiped his streaming eyes and moved quickly and quietly to lock the outside door and then the one that led to his dressing room.

"Seduction in a gray flannel gown," he told her, as he

came back to the fireplace, where she stood waiting with an air of quaint and touching dignity. He touched his fingertips to his mouth and tossed her an airy kiss. "In this, as in everything else, you are an original, my lady."

Ladybeth bit at her lip. Nothing had gone right, or at all the way she expected it to, and her mood had changed. What had seemed a wonderful notion when she was alone in her own room, in fact, the only proper culmination to their mutual love, now seemed the silly fancy of a lovesick schoolgirl.

No wonder he was laughing! Mortified, her face burningly hot, she fled on frozen feet to open the locked door. Her hand was already on the knob when she heard Bay's voice, sounding very much the earl.

"Do not dare even try to leave!" he warned her.

Slowly, reluctantly, Ladybeth let go of the knob and faced him once again.

"You said you were here to seduce me, Ladybeth," Bay remarked crisply. He folded his arms across the burnished red hair on his chest. "So be it. I demand to be seduced!" he insisted sternly.

Ladybeth saw the sparkling delight in his blue, blue eyes and the mischief on his quirkishly lifted mouth. She watched for his eyebrows to scale his forehead in his own unique fashion, first one and then the other.

She didn't care about his insistence and she had no more thought of resistance. Her insides were all melting into one great ball of fire, and it burned, oh how deliciously it burned for him!

Never taking her eyes from him, she undid the long row of buttons at the front of her gown and then untied the little sleeve bows. Finished at last, she pulled the gown over her head and tossed it at his feet.

"Is this more seductive?" asked Ladybeth, standing

naked before him, as though it were the most natural thing in the world.

Without any reply other than the leap of desire in his eyes, the earl stepped across the mound of gray flannel to snatch her irresistible bare body into his arms.

He held her high against him so that the curly, dark red hair of his chest tickled her breasts, while his hard mouth pressed down on hers, loving her, teaching her, telling her. Ladybeth kissed back with equal, if less expert ardor, loving him and learning from him with amazing speed and skill.

They kissed until Ladybeth lay limp against him and Bay's breath sounded as a series of gasps.

"What do we do next?" whispered Ladybeth, standing on his stockinged feet to warm her cold toes and still straining against him for pleasure as well as warmth. She was aware, from his own straining, that an extremely masculine variation of what was happening *inside* her appeared to be happening *outside* to him!

"You're the seducer," chuckled the earl. "Haven't you any bright ideas?"

"I thought we could g-get into b-bed. I'm so h-hot as w-well as so c-cold."

He put her away from him. His hands went down the length of her, incredibly impersonal this time. After taking her icy hands, he even bent to feel her frozen feet.

"You foolish child! You're a lump of ice!" he said as scoldingly as though it wasn't his own challenge that had caused her to remove the flannel gown. Reading her mind, "Have you never heard of slippers?" Bay asked, picking her up quite easily and tossing her across his left shoulder. Then he reached with his right hand for a copper warming pan standing near to the fire.

He strode over to his bed, with Ladybeth still slung

over his shoulder, her head hanging down his back and her bouncing bottom very much on view.

She wriggled a little at the indignity of it, and he growled out, "Keep still, you silly girl, I'm warming the bed for us, so you don't freeze before you are *properly* heated up."

It was hardly a loverlike statement, any more than she was in a loverlike position, but for some reason, the pretendedly grumbling tone and the feel of his one arm holding her and his one hand sliding along her legs made her feel supremely happy.

She stayed just as she was until Bay suddenly dumped her onto the lovely warm sheets and then tucked an even lovelier heap of blankets almost to her chin.

He stood next to the bed, looking down at her, while she lay, toastily content. There was passion in his face, and tenderness, too. It was the passion she craved most, but the loving tenderness almost undid her.

"I expect you to join me here," said Ladybeth with vast dignity.

"I was only waiting for your invitation," said the earl.

With a soldier's economy of movement, he stripped off his stockings and breeches. When he got to his smalls, in a sudden fit of modesty, Ladybeth turned her head away. A moment later she was sorry. She would really have liked to see if he was as splendid-looking below the waist as he was above.

Oh well, there would be other times to look . . .

She gasped as he took her into his arms and she felt for the first time the whole long, bare length of him against her just as bare, if shorter length.

"Oh, God! Oh, God! Oh, God!" she all but screamed a few minutes later.

His head came up from a kissing expedition. "Did I hurt you, Ladybeth?"

"No, it's w-wonderful, utter-ly wonderful. Are you . . . *Please,* are you seduced yet?"

"My lovely, luscious lunatic! I was seduced twenty minutes ago."

"Then do something. Do something. I'm dying!"

"No, you're not, Ladybeth, my Ladybeth, you're just beginning to live."

He was out of bed in a flash and back so soon she had time only for one little whimper at the pain of that momentary separation of flesh from flesh.

She felt flannel being tucked all the way under her and only vaguely understood why, being too caught up in the glory of feeling all of Bay over her, covering her, smothering her, loving her, and finally doing the "something" that her body had been crying out for.

Not just her body cried out; so, too, did she; and so, finally, at the end, did the earl. Then he lay inert upon her, his face nuzzled against her neck, while she put her arms around him, feeling suddenly all-knowing, all-powerful.

When she began to feel his weight and stirred a little, he lifted his head at once. "Am I too much for you?"

"I don't want you to leave me," she said mournfully, "but you're caving me in."

He laughed softly, and in a single quick movement, he was off her and over on his side, pulling her along with him, so that they remained firmly glued together.

"Did I hurt you, little one?" he whispered in her ear.

"I think perhaps you did, just a bit, but so many other important things were happening at the time, it didn't seem to matter at all."

"You're sure?"

"I'm sure." She gave a wriggle of contentment; her

335

laugh was a throaty purr. "I *liked* seducing you, Bay. I think we must try it again."

"If you keep on doing what you're doing, you're liable to seduce me again this very minute. Ladybeth, stop it! Ladybeth . . . don't! Ladybeth . . . Ladybeth . . . oh, what the hell! Go ahead, my lady, seduce me, if you must."

Mr. Franklin;
Since the man John Aitken (called in the British press, John the Painter) was hanged for his setting Fire to British Naval Yards, Americans in London are highly suspect. Because of my Position in Society, I have the good Fortune to be exempt from such Suspicion and can pursue my Activities, but I grieve to tell you that Ebenezer Platt is in a Prison Ship and charged with High Treason. We are all working for his Release. The Treasury has finally established a formal Pension List of annual Allowances to approximately one hundred of the Refugees. The standard Stipend is one hundred pounds, those of lesser Stature receiving forty to eighty. Needless to say, there is great Bitterness and Disillusionment among these unhappy People and not only in the Matter of Money. They resent the contemptuous Treatment they receive and their exclusion from Politickal and Social Importance.

Ladybeth had written her letter in the afternoon and then locked it away in her jewel case. She had retired rather earlier than usual and almost immediately sent Lucy away. Bay had been away for a week, and every night of the seven she had lain awake, longing for him, hungering for him. She had lived over and over again every moment of that wondrous night of love they had shared, from the moment she entered his room until the moment when he lovingly wrapped her in his silk dressing gown and carried her back to her own bed.

"I'll dispose of the gray flannel," he had whispered and, remembering the faint blood stains a lit candle had revealed, she had blushed a little and then looked up at him with loving unconcern. There was nothing, after all, to blush about.

"Thank you, Bay," she said simply.

"Thank *you*, my love, my life, my Ladybeth."

With one final passionless but sweetly tender kiss on her upturned face, he blew out her candle and left her alone in the dark.

The next day, an urgent message about a drainage problem at Shirley Manor had taken him away. But this afternoon, while she was painting in her studio, she was informed that he had arrived home.

Which was why she now sat in her bed in a white and silver-trimmed nightdress of such gossamer weave and such unvirginal cut that she might as well have worn nothing. Except that, looking at herself in the same mirror in which she had once laughed at her gray flannel, she had decided that the cobweb-fine garment, revealing the pale sheen of her skin, was (or at least for a minute or two might be) almost as exciting as though she were to greet him bare.

That he would come to her she had not the slightest doubt. When her door opened and closed, and the earl, dressed in the same silk dressing gown in which he had wrapped her one long-short week ago, stood staring at her gravely, she smiled back happily.

"Good evening, my lord."

"And a very good evening to you, my Lady. I have

come . . ." He paused expectantly, and she did not disappoint him.

"Yes, sir, pray why have you come?"

"It must be obvious to anyone of the meanest intelligence that I am here to seduce you."

"Unlike you, sir, I shall not be so unkind as to laugh." She held out her arms to him, and the increased glimpse this gave him of the shapely body outlined by the gossamer gown caused him to suck in his breath and gulp audibly. "Seduce away, my love," Ladybeth bade him, and his reply to this invitation was given with such prompt and passionate fortitude that through the night they loved and came together in explosive climax, only to rest a while and love and climax again.

Mr. Franklin;

I have met in Chudleigh Court with the wax-works Artist Patience Wright. I abided by your Suggestion (and am now most thankful for it) that she know Nothing of Communication between Us or even my True Identity. I find her Plans alarming. There will be no British Revolution, and to try to foment One would be both foolish and dangerous. Although the Mission for which I originally came to England has not been shiningly successful, I feel the Exhilaration of having served a nobler Purpose. I have been fervently grateful always to two American Sailors who saved my Father and gave me some extra Months of his Life. Now I so thankfully return their Favor. Since last I wrote I have assisted a Total of 11 escaped Naval Prisoners to Freedom. My Place of Work makes a perfect Hiding-Place until these Brave Fellows are supplied with Money and Clothes and new Identities and safe Passage to you in France. You have my Promise that I shall continue to give Sanctuary to those Fugitives, who are escaping the Chains of Tyranny.

"My love," Bay said to her one night, as they at last lay quiet in each other's arms, too weary for love, almost too weary for conversation. "I think that you had better set a wedding date. As your so-delicate grandmother phrased it, I would not like any counting of the fingers when the next Shirley heir is born."

Ladybeth laughed sleepily. "Don't worry. There's no fear of that."

"Indeed?" said Bay politely, and struggled up on an elbow to look down at her. "If by *that,* you refer to pregnancy, then forgive me for pointing out that we . . . that our . . . er . . . activity has made it a very real possibility."

"No, it hasn't," yawned Ladybeth, snuggling closer and impatiently pulling at his arm to bring him back down to her. "I protected myself."

This time he managed to get all the way upright. "You did *what?*"

"I protected myself from pregnancy," she told him sleepily.

"And may I ask, my precocious love," he asked with unusual tartness, "how you came by such information?"

"Ruthanna taught me."

"Mrs. Fielding . . . I mean, Mrs. Ver Loop?"

Ladybeth sat up, too, eyeing him reproachfully for taking away the comfort of his warm body. "Yes," she said simply. "Ruthanna thinks most girls go to their marriage bed woefully ignorant and unprepared. She taught me how to prevent pregnancy so that all my children are wanted."

With unusual prudence, she refrained from adding that the protection Ruthanna spoke of had included the matter-of-fact comment that it had also safeguarded her from venereal disease, which had been another danger of her former profession.

It puzzled Ladybeth now that Bay should look scowling rather than relieved.

"I don't understand you," she told him honestly. "I thought you would be pleased."

"I thought I would be, too! Ah, hell, Ladybeth, it's true I would rather have you to myself a while; but I suppose I just wanted you to set a wedding date, no matter what it took."

He looked so little-boy shamed that Ladybeth couldn't help smiling even as she pulled his head down to her breast and rocked him lovingly. She said nothing about a wedding date, but since Bay suddenly decided he had fresh reserves of strength to draw on, the subject was adroitly avoided. The joy of carnal congress once again prevailed over the pleasure of pillow talk.

Mr. Franklin;

It is no Secret that there in France, you are surrounded by enemy Spies. Alarming Intelligence from the Wife of Lieut. Col F——— indicates that your Life may be in Danger. I pray you for your own and Yr. Country's Sake, take every Care. As to the Exiles, I think I can safely say that Many, if they had it to do over again, would not be here. I well remember not long ago the Ecstasy expressed by one Southern Lady to find herself setting Foot on British Ground. Today she cries of how excessively Dear it is to live in London and how insufficiently the American Sufferers in England are appreciated.

Ladybeth slipped into the earl's room, garbed more sedately than usual in a heavy cream silk nightdress and matching peignoir. It had taken courage for her to come at all because several weeks had gone by with both of them in the same house, and never once had he come to her.

At first she had been puzzled, then furious, then full of angry pride. He could not have tired of her so quickly . . . not when she kept loving him more and more!

She had tried to exhaust herself in painting and socializing; she had immersed herself in the business of saving the American naval prisoners, which seemed so much more noble a service than her spying.

And now there was neither pride nor anger left in her, only the overwhelming need to know the truth. Had he stopped loving her?

The moment his grave, blue eyes met hers across the length of his room, she had her answer. He loved her still; and her heart beat with joy that this was so even as she understood that the new, resolute look of him promised trouble to come.

"I have missed you, Bay," she said with the blunt and simple honesty that at times endeared her to him and at other times made him long to lay violent hands upon her.

This was a time that endeared her. "I have missed you, too, my love," he answered gently.

Ladybeth's heart, which should have been eased, sank lower into the pit of her stomach. There was something much too valedictory about his declaration.

"You had only to cross the hallway," she pointed out. "I was waiting."

"You had only to agree to accept a wedding ring to have me waiting for *you* at the altar."

So there it was at long last: the confrontation so often put off. She could no longer tease or beguile him into forgetting marriage, no more divert him with exhausting lovemaking that kept him too tired to argue.

She asked, wishing to be certain, "May I stay with you tonight, Bay?"

"No, my love," he answered gently. "You see, however delightful a bedmate you may be, I want not just a bedmate but a wife."

Rejection had never been kinder or more flattering, but it was rejection all the same. "I see," said Ladybeth and reached blindly for the door.

His voice stopped her again. "You never intended to marry me, did you? It was all a game."

She turned to glare at him. "That's a lie! I love you. I did intend . . . I do . . . I mean, I would marry you tomorrow if the war were over."

"The war!" he gritted out. "Always the damned war! It could stretch out for years and years more. I love you, Ladybeth, as I never thought to love any woman, but I will not wait on the war. I will not wait on your whim."

"And I cannot wed . . ." She made a helpless gesture, her sentence unfinished. *I cannot marry you one day and betray you the next and the next and the next.*

She slipped out of his room, careless of whether she might be seen. It no longer mattered. Strangely, it was not now so much her promise to Hercules Mulligan and to Gen. Washington, nor her vow to Edmund Crozier that mattered most. It didn't seem important anymore to pull the tail of the British lion.

In truth, none of this mattered as much to Ladybeth anymore—now what concerned her were all the brave, bright young American sailors who had fought for freedom against British tyranny and might die in stinking English prisons without her help. She had saved nearly two score now and, God willing, might save two score more. When matched against that total, a single love story with an unhappy ending could not be said (except by Bay and herself) to matter very much.

"Good-bye, my love," she sobbed against her own closed door. She knew herself too well, she knew Bay too well to doubt that their parting was final.

She was almost glad three weeks later when he accepted a diplomatic posting to Vienna. Her grandmother might fret and fume, but for Ladybeth it became far easier to live the life she must when several countries lay between them, more securely separating her from Bay.

Chapter 37

ᏒᏒᏒᏒ

SOMEONE WAS CRYING ALOUD, MAKING QUITE A RACKET in the process. It was a surprise to wake up, stiff and sore from having huddled so long on the hassock, to discover that the noisy weeping person was no one but me.

I got up gingerly and rubbed the back of my neck, trying to fit together the pieces of my dream before they all faded away into my unconscious.

I looked at the drawing board and gasped a little in shock and surprise. The girl on the canvas was exactly as she had been hours before . . . dancing eyes, smiling mouth, stubborn chin. Only one thing had been added to the portrait. A bare centimeter over the voluptuous breasts, just where the bodice of the green gown began, dangled a six-pointed golden star set with a blue green sapphire.

The same star that even now—I never doubted it for a minute—hung against my I Love New York T-shirt.

The star I had found on a Dingle bomb site, that had made its mark on my palm when I lay sick and its mark on my life ever since.

I stopped sniffling and wiped my eyes. The time had come, I decided, and went first to the telephone book and then to the phone.

"Rabbi Rosen? This is Rilla Scott. I hope you remember me, it would make things easier. We met at the authors' and publishers' luncheon last October. Yes, that's right, the one who is almost Jewish. I wonder if I could come and talk with you. No, please, I think I'll need more than an hour. It's quite a complicated story."

Rabbi Rosen and I made our appointment, and when I turned from the phone, the man in silver gray was there, smiling at me from across the room in his own special, tender way. His nodding head seemed to signify approval. A sudden, great peace descended on me.

"You are going to win through, Amaryllis," he said lovingly. "You will not need me for a while."

"Oh, no!" I held out my arms entreatingly. "I always need you. Don't go away for too long."

"When you need me, really need me, I will be there. Do you not know by now that you are strong, you will survive?"

"But I"—my voice lowered as though I were confessing something shameful—"I want you."

"You want your Cam."

"I thought—" I hesitated. "I had begun to believe you . . . Aren't you the same?"

"Not if it is a flesh-and-blood love you crave, which I think you do."

"God knows I do, but when—"

"I can promise nothing."

He smiled once more, then shook his head and was gone from me. I had a sinking feeling as he faded from my sight that I would not see him again for a long, long time.

I was quite right in thinking so, but they were such full and busy years, in the beginning, it did not so much seem to matter.

Not just my work absorbed me, although Catherine Dingle, art agent, was a hard taskmaster in the volume of production she demanded from the painter Amaryllis, an "overnight success," who first rose to fame with her immigrant series, "Faces in the History of the Bowery," and later received awards for the grace and delicacy of her Oriental watercolors.

Rilla Scott continued to write and illustrate her "charmingly original" juveniles, as Mailer Publishing called my books, quoting my favorite and most flattering reviewer.

I spent winter months at the art colonies in Aruba and Martinique, summer week-ends in Larchmont whenever I was assured that Cam and Irene would not be there. Several times their daughter Bethany week-ended along with me and proved to be just what Maggie had called her, "a delightful child, utterly unlike what one would expect of Irene's daughter."

She was a little dark-haired beauty like her mother, but in pixie humor, impudent intelligence, and independent ways, she was all Mailer, a young female version of my darling Nicky, Jonnie, Jethro, and Chick when they were the same age.

Two years after the night I walked out of Cam's hotel room in London, I went back to England again, briefly . . .

I felt strongly that what I had to tell my Mum and Dad must be said in person, not over the telephone or in a letter.

I didn't think Dad would care, considering the indifference with which he regarded all religions. With Mum, though, it might be different. She was a staunch, if independent Catholic. Even though her disapproval could not change my mind, it would have troubled me to have her mistakenly believe that in turning away from her faith in such an official way, I might be turning away from her.

On the second day of my visit I began my explanation by hauling out a pair of airplane tickets, round trip from Liverpool to London to New York.

"Now what's this?" said Dad.

"A present from me to you," I told them awkwardly. "I want you both to visit me in New York next month. It's high time the two of you came to America. I'll rent a car and we'll travel all about . . . see anything you've a fancy to see, go anywhere you want."

"Oh, my!" Mum clasped the tickets to her ecstatically, but Dad eyed me shrewdly and latched onto the significant point. "What's so special about next month?"

Instinctively my hand reached up to my neck and tugged at the gold chain he had given me so long ago. My fingers caressed the gold star that had once graced Deborah Ben David's neck and later her daughter Ladybeth's. The star that had lain buried, God knows how long, beneath the rubble of the Dingle bomb site. Fate had finally brought it where I fervently believed it had been meant to be, in the hands of a little Scouse mongrel.

Remembering that brought me renewed courage.

"Mum, I hope you don't mind, but this is something I have to do, and I'd give anything, anything at all, to have your blessing."

"You're getting married!" Mum gasped.

"Nooo, not quite," I gulped, "I'm getting converted."

Dad was watching my nervous fingers as they twisted about my gold chain.

"So you're finally doing it," he said with a brief, satisfied nod of his head, almost as though some judgment of his own was being confirmed.

Mum's blue eyes lit up in understanding. "We wondered why it took you so long to make up your mind," she confided.

It was my turn to gasp. "Mum, you don't mind that I'm turning Jewish?"

"Goodness me!" She laughed merrily. "We all knew it was bound to happen one day."

"You did?" I said stupidly. "Then it's more than I knew."

"The time you had your pneumonia," she said softly, "in your delirium you asked for your star. I got it out of your shell box on the dresser and your Dad put it into your hand and pressed your fingers around it. We didn't think you were going to live." Even all these years afterward she wiped her eyes at the memory. "When you woke up, with the fever gone and complaining that you were hungry, the outline of the star was etched in the palm of your hand. It was like a sign from God," she told me solemnly. "I knew then that this day would come to us."

"And you don't mind truly?"

"I want your happiness, our Rilla," which was partly an answer, and more than I had the right to expect.

"How about Auntie Bron?"

"Don't you worry about Bron. I'll sort her if I have to," she assured me sharply.

My father eyed me in that X-ray way he had. "Rilla, is there a man?"

God, but he was the knowing one, my Dad. I was torn between tears and laughter.

"There's always been a man, Dad, since the first year I went to America. Only he's married to someone else. Unhappily, but still married. There was a time when he felt the beginnings of love for me, but it never had the chance to grow." I shrugged. "I don't know what will happen between the two of us or if anything will happen at all, but I'm not doing this for him. I'm not sure he would even care. I just know that it feels right to me. I have—"

I hesitated and decided that I couldn't tell them the whole story, not about the man in gray and Edmund and Deborah and Ladybeth or the earl. It would be too much for them to swallow. Hadn't it taken me years myself?

"I have this—this need," I finished rather helplessly and looked at them, hoping for understanding.

It came to me in overflowing measure.

Five weeks later, on my thirty-first birthday, my parents were with me, one on either side of me, as I stood before the altar and was accepted as a Jew.

"There is a special tenderness supposed to be given to the woman who chooses Judaism," Rabbi Rosen said to my friends and family gathered for the ceremony. "As in the case of our most famous convert Ruth, she may be the mother of our future leaders."

He gave me my Hebrew name—Rachel—everyone cheered. Ben kissed me on each cheek and said heartily, "Mazel tov." Maggie hugged me and whispered, "I hope the next ceremony is for your wedding."

349

I grinned wryly. "So do I," I whispered back.

After which we proceeded to a luncheon the Mailers had arranged, at which the four boys presented me with a piece of Israeli sculpture and a scroll they had drawn up entitling me to all the benefits of persecution!

Then I gave my parents their outstanding desire. The three of us flew down to Disney World for a four-day week-end.

Chapter 38

A<small>S IT HAPPENED, THE NEXT CEREMONY</small> M<small>AGGIE AND</small> I
were asked to attend together *was* for a wedding—only,
unfortunately, not mine. One year after my conversion
Nicky arranged to beat me to the altar, getting engaged
to Francie Loew, the girl he had met in his senior year
at Vassar College when she was just a sophomore.

I offered and they accepted a painting by Amaryllis
as their wedding present, and the two came to my
apartment together one evening to have dinner and
make their choice. Maggie and Ben joined us afterward
in time for coffee and cake.

Nicky favored some of the paintings of the Hester
Street immigrants in the days of his great-grandfather.
Francie leaned to the scenic watercolors. While they
argued together enjoyably, Maggie looked at my current work and Ben poked through a stack of old
paintings piled against one wall.

"There are more in the closet, Ben," I told him absently, as he got up from the floor and dusted off his trousers. "Francie, why don't you take whichever of the watercolors you like best and let Nicky pick out the one he wants from the ethnic group?"

"That would be greedy," she said unconvincingly.

"Go on, be greedy," I urged her. "I would love to see the walls of your home all hung with my paintings. Think of the advertisement it would—" I let out an involuntary shriek. "No, Ben, that's the wrong closet."

But I was too late.

Ben had already opened the door to the small square storeroom, which was not so much a closet as a miniature gallery. The walls were painted a soft white, and the opening of the door had triggered the series of lights rigged over each of the paintings. Not paintings by Amaryllis but the dreamwalker's work. Also, the half-dozen miniatures painted from memory. After each dream-walking experience, when the subjects were fresh and clear in my conscious mind, I had painted one or two and signed them with the same scrolled signature. Ladybeth.

Ben gave a low, long whistle. "Holy Moses!" he said reverently. "I didn't know you collected Ladybeths, too. Good God, Rilla, I hope you carry high insurance. You've got a fortune on these walls."

"Don't be silly, Ben." Even in my own ears, my laugh sounded high-pitched and affected. "There's less than five hundred English pounds' worth hanging up here. These are all copies that I painted myself."

"Copies, huh?"

"Museum copies, mostly," I said airily. "Some from privately owned collections."

"Like these?" he asked sardonically, taking his time

about looking over my small collection before he pointed to the miniatures of Sgt. William Morrison, Hercules Mulligan of the Culper Spy Ring, and Jacob Ver Loop, Dutch merchant of New York. "It so happens my brother Charles owns the originals."

"Really?" I looked at him with a pretense of wide-eyed surprise. "Well, I copied them a few years back when Christie's had them on exhibit. I suppose Cam—Mr. Mailer bought them not too long afterward."

"I would say almost immediately after that," Ben told me dryly.

Maggie had tagged after us into the closet to find out what was going on. Sensing my panic, she tried to pry her husband away.

"Come help Nicky and Francie choose their painting," she urged.

Ben waved away this well-meant attempt to divert him as casually as he would have squashed a mosquito.

"And this one?" he asked, bending over to read the name plaque on the full-length portrait which dominated my treasured collection. "Lady Beth Crozier. By any chance a self-portrait?" he hazarded, lifting one ironic brow. "Strange that I never heard of it, nor, I am willing to bet, has Cam. Stranger even that she appears to be wearing colonial dress and—it is, isn't it, I recognize the sapphire, *your* Star of David? You seem to have your centuries a bit mixed up."

"That one isn't a copy," I added lie on desperate lie. "It's just something I made up myself, imitating Ladybeth's style. You know how interested I've always been in American folk art."

"No, I didn't know," Ben said blandly.

"I—I do it just for fun." If I were the hand-wringing

sort, I would have been doing some fancy manual convolutions.

"Ben, I think we should get back to Nicky and Francie."

Even the most insensitive husband—which Ben wasn't—would have detected the unspoken, wifely warning and dangerous undercurrents in Maggie's sweetly smiling suggestion.

The topic of Ladybeth was dropped, only temporarily, I feared, as we returned to paintings by Amaryllis.

Before the evening ended I managed to call Maggie into the kitchen so we could be alone for a few minutes.

As soon as she joined me, I said without any polite preliminaries, "Maggie, you do understand that Ben mustn't mention either me or my Ladybeths to Cam."

"Why not?" she asked calmly.

"Oh, Maggie."

"Listen, Rilla, there was a time when I used to pray you would get over this passion—obsession—infatuation—whatever you want to call it—that you have for Cam." I started to speak and she held up her hand. "No, hear me out. It was for your own sake I wanted it. I couldn't bear to see you wasting your life in useless longing. Well, your life hasn't been exactly wasted and I know damn well you have never gotten over your feelings for Cam. If it hasn't happened in the past fourteen years, it isn't likely to happen now. So why not *let* Ben mention you and the Ladybeths to his brother?"

"What for?"

"Listen, hon, that marriage is quite definitely headed for the rocks. I don't know about Cam, but it's my honest opinion the fair Irene is fooling around, and when he finds out, that will be the end for him. He's held on a long time because of the kid, but he's not that much of a martyr."

"What's it to do with me?" I asked quietly.

"Plenty of women would love to be around to pick up the pieces. I'd rather it was you than anyone else." She added shrewdly, "You know damn well *you'd* rather it was you, too."

"It will be," I said more confidently than I really felt. "But I want him free when he comes to me. Unencumbered by the past. *I* have to pick the time, Ben can't do it for me. I beg you, Maggie, ask him not to speak to Cam . . . not just yet . . . and see that it sticks."

"Ben will keep his mouth shut," promised Ben's loving wife with a disappointed shrug. "But I still think you're crazy."

"Maybe." I shrugged in turn. "But after fourteen years, a few months more don't seem that important."

"Don't they?" Maggie asked disbelievingly.

I gave her the cheeky smile of the girl from Liverpool. "If you must know," I admitted, "they're agony."

"Oh, Rilla." Her face contorted for a moment in very unlovely, un-actressy grief.

"Oh, Maggie," I mocked. I suppose mine did the same.

We clung together for a moment till Francie provided a dramatic anticlimax, bouncing in cheerfully to offer her help with the dishes.

Shortly after the dishes were done, the three Mailers and Francie went home. I locked and bolted the door after them, for the first time in all my years in America guiltily glad to see them go.

I understood why the moment I ran back to the closet and flung the door wide. The light over each painting went on, and as I stepped inside, I heard the first fluttering beating of the wings. It increased in volume and sound until I felt myself beaten down to my knees, hunched over, sheltering my face and head.

Crouched on the floor of my little closet gallery, with my Dreamwalker's Ladybeths all about me, I was whirled back into Ladybeth's world.

Chapter 39

During the long months, more than eight of them, that Bay had remained in Vienna, she was so caught up in her own life—painting, spying, and above all, rescuing American sailors who had been brought to Britain as prisoners of war—she was able to convince herself that she no longer loved him.

Certainly, on his return, he had become a cool, remote stranger who no longer appeared to love *her*. His role was no longer new to him, and he was very much the earl, very formally her guardian. His voice was brisk rather than caressing when he addressed her. There was a distinct pause between the title and the name. Not only was she Lady Beth to him, but he seemed to expect that to her he would be my lord.

This, from the man who had held her naked in his arms, kissed her lips, kissed her breasts, nibbled her toes, and wound her long hair about a powerful, important portion of himself, muttering, "I adore you. I can't get enough of you. Ladybeth, Ladybeth, witch-woman, I want you. God damn it, I can't untangle your hair! Stop laughing, you little vixen . . . help me, or I'll pull it out by the roots." And they had barely freed her hair, leaving a strand or two about him, when he was plunging lustily into her, hair and all!

Ladybeth closed her eyes, breathing hard, breathing as she had the last nighttime of all they had tumbled together in her bed. Her palms were sweating, her face was damp.

She opened her eyes, and the reality was that she sat across the breakfast table from the very remote Earl of Shirley, who regarded her impassively and told her with chilling indifference, "Your grandmother thinks we should plan a ball for your twenty-first birthday, Lady Beth."

"I would rather not, my lord," she told him quietly.

"I conjecture you have plans of your own in mind?" His voice was grim.

Her eyes fell before his, but she could not deny it. She asked him with some hesitation, "Do you recall that when first I agreed to come to England we—we struck a bargain, you and I? We even shook hands on it."

"At twenty-one you could decide for yourself whether to stay on in England or return to America," he said colorlessly. "I collect you mean to go home then?"

"No, I—I thought I would set up my own apartments. I have seen one in a house on St. Alban's Street near the Pall Mall that would meet my requirements for residence and studio combined."

"You will damn well not set up your own house. Go to America, if you must, go and be damned; but set up your own house, you will not."

"You cannot stop me, not when I reach one-and-twenty, not when I have my own money. Even without your dowry, I earn enough to support myself."

"Try it!" he ground out between tight-clenched teeth. "Just try it and see whether or not I can stop you."

Without another word she turned to leave the room. As she reached the doorway, she heard him ask in a voice of seeming hopelessness, "What happened to us, Ladybeth?"

She froze in her tracks, and when she had the courage to confront him, she saw in his face the same grief for love lost that churned inside her own bruised heart.

"What happened to us, Ladybeth?" he asked again. "Where did all the love go?"

She began to weep silently, helplessly, but even as he reached out to her, she turned and fled the room.

Mrs. Smyth-Carrington, a silly, beautiful society woman, was waiting in the studio for her final sitting. Mrs. Smyth-Carrington was a vain, chattering fool, whose voice was a combination of baby-talk and breathlessness but whose husband was a major with political ties to Whitehall. She had occasionally dropped a nugget of pure ore into her usual babble of fool's gold.

An hour after the sitting began, Ladybeth put down her paint brush and smiled across at her sitter. "Thank you, Mrs. Smyth-Carrington." She managed to infuse some warmth into her voice in relief that this particular portrait was almost done. "You have been most cooperative," she praised. "I shall not need you for the finishing touches."

Mrs. Smyth-Carrington's vapidly pretty face suddenly showed more animation than Ladybeth had seen in any one of their half-dozen sittings.

"Will the drawing be finished tomorrow?" she asked in her baby voice.

"Yes, though I may need an extra day or two, as I said, for the finishing touches."

Two hands clapped together in childlike ecstasy. "I can't wait to show it to my husband."

"I feel sure Major Smyth-Carrington will be pleased with the final result," Ladybeth assured her dutifully.

"Mayn't I take one little look now that you're so near the finish?" Mrs. Smyth-Carrington wheedled in the sugary lisp that nauseated Ladybeth but presumably had captivated her husband.

"If you wish."

Ladybeth stepped aside as her subject rushed across to view the portrait.

"Oh, my!" she breathed reverently. "It's beautiful." She turned to the artist, adding with naïve rapture, "You've made her just like me."

"Thank you," returned Ladybeth politely, supressing her laughter.

Mrs. Smyth-Carrington took one last fond, narcissistic look at her portrait, then went to the pier glass to fit a pink-flowered bonnet over her clustering golden ringlets.

Ladybeth waited impatiently for her to be gone, but Mrs. Smyth-Carrington lingered, reluctant to tear herself away from the glory of her self-image.

"The major plans to hang my portrait on the drawing room wall where his mama's used to be," she announced prettily. "I do so wish he could take a little copy to America with him. Perhaps when you are finished with this great big one, you could copy it in miniature." She opened wide, childlike eyes at Ladybeth and fondled her diamond necklace. "Would it be too terribly expensive?"

"I certainly could not take advantage of you or, if his regiment is actually ordered to America to fight in this ridiculous war, of one of our brave British officers."

"That's just what I told Harry. It's ridiculous he should miss the height of the season. And it isn't even as though the whole regiment is going."

She looked anxious, and Ladybeth cursed herself for not having been more careful until she saw the little beauty's anxiety was lest she should have talked herself out of an inexpensive copy of her portrait.

"Harry will be so lonesome without me and his beloved regiment. He really would love a painting of me to take along with him."

Ladybeth pretended to hesitate. "Well, if Major Smyth-Carrington is going on an important military mission to America, then I must share your patriotic sacrifice, my dear Mrs. Smyth-Carrington."

Mrs. Smyth-Carrington looked at her expectantly, lips parted and pouting, waiting for whatever offer was to come.

"Is it truly an important mission?" Ladybeth hedged.

"Oh, it is, you mustn't tell anyone, even I'm not supposed to know, it's a secret mission for"—she paused impressively—"Lord North and the king himself."

"Good heavens!" cried Ladybeth. "Lord North and the king. And your husband told you so. How very proud you must be, how much he must trust you! I do congratulate you. I must congratulate him."

The pretty face screwed up in alarm. "Oh no, you mustn't do that!" she squeaked. "I mean to say, it's such a secret." Her fingers played nervously with the ribbons of her bonnet. "To tell the truth, I'm not supposed to know. It's just that the men were talking in Harry's study, and I got so weary waiting for them, and I just happened to pass by . . ."

She paused and said pathetically, "You're a woman, Lady Beth. I'm sure you understand. After all, my own husband. I have a *right* to know what's going on . . ."

"Of course you do," Ladybeth assured her heartily. "Any woman would understand and do the same. Naturally, you're concerned if your own husband is going into danger."

Mrs. Smyth-Carrington hesitated. "Not really danger, I suppose," she said scrupulously, then, fearing she had injured her own cause, she hastened to add, "Though one never knows, going to those horrid colonies! I think His Majesty is terribly, terribly generous offering them so much."

"Then I certainly can't be less generous than our king," Ladybeth offered with a beaming smile. "Pray allow me to make a gift of the miniature copy to Major Smyth-Carrington—and to you, of course, if you will be so kind as to accept this small token of appreciation for what your husband is doing."

Mrs. Smyth-Carrington, with all the aplomb of a spoiled beauty, graciously agreed to accept the offered gift. "But Harry mustn't know why you are giving it to me," she added with a slight return of anxiety. "He would be so angry with me for speaking of his affairs. He always says"—her giggle shrilled out gratingly— "that my tongue is hung in the middle. You know how men are."

"Indeed I do. They have no understanding at all. My cousin, the earl, I assure you, is exactly the same." She patted one of the taloned hands with its many rings. "Dear Mrs. Smyth-Carrington. Let us say the miniature is a gift to you and your husband in appreciation of beauty. Any other motive shall remain as secret as"—she paused lightly—"let us say, as your husband's mission. Remember, much as you may miss him during his long, long absence, it must be a comfort to you that he serves the Crown."

"Oh yes, it's my great comfort," Mrs. Smyth-Carrington parroted, once more straightening her bonnet. "But it won't be *that* long. Harry says they must only lay the proposals before representatives of their horrid Congress."

"Proposals? Really? You mean your husband may be instrumental in ending the war?"

"Well, he's an aide to Lord Carlisle and Mr. Eden, but *they* represent the king."

"Just what proposals have they in mind?"

"Well, I didn't hear all of it, only Harry saying they would be fools to refuse when the offer is for all the demands they made previously, except for complete freedom from us. Even titles for some of the rebels."

"Did—"

"Oh goodness, it's getting so late. Harry will be wondering where I am. I really must go." She laid a pretty, if predatory little claw on Ladybeth's arm. "You won't forget my miniature."

"Upon my honor," Ladybeth assured her solemnly.

They parted with smiles of mutual artificiality, and Ladybeth waited only for the last echo of retreating footsteps before she walked swiftly into the small study next to her studio and sat down at her desk.

She did not hear the sound of the footman's entrance, only a loud cough. Her head turned swiftly.

"The earl's compliments, Lady Beth. Luncheon is being served."

"Heavens, I lost track of the time." She glanced

down ruefully at the sacque covering her morning muslin gown and her paint-spattered hands.

"Please make my excuses to the earl. I will not be coming to luncheon today. I would like a tray here in my studio instead. Just a bowl of soup and some bread will do."

As the footman bowed respectfully and turned to leave, she studied her easel and flung a seemingly casual command over her shoulder. "Pray send word to the stables that I should like to ride this afternoon." She looked at the grandfather clock in the far corner of the room. "Say in an hour and a quarter from now."

When she reached the stables at the appointed time, her horse was saddled and ready, but to her dismay, the earl's groom, John Swithin, was waiting to attend her.

"Where is Tom Binkley?" she asked offhandedly, as Swithin helped her to mount.

"He's been let go, my lady," he told her. "Absent without leave. And not," he added with relish, "for the first time."

"I'm sorry to hear it," Ladybeth said, her face a mask of indifference while her heart thumped erratically. "I always found Binkley most proficient in his duties. Has he been replaced?"

The new man comes tomorrow, my lady. He was formerly with the Duke of Devonshire. I am sure you will find him to your satisfaction."

"I am sure I shall," said Ladybeth in a light, bored voice and cantered on ahead.

For appearance's sake, though she was wild to be at home again, she rode her usual full hour. Tom Binkley would get to her, she was sure of that. She must only provide him the opportunity.

Without bothering to change from her riding dress, she waited for him in her mews studio. It had the easiest access to her, and during the day she kept it free of servants, claiming they interfered with her work. Twice over the years Tom Binkley had sought her out there. She was certain that this last time he would again.

When he had not come by the time she should have returned to the house to dress for dinner, she sent a message that she was hard at work finishing a portrait and would not dine with the family.

Then she stopped her pacing, removed her jacket, and readied her paints to put the final touches on the portrait of Mrs. Smyth-Carrington. Presently she became so wrapped up in her work that she did not at first hear Tom's arrival.

He came through the balcony window in the back room, where her canvases were stacked. The faint whistling of "Yankee Doodle" finally penetrated her absorption, and she flung down her brush and flew into the storage room.

"Oh, Tom. Thank God," she greeted him. "I have sore need of you."

"A special message?"

"One that should go straight home, if possible. By way of Franklin in Paris might take too long."

He grinned. "Not with me taking it, my Lady Beth. I'm off to Paris this night. And from there, the first ship home."

"Any reason?" she asked anxiously. "I know you were let go."

"My imposture's not been disclosed," he reassured her, "but it will be if I stay on much longer. That's why I got the boot—for too many odd disappearances. It's time I made my last one." He patted her cheek. After two years they were friends as well as conspirators. "Now what's this message?"

She drew a deep breath. "I've been painting Mrs. Smyth-Carrington, wife of Major Harry Smyth-Carrington. The silliest bit of society fluff imaginable, but she eavesdrops on her husband's private conversations. He appears to have been appointed an aide to Lord Carlisle as part of his special mission to America."

He had been leaning negligently against the wall during the first part of her information, but at the mention of Lord Carlisle, he straightened up, his eyes hard and bright and alert. Every American agent knew that Lord Carlisle was the close friend of William Eden, master of the British intelligence system.

"And the mission?"

"To go to the American colonies and lay proposals before representatives of Congress, granting us all we have asked for in the past, only excepting independence and including titles for rebel leaders."

A short, surprised grunt came from between his pursed lips. She saw his mind go to work and knew of old his way of thinking aloud when they were alone.

"They'll naturally try to get to people who can influence the Congress to their way of thinking . . . cautious people who would just as soon be British . . . who are still afraid of complete independence . . ."

He grabbed at her hand and kissed the paint-smeared fingers. "Take that anxious look off your face, Lady Beth Crozier. You may be sure that I will get there first. This will be dealt with on the highest levels. I will reach the Great Man himself. You know how devoted Washington is to his secret service."

He took her hand again, both her hands. They stood close, no longer smiling, staring into one another's eyes, hand-locked for several minutes.

"I'm afraid this is good-bye, my dear," he said gently.

"Oh Tom, I shall miss you so. I shall"—her voice broke—"I shall feel so alone without you."

He moved their interlaced hands behind her to bring her into his embrace. They kissed fondly but without passion, although the man standing in the doorway could not be expected to discern any difference.

Chapter 40

HE HAD COME UP THE STAIRS IN TIME TO HEAR THEIR words of good-bye, in time to see the seemingly loving embrace.

"Forgive my intrusion on this tender scene," his sardonic voice interrupted them. "I was—most foolish-ly, I realize now—concerned about my cousin's health."

They broke apart in consternation and swung about to face him.

His face remained impassive, his voice quite chilling.

"My bride-to-be and a groom dismissed from my service. No final humiliation to be denied me, I see."

Ladybeth said colorlessly, "You had best go, Tom."

Binkley hesitated a moment even though he knew her words were a reminder of obligation.

Then the earl spoke again, carefully taking a pinch of snuff. "Yes, Tom, you had best go, unless"—he snapped his snuff box shut—"unless you prefer to be thrashed from the premises."

"Good-bye, my lady."

"God speed you, Tom."

He went down the stairs, warily passing the earl to get through the door. When the final clatter of his feet disappeared in the distance, Ladybeth faced the earl, her head held high.

"I am sure that after this you can have no objections to my leaving your home?"

The earl ignored her question. "You must have been thinking me very naïve all these months," he said almost pensively. "I have had many thoughts not altogether kind about you this past year, but never that you would . . ." He shrugged. "I should have left you in your rural fastness. As a little American savage, there was something of splendor in you. As an English lady of the *ton,* tasting all of society's pleasure and decadence, I find you somehow lacking."

She managed not to wince beneath the cruel contempt of his dismissal.

"Then let me go," she said.

"As soon as your grandmother dies," he answered brutally.

"Wh-what?"

"The doctors tell me it will not be long. Her heart is giving out. You have doubtless been too absorbed in your own—er—affairs to observe that she is not well."

Ladybeth walked to the window and stood with her back to him, looking out.

"I should like to announce our formal betrothal as soon as possible," she heard him say and swung about again, stammering incredulously, "I—I d-don't understand."

"After what has gone before what matters a broken betrothal to either one of us?" he asked her disdainfully. "There is nothing your grandmother desires so much as our marriage. Let her die in happiness deeming her dearest wish accomplished; probably, if I know her, in the middle of wedding arrangements. During the year's mourning that follows, we can end the engagement."

"Is there nothing to be done for grandmother?"

"Nothing except to take her out of London and prolong her life by a month or two."

"She gets restless after only a few weeks in the country."

"She is extremely fond of Bath, however, and the air there, as well as the waters, have been recommended by her doctors."

"I will go with her."

"We will both go with her," he said crushingly. "My agents are already looking for a house to rent. I will send the notice of our engagement to the newspapers tonight. Your grandmother has already retired. I suggest you inform her yourself in the morning."

"As you wish, my lord." She gave him a slight formal curtsey.

"As *I* wish, my Lady Beth? Nothing between us has gone as I once wished. Do you know I came to you tonight worried that you might be ill? Hoping as I always hoped whenever we might meet that magically one day things would be as they once were between us? I thought of illness as the reason you might stay away from luncheon and dinner. It did not occur to me that you might be waiting for a rendezvous with your lover."

She could bear no more but stepped past him, as Tom Binkley had done, and hurried down the stairs.

As he followed the fleeing figure at a more leisurely pace, he called down to her, "Pray remember that during the period of our betrothal, I shall expect you to act the part."

When Ladybeth reached her room Lucy was hanging some freshly pressed gowns in her closet. "Would you please do that later?" Ladybeth managed to say without bursting into tears. "I'm—I would like—oh Lucy, please just leave it."

Lucy took one quick, frightened look at her mistress's face, tossed the gowns over the back of a chair, and hurried out the door.

Ladybeth flung herself down on the bed and cried as she had not cried since the day her father died. Deep, wrenching sobs wracked her body from head to foot, and she bit down on her fist, trying to control them. Then she rolled over onto the pillows and wept herself first into exhaustion and finally into sleep.

While she slept, the Earl of Shirley quietly entered the room and stood over her, looking down at the puffy, tear-stained face, trying to understand her restless mutterings.

I can't. I can't. Not when I betrayed him.

In her sleep, quite softly this time, she began to sob again.

Excerpt from letters of Lady Beth Crozier in England to Ruthanna Ver Loop in British-occupied New York . . .

. . . I had not thought that News of an English Betrothal would reach so rapidly from the old World to the new, especially now during such Troubled Times as These. I understand your Reproaches, but my Failing to inform you does not mean that the Years apart have in any way altered my cherished Regard for you. Things are not always what they seem. It is impossible in a Letter to spell out what I mean. If you recall the Past, you will understand why I must occasionally do Incomprehensible Things. . . .

May 1778

. . . I am settled here in Bath for an indeterminate Visit, owing to my grandmother's ill Health. It is a most pleasant City, originally built by the Romans and famous for its Mineral Springs. Everyone flocks to drink the Waters of these Springs, which taste most vilely, though they are considered to be extraordinarily Health-giving. The Earl shares this House, which he has rented for us, but not much of the Social Life which is so dear to my Grandmother. I think she would rise from her Death-bed to attend a Rout. . . .

June 1778

. . . what Joy to learn that you and Mr. Ver Loop have a Daughter of your own. I know you foster the Children of his first Marriage most lovingly, as you did me, dear Ruthanna; but this, I know, answers the deepest Yearning of your Heart. I am most honored that your little Lizzy is to be my Namesake, and I accept with delight the Office of God-mother. . . .

July 1778

. . . Mr. Binkley, the Gentleman you mentioned, was indeed a good Friend of mine during my first Years in England. I had long hoped he would call on you. If you Chance to Meet with him again, pray do not forget to tell him how delighted I was

to hear that the Business which took him Home
from Europe was concluded so successfully. . . .

August 1778

. . . When first I came to Britain, the Earl was able
to find out for me that my Mother's Parents were
both long dead. He has been trying to track down
my other Relations ever since and has just recently
been informed that my Ben David Uncles both
went to the Indies and my Aunt Martha Ben David
Married a Dutchman and lives in Holland. It has
made me melancholy, I admit. I had always hoped
to find my Mother's People. . . .

September 1778

. . . It is three days since my Grandmother and I
went to the Pump Room, where she gossiped most
happily with a half-dozen of her most Intimate
Acquaintance and afterwards won seven Pounds
and some Shillings at Cards. She seemed in the
best of Health and Spirits, and her Maid promises
me that she maintained a cheerful Flow of conversation all the time she was being prepared for Bed.
She died in her Sleep that same Night, and I feel
more bereft, dear Ruthanna, than I could have
believed. . . .

October 1778

. . . His Parliamentary Duties have recalled the
Earl to London, but I am staying on in Bath for
several Months with a hired Chaperone, one Mrs.
Sarah Dudley, a Loyal British Refugee here,
whose Finances are so exigent as to make her
accept, with Tears of Thankfulness, the Post with
me. It is less awkward this Way, as I will now
confess to you what will not be known publicly for

some Months yet. The Earl and I are ending our Betrothal. Out of Respect for my Grandmother, no Public Announcement will be made as yet. . . .

November 1778
. . . Just Yesterday I was speaking to a Clergyman from Boston, who told me most bitterly that the English Clergy look on their American Brethren here with a most jealous Eye and offer them "only Promises" or "compassionable Expressions," but never the Interest or Help or Employment they so desperately require. He assured me quite solemnly that he has advised his Friends in the Colonies to stay at Home if they can safely do so; England has Nothing to offer them. He is by no means the first American to discover that this beauteous Isle of England is not our Home. . . .

December 1778
. . . I am once again in London, as you can see from my Direction, in ample Lodgings of my own in Soho, where most of the Refugees from New York and Pennsylvania choose to live. It is interesting how clannishly we Exiles from America gather together. Most of the New Englanders are settled in Westminster, while the Southerners favor the short Streets between the Strand and Thames River. The Men even have different Coffee Houses, according to the Regions where they hail from. . . .

January 1779
. . . I saw the Earl yesterday on Business of my Grandmother's Estate (All her personal Money and Jewels were left to me). It was agreed between us that we have no formal Notice of the end of our

Betrothal, since it is generally known among our Acquaintance, and only the most ill-mannered venture on Questions. I have become quite adept at parrying these. Usually a freezing Look from the Lady Beth Crozier suffices. You have no Notion, dear Ruthanna, how *very* freezing the Lady Beth (not to be confused with your Friend Ladybeth) can look. . . .

February 1779

. . . I have resumed my Painting after this long Interval, also those of my other Activities which concerned me when I first came to England. It gives an Interest and a Purpose to my Life that has been lacking for some Time. Yes, Mrs. Dudley did come with me on my Return to London, but her Character being somewhat Righteous and her nature highly Inquisitive, I found it expedient to replace her. She has a Sister living in Bristol, and I gave her a handsome Present of Money and sped her on her Way there. . . .

March 1779

. . . Through an agent I have taken a three-year Lease on a House in Brighthelmston, on the Seacoast south of London. To be sure, as you say, London is an exciting City; almost too exciting. One can easily get lost in a ceaseless Round of Pleasure; that is, one who has no other Purpose in Life. Only Yesterday I was in Company with a Gentleman who discussed most agreeably his attending, for the Novelty of it, Sunday Services at Newgate Prison, amongst the Debtors, Thieves, and Murderers, including several in Chains who attracted his Interest because they were under sentence of Death. Another Gentleman, whom I deem not a Gentleman at all, complained of having his Pocket picked, while he enjoyed the Entertainment of a Hanging at Tybrun. Eight Years ago in America, one of these Men was a respected Surgeon and the other a prominent Judge. I have seen Monkeys in the Zoo at the Tower of London who have more the Appearance and Impression of Humanity than such as these.

Chapter 41

"**F**OR HEAVEN'S SAKE, TAKE THAT MOURNFUL LOOK off your face!" warned Ladybeth. "Give me your arm. Smile, I beg you. Try to give the appearance of a man enjoying himself. I assure you, I am considered a prodigiously charming and enjoyable woman to be with."

"Ma'am, I feel certain sure you are. If I were not shaking in my shoes for very fright, I would be flirting with you this moment as delightfully as you are flirting . . ."

"*Trying* to flirt," Ladybeth interrupted merrily.

"Trying to flirt with me."

"You are perfectly safe." She squeezed his arm reassuringly. "Your clothes are in the latest style of the young Bucks about town, your wig freshly curled and powdered. It's a bit large, I observe; just make sure that it doesn't slip."

"London town," she mentioned a moment later, "is

accustomed to seeing the Lady Beth at the Pleasure Gardens and Theatres when she is not in Brighthelmston. If anyone is speculating about you, it will only be about how long you may hold my fickle favor."

He glanced at her curiously. The gaiety of her first remarks had ended on a note slightly tinged with bitterness.

"It seems like a dream to me, ma'am. A few days ago I was in a stinking prison ship, now here I am walking publicly around the famous Vauxhall Gardens with a member of the nobility. I've had naught but nightmares these last two years. This is a dream I am fearful I might wake from."

"'Tis no dream but pleasant reality. We'll parade around obviously a few more times, then slip out and away to the carriage I have waiting. In an hour from now, we should be at my home. Within the week you will be on your way to France."

As they continued their walk, she tried to make pleasant conversation. "You are a Southerner, sir?"

"Yorktown in Virginia, ma'am, on the River York."

"You will see it soon, Lieutenant," she told him softly.

"Please God, ma'am, I hope you may be right."

"Forty-two others before you have reached France safely. Once there, to go home poses no serious problem."

"Good evening, Lady Beth."

The lieutenant felt the trembling of her arm even as she smiled and carelessly answered, "Good evening, my lord."

She would have proceeded on, but the gentleman had plunked himself in their path and stood immovable.

Ladybeth said evenly, "My lord, may I present Mr.

Lee Rawson, a refugee from our southern colony of Virginia? Mr. Rawson, my cousin, the Earl of Shirley."

Both gentlemen bowed and eyed each other like pugilists about to meet in the ring.

Ladybeth said hurriedly, seeking to divert his attention. "You are alone, my lord?" She opened her eyes wide at him and managed to invest her tone with great surprise. "How unusual for you."

"As unusual as it would be for you, my dear Ladybeth, not to have a gentleman—one hopes, a gentleman—in your pocket. Do not fret, Cousin. I will not be alone for long."

"I never doubted it," she said clearly, though his words, like his women, were a dagger in her heart. "If you will excuse me, Cousin."

As he bowed again and stepped to one side, she dragged her fascinated escort past him.

"Was he really an earl?" ventured the lieutenant after an interval of silence.

"Yes."

"It somehow doesn't seem a place an earl would come, or—"

"Or?"

"Forgive me, ma'am, but someone like yourself."

"It's a rowdy, boisterous place, which makes it all the fitter for our purpose. It's noisy and crowded with people bent solely on pleasure. It's easier for escapees to slip in and out here than in a less populated place. You could hardly change your clothes in any other public place as you did back of the bushes in Lovers' Walk."

"But your cousin?"

"The earl," she answered tonelessly, "like many fashionable men, comes to the Pleasure Gardens to choose from among the women of the town. You will have noted there is a plentiful selection. The music is beginning again. I think we can safely leave now."

Four nights later she was at Ranelagh, the more fashionable and select of the two gardens. It had the added advantage of being much closer to her new lodgings in Chelsea.

The meeting had been arranged to take place at the back of the rotunda during one of the special events. She had come alone at the appointed time and gone directly there, wearing the gold brocade gown and carrying the flowered reticule and fan which would identify her.

"We meet again, Cousin."

Her heart gave a great leap of fright as the Earl of Shirley bore down on her, a woman on his arm. The woman was quite remarkably beautiful as to face and figure, but her white-painted face, monstrous head-dress, and a satin dress cut to show her breasts clear down to her nipples also clearly proclaimed her profession.

"Good evening, my lord." Ladybeth dipped down in a curtsey, looking about frantically as she raised her head.

"You should not be alone here like this." The earl frowned, and the woman let go of his arm and fell back a little.

"Won't you introduce me to your friend?" Ladybeth asked him.

"No," he said shortly, "and let us have no pretense that you are unaware why. She is—to put it politely—an actress."

"The English code of manners," said Ladybeth softly. "Escort her publicly, bed her privately, but ignore her claims to a decent show of civility. Do you think because she is a whore she has no feelings?"

Under her steady stare, the earl flushed slightly. Turning, he took the woman's hand and brought her forward.

"Cousin, allow me to introduce my—friend, Miss Marion Trellick. Marion, my cousin, the Lady Elizabeth Crozier."

"How do you do?" Ladybeth smiled.

"P-pleased, I'm sure," stammered Miss Trellick, and then, in a quite audible whisper, "Shirley, are you Bedlam-mad, introducing me to a lady like your cousin?"

The earl gave Ladybeth a smile she had not seen since those long-lost days aboard the packet *Nancy*.

"So much for democracy," he murmured. And then again, quite briskly, "Now Cousin, why are you here alone?"

"I am not," said Ladybeth. "My—my escort had a—a little accident to his clothing and had to—to—"

He eyed her ironically. "To retreat? Leaving you here unprotected. I will wait then till this gallant gentleman reappears."

"No, really, there isn't any need. Oh—oh, there he is now."

Thankfully, she recognized not the gentleman but the suit of clothing striding towards her. He slowed down, recognizing the description of hers at the same moment, but hesitated because of her companion.

Ladybeth hailed him in a quick loud voice.

"Kenneth, here I am." She ran forward to slip her arm through his. "You were gone at least six minutes," she reproached him. "My cousin—this is my cousin the earl of Shirley and his friend Miss Marion Trellick— were quite sure you had basely deserted me."

She pinched his arm, and the gentleman gallantly took up his cue. "As though I ever would," he said with a languishing look at her that set the earl's teeth on edge.

"Lord Shirley, may I introduce *my* friend, Mr. Kenneth Tremaine?" Ladybeth said sweetly.

"Which of the colonies do you call home?" the earl asked, having exchanged bows.

"Mr. Tremaine's accent speaks for him," Ladybeth cut in quickly. "It's pure Boston, as anyone in America would know at once."

"Another sufferer from American injustice, I assume?"

"You assume correctly, sir." The lie came hard to Mr. Tremaine's lips, and Ladybeth intervened again.

"My cousin sits in Parliament, which in its infinite generosity has replaced the annual pension by single grants in settlement of all claims. You can hardly expect *him* to understand our cause," she said.

"I seem to recall that in days gone by you were a fervent American patriot."

"And I recall in those same days you were a plain British soldier."

"Touché." The earl shrugged. "We were both happier then, I believe. Or, at the very least, life was less complex."

Ladybeth held her head higher, blinking back the tears that would have signified agreement. "If you will excuse me, Miss Trellick, my lord, Mr. Tremaine and I are engaged to join a private party."

Mr. Tremaine bowed and smiled, then, obedient to the fingers pinching his arm, turned and headed into the opposite direction from Lord Shirley and his companion.

As he moved away with the actress on his arm, the earl took one lingering look back over his shoulder. Ladybeth had turned around again and stood stock-still, her gray eyes fastened on him, the artificial smile gone from her tucked-in lips, an odd, unguarded expression on her face.

It haunted him, that expression did, the whole endless hour before he put Miss Trellick into a hackeney and out of his life. It haunted him as he rode home alone in his own carriage.

In the dark stretch of the night that came just before dawn, he came awake all at once and jerked himself upright, demanding aloud hoarsely, "How dare she?"

With shaking hands he lit the candle by his bedside, threw back the bedcovers, and stalked about his room in the small clothes that, to his valet's horror, were all he wore for sleep wear.

"Hell's teeth!" he snarled aloud. Then again, "How dare she?" It was *she* who had betrayed *him*. He asked himself for the tenth time as the sun burst through his curtains, what right had she to bestow on him that look of bitter, burning reproach?

Even as he paced his bedroom, angry, impatient, perplexed, in his cousin's house in another part of town, the safe signal of three sets of knocks sounded at the door of the false, mural-painted closet, which served as a door to the concealed attic room.

Most of the night, stripped of his dandy's garments and dressed in servant's garb, the man Ladybeth had introduced as Kenneth Tremaine had exchanged prison stories with Lt. Lee Rawson and Sgt. Herbert Lake of Vermont. Sgt. Lake had been in the attic the longest time of the three, almost a full month.

When the knocks sounded, the men dimmed their lanterns and opened the latch on their side to admit Ladybeth. She carried a pewter candlestick in one hand, a platter of food in the other, and had signaled, as she usually did, with her foot.

Kenneth Tremaine took the candlestick with its single flickering candle, looking admiringly at her ruby red velvet dressing gown and her hair tumbling down her back in glorious confusion. Sgt. Lake, more practical after longer imprisonment, reached eagerly for the platter of cold meats and fruit that she was balancing against her chest.

"It is to be this time tomorrow," Ladybeth told them, her eyes ablaze with excitement.

She laughed aloud, as she always did, in the very teeth of danger. "We shall leave just before dawn for my house in Brighton, traveling in great style with two carriages, several footmen, and numerous outriders. You three will be dispersed amongst the outriders with some Irishmen newly come from Belfast who won't detect your accents."

"Won't such a caravan arouse undue attention?" asked Lt. Rawson, speaking for them all.

"Most unlikely." Ladybeth spoke with calm consideration. "To create a precedent, I have chosen to travel this way several times before. I am known along the way and at an inn where we may stop for refreshment. I shall be in the first carriage with my maid and companion. The other carriage will carry a load of paintings and canvases and several pieces of furniture, which I am having moved to my house."

She put out her hand and touched the sergeant's arm, then smiled impartially upon them all. "Fret not. This mode of travel is not uncommon among the British aristocracy."

She took up the candlestick again, and it seemed to shed a special radiance about her. "I must go now. Sleep well, gentlemen. Two nights from now you will be on your way to France and to freedom."

Chapter 42

Henry Bayard Crozier, seventh Earl of Shirley, striding through the halls of Parliament in a state of weary disgust, nearly bowled over an old army friend, Capt. Royce Albertson.

They shook hands and pounded one another's shoulders with enthusiastic strength, exchanging friendly insults the while.

"An earl, no less. I don't wonder your nose is so high you can't see the rest of the world going by."

"You've gained at least two stone. It's a wonder I recognized you at all."

These jovial preliminaries finished with, Capt. Albertson asked, "Where are you off to with that thunderous expression on your face?"

"Anywhere but here. I have spent the last three hours while the lords of this land bombarded my ears with utterances of the utmost folly on what they are pleased to call our 'differences' with America. I can bear no more at one sitting." He gave his characteristic shrug. "How goes it with you, my friend? Are you but recently back from America? If not, I promise you that you will be in my black books that I have not seen fat hide nor hair of you."

Capt. Albertson held up one hand in laughing alarm. "Pax. Pax. I have been back in England only long enough for a brief visit home. I am expecting to be assigned here in London. I would have called on you by tomorrow at the latest."

"Come to supper with me tonight instead—no, damn, I'm dining at Lord Hurley's. Make that tomorrow night. Do you know where my house is?"

His friend's eyes twinkled. "I haven't much acquaintance amongst the nobility," he said provokingly, and received a cuff on the ear and a card pressed into his hands. "Make it seven o'clock," said the earl. "We have long years of talking to catch up on."

Promptly at seven the next evening a butler ushered Capt. Albertson into the library of Shirley House.

"Whew," he whistled when he was alone with the earl. "You seem to have found the pot of gold hidden behind the rainbow, Bay. A far cry, this, from the barracks in New York where we were last together."

The smile faded from the earl's face as he looked backward into the past. "A far cry," he agreed expressionlessly, pouring two glasses of wine.

Royce eyed him shrewdly. "Still," he said reflectively, "I never remember you happier. You were in love, I recall, with the little colonial you kept so secret. Whatever became of her?"

"What happens to all old loves?" the earl returned cynically, lifting his glass in a silent toast. "Disillusionment. Dissolution. Shall we talk of something else?"

"By all means, your lordship. So far it's been a damned dreary discussion."

The earl's grim mouth relaxed; his eyes lit up with laughter.

"I can see how awed you are by my title, old friend. Tell me about your new assignment."

"I may be working for the ministry you were in such a fury at just yesterday. What was that all about?"

"The American refugees. All these years they have been unrecognized, patronized, or ignored. Now, just when they should *not* be, they are becoming a force in our government." He set down his half-full glass so vigorously that the wine sloshed over the sides. "The exiles say what the ministers wish to hear, so suddenly they speak with the voice of prophets. They echo the false idiocies of Benedict Arnold, whose self-serving reasons for his traitorous defection have made him the new Messiah. This, despite the fact that a full three years ago, while still in the American Army, he was publicly described as a man who worshiped money and would sacrifice his country to get it."

"No soldier can think of Arnold with anything but disgust. Poor André, to be so sacrificed." They both lifted their glasses in another silent acknowledgment.

Royce then laughed ruefully, attempting to throw off his melancholy. "I am not so sure I care for my own proposed assignment: to put stronger teeth into the effort to recapture already-captured Americans here at home. Who can blame the poor devils for trying to escape the purgatory of our prisons? Mills and some of the others make Newgate seem a veritable paradise."

"Are there so many escapees then?"

"'Twixt you and me, Bay, more than the ministry wishes to be known. 'Tis none so hard, the language being more or less the same, not as though they were Frenchies or some other tongue-twisting race. Here in London or in the country, they can mingle with the refugees. In the seacoast towns, I have no doubt, they form a thriving business for the smugglers. All they need is friends sympathetic to their cause."

"Friends sympathetic to their cause," the earl repeated slowly. Refraining with difficulty from shouting those same words aloud, he sank down suddenly in a chair with his head lowered against his raised hands.

"I say, Bay, is something wrong?"

"I'm wrong," said the earl thickly. "I suspect it's possible that I have been the biggest, damndest, dumbest idiot that ever was."

"Oh, if that's all"—Royce swallowed the last of his wine and reached for the decanter—"I'm not about to argue with you on that point, old friend."

They were somewhat foxed by the time the butler returned to announce dinner, the earl seeming to go out of his way to pour as much wine as possible down his friend's willing throat. He continued to signal to his servants for no glass ever to remain empty all during the meal.

By the time that apricot tarts and the trifle were served, the earl judged it safe to banish all servants from the room and return to the subject of most interest to him.

"In the matter of the escaped prisoners," he said idly, smoothing out the wrist ruffles of his shirt with apparent concentration. "Are there any lists of names?"

Royce took a bit of the tart between his fingers, swallowed, and nodded his appreciation. "Damn me, but that was good. Names," he repeated vaguely. "We have some, to be sure, but there's no knowing how accurate they are. They change identities often as not; live men take the place of dead."

"But there are lists, however inaccurate?" the earl persisted.

"Oh, aye, there are, but not much good to us."

"They might," the earl said softly, "be of much good to *me*. Is it possible, Royce, that I might see such a list?"

Capt. Albertson, not quite so befuddled as he appeared, blinked owlishly at his friend. "Any particular reason, Bay? I may not like my duty, but I'm a soldier of the king."

"And I—despite my Whiggery—one of his earls." He smiled derisively. "How can my knowing the names of a handful of escaped Americans harm England? Even"—his voice hardened—"if you think I would be willing to."

"No need to poker up so, Bay. I think no such thing." Royce nodded wisely. "But don't try to humbug me either. We've been friends long enough for me to know when you are up to something. Don't bother to deny it, or even," he added hastily, "to tell me any details. I think I would rather not know." He took another bite of the tart and then, with a wistful look at his bulging waistband, pushed away his serving of trifle. "Come to my rooms tomorrow . . . in the early afternoon after I've been to the war office."

The earl slept badly again that night, his sleep disturbed by memories of a warm, eager body squirming on his lap, of kisses once freely given and returned. Kisses that he had come to believe meant nothing. She had dispensed them all too freely. Or had she? Waking, he was tormented by the recollection of great brooding gray eyes with their look of burning reproach.

He arrived early at Capt. Albertson's room to be

admitted by his batman and kept waiting for three quarters of an hour.

Royce raised his eyebrows when he returned and saw the earl sitting in his best armchair staring moodily at the fire. "Your eagerness to see me is quite flattering," he murmured. Then, seeing his friend's white, strained face, his teasing ended. Wordlessly he dug into the pocket of his coat and came up with a sheaf of papers.

Bay grabbed at them without any thanks. There were six pages to be gone through. He scanned them quickly but thoroughly, mouthing each name aloud in his mind. On the very last page he found what he was seeking. *Lee, Dawson W.* "Dawson Lee," he murmured aloud. In his mind echoed that introduction of just one week ago. *My lord, may I present Mr. Lee Rawson, a refugee from our southern colony of Virginia?*

One week. He checked the date on his list. Just twenty-four hours after Dawson Lee's escape from the prison ship, Mr. Lee Rawson had turned up with Ladybeth at Vauxhall.

He continued on down the list and found the final entry of an escapee from Mills Prison. Kennedy Tremont. *Lord Shirley, may I introduce my friend Mr. Kenneth Tremaine?*

He started to crush the papers between his hands and found them quickly rescued and removed from him by Royce. "Here, I say, I need those."

The earl walked over to the fireplace and stood there, his back to the room, his head down on the mantel. When he straightened up and turned around, his face was still ravaged, but his eyes were wondrously bright and clear.

"My thanks to you, old friend. If you will excuse me, I have pressing business."

"I don't suppose you care to tell me what it is."

The earl was already out the door, but he popped his head back into the room, laughing deep in his throat. "Strangulation," he said. "And marriage. Not necessarily in that order."

Chapter 43

"**L**ADY BETH LEFT FOR HER HOUSE IN BRIGHT-helmston at first light this morning, my lord," said her Chelsea landlady respectfully.

"Was she alone?"

"Oh, no, indeed, my lord. She was accompanied by her maid as well as her companion, Mrs. Bostwick, a most respectable elderly lady."

"No men servants?"

"Oh, yes, indeed, my lord, there were two footmen and at least four coachmen. She took two carriages, Lady Beth did, being wishful to transport a few pieces of her furniture and a dozen of those big canvases of hers. She's making a long stay this time, I believe."

"My cousin most scatter-brainedly neglected to inform me of the exact date of her departure. Thank you, Mrs. Halliday. You relieve my mind about her safety on the road."

The earl held out his hand, and when Mrs. Halliday

accepted it, she felt the rustle of paper between their fingers. "Oh, thank *you,* my lord."

The earl spent most of the day in preparations of his own. After so many miserable years, he told himself, curbing his desperate impatience, he could afford to take another twenty-four hours for careful planning.

He retired early and was deep in sleep when his butler Badleigh came quietly into the room. With the alertness of an old soldier, Bay was awake and up at once.

"Has something happened?"

"I am sorry to disturb you, my lord, but Captain Albertson begs to see you on a matter of the utmost import."

"What is the time?"

"Just getting on to midnight, my lord."

"Send him right up."

He was tying the sash of his dressing gown and had thrown a log on the fire by the time Royce entered the room right behind the butler.

"You may return to bed, Badleigh," Lord Shirley announced firmly. "I will see Captain Albertson out myself."

When the door closed after Badleigh, he held up a hand in signal for Royce to maintain silence. Then he opened the door swiftly to check that the hall was empty.

At his next signal, Royce spoke low but clearly. "I cannot, of course, give you private information or tell you my sources. I can only say that if I were the Earl of Shirley, I would be concerned about my American-born cousin who was believed to have shifted her loyalties after she came to England. It would go hard with her if she is discovered with any escaped prisoners of war."

"How did she come to be suspected?" the earl asked quietly.

"She was never mentioned specifically in any report. . . but there appears to be only one American-born ladyship with a convenient house in Brighthelmston near the ocean, who is cousin to an earl, friend of the refugees, and a society portrait painter. Was it to Brighthelmston you meant to go for the purposes of strangulation and marriage, Bay?"

"I was planning to leave at first light."

"Interesting. I was planning to leave town at the same time." Royce flicked an imaginary speck of lint from off his sleeve. "If I were concerned with—er—the lady in question, I think I should not wait so long."

They eyed each other steadily.

"Thank you, Royce."

"For what, my lord? I have not even been here."

Before the door closed noiselessly behind him, the earl was pulling on his riding breeches.

It was midmorning when he reached the outskirts of Brighthelmston and stopped at a local inn to make inquiries and get food and water for his sweating horse.

He had to stop twice more at private homes before he was directed to a rather stark stone house in the sparsely populated section of the eastern shore. It stood gray and bare and faintly menacing just above the chalk cliffs that rose sharply behind a raised stretch of sand.

He tied his horse to a tree inside the front gate and walked around to the gardens in back. They were contained by unnaturally high and wild-growing hedges that provided a perfect cover for a pebbled path leading to the very edge of the cliffs and straight down to the beach.

"Smuggler's delight," he said aloud cynically, as he

returned to the front to pound with the butt of his riding whip on the front door.

An elderly lady—no doubt, the "respectable Mrs. Bostwick"—opened the door to him.

"I'm Lord Shirley." He stepped inside without invitation. "Please send my cousin to me."

She peered at him with faded, squinting eyes, alarmed by this male invasion. With both hands to her ears, she begged him to repeat his remarks. When he took to shouting, he finally managed to convey his message, and she smiled agreeably and ushered him into a small drawing room while she went to fetch Lady Beth.

It was obvious why Mrs. Bostwick had been picked as chaperone, he thought grimly, marching up and down in front of windows that overlooked the front of the house without any glimpse of the cliffs.

When Lady Beth, in a simple flowered muslin, came breathlessly into the room, he greeted her with his conclusion. "Half blind and almost wholly deaf, the ideal chaperone for someone in your occupation," he announced coolly.

She ignored this.

"What on earth are you doing here, my lord?"

"Can we be overheard?"

"The cook is in the kitchen. The maids are up in the bedrooms. Only Mrs. Bostwick is anywhere near."

"What about your escapees Dawson Lee and Kennedy Tremont? Are they already gone?"

"I don't understand. Of whom are you talking?" she asked composedly. Only the faintest flicker of the gray eyes betrayed concern.

"No more games, Ladybeth. There isn't time," he told her roughly. "There will be soldiers at the door before many hours have passed to make the same inquiries. If your men are not already gone from here, then they must—for their own safety and yours—be gotten away or safely hidden. For God's sake, don't look at me like that. Do you think I would"—his voice shook—"*could* ever harm you?"

In a single exchange of glances, years of bitterness and misunderstanding slipped away. She gave him the greatest gift she could.

"They are in the attics, the three of them," she said fearlessly.

"*Three* of them?"

"Three."

He began to laugh. He laughed so hard that tears stood in his eyes and finally slid down his cheeks. She watched him gravely while this excess of merriment continued.

"Would you fetch me some breakfast, my dear," he gasped finally. "I'm not only devilishly sharp-set, but I need a short time alone to work out our problem."

"*Our* problem?" She lifted her head proudly. "You are English. I am American."

"*Our* problem." He held out his hand to her. "Regardless of nations, we are one."

She lowered her head, unwilling to let him see the tears now standing in her own eyes, but his hand went under her chin and lifted her face.

"Ladybeth, my dear impossible Ladybeth, why did you do this to us?"

Before she could answer, she was yanked hard against his chest, his arms, which she had never thought to feel again, breathlessly confining her, his lips crushing hers.

She emerged, quaking, from his kiss and managed to say with seeming nonchalance, "You reek of horse."

He gave her the wicked, gleaming smile that still sent her heart down to her knees.

"When there is more time, I shall describe to you very fully what you smell of, my lovely. Now will you please fetch me some food before I faint?"

She fled the room, stumbling over a footstool, followed by his gently mocking laughter.

Twenty minutes later he was wiping up the last of his egg yolks with a crust of bread and washing the whole down with great gulps of ale while she sat silently by.

He pushed back his tray and turned to her. "Do you know many local people?"

"Almost all who are of social importance. When the Lady Beth Crozier first moved here, the locals, of course, were anxious to make my acquaintance. I accepted their attentions; they were useful in lending color to my performance."

"Excellent." He gave a short sharp nod. "And do you have any men servants?"

"The gardeners who come in by the day. My groom here. A stablehand. One young footman."

"Get to your desk then. Start writing notes. The Lady Beth Crozier is about to give an elaborate tea party."

"When?"

"This afternoon."

"This afternoon? That's—don't be ridiculous. I could never gather people together quickly enough."

"Don't *you* be ridiculous. You underestimate *my* importance. The Earl of Shirley, your very eligible bachelor cousin, is the guest of honor. You hope your invited guests will excuse the short notice, as he is only here unexpectedly for the day. Write your notes. If you have not enough horses, we'll hire carriages for your men to dispatch them by hand. The locals will be tumbling over themselves to attend."

"You conceited oaf!"

"Not at all, my sweet. Only a realist. Go to your desk and start writing. I'll return to the inn and order food. Can your Mrs. Bostwick cope?"

"Yes, indeed, she's very efficient at supervising. It's just her eyes and ears that are bad."

"Did you advertise for those very qualities?" he asked sardonically.

"No, indeed, I just found her playing the unenviable part of poor relation in the house of a British aristocrat." She smiled sweetly. "She was most happy to make the change I suggested."

Mrs. Bostwick was summoned and the party plans outlined to her by Ladybeth. She nodded her understanding and went bustling off to organize the kitchen and the maids.

The earl borrowed Ladybeth's mare and rode off to the inn, while she sat scribbling at her desk. She was still sitting there, with a smudge of ink across her nose, on his return.

"The first batch of invitations has gone out." She showed him a pile of envelopes. "I have another dozen ready when the men return."

"Did you make up a guest list?"

"Yes, here it is."

He ran his eye down it. "Mmm, not bad . . . Wilkes-Barton, most impressive . . . McCallum . . . thought she was dead . . . the Palfreys . . . I had no idea they were here . . . Good God! Sir Stanfield Kincaid!" He eyed her severely. "I hope you haven't had anything to do with him?"

"Not without Mrs. Bostwick present," she said demurely.

"Thank God for Mrs. Bostwick then . . . the Dalbys; old fogeys, but they'll fit the picture . . . Ah, Mr. Darlington, the vicar, and his wife, just what I wanted . . . How soon will you be done?"

"Just a few more."

"Let Mrs. Bostwick finish the invitations. It's time I met your guests in the attics."

She hesitated a moment, and he said impatiently, "Come now, it's too late to draw back. You have no alternative, nor have they."

The attics were portioned off into two large rooms. Behind the first room, Ladybeth gave the familiar signal of three sets of knocks, and a door set in the wall swung open from inside.

The inner room was well lit, and the men all jumped up, startled, as the earl stepped inside after Ladybeth.

"We meet again, Mr. Rawson, Mr. Tremaine," the earl said easily, and looked inquiringly at the third man.

"Sergeant Lake," Ladybeth introduced him, then added calmly, "Gentlemen, my apologies. The earl rode from London to tell me that I am under suspicion and you are all in danger of recapture."

"Jeez," whispered Sgt. Lake.

"Can't we get out now?"

"Let's make a run for it."

"If we keep our heads," the earl interrupted sharply, "all will still be well." While he looked the men over critically, he flung back over his shoulder to Ladybeth, "When were they to leave?"

"Tonight, after dark, on the tide."

"Smugglers?"

"Sympathizer-smugglers."

"It's the last time for you—and for them."

"What do you mean?" she breathed.

"I am, after all, English. I want a parole from each of you: your pledge, in return for freedom, never again to take up arms against England. For you, my lady, that means *all* your activities against England."

In the dead silence of their hostility, he spoke impatiently, "For God's sake, I'm only asking neutrality. You would not be helping your cause if you were imprisoned."

Sheepishly, each man in turn gave his parole, and the earl turned to the still woman.

"Ladybeth?"

"I give you my parole," she said, each word seeming to be wrenched out of her.

"And your promise, too. You will follow every direction I give today that will bring us all safely out of this?"

She stared at him unhappily, and he stared back implacably.

"I promise," she gulped at last, and he nodded, satisfied, and turned back to the men.

"Gentlemen," he said, "we're about to give a party. Do any of you speak English?"

He grinned at the chorus of catcalls.

"I meant English as it's spoken here in England, not America."

"My father was from Yorkshire," the self-styled Mr. Tremaine contributed unexpectedly. "I can speak like him any time, not proper English as it's spoken in the *States,* sir."

The earl accepted this correction with just the slightest twitch of his lips. "In that case, *you,* Mr. Tremaine, will be a guest," he said. "We had better change your name again, for safety's sake. Mr. Hadley, I think. Mr. Hinton Hadley, a wealthy mill owner from Yorkshire."

"You other two, I believe, must remain speechless,

so, let us say, footmen. Do you have some fancy footmen's garb, Ladybeth? Good. Then better get down to the kitchen and start whipping up that noxious white powdered confection for their hair."

"I don't know how."

"The cook or one of the maids will know, or the inestimable Mrs. Bostwick. Run along now . . . it takes time to harden and dry on their heads."

"It's a barbaric custom," she grumbled as she was shooed out of the room.

"Gentlemen," the earl said, as her footsteps faded in the distance, "there is just a bit more to our plan."

Chapter 44

THE DOWNSTAIRS ROOMS OF LADYBETH'S HOUSE WERE so crammed with guests they seemed incapable of holding more. Yet still the door knocker sounded, and the eager company poured in.

The earl was the handsomest man that ever was, the ladies whispered behind their fans. A sportsman, he was, no titled nonsense about him, said the men. Extraordinarily affable for a member of the nobility, they all agreed. Just as pleasant as Lady Beth, who was looking much grander than usual in a creamy satin gown, its brocade underskirt and lace-edged sleeves embroidered over in daisies.

The elegant Mr. Hinton Hadley came in for his fair share of praise. A pity he was in trade, of course, but *owning* mills was not exactly work . . . and considering all that money, much could be overlooked.

The two footmen in their smart blue jackets and high-powdered waves moved about the rooms along with the extra inn servants, serving cakes, pouring sherry, collecting glasses, correctly silent.

Between his homely tasks, one of the two stationed near the door kept a constant watch. Presently he pushed his way through the throng to draw the earl's attention.

"Coming?" asked the earl.

The footman nodded his white head.

The earl moved swiftly to the rear of the drawing room, collecting Ladybeth along the way, and stationed himself in front of the fireplace. A nod from him to Mr. Darlington and Mr. Hadley, and the vicar and the "mill owner" came to join them.

"Ladies and gentlemen," the earl called out, "I hope the purpose for which I have invited you here today is as much a pleasure to all of you as I expect it to be to me. My cousin and your neighbor, Lady Beth Crozier, has just agreed to marry me, and before the lady can change her mind—again—the vicar is prepared to perform the ceremony."

In the midst of the laughter and hubbub and murmurs of congratulations and (from some green-eyed ladies) disappointment, Ladybeth clawed frantically at the earl's arm. "Are you crazed?" she demanded.

"Not at all. I obtained the special license yesterday from the bishop of my parish."

"I don't mean that—why now?"

"I think you would be more protected as the countess of Shirley, besides which . . . ah Reverend, good, you are ready . . . Ladybeth"—his eyes bored into hers—"the talking can come later. You gave me your promise."

In a walking dream she found herself standing beside the earl and facing the vicar. She heard "Mr. Hadley, the mill owner" say "I do" when the company was asked, "Who giveth this woman to be married to this man?"

Then she was saying, "I do" as well, and so was Bay, looking at her with eyes of such fierce love as he pledged, "I, Henry Bayard take thee, Elizabeth Esther, to be my wedded wife . . ." that her pride and anger and resistance were swept away in a tide of overwhelming passion and joy.

In the slight pause before Mr. Darlington commenced again, there was a loud knocking on the door.

Noise, confusion, whispering, and tumult followed. Guests turned around, craning their necks. Servants flocked to the door.

"Pray continue," the earl told Mr. Darlington in a soft but menacing voice.

The ceremony continued. They were pronounced to be man and wife, and Mr. Darlington was prepared to pray on, but the earl interrupted firmly, "Thank you, sir," and in the most leisurely fashion, took his wife into his arms.

"I have you at last," he said softly into one of her ears, "and I shall never let you go again."

Then he kissed her so deep and so long that the room tilted under her feet and fireworks like Vauxhall's exploded inside her head. The ladies tittered behind their fans and the gentlemen's breeches grew sympathetically tight.

Hand in hand with his bride, breathless but not abashed, the earl faced around to their guests.

"What was all that commotion I heard?" he inquired civilly of all.

One of the inn servants came forward. "There's a Captain Albertson to see you, m'lord, and a whole troop of soldiers outside with him."

"Our first wedded guests, my love," the earl said

aloud to his wife. His eyes twinkled a challenge at her, and she thrust her chin up to meet it. "We must greet them as proper husband and wife."

"Of course, we must, my dear."

As they proceeded across the room, their guests made a path for them. At the end of it, Capt. Royce Albertson and two soldiers stood waiting.

"Royce, what happy timing!" the earl greeted him. "I wondered if it might be you. My dear, may I present a good friend of my soldiering days, Captain Royce Albertson. Royce, my bride, Lady Beth Crozier. You missed the wedding by scant minutes, but I hope you will join in the feasting."

"My felicitations, Lady Beth. Bay, you always were a lucky devil. I am sorry to interrupt such a happy occasion." His eyes gleamed appreciation of the master stroke that had inspired the happy occasion. "Some escaped prisoners of war are believed to be in this area, and we are forced to conduct a search."

"I believe we must have seen them if they were here." The earl advanced this opinion in a mild, thoughtful manner. "Search by all means, though. Would you like some servants to assist you? Or myself, perhaps? My wife can see to our guests."

"Perhaps *you* should stay with our guests, my dear," said Ladybeth in a firm, clear voice. "After all, I know the house better."

Several more soldiers were called in, and with Ladybeth sweeping along beside him, chatting agreeably of his years of service in America, Royce and his men went over the house from cellars to rooftop.

She even showed him the second room in the attic, making a game of it to see if they could find the hidden door by themselves. The concealed room was carefully clean, containing only a few bits of furniture, and a number of Ladybeth's canvases stacked against each wall.

"I understand in the old days," she told Capt. Albertson, her eyes wide and limpid, her voice hushed, "this room was used to conceal *illegal contraband.*"

His eyes met hers in perfect understanding. "Just so, ma'am," he said repressively.

"My congratulations again, Bay," he repeated when he returned to the entranceway at the foot of the steps. A wave of his hand dismissed the soldiers. "My double congratulations."

"Are you sure you cannot stay to eat or drink a toast with us?" asked Ladybeth with innocent regret.

"Positive, ma'am. I have to search the stables and outbuildings. Just a matter of form, you understand. Naturally, I will find nothing."

"Naturally." Ladybeth smiled brilliantly at him. "Why would escaped prisoners be so foolish as to stay around and be caught?"

"Why, indeed?" said Royce, and kissed her hand in mingled respect and alarm.

The earl accompanied him to the stables, where his soldiers made a cursory inspection of stalls, storeroom, and then the grounds.

"By God, Bay!" he said feelingly to the earl in one of their few moments alone. "I don't know whether I should congratulate or commiserate with you. That's a rare handful you've taken to your bosom."

"I was never one for the quiet life," the earl remarked with a grin.

"Intelligent, too," added Royce gloomily. "A woman with brains can tax a man. Who wants to exercise his wits over the dinner table?"

"I do."

"Damn, man, you're besotted."

"That's a good word, Royce." This time there was not the glimmer of a smile in the earl's eyes. "Besotted exactly describes it. From now till the end of time."

"Just keep her out of *one* kind of trouble. In conscience, I can do no more."

"Old friend. My thanks, whether you want them or not, and do not fear. I have her word. In honor, this has been the last escape." They clasped hands cordially. "My carriage has arrived from town. We leave shortly on our honeymoon. As soon as we return to London, we expect you to be our first visitor."

He watched Royce ride away at the head of his soldiers and then returned to the house, thankful to find that some of his guests were taking their leave.

"Has the captain really gone?" Ladybeth whispered.

The earl frowned. "I thought it unwise to ask him if he was proceeding directly to town. For all I know, he may be putting up with his men locally."

They exchanged worried looks.

"Do you think he's suspicious?" she whispered even lower.

"My love, he's more than suspicious. He knows. The real question is, will he keep a watch on this house?"

They were interrupted by more guests coming to wish them joy and say farewell. An ominous crack of thunder sounded outside, leading to the hasty exodus of all.

In the midst of a whipping wind, the earl and his new countess stood at the door and thankfully bid the last lingering guest good-bye.

The storm raged all the rest of the afternoon and into the evening. No boat could possibly put to sea.

While the inn servants and footmen cleared away the

traces of the party, Lord Shirley and Lady Beth and Mr. Hinton Hadley sat in the library discussing alternative plans.

It was the earl who finally decided.

"We will return to London at daylight, where I shall make arrangements to hire a yacht for a honeymoon cruise of the Greek Isles. Let Mrs. Bostwick stay here in charge. Mr. Hadley and his two servants will travel by hired inn carriage home to Yorkshire."

"Oh, no, that would never do!" Ladybeth interrupted in distress. "They would never make it so far. The servants would have to speak—"

The earl hushed her. "My valet Wilkerson will be with them to do the talking; he was formerly my batman in the army and is the soul of discretion and wisdom. He will ask no questions and carry out my orders."

"But—"

He shook his head at her. "Oh, doubting one," he reproached her. "There is no question of their attempting to get to Yorkshire. That is merely an acceptable story to be spread around in case the soldiers remain, though I think myself they are far more likely to be scouting us. Royce will see to that. To continue, Mr. Hadley's entourage will proceed along the coastal route only so far as Dover. There some fault will be found with . . . let us say . . . a carriage wheel; Mr. Hadley will, of course, put up at the inn and, charmed by the region, will decide to stay on for a few days. Or until the Crozier honeymoon yacht arrives in port. Under cover of night, he and his servants will come onto the yacht and be put off at the first neutral port on our way to the Greek Isles. They will have their passage money to go home, of course. Well?"

She flung herself at him. "Inspired!"

"It's a reet good notion, sir!" said Mr. Hadley in the broadest Yorkshire.

They started on their way at dawn, proceeding rapidly till halfway to London, when the carriage suddenly stopped short. The earl swung open the door and, without putting down the steps, jumped out onto the ground. After waiting five minutes, Ladybeth stuck her face through the window.

"Is there trouble, Bay?"

"A tree brought down by last night's storm is obstructing the road."

He and the coachmen were hard at work removing it when Ladybeth also jumped down from the carriage. There was a loud crackling sound, and she looked about in surprise for the source.

The men looked up in the same moment, and the earl sprang toward her, crying out a warning.

Backed against the carriage as far as she could get, she flung up her arms to protect her face and head. The huge thick branch, split from the trunk of an old oak by the storm and just now breaking free, hurtled to the ground, one splintered end of it dashing against her right hand.

With just one single cry of pain, she crumpled to the ground.

Chapter 45

THE EARL AND THE DOCTOR WERE LEAVING LADY-
beth's room together when she called him back in a
voice weak with shock and dulled by laudanum for her
pain.

"What is it, my darling? You must rest now."

He had to bend close to hear her whisper. "Not here.
You must do as we said. Arrange for—yacht."

"Sweetheart, you can't—"

"Be fine on ship. Bring maids—take care—" Her
eyes closed; she forced them to open. "Bring doctor—if
you must. Two doctors. Must—promised . . . get to
Dover. Want my honeymoon. Please, Bay—my men.
Promised last time."

"My brave soldier. It shall be as you wish."

Thus it was that two mornings after a solemn little
procession marched onto the yacht *Orion*. First, the
earl, carrying a blanket-wrapped Ladybeth in his arms,
then her maid Lucy and an extra maid. Doctors, valets,

and servants followed in swift succession to be greeted by crew members and shown to their various quarters.

Ladybeth, attended by the doctors and two maids, had been settled as comfortably as possible in the wide, nailed-down bed arranged for by the earl. As soon as he came to tell her they were safely afloat, she consented to another dose of laudanum and drifted into a restless, whimpering sleep.

She slept most of the way to Dover, where Mr. Hadley and his two servants were taken on. She slept much of the way to the Greek harbor of Piraeus. When she arrived there, she was no longer taking laudanum, so she was sufficiently alert and awake to say good-bye to the three Americans, who slipped silently through the connecting door from the earl's room to express their heartfelt thanks.

A few days later, as she scrambled over the rocks on the Isle of Hydra, with her right hand and arm in a silk sling, the earl carefully holding onto her left hand, she said to him, "Can't we send the doctors home, too? You can fix this"—she ruefully indicated the sling—"as well as either of them."

"If you're sure—"

"I'm sure."

The yacht returned to Piraeus. Passage for the doctors and the extra servants was soon arranged. Then the *Orion* sailed on.

Before very long the sling, too, was unnecessary, only light bandaging for her hand. The earl attended to the bandaging each morning. Punctiliously each night he kissed her forehead and vanished through the connecting door to his own small room.

They journeyed all over the Islands, anchoring whatever place took their fancy.

The day they stood amongst the ruins of the Temple

to Poseidon, high atop Sunion, for the first time a cry of passionate longing was wrung from her. "Oh God, if only I could paint it!"

In a sudden movement, the earl turned from her. Slowly she came around to face him, and to her amazement saw tears standing in his eyes.

"Bay," she said wonderingly, "my darling Bay. Did you think I did not know?"

"Not know what?" he managed huskily.

"That I may never paint again. Dear one." She stroked his sleeve lovingly. "I have known from the very beginning."

"But you never said anything. You never seemed to . . . God! I woke each day in horror, wondering if this was going to be the day I would have to tell you."

"I knew immediately. I could *feel* it. And I heard the doctors whispering about the crushed bones and severed muscles."

"You must mind more than you are saying."

She looked out toward the sea, blinking her eyes. "Dear husband, when none of you have been by me, I have shed a veritable ocean of tears. Doubtless, there are times in the future when I shall shed some more. But I am not such a poor creature that I—" A slight smile trembled on her lips. "I have my life, my health, and I have you. If I cannot paint, I shall teach. Possessing a wealthy and generous husband"—she sketched him a mock-curtsey—"I will be able to take promising pupils who cannot pay. I shall perhaps set up a gallery and give exhibitions. My husband will work hard in Parliament on behalf of the American cause, and I shall make an excellent political hostess."

She looked out over the blue sea and then back to him. "Both my arms are strong, even if one hand is useless; I shall be able to hold my babies in them. And understand this," she told him belligerently, "our children shall not be reared and educated as my father was, with nurses and nannies and governesses and tutors standing betwixt them and us. *Our* children will know their parents. I am presuming, of course," she added ever so nonchalantly, "that you give me the opportunity to become a parent."

The earl's eyes were narrowed, the stubborn Crozier chin—their joint inheritance—thrust out at her. "You are saying?" he asked softly.

"You were kind and considerate, gentle and loving, when I was in pain, feeling ill and bereft. I am as well now as I will ever be; I have been so for some time. For a honeymoon—not that I mean to cast aspersions on your—er—abilities, Bay—but doesn't *something* seem to be lacking?"

The earl cast a look at her solemn face and eyes brimful of mischief. He held out his hand and said only, "Come."

"I'll fall," she warned as he pulled her down the rocky path.

"Pick up your feet," he suggested unchivalrously, dragging her on.

They rode their hired mules to the harbor and the ship's boat took them out to the *Orion*.

Once aboard, the earl calmly lifted Ladybeth into his arms and proceeded along the deck. His valet Wilkerson approached. "Where would you wish your luncheon to be served, my lord? Indoors or on the deck?"

"Nowhere," said the earl. "We are not hungry. Not hungry for luncheon," he added scrupulously, and Ladybeth, choking with laughter and blushing with embarrassment, hid her face in his shoulder.

"We will not be hungry until dinner," continued the earl imperturbably to the equally red-faced Wilkerson, "at which time we would like trays to be served in her ladyship's cabin. Her ladyship and I are planning to retire now. We do not wish to be disturbed."

"You wretch!" Ladybeth upbraided him as he dropped her onto her bed and locked the door of the cabin. "I will never be able to face that man again—or anyone on this ship, for that matter. What you said will be repeated to everyone."

"Good," said the earl, pulling off his seaman's shirt. "Then everyone will be sure to stay away from us. Turn over."

"Why?" Suspiciously.

"I shall have to play lady's maid for you."

She turned over, well content to have him maid her, and he immediately set to work on her buttons. When he had slipped the gown over her head, he started sliding down her petticoats.

"You do this too damn well," she grumbled.

"Thanks to you, I have had considerable experience."

Ladybeth sat upright, pulling away from him. "Why thanks to me?"

"If you had married me when you should have, my experience would have been vastly less."

"I suppose I *forced* you to chase all the Drury Lane doxies and actresses and the whores who ply their trade at Vauxhall."

"Since *you* frequented Drury Lane and Vauxhall, how else could I expect to see you? If you think I bedded all those women you saw me with, you exaggerate my prowess in the bedchamber and may well have to—er—how did you express it?—'cast aspersions on my abilities'?"

She gripped her underlip between her teeth, remembering the pain of countless encounters in the past.

"I thought you—"

"I know what you thought. You were wrong. Oh, I had my flings over the years. I had to; I am not celibate by nature. But I have loved only you and wanted only you since the early days in New York. If you suffered seeing me with other women, do you know what it meant to me, after we came home to England, feeling you slip away from me bit by bit without knowing why or what I had done? I came to your room the day I asked you what had become of us and heard you crying in your sleep about betraying me. And to find you in the arms of my groom."

He stared somberly down at her. "You blamed *me* for believing that was your betrayal. I knew it the night at Ranelagh when you gave me that bitter, reproachful look. I kept asking myself, what has *she* got to reproach *me* about?"

She said pleadingly, "I wanted you to believe in me in the teeth of all evidence. I wanted you to believe in me even if it meant disbelieving your own eyes and ears and senses."

"Yet you couldn't trust *me!*"

"Tom Binkley wasn't an escaped prisoner. I might have trusted you to help him if he was *that*. But he was an agent. An enemy agent. And you are an Englishman. I could not be sure which way you would see your duty."

"Was that the betrayal you meant?"

"No." She lifted her eyes to his. "Somehow I never thought of the information I gave as betrayal, certainly not helping the escapees. But there were times you brought papers home from Parliament, and I went through them in the library when you weren't there. Your *private* papers! I felt ashamed of that, but I had to do it. Some of the information seemed important

. . . There was a plan once, I remember, for crushing the colonies by separating them from one another by sea and land, so they would be starved into compliance."

"My dear heart, many such idiocies were proposed. There were always men like Fox and Burke, and even me, to oppose them."

"I know," she said simply. "Only it wasn't for me to pick and choose but just to send whatever information I could get. I could not marry you and work against you behind your back."

"Was it worth the separation and pain?"

"It wasn't a question of worth," she explained earnestly. "I had no choice."

"I suppose I must try to understand then, since I had no choice either about loving you. God knows I would have stopped if I could. I paid with years of agony and frustration for a very few short months of happiness."

Her mouth quivered. "I never meant to hurt you so."

He said softly, "Your life is pledged to me now as mine is to you. Will you give me the same loyalty that you gave your cause?"

She knelt on the bed close to him and tightened her arms about his waist, one cheek against his chest. Dexterously his hands slid up her bare legs, pulling the bands of her petticoats to turn them inside out and whisk them off.

As his hands slid down her legs again, she tensed them together, holding her breath for just seconds before she gave a deep, prolonged sigh that somehow, as he joined his mouth with hers, kindled into the rapture of a kiss.

When he lay down beside her, tugging her into his

arms, her eyes glowed at him, jewellike. "I shall love you, Bay, and be loyal to you all of my life," she vowed.

He shed her of her chemise and shift and lifted her, splendidly naked, high in his arms.

Huskily he told her, "One lifetime is not enough to encompass all the love that I have to give you."

With her bandaged hand lightly tangled in his hair and her other reaching out to bring them close to one another, Ladybeth threw back her head and laughed joyously aloud. "Then perhaps we should return and live another time," she proposed.

As he lowered her onto his body, her face nuzzled against his, a strange, eerie buzzing sounded in his ears. His head whirled round and round on his shoulders. Her great gray eyes were suddenly gleaming at him, greenly catlike. The disarrayed curls, instead of tumbling about her face, had suddenly turned into a red brown mane tossed down a tanned back.

He heard the sound of distant laughter and a peculiar voice saying in his ear, "I will wait forever for you, I will, me fine lordship."

Then the picture dissolved, and there was only Ladybeth. Ladybeth, lying nude and natural, her gray eyes expectant, her smiling face eager, and her body as it yielded to him, utterly, anxiously ardent.

The cat-eyed girl retreated to a far corner of his mind.

"If you will come back, then I will," pledged the earl.

Chapter 46

IT WAS MORNING WHEN I AWOKE, LYING IN A SODDEN little heap on the floor of my closet gallery. I had several times before awakened just so, still crying bitterly, weeping for the past that I wanted to cling to and could not.

This time I was sobbing with pain. My hand! My right hand. It hurt so horribly. As far as I could see, turning it over, touching it gingerly, there was not a thing wrong with it. Just that red-hot agony from the finger-tips to the wrists.

I thought of Ladybeth and what it must have meant to her never to paint again. Her career had ended when she was a good ten years younger than I was now. No wonder there were so few Ladybeths in existence; she had not painted long enough for many to survive.

On wobbly feet I headed for my studio, stumbling and swaying as I walked. There had been a fresh blank canvas on my easel before the gathering of the Mailers yesterday. I don't know what I expected to see on it now . . . probably the vapidly pretty face of Mrs. Smyth-Carrington, done in the vivid coloring and with the slashing strokes so typical of Ladybeth.

I stared at the canvas, my heart beating erratically, my breathing jerky and ragged. It stood on the easel as virginally bare as it had been before my dinner party the night before.

I had blanked out last night when the wings beat around me. I had drifted back, as always, through the centuries. But *I had not painted!*

For the first time in my life since I began my journey into the past, my blackout had not produced a Ladybeth portrait.

So I must not have dreamwalked either!

"Ladybeth!" I cried aloud. And then, cradling my flaming hand protectively to me, I whispered low and pleadingly, "Ladybeth, it's time you were done with me or I with you."

I felt no response in the stillness of the room around me, and I started to cry bitterly again, half with disappointment, half because I was mad with the pain of my hand.

I went back and turned off the lights over the pictures in the gallery and slammed the closet door shut.

"I'll burn you all! I'll tear you up!" I raged. "I'm Rilla Scott, not Lady Beth Crozier. Damn you, I have a life of my own to lead. You had yours. Why can't I have mine?"

I flung myself onto a big armchair, sobbing against the cushions. "You had your Bay," I wept over and over. "Why can't I have Cam?"

There was music, wonderful music all around me,

and the pain—that terrible pain that Ladybeth must have felt to need so much laudanum—was ebbing away, leaving my hand mercifully eased.

"You can," I thought I heard a voice say. A dim, distant voice. I sat up, wiping my eyes and face, looking expectantly for the man in silver gray.

He was not there.

"Good-bye," said his voice ever so faintly, and I suddenly realized in an agony of longing and regret that he meant good-bye for good.

"Oh, please," I cried, reaching out with both my arms. "Oh, please don't leave me."

His face, his dear, dear face, hovered over me just for seconds.

"It's either shadow or substance now. You can't have us both. Good-bye, good-bye till the next time, my very own dear love."

I was right. He was never coming back to me.

I jumped up out of my chair. "Good-bye, my love, my lord," I flung after him into the empty space filled with his presence. I heard a faint chuckle and then I was alone.

Startlingly, shrilly, the ring of the telephone pierced the thick silence. I answered it in half a daze. "Hel-lo?"

Through the telephone, the reality of prosaic, every-day life spoke to me in the flat, nasal voice of the building superintendent. "Miss Scott? Excuse me, I know you like *Ms.* Scott—sounds the same to me— Listen, I can put you ahead on the waiting list for painting your apartment if you are willing to have it done today."

"Today!" said Rilla, aghast, looking rather helplessly about her. "I could never get ready in time."

"Listen, I could send up a couple of men, myself, too. The size of your apartment, we could prepare it in an hour, maybe a little more. You see, it's this way, the painters are already on their way here to do Mrs. Rosen's place, and she's sick. If you don't take this chance, you'll have to wait till summer. Believe me, it's better a little unprepared than painters in the summer."

"I believe you. I believe you. Thanks, Mr. Hatch. I'm going to make arrangements to sleep out tonight. I don't want a migraine from the smell of the paint like last time. Will that be all right?"

"Believe me, you can leave everything in my hands."

"I believe you," Rilla found herself saying again, and before she could laugh, repeated a hasty "Thank you" and hung up.

A moment later she was dialing Larchmont. "Maggie? It's Rilla. I need a favor."

"You want me to put you in touch with Cam!" Maggie declared ecstatically.

"I want to borrow your apartment tonight if it isn't on loan to anyone else. Mine's being painted."

There was a long pause.

"For a moment," said Maggie in her most throbbingly actressy voice, "I thought that you were about to do something sensible."

"I am," laughed Rilla. "I am trying to avoid a headache. Of course, if you would rather not—"

"I shall phone the front desk to give you the spare key," said Maggie with vast dignity. "I noticed last week that we were a little low on coffee."

"That doesn't bother a little old tea-drinker from Liverpool. Ta, Maggie."

"You are welcome, I'm sure."

I was laughing, but I had lost enough of my native Liverpool shrewdness to forget to hang up before she could slam down the phone against my unprotected ear.

DREAM WALKER

A few hours later, with only a large shoulder bag containing a toothbrush, a change of bra and panties, and a leotard, I hopped a cab to take me the mile or so to the Mailers' New York apartment.

I spent a thoroughly lovely and lazy day. No work to do. No obligations. No one, except Maggie, knew where I could be found.

I made eggs and chips for lunch, with tea instead of coffee from the diminishing supply. About six I called the Chinese restaurant two blocks west, and it delivered a luscious dinner, complete from egg roll to almond cookie.

I ate and read and watched television. Then I took a long hot bath and washed my hair, slipping on my leotard afterward instead of getting dressed again.

While I read some more, I played a few cassettes, some nice schmaltzy music suited to my mood. It was getting colder. Instead of turning up the thermostat, I tossed a match on the neatly arranged logs and sat cross-legged before the fire, just drifting and dreaming.

I don't remember how much later it was—time seemed to be standing strangely still—I switched from the music to one of Maggie's exercise tapes, wrinkling my nose a little in distaste at the syrupy voice that told me that, even if I was now pudgy, an exquisite figure was easily within my grasp.

"You are trying to deceive the consumer!" I accused the cassette. "Most pudgy figures can*not* be made exquisite."

In spite of which, I lay flat on my back, kicking my feet in the air at command and bringing them back over my head, toes touching down behind.

"Fooled you!" I thumbed my nose at the tape, which was sorrowfully acknowledging that this was a difficult exercise and would take much practice.

422

As I was rolling back and forth on my bottom (to reduce its size), I noticed that the fire was going out and opened the screens to poke at it with the brass poker. When that didn't work, I tried using a lighted twist of paper.

On the third try, I had my fire back and once again sat there, toasting in dreamy contentment until the syrupy voice admonished, "Let's try it one more time."

The next few minutes were rather energetic. I was on my back, ready to give up, when the door slammed shut, half-scaring me to death.

When I saw the man standing there in the hallway, staring at *me,* I came upright in a hurry. I couldn't believe my eyes . . . it couldn't be . . .

"C-Cam," I stammered, "wh-what are you d-doing here?" And at exactly the same moment, he asked me, "Who the devil are you?"

And even as he spoke the hurting words, another voice seemed to fill the void between us. In his clear voice, the man in gray said, "Did I not promise you, Rilla?" And then, fading fast . . . *Good-bye, my own true love.*

Chapter 47

THROUGH LONG YEARS OF MY LIFE, IN MY DREAM-state, I had been force-fed the bits and pieces of my past. After I came home to my newly painted apartment from Maggie's, the entire jigsaw seemed to be complete.

The man in silver gray had gone from my life forever, but his farewell gift had been last night's encounter with Cam. This morning's charade was just the first step I planned to take.

I was not only prepared to meet my future now; I intended to confront it.

While the kettle boiled and my bread toasted, I readied my paints and brushes.

With a mug of coffee and a plate of dry toast standing by, I started to paint. Not as the illustrator Rilla Scott. Not as the painter Amaryllis. The portrait I did was in Ladybeth's style, and my subject was my beloved apparition—the man in silver gray.

Everything I painted about him was as I had always seen him, satin breeches, brocade vest, fitted waistcoat on his tall, spare frame. Everything except for his face. His face was Cam's as it had been that night in Maggie's apartment, unhandsome but ruggedly sexual, tanned skin, black hair lightly powdered with snow, blue eyes darkening with the promise of passion.

It took me the better part of the day. When I had finished, I added the final important touch . . . the scrolled, scribbled "Ladybeth" in the corner.

I had to hold the canvas carefully in the cab going to Ben's office; the paint was not completely dry.

"Hi, Ms. Scott," said Ben's secretary, looking doubtfully down at her appointment book. "Is Mr. Mailer expecting you? He didn't mention that you were stopping by, and I know he's trying to make the five thirty-six train."

"He didn't know. I have to see him," I told her baldly. "Is he alone?"

"Yes, but—"

"I'll go right in."

Carrying the painting at an awkward angle away from my body, I sidled past her desk and went loping down the hallway. Ben looked up in surprise from the briefcase he was jamming full of papers from his desk.

"Something up, Rilla?" he asked me, and I propped the canvas up on an end table, letting it lean tipsily against the wall while I got straight to the point.

"I want you to call your brother . . . your brother Cam," I amended breathlessly, "and ask him to come see this painting."

"I thought it was my brother Cam you meant," said Ben dryly, and this time his brows angled into positive pyramids. "And just what am I supposed to say," he inquired courteously, "when he asks me what the hell this painting is all about?"

"He won't ask that . . . or, at least, if he does . . . what he's going to want to know most is where you got it. I want—" I swallowed convulsively and managed to get the words out. "I want you to tell him."

"Your name?"

"Yes," I whispered.

"Your address?"

"Yes," I nodded.

"Well, hallelujah," said Ben. "It's about time."

I blinked a little, and then I smiled through eyes brimming over with tears. Maggie had talked, of course. How could she not? Or maybe, some time, some way, over the years, I had just given myself away. How could I not?

"There's just one little problem, Rilla. It's not going to be as fast as you intended."

"Wh-why not?" I quavered.

"Cam called me yesterday to say he was going out of town."

I plunked myself down on the nearest chair and burst into tears. "I wanted it to be t-t-tonight," I wailed like a three-year-old.

Ben patted my head as though I were his beloved golden retriever and offered me a spotlessly clean handkerchief from his jacket pocket. "That's the bad news," he said. "The good news is that when he comes back, he and Irene are going to be divorced."

I sobbed noisily into his handkerchief.

"Is he—is he—very un-happy?" I hiccupped.

"I think the right word is relieved," said Ben. "He faced the failure of his marriage a while back. As long as there's not too much upheaval for Bethany, Cam will be fine."

I saw him cast a look at the digital clock on his desk. "Rilla, why don't you come home to Larchmont with me? A couple of the boys will be there for dinner. Maggie will be good for you."

What he meant was that Maggie would be better able to cope with tears and turmoil.

"No, thanks." I gave him a watered-down grin and returned his soggy handkerchief. "I need to be by myself," which wasn't true, "but call me, please, and tell me the minute Cam gets back."

"Scout's honor," said Ben, and I waved good-bye and trudged the short distance home prepared for a long and very lonely evening.

It was a relief to hear the phone ringing almost as soon as I got in the door.

A public relations friend, G. F. Driscoll, wanted my company at the opening of a new club on First Avenue. I nourished an overwhelming dislike for the crowds, the confusion, and the cacophony of places like this. G.F. had turned seduction into such a fine art: an evening spent repelling him was one of the most strenuous forms of exercise known to woman.

In spite of which, I gasped out an eager yes almost before he finished inviting me. Anything was better tonight than to be by myself.

I looked through my closet and decided, rather sadistically, to wear my black jersey dress. It would drive G.F. wild, not just because of the way it molded itself to my figure, outlining every outlinable contour, but because the complicated series of cross straps around the back and shoulders would require a Houdini to figure out how it could be removed.

I was tired even before the evening began. I hoped that by the time I had danced and drunk my way through the next several hours and then fought the good fight against G.F., with any luck I would be much too tired to be able to think and just tired enough to fall asleep.

Chapter 48

"YOUR BROTHER CHARLES IS HERE, MR. MAILER."
The receptionist reared back in alarm as a roar sounded through the intercom. "Send the so-and-so in!"

Cam strolled nonchalantly into the office a moment later, a gabardine raincoat over his arm. He was wearing summer-weight dark blue slacks, a checked jacket, and a white sports shirt unbuttoned at the throat to show that his chest and neck were sun-roasted to a rich, red brown mahogany.

"Where the hell have you been?" snarled Ben. "We've all been worried sick."

Cam raised pained eyebrows. "To the Dominican Republic getting a divorce. I thought my lawyer informed you."

"That was two weeks ago." Ben allowed himself to be diverted. "Is it all finished with?"

"Nice and tight, quick but legal." He grinned. "I'm a free man."

"So what have you been doing with your freedom?"

"Obviously," Cam told him kindly, *"not* what you think, Ben. Though this brotherly concern is touching, you might remember that I am all grown up now. Though I confess," he admitted charitably, "that marrying anyone so obviously unmarriageable as Irene wasn't the most adult move I ever made."

Ben grunted, "Ummm," and Cam gave a rueful laugh. "Anyhow it's all undone, and I've got Bethany, except for a month in summer and two weeks every winter."

"My God! How did you get Irene to agree to that?"

"Easy," said Cam cheerfully. "Her new husband wasn't too crazy about taking on another man's kid."

"She's married again!"

"That's what took so long. After the divorce, I went to Greece with her to help smooth out the legal tangles so she could be married without any impediments. It was all very hush-hush, but you'll read about it in the newspapers tomorrow when they make the big announcement from their honeymoon paradise."

"Who'd she marry?"

"Cornelius Drachos."

Ben gave a long, loud whistle. "Whew. The shipping magnate. She really hit the big time. And you were at the wedding?"

Cam sat down in a leather chair and grinned across the desk. "I was best man."

"Jee-sus Christ! This is all too civilized for me," Ben complained. "I guess I'm just an old-fashioned guy at heart. Anyhow, you're well shut of her."

Cam said quietly, "I know you never liked Irene, but to give her her due, it was as much my fault as hers that the marriage failed. I don't think it ever would have worked—we want such different kinds of lives—but it's not easy to hold a marriage together when your husband is obsessed with—with someone who doesn't exist."

"Ladybeth?"

"Ladybeth," confirmed Cam and cocked his head at his brother. "You don't miss much, do you, Ben?" he inquired with easy affection. "I found her first miniature in that upstate flea market soon after Irene and I got engaged . . . and immediately I started having dreams of a girl I had never met, tall and slender, thick chestnut hair, huge gray eyes. Lovely, but not a patch on Irene for looks. Yet every time I held my wife in my arms, I dreamed of my unknown girl, and what was happening for real couldn't compare to my fantasy. It happened for weeks, sometimes months, each time after I acquired a Ladybeth portrait. Then I went to England to the Christie auction, and I met . . . She wasn't my girl of the dreams, but she was . . ."

His voice husked up. "All in the space of a few hours I found her and fell in love with her and lost her. And it took me years to realize what had happened to me. By the time I understood, it was too late."

He got up from the chair and started wandering restlessly about the office. "Irene would have cheated sooner or later, she's got jet-set burned in her brain . . . just the same, I cheated her first. I never from the start had a whole heart to give her."

"What now?" asked Ben.

Cam said slowly and deliberately, "It was, after all, just a few hours in an English pub five years ago, and I admit I got drunk as a lord on his wedding night when Irene told me about Drachos, but not so drunk that I didn't finally put a name to that hauntingly familiar face and voice . . . and recognize the star, too. It was Katy Dingle that night in your apartment."

He did a 180-degree turn to face Ben squarely. "Your wife has done some artful fabrication, and either before or after I wring her neck, she's going to have some tall explaining to do. Or maybe, just maybe, brother, you can do it for her."

Ben said quietly, "Go into the connecting office."

Cam hesitated, looking at him inquiringly.

"Go on," Ben urged. "There's something you'll want to see."

Cam opened the door, took two steps into the room, and stopped—paralyzed. Staring at him from the wall was his own face on the body of an eighteenth-century aristocrat, painted in Ladybeth's style. A man in silver gray.

"How—where—?"

"She brought it in for you to see."

Cam said painfully, "She *wanted* me to see it?"

"You're damn right she did. She's been driving me crazy with phone calls twice a day for two weeks now screaming to know your whereabouts."

"Katy Dingle." Cam murmured the name caressingly under his breath, but his brother heard him.

"She agents as Mrs. Dingle," he said dryly, "but the right name is Amaryllis."

Cam stared incredulously.

"The ethnic painter?"

While he was still reeling with the shock of the first blow, Ben kayoed him completely. "In our family," he stated deliberately, "we know her best as Rilla. Rilla Scott."

"Rilla Scott. You mean, *your* Rilla? The one the boys always talk about, who lived with you when . . ."

His voice trailed off. Suddenly, vividly, it was coming back to him . . . a summer day in Larchmont . . .

He had gone to the garage for some suntan oil when he heard a call from the shower. It sounded like "Come-a-love." As he paused slightly, the shower door swung open and the same voice, sounding as though her mouth was full of spray, ordered, "Come in here this minute so I can close the door!"

He knew damn well by then that neither the invitation nor the command was meant for him—but he couldn't resist!

"All right, but just remember *you* were the one who insisted!" he had said, stepping into the shower.

He could remember as though it were yesterday the wide, horrified eyes . . . *Hell!* How *could* he have forgotten that they were gleaming blue green cat eyes? No wonder Katy Dingle in London had seemed to be someone he knew before!

Standing here, so many years and one broken marriage later, he could picture her still, bare as a baby's bottom and lovely as a Greek goddess. Every time she tried to conceal a part of her, he got a better view of another part. And after *she* cried with embarrassment and *he* cried with laughter, they wound up on the shower floor in each other's arms. God, how he had wanted her . . . and God, how willing she had been . . . until they heard Maggie's voice calling Chick.

He had thought at the time that the nymph in the shower was not only beautiful but witty as well, one of Maggie's young actress friends putting on a cockney accent.

Until the awful realization later when they were introduced that the harsh accent—Scouse, not Cockney —was not put on.

Later he had plucked her out of the water, choking and sputtering; filled her dinner plate, exchanging commonplaces, that atrociously dressed, shrill-accented girl, who looked at him with the cow-eyed adoration of adolescent infatuation, reeking of cheap perfume and cigarette smoke.

The worst shock of all was that he had continued to be attracted, violently attracted to her, in spite of *him*self and in spite of *her*self. He had wanted her still; he had intuitively felt that she could be had.

But one didn't do that sort of thing, not with a girl who worked for the family. He had felt very noble, relinquishing what hadn't been offered. When he discussed her with Maggie, he had been almost savage, refusing to acknowledge his disappointment.

And all along . . . all along . . .

He sat down hard in the nearest chair. His head was spinning on his shoulders. From far off he heard faintly mocking but not unkind laughter . . . and a face was there before his eyes . . . two faces, one with great, gray eyes and the other with gleaming cat eyes . . . both with stubborn chins.

They were laughing at him. Why shouldn't they laugh? Thirteen . . . fourteen years he had been searching, and all along she had been within easy reach, his for the finding.

Katy Dingle. Rilla Scott. Ladybeth?

The next thing he knew Ben was shaking him by the shoulders, trying to pour brandy down his throat straight from the bottle.

He accepted a generous swig and stood up.

"I'm okay, Ben."

Ben capped the bottle with shaking hands. "Christ, you scared me, conking out like that."

"Where does Rilla live?"

Ben supplied the address, though "God knows if she's there," he added. "Ever since you've been gone, she's been hitting the night spots. It's completely unlike her, but she's practically taken a lease on the Artists and Models Studio, a new place in the west fifties."

Cam looked at his watch. I doubt if any club in New York is open at five o'clock . . . but it's just as well. I have some arrangements of my own to make, and I promised to take Bethany out to dinner. If she calls"—He plucked his raincoat off the chair and started for the door—"as far as you know, I'm not home yet."

"But Cam, the poor girl's going out of her mind."

"The poor girl has led me one hell of a merry chase. The ball is in my court now. Don't ruin my game, Ben. You and Maggie have lied plenty for her; you can lie a few more hours for me. And don't worry. I finally know where I'm going and what to do."

Chapter 49

I UNLOADED G.F. IN THE LOBBY OF MY APARTMENT building, telling him straight out in front of the grinning elevator man that I was much too tired for our usual 2 A.M. tussle.

"Good night, Bob," I said, hobbling off the elevator at the seventh floor.

"Good *morning,* Miss Scott," he chirped impudently.

The first thing I did after double-bolting the door to my apartment was to kick off my high-heeled shoes. Dancing might be healthier for insomnia than Valium, but God, it was hard on the arches!

I padded into the bedroom. There was nothing surprising about the fact that the reading lamp on my night table was lit. I always switched it on before I left the apartment to welcome me home. What stopped me in my tracks were the folded-back blankets, the propped-up, dented-in pillows.

Someone, to paraphrase the three bears, had been sleeping—well, at least sitting—in *my* bed.

I gave a violent start as the door to the bathroom swung open. Cam, with one of my bath towels tucked around his middle, strolled casually into the room. His hair was wet, his skin glistening with water from the shower. He was hard flesh and bones and brown all over, except for the part of him I couldn't see.

"You're late," he said casually, and discarded the towel, draping it across the nearest chair. As he climbed back into my bed, I was given brief but overwhelming evidence that he was brown all over. I couldn't help a bit of speculation—even at this critical moment in our lives—as to just where he had been sunning himself without any trunks.

I stood there, gaping at him, and Cam suggested pleasantly, "Won't you join me?"

I couldn't answer him. I couldn't move.

"I've been waiting five years," Cam said in a quiet, persuasive voice. "Ever since the last time you accepted that invitation."

It was a matter-of-fact statement without any element of reproach. But I felt his pain as keenly as I remembered my own the night I left him.

I moved closer to the bed.

"I didn't want to leave you that night in London," I said breathlessly. "It almost—I—it was the hardest thing I ever did in my life, walking out on you like that."

"Then?"

"Oh, my God, it's such a long, long story. And so—involved. I don't know how I'll ever make you understand."

"Come here," said Cam softly.

I came.

"Sit beside me."

I sat.

One of his hands reached for my chin; the other he stretched out so I could see that Deborah Ben David Crozier's Star of David, on the same chain my father had given me years before, was dangling from his middle finger.

It was such a small thing, that he had taken the time to have the chain mended, but it touched me strangely. My heart was singing with gladness even before his hands were on my shoulders, turning me to him.

"I'm sorry I didn't recognize *you* right away, Rilla Scott," he said, his eyes blazing into mine. Then he put the chain around my neck, kissing the top of my head as he clasped it. "I have loved Ladybeth," he murmured huskily, "as long as—"

"As long as I've loved you?" I suggested.

"Longer than that," Cam told me. "Long before our lives began."

I had waited almost half my Rilla Scott lifetime to hear those words. I had waited, it sometimes seemed, since the beginning of time to see the light of love shining for me in his coal black eyes.

While he got me out of my dress, I rolled off my panty hose. While he unhooked my bra, I snuggled up against him, crying for very joy.

He kissed my tear-damp face, up and down and all around, then he kissed my quivering mouth until the long-forgotten art of kissing seemed to come back to me and I was able to give him just as good as I got.

Lots of forgotten things were coming back to me under his expert tutelage.

I remember once saying, "But Cam, we have so much to talk about," and his smothered laugh, as he told me soothingly, the way he might have spoken to Bethany, "We will talk tomorrow, beloved."

"B-but C-Cam," I stuttered out even as I thrilled to that wonderful word, *beloved* . . .

"Tomorrow is for talking. Tonight we are going to love." His hand laced with mine as we lay side by side, pressed tightly against one another, sardine style. "I need your love, darling. If only you knew how much I needed it. Going to bed with a woman is not what I call loving. I've been hungry for the other a lot longer than you know."

I turned away my head to hide a smile. Before many moments passed, he would find out that his last remark had not exactly been true. I had been needy for much, much longer than he.

I sat up and held out my arms to him, welcoming him into them, welcoming him to all of me.

As he switched out the bed lamp, I smiled again in the darkness. Soon he would know all there was to know.

There was a distant ringing in my ears that I thought at first was the familiar, knowing chuckle of my man in silver gray, but it turned out to be Cam's joyous laughter as he showed me the way to love.

Author's Note

Although the main characters in the historic section of *Dream Walker* are fictitious, several of the minor ones are not. For example, Hercules Mulligan, the New York tailor, was suspected by the British to be a spy and arrested several times, only to be released, as no real evidence was ever supplied against him. Gen. George Washington supplied proof of his own on the day in 1783 that the British sailed out of New York, with the Americans marching in right behind them. The first person the commander-in-chief called on was Mulligan, and he is supposed to have given him a bag of coins. Later he ordered a full set of clothes from the tailor-spy.

The sequence of certain events of the time have been kaleidoscoped to suit the needs of the hero and heroine. The use of the invisible ink, "stain," was first brought to the attention of the American intelligence by John Jay and his brother, but it was not in general use among agents until about 1779.

Sir Henry Clinton succeeded Sir William Howe as Commander of the British Armies in 1778; and he was the leader of the military "gentlemen" who later rode madly down the streets of New York each morning in pursuit of sport.

Trinity Church was almost destroyed during the occupation in the (probably patriot-set) fire of 1776. Later the cemetery stones were pulled down to form paving stones. It is true that while the military band played concerts, British soldiers and their ladies danced on this cemetery floor.